# THE ANGLE OF THE *Angels*

## DAVID LEE HOWE

*Relax. Read. Repeat.*

THE ANGLE OF THE ANGELS
David lee Howe
Published by TouchPoint Press
Brookland, AR 72417
www.touchpointpress.com

ISBN-13: 978-1-952816-46-8

Editor: Jenn Haskin
Cover Design: Colbie Myles
Cover images: Shutterstock, Portrait of young couple in love embracing at beach and enjoying time being together by Milles Studio

Visit the author's website at www.davidleehowe.com

 @ DavidLeeHowe  @ DLeeHowe

First Edition

Printed in the United States of America.

Thank you to Ms. Jillian Mason for the input you provided to me as both a developing author and professor. To Mom, thank you for always pushing me to grow and to do better. To Dad, thank you for your guidance. You were the best father anyone could have ever asked for. To my lovely wife, Dawn, a very special thank you. Without you, my dear, none of this would have been possible. 143.

# Chapter 1

## The Consequential Encounter

JULIE CHRISTIANSON SUSPECTS the moment she first lays eyes on him that her future might be intertwined with the young man on stage. Watching him perform, she begins to envision recruiting him one day for her own musical project. His stage presence is irresistible, and her training makes it easy to recognize talent when she hears it. With her current music studies and her creative writing struggle, she casts aside any immediate sense of urgency.

"What is his name, Zoey?" she asks, knowing her roommate would find out if she didn't know already.

"I'm fairly sure his name is Hunter Watkins. He plays here every month. Why, do you like him?"

"What's not to like? He can sing, he has a stage presence, and he is a good-looking man. Looks help when you are forming a band, Zoey."

"Well, you have a slight problem. The singer on stage with him is his sister. I don't think there is anything that can pry them apart." Zoey pushes her glasses to the bridge of her nose.

"She's a good singer. I will give her that much. And she's really beautiful."

"She isn't as good as you are, and you know it. Nor is she as beautiful," Zoey says.

"Success isn't about who is better. Success is a combination of timing, planning, and networking," Julie replies.

"Check, check, and check. You have her in all those departments too. You should go introduce yourself when they go on break. You just never know, Julie."

"I'm not ready to put a band together yet. That's a full year or more down the road. You are from the area. What do you know about him?" Julie asks. She slides her long blonde hair behind her ears, cocking her head to the side as she questions her friend.

"He's from Ithaca or one of the surrounding towns. Newfield, I think. I have seen him at parties before. He's kind of magnetic, isn't he?"

"Yes, he is." As Julie watches the performer, the two lock eyes for a brief moment. Julie smiles as she continues to study him. It is as if she can feel something more than what she sees, something purely magical. Hunter's eyes are warm and inviting, and her heart slightly flutters when he smiles back at her.

Julie notices their other roommate, LaShonda, across the crowded room. She takes Zoey's hand, pulling her to their table.

"Girl, I don't know what you have to do to get a band going, but that boy up there knows how to play that guitar. All he needs is a singer of your caliber, and you can put Zoey and me down for backstage passes because we're coming along for the ride." LaShonda laughs as she puts her phone down on the table.

Julie looks back up as Hunter addresses the crowd. She shakes her head as he begins to play a synthesizer. The performer is mesmerizing, and she listens closely as he addresses the crowd.

"This next song is about following your dreams and how you must never, ever, allow anyone to steal them. Often, they're all that we have." Hunter grins in a theatrical fashion as he continues to address the crowd. "And remember, you can't get there from this side of the moon." He laughs out like the devil.

Julie seems intrigued by the mournful sounding introduction and captivated that Hunter has mastered the guitar and the keyboards as well. Impressed, she smiles at her roommates, who are now oblivious to the performance, immersed in their habitual texting habits. She quickly turns her attention back to the stage and listens closely to the lyrics of the song that is being performed.

*This Side of the Moon*

*"Pins and needles, nails on the chalkboard.*
*You clip your wings every time you are bored.*
*Your best plan lays in the center of your broken heart.*

*Books and baggage you cart off to school.*
*Education is how the rich indenture fools.*
*Your best hope lays in wait for a brand-new start.*

*You can't get there from this side of the moon.*
*Fly too high, they'll come for you.*
*You can't get there from this side of the moon.*
*Be careful if you dream.*

*If you can see beyond the darkest of nights.*
*If you can see beyond all that is right.*
*Then where you go will always be in the light,*
*in the kingdom of your desires.*

*You can't get there from this side of the moon.*
*Fly too high, they'll torment you.*
*You can't get there from this side of the moon.*
*Be careful if you sing.*

*Selfishness is the way of the West.*
*Who cares if you are the best?*
*They'll treat you like you're one of the rest.*
*Be careful if you dream."*

Julie leans over to Zoey. "Does he write all of their music?" she asks.

"Yes, he does. He has some really good songs. I have seen him play for a couple of years now. That one they just played must be a new one. I've never heard it. It had a pretty cool dance beat, for such a dark sounding song."

"I thought the same thing, but they played it in the key of E minor. That's not typically a key you write a dance song in. Who is this guy?" she asks. Immediately she turns her full attention back to the stage.

"No, it's not. Go and introduce yourself, Julie. What do you have to lose?" Zoey urges as she texts.

"I have four very long and hard semesters left. The last thing I need right now is to get into a band, or worse, get mixed up with a boy. I shouldn't even be here right now. I have so much homework to do it's not funny."

"But you are a straight-A student, and you always are so far ahead of everything it's just disgusting. It's only the first week of classes, Julie, lighten up," Zoey jabs at her roommate.

"I am always ahead, and that's because I don't waste time. When I'm ready, perhaps I can use him. We'll see. Until then, I have a whole book of music theory that I have to understand, countless term papers to write, and somehow manage to get through Professor Pistorovski's Diction class."

"Oh, you have him this semester?" Zoey asks. A look of dread overwhelms her.

"No, I'm saving that for next year."

"That's a good idea. He's the most stressful professor on campus. But he'll like you. I think you worry too much. I'm buying. What do you two want to drink?" Zoey asks her roommates. She reaches into her purse to retrieve her credit card.

"Margarita," LaShonda replies as she looks up from her phone.

"Iced tea, and three lemons, please," Julie orders. She quickly turns her attention back to the band.

"It's Friday night, Julie. You can have a drink, you know," Zoey says.

"Iced tea is a drink, my dear," she replies. She smiles as she wrinkles her nose at her friend.

Zoey shakes her head and laughs as she rises from her seat.

# Chapter 2

## Music as Magic

THE FOLLOWING EVENING FINDS Hunter Watkins and his band in the recording studio. The band performs many different takes of the final cut on their debut album.

"Hunter, this is simply an amazing song. Give me one more take, just like that, folks," Alex suggests from the studio's control booth. The band members check the tuning of their instruments and await the producer's cue from their station. Hunter nods to his producer, acknowledging the compliment.

"Okay, from the top, please. I will give you all eight counts with the click track, then hit it," he instructs over the PA system. As the band begins to play, Hunter looks at Alex and smiles, knowing this particular song will be the icing on the band's debut CD.

"Excellent. That's a take, guys. All I need now is Krystal in the isolation booth for the lead vocal track. The rest of you can come on in here, please."

Krystal steps into the chamber and places the headphones on, awaiting her cue from the producer. Alex starts the recording and points to her to begin singing. The rest of the band settles into the control room, quietly watching and listening to their singer as she completes the most essential part of the recording.

## Western Town

*"Is there a way to your heart? Would you show me where to start?*
*Is there something you desire? I would like to set that fire!*
*Do you really want to know? Will you really let it show? Will you now?*

*What if we live? What if we love? What if we need a little luck?*
*What if we scream. What if we shout? What about now?*

*Is there something on your mind? I would gladly lend some time to.*
*What's that notion deep within? Maybe I feel akin to.*
*Let me in or let me see that we're really meant to be. Let me see.*

*What if we live? What if we love? What if we need a little luck?*
*What if we scream? What if we shout? What about now?*
*What if we dream? What if we dare?*
*What if we take some time to care?*
*What if we live? What if we love? What about now?*
*In this Western Town.*
*In this Western Town*
*In this Western Town."*

"That's a wrap. Fantastic job, everybody. Come on in here, Krystal, and let's give this a quick listen," Alex instructs over the PA system.

"Little sister, that was perfect." Hunter gives her a big hug.

"Thank you, I hope we sell a million overnight," she replies.

Alex smiles as he plays the nearly perfect cut for everyone. "That would be more than ideal. Tomorrow Krystal, before we finish mixing, we will have you and Hunter layer some backing vocals on the ending, so get a good night's rest. Other than that, this song is relatively finished. Hunter, I will need you and Johnny for some minor finishing touches in the control room tonight. As for the rest of you, go celebrate. I have great feelings about all of this material. Krystal, I doubt there is anything that can stop that voice of yours from hitting the top of the charts."

"Thanks, Alex. We're going to grab some drinks and dinner at the Boatyard Grill. You'll join us when you finish, won't you?" she asks.

"I have to check out another band tonight, but thank you for the invitation."

"See you in a bit?" Krystal asks her brother.

"Yes, Johnny and I will be right there. And be careful going down the hill. The snow is beginning to pile up out there," Hunter says as he looks out the studio window.

"I will," she says as she and the two other band members turn to leave the studio. Krystal smiles at her brother and steps out into the long winter's night.

Alex hands Hunter and Johnny a pair of headphones. "With your writing and her voice, you guys will have a good shot with this album. God willing, of course. I'm surprised that as good of a singer as you are, Hunter, that you ever let anyone take the microphone away from you. But the two of you together are amazing. And your sister has the looks and talent to help assure you guys go all the way."

"You think so?"

"Yes. Pretty and talented can go a long way in the industry." He turns his attention back to the soundboard, adjusting some sound effects.

"That's why she's the singer and not Hunter," Johnny says to the producer. Hunter laughs as he leans back into the leather seat.

The three of them work together, placing more effects on the song. Johnny sits twirling his drumsticks, giving suggestions when asked. "It's perfect," Hunter finally says, and Johnny nods his head in agreement.

"The hill is going to be getting pretty slippery. You guys better get going. I will see you tomorrow. Get out of here," Alex says to them.

"I will see you at the restaurant, Hunter," Johnny says.

"Okay, I'll be right there."

"If you have nothing going on Friday night, Hunter, I have some open studio time if you and the band want to get started on a second album," Alex says as they step out of the studio.

"Sounds good, Alex. I will check with everyone in a few minutes. Have a good night," he replies.

Hunter takes off from the parking lot, losing traction the moment he turns onto the slippery street. The vehicle fails to respond as he slides into the curb. His eyes open wide as he comes to a complete stop, narrowly missing a parked car. He shakes his head and lets out a sigh of relief. He quickly reaches to the dashboard to engage the four-wheel-drive switch to the vehicle. "Thank you, Father," he says as he continues on his way. Flashing lights at the bottom of the hill heightens his concern. Through the flurry of the falling snow, he observes an emergency flagman waving traffic onto a side street. He rolls down his window as he approaches the first responder.

"You'll need to detour down Buffalo Street. We had to close State Street. There was a bad accident at the bottom of the hill."

"Is everyone all right?" Hunter asks.

"I'm not sure. Please proceed," the emergency worker replies as he continues to wave Hunter into the detour.

He turns onto the adjoining street and reaches for his cell phone to call his sister. The phone immediately transfers into her voice mail. He hangs up the phone, looking very concerned.

As Hunter reaches the parking lot of the Boatyard Grill, his worst fears are suddenly realized. Johnny races to Hunter's truck. A look of horror overwhelms his friend's face. Hunter rolls down the window out of concern.

"Krystal is being taken to the emergency room. She wrecked her car going down the hill. Mathew and Luke are also being taken there. We need to go to the hospital right away," Johnny says with desperation in his voice.

"Get in," Hunter says. Given the weather conditions, he drives as quickly as he can toward the Cayuga Medical Center.

# Chapter 3

## Cold Winds and Dark Clouds

THE COLD DECEMBER AIR AND overcast sky do very little to help lift Hunter's spirit. He and Johnny arrive at the Church together, still in a state of shock that Krystal and the others are no longer with them. The street is lined with grieving friends and local fans, all of them mourning the loss of the three aspiring musicians.

Hunter and Johnny are ushered into the side entrance of the Church. The finality of the tragic event brings Hunter to a steady flow of tears. The sight of his sister's casket is too much for him to bear, and he weeps into his hands.

Hunter turns to his family, already seated in the pews. His mother gently begins to cry at the sight of her son's tears. He takes a seat next to his two brothers and waits for the service to begin. As the minister speaks, he slumps into his pew. The service is filled with beautiful memories of Krystal. The kind words spoken by family and friends are certainly not enough to ease his pain. After the memorial service, he wanders home to his empty loft. He sits on his bed and looks up at the poster of John Lennon mounted on the wall. He pauses a moment to read the lyrics of the famous song '*Imagine*.'

"It's not easy living for today, John," he whispers to the picture. He grabs the guitar that rests on a stand near his bed and gently strums the instrument. He starts to play a melancholy chord progression for several minutes, then abruptly stops, placing the guitar back on its rest. He reaches for his notebook that he keeps on the nightstand. As he writes, the lyrics flow perfectly onto the page.

*Long Way Home*

*Lost a good friend yesterday. He missed a turn on the highway.*
*Now my whole world is upside down. They said he was heading my way.*

*So take the long way home. It makes me feel lighter.*
*Take the long way home. Hold me a little tighter.*
*I feel I'm growing old. I used to be a fighter.*
*So take the long way home. Hold me a little tighter.*

*Hold me tighter, it's the right time. Let me know you're there.*
*Slap me harder. Pour your heart out. Kiss me if you care.*

*We used to laugh until the early hours, and raise hell with the neighbors.*
*Then go fishing after summer showers, and drink like we were sailors.*
*Take the long way home. It makes me feel lighter.*
*Take the long way home. Hold me a little tighter.*
*I know I'm growing old. I used to be a fighter.*
*So take the long way home. Hold me a little tighter.*

*Hold me tighter, it's the right time. Let me know you're there.*
*Slap me harder. Pour your heart out. Kiss me if you care.*

*Kiss me if you dare.*
*Kiss me if you dare.*
*Kiss me if you dare.*

Hunter looks over the words. They solicit a broken-hearted smile as he reads. He glances through the book of songs that he has been composing, many of them inspired by his little sister. He shakes his head and places the book back where he had claimed it only moments before, and he dozes off into a much-needed sleep.

OVER THE COURSE OF THE winter, Johnny makes several attempts to lift Hunter's spirit, urging him to begin playing again. Desperate to make something of himself, he tries one last time to coax Hunter to pick up where they had left off. He knocks on Hunter's apartment door and enters as if he were family. The two exchange greetings as Johnny hands Hunter a coffee he bought for his friend.

"I need to do something. We need to play. We have an album and can form a new band. Your sister would want that," Johnny urges.

"No. It just wouldn't be the same, Johnny."

"Well, if you are not going to try and put a band together, then I have to do something with my life," Johnny says.

"I just don't think that I can ever create like that again," Hunter replies.

Johnny looks down at his coffee with sadness in his eyes. "There is nothing in this town for me, and there never will be. I have to do something. I can't stay here anymore." He takes a sip from his cup and looks at Hunter.

"I just don't feel it, Johnny. I'm sorry." Hunter pulls a thread off his shirt and lets it drop to the floor. "Krystal was that special little spark that helped me create that music. She was the inspiration to write almost all of those songs. Growing up, she looked at me like an idol, and we dreamed together. She started singing because of me."

"You can't live life like you are, Hunter. You have to pick yourself back up. She's gone. There is nothing that's ever going to change that. I miss her too, you know."

"I know," he replies.

"Come on, write about it, man. You have been given a gift that so very few people have. You have a talent that most people would sell their soul to have. It's a chapter of your life that God has given to you. It all happens for a reason. So we have been dealt a serious loss. Let's deal with it together. Let's write something new. They all would want us to keep going, don't you think?

"I just need some more time, Johnny."

"Well, I can't wait anymore. Jane is pregnant, and I have a family to support now."

Hunter looks at him as his mouth opens wide. "Wow, congratulations. You just got married last year. I thought you both wanted to wait a while to have kids," he replies. He looks at Johnny rather confused.

Johnny takes a deep breath. "We did, but that doesn't matter now. I met with a recruiter yesterday. If you are not going to put a band back together, I'm going to enlist in the Army. If you're not willing to take a shot at the big leagues, Hunter, then I am off next week. I have to move on."

"I understand," he says. He puts on a half-hearted smile for his friend as Johnny turns to leave.

"I have to go so I'll see you later. Have a good day," Johnny says.

Hunter shakes his head as his friend closes the door. He looks over at his lyrics book that sits on the nightstand. He retrieves it, then rubs his eyes for a moment. He reads what he had last written, shaking his head as anger overwhelms his face. He reads for a moment, then slams the book shut, flinging it across the room. He lays his head back on the couch, silently crying as he stares at the wall in front of him.

With Hunter unwilling to change, Johnny leaves to join the armed forces. Hunter takes a job with a local contractor as a carpenter's apprentice. The smile he once wore so brilliantly seems to have found a permanent hiding place deep within his soul. He begins drinking, and sometimes heavily. People around the town start to whisper that Hunter Watkins died that day along with his sister. What they didn't know was that he was about to be blessed with some warming rays of hope.

# Chapter 4

## All the Queen's Men

ZOEY WANDERS DOWN THE stairway in the early morning light, not surprised that Julie is already up and immersed in reading a textbook. "Do you ever sleep?" she asks. She trudges her way into the kitchen for her morning coffee.

"Of course, silly," Julie replies. She briefly looks up from her book. She smiles at her half-asleep roommate, still dressed in her blue and white polka dot pajamas. She shakes her head as she continues to read.

"I swear you're not human," Zoey calls out from the kitchen. She pours her coffee and wanders back into the living room, sitting down next to her roommate on the living room couch.

"Did you go out last night?" Julie asks. She closes her book, knowing Zoey will want to talk for a few minutes.

"Yeah. We went to the Ale House," Zoey replies. She takes a sip from her cup, cradling it in both hands.

"Oh, did you have fun?"

"Sure did. There was a really good guitar player there."

"Do tell," Julie says with interest.

"Oh, wow. He played stuff with such perfection it would make our professors feel inferior," Zoey replies. Her eyes open wide behind her oversized reading glasses.

"Really?" Julie asks.

"He played a rendition of Beethoven's '5th Symphony' on a classical guitar, and it was amazing. But the last set he played Mozart's 'Turkish March,' and it was just unbelievable."

"On guitar? I guess I should've gone with you."

"You should have. You would have been impressed. He played that one on his electric guitar, with all of his sound effects. Julie, he captivated everyone there."

"The producer I met with yesterday may have suggested him as a potential band member. He's not from England, is he?" Julie puts her feet on the coffee table and sets her book aside.

"He has to be. He spoke in an English accent when he introduced the Mozart piece."

"Daddy arranged for recording time at the studio here in town. I went down to meet with the owner. Oh, and he played me some of Hunter Watkins' music, that one musician you took me to see perform last year," Julie says. She smiles as she speaks, resting her head on the back of the couch.

"It was good, wasn't it?" she asks. Zoey sips some more of her coffee.

"Oh my God, I love his music. He's a really gifted writer."

"I haven't seen him around much since his sister was killed. I heard he wasn't taking it very well," Zoey quotes the local gossip.

Julie lifts her head off the back of the couch. "That's just what the producer said. He told me the guy was meant to write songs, and I should try to recruit him for my project."

"You should."

"Actually, I'm going to," Julie replies, leaning toward her roommate and nodding her head with a grin.

"You should recruit him as a boy toy as well. He's a really good-looking man. Though I never remember seeing him with a girl," Zoey replies. She looks away for a moment as if puzzled by her own statement.

"Maybe he's gay?" Julie wonders out loud.

"Maybe. Or maybe he's just like someone else I know who people also wonder if she is gay. Or maybe he's just someone who does not want to be tied down while he attempts to make it big. Know anyone like that, Julie?" Zoey stares at her roommate, casually taking another sip of her coffee.

"Touché, my dear, touché." Julie smiles as she nods her head.

"So you are ready to start a band then?"

"Yes, and after hearing more of his music, he is on my list." Julie turns her head like a movie star who is smiling for the camera eye.

"Do you want me to find out his phone number for you? I have a few mutual friends. I'm sure they could get it for me," Zoey asks.

"I think I know right where to find him. The producer told me where he tends to hang out after work. I would rather meet him in person. If that does not work, I actually have his phone number." Julie pulls the card from her book that the producer gave to her. She turns the card around to display the handwritten number.

"That's what I love about you, Julie. You just seem to think of everything."

"I don't know that I think of everything. If I did, I wouldn't need a good songwriter."

"When are you going to track him down and tell him he's now playing in your band?" Zoey asks in a monotone voice.

"Friday night, I understand he habitually goes to a specific bar when he gets done with work."

"I wish I could go, but I have a group project to work on. I would love to see the look on his face when you walk up and tell him, 'Congratulations, you are my new band member.'"

"It worked on the keyboard player, didn't it?"

"Well, yeah. What man can resist a beautiful woman with long legs, blond hair, and blue eyes telling them what to do?" Zoey bats her eyes.

"None that I know of," Julie says. She smiles as she rises from her seat to get ready for her morning class.

# Chapter 5

## Letting Go

HUNTER AWAKENS TO THE sound of a cooing Mourning Dove. He rolls over and gazes out the window at the lonely little bird. The dove struts underneath a lilac tree, calling out for a companion. "Who knew, who who who," the bird seems to cry out.

"Wish I knew," he quietly answers the dove. He momentarily pauses to watch the bird as it continues to lament and broadcast his loneliness. He suddenly rises to grab the note pad on the nightstand. "Pen…where is a pen?" he mutters. He races to the living room to locate his jean jacket, where he always keeps one handy. As he retrieves it, he runs back to his room and jumps onto the bed. Quickly he begins to write.

_I Stand Down_

_How do you melt away a frozen heart? How do you turn your cheek? When I'm in desperate need of a brand-new start, and wolves are at my feet._

*I shout up often at your lofty sky. You never answer me.*
*Just to sit here and to ask you why I'm lost, but I believe.*
*I cry out… I cry out.*

*When I laugh too loud or just too proud, scorched on this rocky path.*
*And the shadow that two crossed sticks cast, that tends to bring me*
*back.*
*When my pride deceives, and I'm on my knees, I find humility.*
*Now I see it must be you've answered me. I'm lost, but I believe.*
*I cry out… I cry out… I stand down.*

*Oh, the time may find you.*
*You know, when you've come undone.*
*Oh, and I may remind you, you're not the only one!*
*Oh, and don't you ever leave me.*
*You know, when you've come undone.*
*Oh, and don't you deceive me. You're not the only one.*
*You're a rising, not a setting sun.*

*I stand down. I stand down. I stand down.*

As he finishes writing, he glances up at the clock. Placing the notebook back on the stand, he turns his attention to get ready for work. As he puts on his clothes, he smiles at the sound of the dove still broadcasting his song of hope. Hunter looks out the window and marvels in appreciation at the bird. "Thank you, sir," he says to his little winged friend. He starts to turn away but quickly turns back to the window. Looking up toward the sky, he smiles and whispers to the wind, "Thank you, too, Father. I needed that."

# Chapter 6

## Golf, God, and Satan

DRAKE, THE DIRECTOR OF Angel Affairs, responds to an alert on his handheld Universe Observation device. "Oh dear," he says. He turns and frantically inputs data into the central computer of Heaven.

"What is it?" Oliver, his young angel apprentice, asks.

"We have a bit of a problem."

"What problem?"

"The timeline continuum, it's becoming terribly eschewed."

"Oh, and, um, what does that mean?" Oliver cocks his head like a curious child as he watches his mentor.

"It means that he's up to something."

"And, uh, who is he?" Oliver asks.

"The problematic one, who else do you think?" Drake replies.

"Oh, him again, eh?"

"Yes, I'm afraid so."

"What's he up to now?"

"He is about to tempt several of our influential mortals. It could have grave

18

consequences. God has placed positive messages of faith, and hope, inside their constitutions. Once they write their songs, those messages will appeal to the masses. That will draw many of them to a burning desire to discover the Kingdom of Heaven. Those messages lay dormant within them, but if Satan sabotages their project, they will be forever lost. He would then be able to twist their messages into his own. Failure to stop it now may result in a significant and unfortunate loss and might subsequently affect the anticipated continuum of events."

"And, uh, what do we do about that?" Oliver asks.

"We interrupt," Drake replies.

"Don't you mean we intervene?"

"No, we interrupt. Then we get permission to intervene."

A slight degree of concern appears in his assistant's voice. "You mean we interrupt the Big Guy?" Oliver asks.

"Yes, I'm afraid it is absolutely necessary."

"You know He doesn't like to be disturbed when He is shooting His morning round of golf." Oliver's voice raises in pitch, and his eyes open wide with concern.

"Well, I know that, but this problem needs His immediate attention."

"Oh, okay, well, I will wait here for you and watch the computer display."

"No, you won't. You will follow me right this very minute. Now let's go," Drake says.

The two angels walk down the Hallway of Eternity and out onto a fairway. They approach God from behind as He readies His shot. The two of them overhear God talking to Himself on the putting green. Hobbs, God's caddy, places his finger to his nose shushing the two well-intentioned angels as they draw near.

God, ever observant to the slightest movement in the universe, senses His assistant's approach. He looks over to Hobbs, smiles, and winks. Hobbs drops his head and rubs his face to hide his smile, knowing that God will somehow toy with the two of them.

"Steady, steady, head down, let's feel the roar of the crowd. Give them something to cheer about," God says out loud. He takes several practice swings at the ball. Oliver looks around, perplexed, unable to see anyone other than the Almighty and His caddy.

"Father, we hate to disturb you, but we have a problem," Drake says, and God abandons His backswing.

"Ah, hello, Drake. Hello, Oliver. Be with you in one moment. I have a difficult putt here. Not rightly sure how I am going to make this shot," God says with a smile.

"But you're God, you can do anything you want," Oliver says.

"Oh right, I forget that sometimes." He laughs as He once again abandons His attention to the shot. "I hate to cheat, though, unless *he's* around," He says directly to Oliver.

"He *is* around. He's about to attempt to steal Julie Christianson's and Hunter Watkins's souls as well as the rest of the band that they're about to put together."

"He is, is he?" God asks. "Well, he can have the drummer. He's a little too goofy for my liking." Again, He winks at Hobbs.

"Hunter hasn't even met the drummer yet, Father, nor has he met Julie. Without her, he'll never write all the songs you have placed within him, as they still lay dormant in his mind. Without Hunter, Julie won't write her songs of love and hope either. In fact, they won't be able to do anything else you have planned for the two of them. He's going to try and take them all, Father," Drake says. A sense of urgency resonates in his voice.

"Well, what do you want me to do about it? I suppose you want me to allow you to interfere in their lives? They all have free will, you know?" God pleasantly asks. He turns to focus on His shot at the cup.

"You have to allow us to put an end to it, Father. I advise that you allow me to provide an assignment to an angel to help protect them," Drake says. He looks into his observation device to monitor current developments.

"Can I do that?" He quietly asks Hobbs, smiling once again with a confused and bewildered look.

"Yes, Father, you certainly can," Hobbs replies. "However, it would require your immediate assessment of the situation to see whether it merits your approval to do so, Sir. If so, then you can enable the two of them to follow through for you." He takes the golf bag off his shoulder and smiles, knowing that God will grant his assistant's wish.

"Oh, all right," God says as He agrees to the request and hands His putter to the caddy. He reaches into the bag retrieving the pitching wedge, and rests it over His shoulder. "Hobbs, take the clubs back to the clubhouse and wash them all for me, would you please? I'll keep this one, though."

"Yes, Sir," Hobbs replies. He turns, making his way back to the clubhouse.

"Well, where are they?" God asks. Curiosity lingers in His voice as He begins to scan the heavens.

"Here." Drake snaps his fingers. The three instantly appear on the granite rim of the campus fountain at Ithaca College, which overlooks Cayuga Lake.

"Drake, I must say that you are getting rather good at using that power, my compliments. But you know that bothers me a little when you do that. Remind me to revoke that power when we get back, would you?"

"Sorry, Father, it was rather unavoidable. And I remind you that you made that power irrevocable back in the fifteenth century," Drake reminds His boss.

"I did, didn't I?"

"Yes, Sir, you did."

"Oh, right. Hey, we're in Ithaca," God says with great excitement in His voice. Appearing very pleased, He looks down upon the waters of the longest Finger Lake that He purposefully created during the last Ice Age.

"Yes, Sir. Just over there, around that crook in the lake, is your most favorite waterfall of all, at Taughannock Park," Oliver points.

"Oh, goodie, do we have time to shoot nine holes at the country club?" God asks. He takes a practice swing toward the lake with His pitching wedge still in His grasp.

"No, Sir, we do not have time. The evil one is down there somewhere lurking about and getting ready to tempt Hunter and his soon-to-be friends," Drake replies. He nods his head toward the City of Ithaca.

"Ah, I see him down there now," God says. He takes another practice swing with His club toward the lake.

21

"I don't see him. Where is he?" Oliver quietly asks.

"Hush up," Drake says to his assistant. "You are here to learn. You can't do that with your mouth open."

Satan suddenly appears standing next to God, with a smug look fixed upon his face. "Always loved this view, Old Man. I think it the finest view in the entire galaxy, actually, my compliments."

"What are you doing here?" God asks. He turns His attention away from the angels.

"Oh, I'm just loitering about, enjoying the day. Is that a problem?"

"Everything you do is a problem, my troubled little child," God says.

"You didn't think it a problem when I played music for you in Heaven. It seemed to make you very happy as I seem to recollect," Satan says with pride.

"I'll give you that one," God says.

"Yes, well, I think it's time you pay me for that one, Old Man, you know what I mean?" Satan suggests.

"Pay you? Be thankful I don't put you in a bottle for a millennium or two and throw you to the bottom of that lake down there." God laughs as He quickly looks over at Drake.

"You'd never do that. You're too nice. That's part of your problem, you know. You are disgustingly nice, really. Besides, who would roam about the planet tempting people's poor little souls?"

God turns back again to Drake and quietly asks, "Would that be a dilemma?"

"Indeed, it would. Besides, I don't ask much," Satan replies. He folds his arms as he also continues to admire the view of Cayuga Lake.

"What do you want?" God asks.

"How about that lovely girl down there named Julie Christianson, and that young man Hunter Watkins. Hell, throw in the rest of the band they're about to put together. Give me their souls, and I won't trouble you again, at least for another century or so."

"No, but you can have the drummer," God replies jokingly. He winks at Drake then takes another practice swing toward the lake. Drake shakes his head as he smiles.

"Actually, I was going to offer that you keep him. He is a big boy, and he scares me a little bit," Satan replies.

"You, scared, eh?" God asks.

"Not really, but I'm not asking very much, just a few souls."

"Why are you troubling yourself with them anyway? Haven't you got enough to do?" God asks. He smiles once again as He continues to enjoy the magnificent view.

"That Hunter Watkins likely has a wonderful temper that no one has ever really tested yet. I can use that, you know? And I like some of the songs that he has already written."

"Why don't you simply wait and buy their CD when it comes out?" God asks.

"They haven't made it big yet, and you know that I do so hate to wait. It's so much more enjoyable to purloin their material, you know? I hate to pay for things. It's so ... it's so uncivilized."

"But if you had your way, there would be no civilization left at all," Drake says with contempt in his voice.

"Oh, got me on that one, you little wanker."

"No, they're off-limits. Do not interfere with them, or I will not be happy with you," God says.

"Oh no, not that again," Satan replies. He places his hand on his head in an exaggerated theatrical display as if on stage. "God is unhappy, oh, no."

God looks at him in silence for a moment. "You never were a good actor. Got time for Nine Holes? I'll play you for them," God calmly offers as He smiles at His rival.

"Father, you can't do that," Drake says with great concern in his voice.

Satan snaps at Drake. "Why don't you stay out of it, you slimy little limey, lest I rip your bloody wings off?"

"Limey? You are just as much a limey as I am. Why don't you go do something useful, like go haunt a house?" Drake quickly retorts.

"I do, regularly. I've got people, you know," Satan says. He laughs as he smirks at Drake.

"Stop it, both of you, right now," God orders. "And you, nine holes or not?"

"Are you serious?" Satan asks.

"Yes, of course, I am," God says.

"But you cheat!"

"I do not," God replies. He looks down the hill, taking another practice swing toward the lake.

"Oh really?" he asks. "What do you call the Big Bang, a bloody bonfire? That was cheating on the grandest of scale, using your powers to keep the whole thing from imploding back upon itself. You are the biggest cheater in the entire known universe."

"I just bend the rules of physics a little once in a while, if need be. You playing a round with me or not? We can make the country club from here in five minutes."

"Oh, look at the time. No, thank you, just the same. I have some other things to attend to, unfortunately," Satan says. He looks to his wrist, checking his watch.

"Do you want me to guarantee that you end up with the drummer for eternity?" God asks.

"Oh, all right then, but just for fun. No wager on the souls or anything. Will that be nine holes or eighteen?" Satan asks.

"Nine is fine," God replies. He and Satan turn and begin to walk toward the College Student Center.

Oliver watches them walk away, then looks at Drake. "They're going to actually go play golf together?" he asks, puzzled that arch-enemies would do such a thing.

"Yes, they're going to go play golf. Come, we have work to do," Drake replies. He begins to punch in some data into the hand-held observation device.

"I thought we didn't have time, and they're going to go play golf," Oliver says.

"God made time. Come along. We have work to do," Drake says.

# Chapter 7

## A Turn in the River

AFTER DRINKING THE NIGHT away, Hunter awakens with a slight hangover. The nagging beat of drums emanates from the apartment down the hall. The noise seems to bother him, and he grabs his head to try and ease the tension. He moans as he rolls out of bed and stumbles into the bathroom.

"Remind me to kill whoever that is when I meet him," he says to the reflection in the mirror. He quickly showers, then throws on his favorite white t-shirt. He is nearly ready for work when his boss enters the apartment.

"Are you ready or not?" Nick asks. He hands Hunter a cup of coffee.

"Almost, thanks," Hunter replies. He takes the cup and slowly sips from it.

"Let's attack this day. Tonight I have plans for you, little buddy."

"Yeah, what plans?" Hunter asks. He takes another sip as he leans up against the counter.

"I think I found you a new guitar player to get you a rock band rolling again."

"Oh, yeah? Good guitar players are hard to find, Nick. What makes you think he's any good, let alone why do you think I want to play in a band again?" he asks.

"Because I know a good guitar player when I hear one, and you know you want to play again because you're a Diva. It's in your blood, old boy. And this guy is unbelievable."

"Diva? I'm not a Diva, you twit."

"Oh, you're a Diva, buddy. You probably spent the last ten minutes doing your hair."

"I did not. I don't engage in such vanity." He tucks his shoulder-length hair behind his ears.

"Well, you should have because you're goddamn ugly. Come on, or we're going to be late. Let's go, Diva."

The drummer still bangs upon his drums as Nick looks down the hallway. "I would say that there is your drummer. But if he were my neighbor banging on those things this early, I would make a Popsicle out of him with his drumsticks."

"That very thought had crossed my mind," Hunter replies. He looks down the hallway then pulls his apartment door shut. "He is good, though. I will give him that."

They exit the building and get into Nick's truck. He looks over at Hunter as he starts the vehicle. "What did you do last night? You seem a little slower than you normally are," Nick asks. He engages the vehicle and begins to drive off.

"I made the mistake of walking down to the Chanticleer," Hunter replies.

"You've been drinking a lot lately, old boy. You've got to slow down."

"Yeah, yeah, I know. So what did you do after work that you found this guitar player?"

"I went up to the Scale House. They have a Thursday night blues jam that they put on. It's generally good for a laugh or two. But this one guy got up and just smoked them all away. He was insane. I instantly thought of you. I texted you to come up. You didn't answer me. You missed it," Nick informs as he turns onto the main thoroughfare.

Hunter looks at his phone and notices that there is an unread text from him. "Yeah, pretty good, is he?" he asks as he reads the message.

"Yes, I actually talked to the guy. He's new to the area, and he's looking to get a band together. He asked if I knew any singers, drummers, or bass players. I told him about you."

"I guess I have been getting a little itchy to play again."

"This guy is one of the best I have ever heard," Nick states with excitement.

"What's his name?"

"He goes by the name of Scratch."

"Scratch?" Hunter questions in an elevated and curious voice.

"Scratch, yup, that's it."

"What kind of a name is Scratch?" Hunter asks as he rolls down the window.

"Wake-up puss-head, it's a nickname, and he's playing again tonight at the Dock Bar with the house band," Nick says as they pull onto the job site. He tosses his empty coffee cup at Hunter's head. "Let's go, Diva."

"I'm not a Diva." Hunter's voice is laced with a little irritation as they grab their tools from the back of the truck.

The two of them work the day away, cutting and connecting wooden planks for a stud wall. Hunter watches his boss closely, learning all he can from the master carpenter.

As quitting time arrives, they make their way to their favorite watering hole. They both order their usual draft beer. Nick cannot help but notice a very slender and attractive blonde-haired girl at the end of the bar. She watches Hunter as a smile gleams across her face. Hunter, busy pecking away at sending a text message, doesn't seem to notice the girl.

"Don't look now, buddy, but I think you may have a more important plan in store for this evening than what I was planning," Nick says quietly. Nick continues to casually watch the girl as she whispers something to her friend seated next to her.

"What are you talking about?" Hunter asks as he looks at Nick.

"The pretty blonde at the end of the bar has been watching you ever since you walked in."

"Blonde? What blonde?" Hunter questions with interest.

"The one that's coming right this way at this very moment," Nick says quietly as he lifts his mug, appearing not to notice the girl approaching.

Julie spins the barstool next to Hunter and takes a seat. His eyes open wide, and he smiles at the stunningly beautiful girl. Fixated on her every move, he watches as she places her beer bottle on the bar, and she waves the bartender over to order some drinks.

"Excuse me, are you Hunter Watkins?" she asks as she places a $20 bill on the bar. She motions to the waitress to get both Hunter and Nick a drink.

Hunter appears to be taken by her beauty and her captivating smile. Her eyes are blue, wide, and inviting, and he struggles to turn away from her stare. "Yes, I am, and you are?" he asks as he extends his hand for a proper introduction.

"I'm Julie Christianson. Some friends told me I might find you here right about now." The girl shakes Hunter's hand. Her palm is warm and velvety to the touch. Hunter struggles to take a deep breath.

"Friends, oh yeah, who might that be?" he asks, doing his best to appear nonchalant.

"Old fans of yours," she replies.

"Fans, ha." He turns to Nick and laughs. "Hey, she met my mom and dad."

"Good one. You have a sense of humor, too," Julie replies. She uses her charm to try and pique his curiosity. "I was told you might be interested in being a part of what I'm attempting to do."

"She must be studying psychiatry, Hunter. Your mom probably told her that you would make a great case study," Nick says.

"No, actually, I study music at Ithaca College, and I am putting together a band. I need a few talented players," Julie replies. She raises her eyebrows as she looks back at Hunter.

"I knew I should've picked up a guitar. Hi, I'm Nick Kincade," he says. He reaches over to shake the girl's hand. She reciprocates with a firm businesslike handshake.

"Hi, Nick," she greets him in pleasant acknowledgment, quickly turning her attention back to Hunter.

"But you have no talent, Nick," Hunter replies. He casually takes another drink from his beer.

"Oh, you two are terrible." She laughs at the ongoing prodding the two are dishing out to one another. "I love it," she says with genuine amusement.

"So what do you need me for, Julie?" he asks.

"I would like you to play guitar for us and sing with me on some duets that my keyboard player and I are working on."

"I'm flattered. Let me be honest. I haven't played in a while. I'm seriously out of practice. If you go to Ithaca College, there are far more talented players up there than I am. Some things happened to me, and to be completely honest, I kind of lost my passion for playing music."

"Yes, I heard what happened. That was just horrible. I would have taken some time off myself."

"It kind of took all the fun out of playing for me." Hunter stares briefly into the bottom of his glass.

"Well, everyone needs some time away, Hunter. What people tell me about you, though, is that you are a very gifted musician, and they seem to think that you have it in you to play again, so what do you say?"

"Oh, I don't know. I'm so out of practice."

"That's odd?" she states, speaking directly to Nick.

"What's odd?" he asks. He looks at her as he takes another drink from his beer.

"They told me that Hunter Watkins is the best. They didn't tell me he's also a Diva." Julie grins, laying down a dare. Nick, caught completely off guard by her statement, begins to uncontrollably blow beer through his nose, nearly drowning himself in the process.

Hunter laughs at Nick's stupidity. "Easy, Nick, you twit. Diva?" he questions with excitement, quickly turning his full attention back to the girl. He nods his head as he tightens his lips, smiling at her with his eyes.

"Now, we all know that can't be the case, so practice, Thursday night, my place, yes or no?" she asks. She extends her hand for Hunter to shake in agreement to the commitment.

"I guess with that challenge, yes it is." Hunter shakes her hand.

"Get them whatever they're drinking, and three shots of Tennessee's finest," Julie says to the bartender. "And grab a bib for Mr. foamy-nose over here if you would, please."

"Good one," Nick replies. He raises his glass toward Julie while simultaneously laughing at his embarrassment.

"You are a natural entertainer," Hunter says to the girl.

"I know, it's what I want to do," she says. "You okay, Nick?" she asks with sincerity.

"Yeah, I'm good," he replies.

The bartender serves the drinks, and Julie takes the shot glass as she holds it up for a toast with Hunter and Nick. They both oblige the girl, joining their glasses together in a toast to the new venture. As soon as she finishes the shot, she places the glass on the bar and reaches for her phone. "Here, call your number," she says. She hands it to him, and he does as instructed. When his phone begins to ring, he gives her phone back and answers the incoming call. "Hello," he says.

"Hi," she replies softly. She smiles as she looks at him, allowing Hunter the opportunity to stare deep into her eyes. He watches her closely as she saves his contact information.

She curls her index finger to the man at the other end of the bar, tucking her phone into her tight white Levi jeans as her friend approaches the group. "This is Chad," Julie says. "He's my piano player."

"Pleased to meet you, Chad," Hunter replies.

"Nice to meet you. I used to come to watch you play in your band a couple of years ago. I really like how you write music."

"Thank you," Hunter replies.

"You still have it, don't you?" Julie asks.

"Have what?" he asks. Hunter looks at her with curiosity.

"The writer's fire."

"The writer's fire? I have never heard that statement," Hunter replies. He looks at her with curiosity.

"They say that you wrote some songs that were simply amazing. They say you have it, that you are an extraordinarily gifted musician. I actually heard you play one night, but only for a few songs. I was impressed with what I heard."

"*It*, you mean a potential?"

"Yes, a potential is another way of saying it, I guess. You still have it in you to write, don't you?" she asks.

"I hate to make his big head grow any bigger, Julie, but the boy can write about anything, anytime, anywhere, and he needs to start playing again," Nick brags. "Whip him into shape, will you?"

"Whip him, oh, that sounds kind of fun," she replies. She looks over at Nick with a devious grin.

"Wow," Chad and Nick both reply in unison. Hunter drops his jaw and quickly begins to blush.

He turns to Chad, asking, "Where did you find this girl?" He looks back at Julie with a big smile and astonished look.

"I didn't. She found me. I was sitting in with a band on the Ithaca Commons, and she pulled me aside after the gig, introduced herself, and told me congratulations, I was her new keyboard player."

"Just like that?" Hunter asks.

"Just like that," Chad replies. "Somehow, I wasn't able to argue."

"Just like that," Julie says. She snaps her fingers.

"You have some strange powers," Hunter says. He shakes his head, fascinated by her complete sense of control.

"Yes, I do... don't cross it," she replies with a look of seriousness. Quickly she surrenders an infectious laugh that overwhelms her face with a warm and inviting glow. "We have to go. I will call you Thursday with directions to where we practice. Sound good, Hunter?"

"Okay," he replies.

"We'll see you Thursday then. Bye."

"Nice meeting you guys," Chad says.

Julie smiles as she turns away. Chad walks with her, holding the door open for her as they exit the establishment.

Nick and Hunter watch as she walks away. They stare at her perfect hourglass figure as she steps through the doorway. Both of them simultaneously take a deep breath.

"I was outdone," Nick says. He turns back to the bar, retrieving his drink.

"How's that?" Hunter asks.

"I said I had plans for you this evening, but that girl just made plans for your lifetime. Congratulations, man, you not only have a new singer but a smoking hot new girlfriend. I think I'm starting to hate you."

"Nick, that's the most beautiful woman I have ever seen in my life."

"I Agree. That girl is one in a million."

"I'm thinking more like one in a billion."

"Actually, you're probably right," Nick replies.

"Do you think love at first sight is possible?" Hunter asks.

"They say it happens all the time, and I saw the way she looked at you. I'm pretty sure she likes you, old boy. I also saw an assured woman who wants fame, fortune, and the house on the hill as well. I just can't believe she might like your sorry little ass."

"Why do I think she may get all that?

"Because she probably will," Nick says. He lifts his glass for a toast.

"That remains to be seen," Hunter replies as he taps his mug with Nick.

"Hey, drink up. That guitar player is at the Dockside Bar. Let's go check him out."

"Oh right, I almost forgot about that," Hunter says. They both finish their beer and leave the bartender a tip.

Nick taps Hunter on the shoulder as the two leave the tavern. "You are a fortunate man, Mr. Watkins."

# Chapter 8

## A Flame on the Rise

NICK AND HUNTER ARRIVE AT the Dockside bar on the western end of town. The tavern is filled with patrons, a peculiar sight as most of the students from nearby colleges are away on summer break.

"Wow, are there a few people here tonight, or what? This guy must be pretty decent," Hunter says. They get out of Nick's truck and approach the entryway.

"Decent? The guy is pure evil on guitar," Nick replies.

"Pure evil, eh? We will see about that," Hunter says.

Upon entering the tavern, the crowd cheers as the band finish playing one of their songs. Nick and Hunter make their way to the bar. "Two drafts," Hunter says. The bartender grabs two plastic cups, then pauses a moment as she looks at him.

"Hey, you're Hunter Watkins, aren't you?" the attractive bartender asks.

"Yes, I am," he replies.

"Are you ever going to get a band together? I'm doing all the bookings here and would love to see you play again." She begins to fill the cups as she smiles at him.

"That may be in the works. We'll see," Hunter replies.

"Well, you should get this guy to play for you. He's been coming in here for a couple of weeks now and sitting in with the house band. He's looking to get into a local group, and frankly, he's one of the best I have ever heard. I mentioned you as a possible frontman," she says.

"That's why I came. My friend here dragged me out to see just how good he is."

"If you promise to put a band together, then these are on me," she replies. She slides him the beers and nods her head.

"It's a deal," Hunter replies. He leaves the girl a tip, then turns his attention to the band.

"Ladies and gentleman, all the way from jolly old England, please give a huge Dockside Bar welcome to our guest guitarist, Scratch." The crowd lets out boisterous applause.

Hunter studies the musician like a hawk. He notices the guitar player has a vintage Gibson Les Paul Sunburst. The beam from the spotlight scatters off the polished finish as if emanating from an exploding star. The man, dressed all in black, begins to play an eerie melody with only one hand as he grabs an empty beer bottle with his other hand. The music he is playing is suddenly accompanied by a haunting chorus of slide orchestration from the beer bottle. It creates an entirely mesmerizing guitar solo and the crowd cheers at the guitar player's abuse of the fretboard. Hunter watches, captivated and fascinated.

"Is he phenomenal or what?" Nick asks.

"Of that, there is no doubt." Hunter continues to watch and listen as the guitar player seems to perform the impossible.

Scratch finishes his solo, leading the band into the next song. Hunter cocks his head as they begin the piece. The singer puts on a dark pair of sunglasses as he begins to sing to the dark and bluesy song.

*Flames on the Rise*

*"Caught the latest feed that was beamed in from the satellites.*
*You never know what to expect on the other side... of tomorrow.*

*I don't know what you're feeling.*
*I don't like what you're feeding me... with flames on the rise.*

*Little tyrants ruled with impunity in foreign lands.*
*Kept tearing at the giant, who reduced them down to grains of sand.*
*So shallow all you're screaming.*
*I don't know why you're bleeding me... with flames on the rise.*

*Stop your crying. Wipe your tears away.*
*I can see you, one, two, three, and*
*I might hit you while you're sleeping.*
*With flames on the rise.*
*Flames on the rise."*

Scratch solos over the piece. The crowd screams as if under some demonic trance. Hunter listens closely as the guitar player tears into the fretboard with ferocity and precision that seems to border on sheer anger. The singer leads Scratch out of the solo by continuing to sing the lyrics.

*"Subversives check their courage as they slit the throats of diplomats.*
*Then wonder why it's raining lead and fire down upon their lands.*
*I don't care what you're feeling.*
*I hope you've been expecting me... and the flames on the rise.*

*Stop your crying, wipe your tears away.*
*I can see you, one, two, three, and*
*I might hit you while you're sleeping.*
*With flames on the rise.*
*Flames on the rise.*
*With flames on the rise.*
*Flames on the rise."*

"Does Scratch know how to burn or what? Give it up for Scratch, ladies, and gentlemen," the singer shouts out. The crowd screams for more. The singer points to Scratch and raises his arms, signaling for the crowd's applause. "We're going to take a short break, but we have more red-hot Blues coming right your way, and Scratch is going to tear it up some more for you, so don't go away. We'll be right back. And whatever you do, don't forget to tip your bartenders," the singer says. He places the microphone back on the stand and turns to go backstage.

Hunter and Nick look at each other in amazement. Both have finished their beers and simultaneously spin on their stools to face the bartender.

"What did you think?" she asks Hunter. She takes both cups to fill them.

"Holy shit, the guy is unbelievable," Hunter replies.

"You ought to go introduce yourself. They're in the band room out back," she says.

"That's a great idea." Hunter looks over his shoulder toward the stage room door. The barmaid pours the beers, again refusing payment. "Thanks, Kid," Hunter says. He winks at the girl, then turns on his stool. He slides Nick his beer. "Leave her a tip, then let's head out back," Hunter says, nodding his head toward the band room.

"I'm good. I'll hold the seat here for you," he replies.

As Hunter approaches the dressing room, the singer from the band recognizes him. "Hey, you're Hunter Watkins. I haven't seen you in a while. Can I get you to sit in for a few songs tonight?"

"Hi, how have you been? Thanks that would be fun, but no, not tonight. It's your show. I just came by to check out your band. I don't think I ever caught your name, though, my friend?" Hunter asks as he firmly shakes the young man's hand.

"I'm Paul. I used to love to watch you play. You gave me some great advice a while ago that really helped me out."

"I did? Hunter asks.

"Yes. I told you I wanted to sing in a band, and you told me the best way to do that was to get out and get some experience here at the Dock. So I came down here, sang some songs, and they asked me to join their house band. Thank you. If you had not advised me to do that, I would still be thinking about doing it instead of actually doing it. I love it."

"Oh, I remember now. That was at the Haunt, just over a year ago," Hunter says.

"Yes, it was. Are you playing again? the singer asks.

"Well, I might be putting something together. We'll see if it can take flight."

"Hunter, this guy that has been sitting in is looking for a permanent band. Let me introduce you."

"Would you? That would be great," Hunter replies. The two of them walk toward the dressing room.

"I will if I can tear him away from the two hot girls with him backstage," Paul says.

"He has two girls?" Hunter asks.

"They're as red-hot as his playing. To-die-for gorgeous, really. I think only one is his girlfriend, though, but come on in."

The two enter the dressing room, where the rest of the band members are hanging out with a few quests. The guitar player is seated in the corner of the room, accompanied by two beautiful redheaded women.

Paul gains Scratch's attention. "Scratch, I want to introduce you to a very gifted songwriter. This is Hunter Watkins."

"Hey, pleased to meet you. I'm Nick Pocker, but you can call me Scratch. Everyone else does. Have a seat, mate," he says to Hunter.

"That was some incredible abuse of the Les Paul with the beer bottle you just did, sir. I've never seen it done quite that way. Pretty impressive, really. My compliments," Hunter says. The two girls at the table grin at Hunter, then look at Scratch.

"Yeah, it's something that makes the kiddies yell and scream, isn't it?"

"Indeed, and the picking technique you have developed is equally as impressive. It is a pleasure to meet such an exceptionally talented player. Where the hell did you learn to play like that?"

"Ah, you are too kind, mate. That's something I picked up in my Delta Blues days," Scratch says. He takes a drag from his cigarette. "A few people have told me about you and your previous band. Terrible what happened. My condolences. Do you ever think about starting a new one?" he asks.

"Yes. I'm starting to consider it. I haven't played in a while, but I'm certainly getting the itch to play again."

"From what I hear, I'd be interested in jamming with you. People keep telling me I have to hook up with this Hunter guy. They tell me that you've got what it takes to make it big. I've always wanted to make it in the music industry. I spent my whole life trying to get somewhere. It's tough, you know?"

"Yes, I sure do," Hunter says. He lets out a brief laugh as he looks at the two women.

"You need a plan. It's so difficult to do it alone. I'm sure you know that already. You need allies, mate. Don't you agree?" Scratch asks, taking another drag from his cigarette.

"Yes, you're absolutely right. Are you free next week?" Hunter asks. "I would love to get together and see what we can come up with."

Hunter smiles at the two gorgeous women situated on both sides of the musician. The more attractive of the two stares at him, flirting with her eyes. Twirling a strand of her long red hair, she bites the corner of her lip as if hinting that she could be much closer to Hunter should he prefer.

Scratch notices Hunter's observation of the girls. "Oh, how despicable of me. I did not introduce you to my two dearest friends. Please forgive me, this is Naamah, and this is Aphrodite," Scratch says. "They're both responsible for running my fan club."

"Hello," Aphrodite says.

"Nice to meet you," he replies.

"Hi, I'm Naamah." She reaches out to shake his hand. "I'm really pleased to meet you." she says. As she slowly withdraws her hand from the greeting, she slides her index finger across Hunter's palm.

"Hello, Naamah. Pleased to meet you as well," he replies.

"I'm a musician, mate. I am always free. Give me a call anytime," Scratch says. He rips the tab off of his cigarette pack and writes down his cell phone number. He hands it to Hunter and shakes his hand. Scratch's handshake is firm and cold as ice.

"I will. I look forward to getting together with you," Hunter replies. He looks up and notices that Alex has entered the room.

"Hunter, how the hell have you been?" Alex asks.

"Good, Alex, how about yourself?" he asks.

"Not bad. I have been hearing about this amazing guitar player. The owner of the club has been urging me to come down here to listen to him. You are one imposing guitar player," Alex says to Scratch.

"Scratch, this is Alex Cirelli. He's the man when it comes to recording," Hunter says.

"Nice to meet you, Alex," Scratch replies.

"That was some unbelievable riffs you were pulling off there. I can always use a good studio musician if you are interested." Always a salesman, Alex hands Scratch his card.

"Thanks, my friend. I will keep that in mind."

"You should hear some of the songs that Hunter, here, has written. You two should swing by together and toy around with some of it," he says.

The singer interrupts the conversation as the house band begins to leave the room for another set. "Scratch, are you ready to rock some more?"

"Yeah, I'll be right with you," he replies. He reaches over to grab his guitar, kissing Aphrodite as he rises. "Give me a call when you get the chance, Hunter, and we'll rip-off something worth selling our souls. Pleasure meeting both of you," Scratch says. He steps around the girls and heads toward the stage.

Hunter turns to the girls. "Pleasure meeting both of you," he says.

"I look forward to seeing you again, Mr. Watkins. Is there a Mrs. Watkins that we can hang out with when you and Scratch get together?" Naamah asks.

Hunter begins to laugh. "No, there is no Mrs. Watkins on the immediate horizon that I'm aware of," he replies.

"Well, even better. Then you are free to party with Aphrodite and me when you are done playing and want to unwind. We look forward to possibly working with you, Hunter," she says.

"The pleasure will be all mine," he replies. As Hunter is about to exit the room, he takes one last look back at the sultry redhead, and she flicks her hair as she smiles back at him.

"I figured the buzz of this player might lure you out of the woodwork, Hunter. I knew you would soon start thinking about playing again," Alex says.

"You're a very wise man, Alex."

"You should know that there is a girl in town who came to see me. She's a voice major at Ithaca College. She seems pretty serious about forming a band. I received a call from an attorney friend downstate about her. I met with her and listened to a couple of demos she had, and she blew me away. When she asked who might be worth investigating for local songwriters, the first person I told her about was you."

"Oh, thank you."

"You have to get back out there, Hunter. I hope you don't mind, but I played a couple of your songs that you did with Krystal. She really liked them. She'll be looking you up."

"Her name isn't Julie, is it?"

"Why, yes, it is," he acknowledges. "She has contacted you already; I take it?"

"Yes, and that girl is something else," Hunter says.

"Hunter, let me tell you something from a purely professional point of view. Your sister was an excellent singer, but this girl, Julie, is the real deal. She is, without question, the best voice I have ever heard in my studio. You are a great songwriter, and your first album, that's all but done. You simply can't leave it abandoned in my studio. You need to write some new material, with this girl, preferably. I always thought you had what it takes to make it out of this town and on to some level of stardom. Land this guy Scratch and this girl Julie and let's get the thing rolling and make some money."

"I'll do my best," Hunter replies.

"I would expect nothing less, Hunter. Come on, let's go get a beer."

"That's what I like about you, Alex. You always have great ideas."

# Chapter 9

## A Meeting of Masters

HUNTER AWAKENS THE NEXT morning and prepares a pot of coffee. Looking out his window, he notices that the mailman is making the morning rounds. He finishes his first cup and makes his way down the stairwell to retrieve his post. As he reaches the mailbox, the new tenant begins to approach from the parking lot.

"Hi. You must be my new neighbor," he says to Hunter.

"Yes, I believe I am," he replies.

The stranger introduces himself, "Nice to meet you. I'm Chris."

"Hi. I'm Hunter," he replies as he shakes his hand. He notices the man has a grip that could crush a walnut and a physical frame more akin to a bodybuilder.

"I'm pleased to meet you. I take it you're a drummer?" Hunter asks.

"Yes. An aspiring one anyway," Chris says. He reaches into his mailbox.

"I heard you play yesterday. You're very talented."

"Thanks, I try. I sure hope I didn't bother you. I normally don't play in the morning, but I just moved in and finished setting up my drum set. I had to play it a little bit."

"Not a problem, I understand. Next time I will just kill you when you start that early." Hunter smiles as he jokes with his neighbor.

"That's fair." Chris laughs as he glances at his mail.

"I did notice that you have some nice chops. How long have you been playing?" Hunter asks.

"Since I was a kid. It's a great stress relief from my studies."

"So you are a student?"

"Yes, I go to Cornell, but I also take music classes at Ithaca College."

"Oh, cool. What are you studying?"

"I'm doing my master's degree in business at Cornell. Up at Ithaca College, I'm taking some advanced percussion classes, and I conduct some tutoring hours."

"Nice, what do you plan to go into?" Hunter asks.

"The entertainment industry. I really would like to form a band. That is how I initially would like to break into the industry. I have a few connections, but Ithaca is so full of talented people and an ideal place to find good writers."

"Yes, I hear there are a few around. I would love to do a jam session with you. I'm actually looking for a drummer at the moment to get a band rolling."

"You play?"

"I do."

"Cool, what do you play?" Chris asks.

"Oh, guitar, bass, piano. Whatever I can put my hands on," Hunter says.

"I prefer to get my hands on blondes, brunettes, and redheads myself." He grins as he looks at Hunter.

"Nice." Hunter laughs with his new friend. "Let me know if you ever end up some night with too many instruments to play. I'll give you a hand."

Chris opens one of several letters he's received and begins to look it over as they walk. "I will do that. What is on your agenda tonight? I have a guitar player coming over that I met at the music store. He and my bass player friend, Franklin, are coming over this evening. You want to join us?"

"Guitar players are hard to come by, is he any good?" Hunter asks.

"Oh, man, he's absolutely phenomenal. He just showed up in town and is creating quite an impression."

"His name is Scratch, isn't it?"

"Yes. It is." Chris glances up from reading his mail.

"I caught him last night," Hunter replies.

"Oh, you were at the bar then," he says.

"Yes, he's unbelievable."

"Do you think?" Chris asks.

"What time are you getting together?" Hunter asks.

"Six o'clock. Can you make it?"

"Yes, I can do that. He gave me his number. I was going to set something up for next week, but tonight would be even better. Great, let's do it. I'll grab my guitar and be there by six."

"Pleasure meeting you, Hunter. I'll see you in a bit." They both turn into their apartments, and Hunter immediately places his equipment by the door. The phone rings, and he smiles in reading the contact name.

"Hey Stranger, it's Julie."

"Hi, yes, I see that," he says. "How are you?"

"Good. I'll be better when we can get together and write some music," she says softly into the phone.

"I'm ready any time you have in mind," Hunter replies.

"I have everything ready for Thursday, but I was wondering what you were doing tomorrow afternoon. I have a couple of musicians coming over, and I would love it if you could come over as well. I would like to see if you can write something to a particular song my keyboard player created. I hear a big love song out of it, but I can't seem to find the words to it. I thought it would be a great idea if we could get together sooner to see if you can come up with something."

"You're too flattering, Julie. That will get you everywhere with me, you know. Sure I can make it. What time are you thinking?" Hunter asks.

"Great, why don't you come over tomorrow around four o'clock?"

"All right. That sounds perfect. Where is your apartment?"

"Do you know where Buttermilk Falls Park is?" she asks.

"Yes, of course," Hunter replies.

"I'm in the red house with the long driveway, slightly past the park's upper entrance. So four o'clock? I'll see you then, okay?"

"I look forward to it." Hunter smiles as he takes a deep breath.

"Bye," she says.

"Goodbye," he replies.

Hunter plays his guitar for a few hours and takes his time getting ready. As he makes his way to Chris's apartment, it is clear Scratch has arrived in hearing him play some guitar scales.

"Glad that you could make it," Chris says as he helps Hunter by taking the practice amplifier from him. The two enter the living room, where Scratch stops playing long enough to acknowledge Hunter's arrival.

"Hunter, I know you have met Scratch, and this is Franklin on the bass guitar," Chris says as he directs Hunter's attention to the other musician.

"Hi, Franklin. It's a pleasure to meet you."

"Nice to meet you, Hunter. Seen you play before, man. I am excited to sit down with you all tonight," Franklin replies.

Scratch greets him from across the room. "Hey, mate. Good to see you again."

"How are you doing, Scratch?" Hunter asks.

"Not bad. Are you ready to rock?"

"Yeah. I think I can keep up with you guys. Let's do it," Hunter replies. He slings his guitar over his shoulder and reaches into his pocket for a guitar pick.

Chris takes his place behind his drum set, reaches over to a micro-fridge, and grabs a beer. "You guys want one?" he asks. He pops the top and takes a quick swig.

"Yeah and hell yeah," Scratch says. He reaches for the handout Chris is offering, and Hunter takes him up on the offer as well. Chris offers a beer to Franklin, but he waves off the libation. The two guitar players tap their bottles in a toast.

"Let's burn. Follow me, boys," Scratch says. Setting his beer bottle down, he begins to play a four-bar musical progression.

They play the progression for several minutes when Hunter motions the others to stop. He takes out his notepad and frantically begins to write. He glances at the myriad of electronics that Chris has set up. "Do those keyboards work?" Hunter asks as he continues to write. The others look at him with curiosity as his hand races across the page.

"Sure. Just turn it on. The power is on the top left, and the amp is next to it," Chris replies. He turns from his drums and reaches into his drum bag. Retrieving a small pocket pen recorder, he turns it on, setting it on his music stand. Scratch does the same, retrieving a similar device from his shirt pocket, and puts it on top of his amplifier.

Hunter looks to Scratch. "You are playing that riff in E Major," he says. He presses the power button to the keyboard, then turns on the amplifier.

"Yes, I am. It's a simple turn-around of E, B, D, then A. If you would like, I can switch it to a minor key. It would give it a nice darker sound."

"No, that progression is perfect. Hold on a minute," Hunter says. He reads the program numbers listed on the keyboard, punching a number that yields a synthesizer sound. He puts down his lyric sheet and finds the piano chords.

Scratch listens to what Hunter begins to play. He nods his head as he grins, appearing impressed that Hunter is attempting to play two instruments simultaneously.

Hunter quickly comes up with a melody for Scratch's progression. "Oh, I like that, mate. You're good. You're really good. I don't suppose you hear words to it as well, do ya?" he asks.

"Yes. I do. I just wrote the words down. I will play this simple melody in between the lyrics. After I play this a second time, go ahead and lay down a solo for the same amount of measures in the middle of the song, all right?"

"No problem, Mate. Can do," Scratch replies.

"Chris, can you slow the tempo just a bit, please?" Hunter asks. He positions himself beside the keyboard to be free to play the guitar as well. Hunter nods to Chris, and the drummer taps a four-count. The four of them begin to play the song again. The others listen as Hunter belts out the song lyrics without the aid of a microphone.

## Only Me

"I drove in just the other night, and you all stood still.
This old boy is back in town, and I came for your sweet will.
I may be crazy, but I know I'm right when I say I need you so.
And if you take my hand tonight, then I will need you more and more.
It wasn't long ago, but some things never change.
I would have thought by now that things would have been rearranged.
Everything's the same as it used to be.
The only thing that changed is only me.

I've been all around this great big world, and I've seen all there is
to see.
Now I'm back in town, and I know you are the only one for me.
I may be crazy, but I know I'm right when I say I need you so.
And if you take my hand tonight, then I will need you more and more.
It wasn't long ago, but some things never change.
I would have thought by now that things would have been rearranged.
Everything's the same as it used to be.
The only thing that changed is only me.

Now I have led a golden life. My dreams they've all come true.
Yet through the years, I have met no one who can move me quite like
you.
I'm talking fast, and my words are hyped as I hold you tighter still.
I said I loved you one lonely night, and babe, I guess I always will.
It wasn't long ago, but some things never change.
I would have thought by now that things would have been rearranged.
Everything's the same as it used to be.
The only thing that changed is only me.
Only Me, Only Me, Only Me, Only Me."

"I love it. I absolutely love it, mate. It's simply brilliant. I don't think I have ever seen someone come up with such a perfect piece as quickly as you just did. You have a serious gift, my friend. How the hell do you create lyrics that fast is what I would like to know?" Scratch asks.

"Well, it's as if He slips it to me," Hunter replies.

Scratch looks over at the other musicians. "He slips it to him," he says. "Who slips it to you, some ghost?" Scratch asks.

"No, the Big Guy," Hunter replies.

"The Big Guy. You mean God?"

"Yes, of course," Hunter says.

"I didn't know God was in the Rock and Roll business. I thought he was more into Mozart, really."

"Mozart had to have had a direct line to him. Mine is more long-distance," Hunter replies. He begins to laugh as Chris and Franklin do the same.

"Well, may He slip you many more like that. Can we go through that song again? I think I would like to mimic some of that melody in the guitar lead to what you just wrote, or He wrote," Scratch says. Like a true master, Scratch spends only a moment figuring out the melody that Hunter has created.

The musicians spend the next several hours fine-tuning the song and working on some cover material. As the evening progresses, a comradery begins to form with the musicians.

# Chapter 10

## An Angel's Arsenal

DRAKE LOOKS AT HIS Universe Observation device. He notices that Hunter has met with and is about to meet again with Satan. Oliver is sound asleep at the main control board of Heaven.

"Wake-up," he says to Oliver.

"What... what?" Oliver asks as he lifts his head off the console, startled out of his slumber.

"It's him again."

"What's he doing now, Drake?" Oliver asks. He rubs his eyes and looks at the monitor in front of him.

"He's up to something. I can see it. He met with Hunter and is about to meet again to play some music."

"What do we do?"

"I'm not sure what to do yet, but he is up to something, so we better prepare for it."

"How do we prepare for it if we don't know what he's doing?

"We apply some logic."

"I'm not so good at that, Drake."

"Yes, I know. Hence why you are my assistant and not the Director, but you will learn quickly. Watch what I am doing," he replies.

Drake begins to enter the parameters of the emerging scenario in the Probabilities Calculator Computer.

"What will that do, Drake?"

"It will spit out the highest probability of what we should do."

Oliver continues to watch as Drake enters the data into the calculator. When he finishes, Oliver reads the results. "It says, Drake, to 'Offer Krystal Watkins, apprentice angel, the *Mortal Intervention Assignment.* She will provide solutions to potential problems that may arise with the forthcoming anticipated events. Send the *'Wings Acquisition'* contract now for her to accept or reject the assignment.'"

"Yes, I see that," Drake replies. "I have been able to read since the Dark Ages, Oliver. Thank you. Now touch that icon to send her the assignment contract." Drake smiles at his assistant.

"Okay, I sent it. That's it? That's all we're supposed to arrange?"

"For now. If the parameters don't change, then that is all we are supposed to do for the moment."

"I thought we are not supposed to send angels unless God says it's okay."

"Good. You are learning. That is why we met with God, to explain our request. As Director, the approval is sent directly to me. Once He approves our request to intervene, I run the computer parameters, and that gives us the direction to proceed."

"So now we have to summon the apprentice angel?" Oliver asks. A little excitement builds within his voice.

"Yes, and you just did when you sent her the contract. You catch on quickly, Oliver."

"I see. He sure does think of everything, doesn't He? Oliver asks.

"Yes. He does. Now pay close attention to what I'm doing. We have an assignment for a new angel so that she might gain her wings," Drake says.

He begins touching some icons on the computer screen. Quickly an angel appears in the Hallway of Eternity and walks directly toward them. Oliver taps Drake on the shoulder, who is preoccupied with the computer. Drake briefly looks up in acknowledgment as he continues analyzing computer data.

"Come in," Drake instructs the angel who is now standing in the doorway. "Krystal Watkins, is that correct?" Drake asks the angel.

"Hello. Yes, I am. I was told to see the Director of Angel Affairs. Do you know where I can find him?"

"Hello, I'm Drake. Sit down, please."

"Beautiful day, isn't it?" Oliver asks the girl.

"They're all beautiful if you know what to look for, this one especially. I was told I might be able to get my wings," Krystal replies. She smiles at both Oliver and Drake.

"We have an assignment for you that would make it possible to do precisely that," Drake says to her.

"What can I do to help?" she asks.

"Please call me Drake, and this is Oliver. You must try and protect a particular human that you are very familiar with."

"Oh, and who is that?" she asks.

"Your brother, Hunter Watkins," Oliver says.

"Oh, wonderful, how is he? I hope he gets here one day."

Drake looks at the girl with reassurance. "At the moment, he's fine. If we are not careful, however, he might not make it here as you hope."

"Oh, and you want me to do something about that?" she asks.

"Yes, that will be your assignment. You will be returned to Earth and appear as a mortal but still retain your angelic powers. See to it that Satan's effects are diminished so that he does not end up stealing Hunter's soul. You are to aid Hunter in any way that you find necessary. You are to help him make the right choices if you can, including, but not limited to, aiding any of his friends. Specifically, when we inform you to do so, you are to become friends with one of his bandmates named Chris. So far, so good?" Drake asks.

"If this is what it takes to get my wings, then you can count on me," she replies.

"Good. Oliver will give you a few items and some information on the assignment in a moment. These items, however, I will give to you now. You may or may not use them. It is entirely up to you. Hold out your hands, please," he says.

The girl does as instructed. Drake reaches into a small white satin pouch and retrieves a walnut. He holds it before her eyes then places it into her in her hands.

She looks at it perplexed. "A walnut?" she asks.

"Oh, it may look like a walnut. That is where the similarity ends. If you feel the need, then you are to throw this only at a mortal's back. It will protect him for one night only against Satan and his power, or any of his agents for that matter. It may also cause the individual to undergo a great deal of creativity while under its protection. Use it wisely. It will burst into a thousand points of light when it strikes the target then instantly disappear before your eyes." Drake reaches into the pouch and retrieves a second nut. Again he holds it briefly before her eyes.

"What is that?" she asks.

"This is a Hickory nut. Again, it is only a disguise. If you feel the need, you are to throw this only at a mortal's back. Doing so will enable someone to share their true feelings. Like the walnut, it too will burst into a thousand points of light then instantly disappear before your eyes." He places it into her hands and retrieves one last nut. He holds it before her eyes.

"An acorn," she says.

"Yes, but again it is only a disguise. This one is only to be used against Satan. It also must be thrown against his back. Like the others, it too will burst into a thousand points of light then instantly disappear before your eyes. It will temporarily immobilize him. A few seconds at best. He goes by the name of Scratch." Drake hands her the pouch. "Keep them in this until you decide you need to use them. Now I will leave you with Oliver. You will be cloaked so that Satan nor any of his demons will recognize you as an angel. Other angels, however, will aid you in your assignment, as they will be able to see you. In essence, you are now a secret angel agent on assignment, alright, my dear?" he asks.

"Yes, sir. It will be my pleasure," she says.

"Drake. You can call me Drake."

"It will be my pleasure, Drake," she says with a degree of excitement.

"Have a pleasant stay back on Earth, Miss Watkins. Good day. Oliver, take her to the Cloaking Preparations and Hologram booth, please. See to it that she is altered appropriately so as not to be recognized by her friends or her family and, more importantly, the Evil one or any of his temptresses. Good luck, my dear. I trust you will earn your wings."

"Thank you, Drake. Have a lovely day," Krystal replies.

Oliver and Krystal walk down a long golden-tiled hallway. As they arrive at the cloaking room, Krystal appears to be amazed at the sight of a large booth. It is constructed of only glass and large golden support frames. Her eyes open wide at the sight, and Oliver motions for her to step up into it.

"This will not hurt at all," Oliver says. He opens the door and touches a couple of icons on a large computer screen next to the booth.

"What will it do?" she asks.

"It will change some of your physical features. These changes are purely temporary. Once the assignment is over, and you are back here in heaven, you will become your normal self. For now, we will assign you a new body. Your facial features will change ever so slightly. We must also change the color of your hair and alter your height by a few inches. Too many similarities to how you once looked would arouse suspicions among those who knew you when you were a mortal. Your hair is blonde. How would you like to be a brunette for this mission?"

"Oh, that would be lovely," Krystal says. She looks out from the booth with excitement.

"Brunette it is. Taller or shorter?"

"Well, if I was a little shorter, I might be a little quicker on my feet, wouldn't I?" she asks.

"Oh, yes, you would, good thinking," Oliver says in agreement. "Shorter it is."

"This is going to be fun, isn't it?" she asks.

"Almost all angels have fun on this type of mission. Maybe it's because they get to prove themselves all while helping to defeat Satan. You are protected so that no harm can come to you. Now, what type of sunglasses? Rectangular, semi-rimless, cat's-eye, what will it be?" he asks. Oliver scrolls through the options on the viewing screen for her.

"I like those. I could wear those inside and outside all the time," Krystal says. She points to the yellow sunglasses.

"Oh, excellent choice. Unisex Round it is. Those are my favorite as well. I believe they call them John Lennon's on Earth," Oliver says. He continues to punch in the parameters.

"What about your attire, Krystal? Jeans, slacks, shoes, shirts. What are your preferences?"

"I love blue jeans. And it is summer down there, so how about faded blue jeans and a yellow short-sleeved shirt to match my sunglasses. Oh, and a pair of white sneakers. Can we do that?"

"Yes, no problem at all. You will be provided with plenty of money once you arrive, should you wish to change your attire," he says.

"Should I shut the door now?"

"Yes, thank you. Are you ready?" he asks.

"Yes, I'm ready," she says. She reaches over, gently pulling the door shut, and Oliver starts the machine.

It makes an array of harmonic sounds. The glass chamber quickly fills with a dense white mist. The process takes only a few moments, and the computer screen flashes that the process is complete. Oliver opens the door, and the foggy mist inside the booth rolls onto the floor. Krystal steps out of the booth, now disguised as a brunette in white sneakers, faded blue jeans, a yellow short-sleeved shirt, and sunglasses.

"Oh, you look absolutely marvelous, my dear," Oliver says. He closes the door and touches an icon on the computer screen. The glass door instantly transforms into a full-length mirror. Krystal laughs upon seeing herself disguised as a brunette. Oliver takes her hand and lifts it above her head, twirling her around in front of her reflection.

Oliver touches another icon that is flashing on the computer. The mirror transforms back into glass, and Hunter instantly appears on a real-time hologram projection inside the booth. The two angels watch as he drives into Buttermilk Falls State Park on his way to meet Julie for their writing session. He parks his truck and stares into the park. The two angels continue to observe as Hunter steps out of his truck and straps a guitar over his shoulder. Slowly he walks up the gorge trail, looking continually into the stream that flows beside the path.

The park is empty with no one in sight. He takes a seat on a bench and gazes at the water as it tumbles down the channel that is carved into the hillside. In the early afternoon sunlight, the area glistens as a rainbow effect is created from the water as it cascades into the natural pool. He sits quietly, appearing as if in a state of deep reflection.

"We used to go there together," Krystal says. The two of them both continue to watch Hunter. "He's thinking about me, isn't he?" she asks.

"It appears to be a moment of reminiscence, yes. Only God, or Drake to some extent, knows the exact true answer to what he's thinking. Drake always says, however, that if you listen really closely, you can hear their thoughts."

The words to a new song appear to come quickly to Hunter as if out of nowhere. He reaches into his pocket and retrieves his notepad, quickly jotting down some lyrics. Both angels turn their full attention to the hologram as he begins to sing.

*Find a Way*

*"See the stream that's flowing wide. It's fairly clean, and such a nice surprise. I'm flowing through another day. A simple choice, I'd like to stay awhile. Get out and live it, that's my feelings. Make every day a Saturday.*

*Hold this rose as it's blushing red. It's hanging on by such slender threads. Don't you know what this does to me? Oh, this life's such a mystery! Get out and live it, that's my feelings. Make every day a Saturday. If I could find a way!*

*Take time to laugh, but save some time to cry.*
*A silly boy, quiescent, wondering why.*
*Watch the clock, and the moments pass. Don't you know it's ticking*
*by too fast?*
*Get out and live it, that's my feelings. Make every day a Saturday.*
*If I could find a way!*

*See the gull gliding over the tide, hanging on to a new sunrise.*
*Dodge the day from the birds of prey. No other choice, I'd like to stay*
*awhile.*
*Get out and live it, that's my feelings. Make every day a Saturday.*
*If I could find a way!*
*If I could find a way!*
*If I could find a way!"*

Oliver watches the girl out of the corner of his eye. He can see that despite her heavenly happiness, there still exists a bit of yearning for her previous life on Earth.

"He is a pretty talented lad, isn't he, Krystal?"

"Yes, he is. He certainly is," she slowly replies. She turns her attention back to Oliver. A quick half-hearted smile signals to Oliver that she is ready for the mission.

"Here is a key to a fully furnished apartment on the Ithaca Commons. The address is written on it," he says to her. He places it into the satin pouch she is holding in her hand. "That will be the base of your operations," Oliver instructs. "And this is your communication device. It is both a phone and a real-time video interface with us in the Main Control room."

He hands her the device, and she looks it over in her hand. "I see," she says.

"If you have any questions that need an immediate answer, then shake it, and I, or Drake, will be able to communicate with you instantly. Any questions before you go, my dear? Oh, sorry, I mean Miss McCarthy."

She looks at him with curiosity. "Miss McCarthy?" she asks, appearing perplexed by the statement.

"Yes, I almost forgot. Your name for this assignment is Jennifer McCarthy. You can appear either in mortal form or as an angel. It's your call. In angelic form, you will be completely invisible to humans, but you'll be allowed to interact with humans in mortal form. Most angels report that they prefer to operate completely in mortal form. You likely will achieve more in mortal form. Either way, if you whisper a suggestion onto the wind, mortals tend to act upon that suggestion. They seem inclined to do what an angel suggests for them to do. Humans call it 'gut instinct,' but it is what it is. So, your name for the assignment is Jennifer, or Jenny, whichever you prefer. Do you have any questions?"

"I like Jenny better," she says.

"Jenny, it is," Oliver says.

"No, I don't have any questions at the moment, but if I do, I will give you a shake," she says. She holds the phone up and quickly shakes it. Instantly she appears on a large monitor.

"Splendid. You see, it works. Oh, I almost forgot. You are also enrolled in Ithaca College as a Philosophy and Religion major. We will place you on campus when we send you back. Make your way to the Registrar's Office and get your schedule when you arrive. And one last thing. Do not eat ice cream," Oliver says.

"Ice cream. Why no ice cream?"

"It's what angels most want to indulge in on their assignments. They seem to find it nearly impossible to resist. It could result in interfering with your mission or delaying you acquiring your wings."

"Oh, well, we wouldn't want that," Krystal says. "I guess I'm ready then."

Oliver takes her hand and helps her back into the glass booth. "Good luck," he says. As he closes the glass door, he points to the latch on the door. "Press the transport icon there on the doorknob when you are ready. And remember, no ice cream."

"Not a lick." She laughs as she notices a small screen in the center of the golden door latch. She waves goodbye, then presses the transport icon as instructed.

CHRIS WALKS ACROSS the Ithaca College campus, and one of his books slips out from underneath his arm. He drops to his knee to pick it up just as Jenny suddenly appears standing above him. The sun shines brightly, and her figure instantly casts a shadow on him as she looks down from the granite rim of the campus fountain.

He appears shocked as he stands, having not seen her standing there only a moment before. "Holy shit! Where the hell did you come from?" he asks. He appears astonished as he looks up at her.

"Hello," Jenny says.

"Hello," he replies. He places his books on the granite and rubs his eyes as if in disbelief.

She smiles at him as she looks down. "What's your name?" she asks.

"Chris. What's yours?"

"Jennifer."

"Hi, Jennifer," he says.

"You can call me Jenny if you'd like."

"Hi, Jenny."

"Don't you just love this view?" she asks. She looks toward the lake.

He continues to look up at her. "Yes... I... I do," he says.

"Is that the Registrar's Office over there?" Jenny asks. She points toward a long building at the end of the quad.

"No, that's the Student Union Center. The Registrar's Office is this building right here," he replies. He points to the building that is only yards away.

"Thank you, Chris." She extends her hand for him to help her down from the granite. He does not hesitate to help her, quickly taking her hand. "Thank you. Maybe I will see you around," she says. She steps down from the platform and smiles at him once again.

"I sure hope so," he says. He shakes his head as she walks away.

# Chapter 11

## Must Be Love

A HAWK SCREECHES AS IT soars above the park forcing Hunter out of his writing session and into the current moment. He looks at the time on his phone. Rushing back to his truck, he proceeds up the winding mountain road for his rendezvous with Julie. As he arrives, she steps out onto the porch and into the late afternoon sunlight. Hunter takes a deep breath upon seeing her. "Oh my God," he slowly and quietly says to himself. Her royal blue shorts and matching top hug her body's curves and likely stir the young man's emotions. Any thought about love at first sight is undoubtedly confirmed by his second encounter with the beautiful girl.

"Hi Julie," Hunter says. His eyes open wide as he approaches her.

"Hello. I'm so glad you could make it," she replies. She sits down on top of the steps next to one of the large white support pillars. Her slightly tanned legs seem to glisten in the sun.

"What a beautiful property," Hunter says. He surveys the flora that graces the Victorian estate. "So many flowers, they're all so beautiful."

"It is one of the things I fell in love with when I came to see the apartment. The landlady is so wonderful. She's always tending to the garden or running downtown to get some wonderful pastry treats that we often sit here on the porch and share in the evening. I told her that she should make the place a bed-and-breakfast. The garden that she has created in the back of the house is even more beautiful."

He leans slightly forward toward the girl. "Maybe she'll adopt you," he replies.

"Maybe," she laughs at the idea. "She's just a dear. If she ever sells it, I want to buy the place," she says. She reaches into her shorts for her lip balm. She takes the top off the stick, and he watches her as she applies it.

Hunter sits down next to her. "We won't be disturbing her tonight, will we?" he asks.

"No. She's traveling for the next month," Julie says. She places the top back on the moisturizing stick, then pulls her hair around her neck to the right side of her shoulder. Her slight movement allows her sweet-smelling perfume to permeate the air. Hunter briefly closes his eyes as he breathes in the scent as if enchanted by the memory of the moment.

Julie is looking at him as he opens his eyes. "Are you alright?" she asks.

"That depends on who you ask, I guess," he replies.

"You're funny. You make me laugh. That's a good quality to have, Hunter. Where do you get your sense of humor?"

He leans toward her as he smiles, "I'm the youngest of three brothers. What you think is funny is likely more of a coping mechanism."

Julie lifts her hand to her lips as her mouth opens wide. "Oh my God, you are too much." She shakes her head as she laughs then looks back at him. "You are funny, Mr. Watkins. I must say."

"I think the others are here," Hunter says as he looks toward the road.

"I think you're right," she replies as two cars begin to pull into the driveway.

Chad, Chris, and Franklin wave as they approach from the parking lot. Chad greets Hunter and Julie as Franklin and Chris pause for a moment, admiring the 1800's farmhouse.

Franklin strokes his goatee as he looks up at the Mansard roof and dormers. "Oh, Lord, I bet this old house could tell some stories," he says.

59

"I bet we could make it tell some more," Julie replies.

"I bet you're right," Franklin says.

"Do you have this whole house to yourself?" Chris asks as he approaches the porch.

"No. The landlady lives in the back half. The front half is a three-bedroom apartment that I share with my two roommates," Julie replies.

Hunter greets the three musicians as they come closer. "Good to see you all again," he says.

"Oh, you all know each other already?" Julie asks Hunter.

"Yes, Chris and I live in the same building. I just met him and Franklin yesterday, and you already introduced me to Chad," Hunter replies.

"Well then, are you all ready to make some music?" she asks.

"Sounds good. Let's do it," Chad replies.

Hunter retrieves his guitar from his truck as Julie leads the others into the house.

A baby grand piano gleams in the afternoon sunlight, just inside the Victorian Parlor. Hunter looks up as he enters the room, appearing to admire the ornate crown molding that wraps around the edge of the lofty ceiling. The tan Damask wallpaper and large Mahogany doors also seem to capture his attention.

"Wow, what a wonderful home, Julie," Hunter says.

"You like?" she asks.

"Yes, I do. I really do."

"I'll be right back," Julie says. Hunter watches her closely as she leaves the room.

Chris quickly finds the simple drum set in the corner of the room as Chad begins to play a ragtime piece on the upright piano. Hunter grins as Chad demonstrates that he is an exceptionally talented pianist. Franklin plugs his guitar into a bass amplifier and begins to play along.

"How long have you been playing, Chad?" Hunter asks.

"All my life," he replies. "My mother is a music professor at Ithaca College. They say that you need to find what makes you the happiest in life.

Music is what makes me the happiest. Trying to make a living off it is what I need to figure out. That seems to be the tricky part."

"Julie said you wrote a love song. Would you play it for us?"

"Sure. It goes something like this." Chad begins the song. The room's natural acoustics allows the piano's orchestration to fully resonate, which seems to spark Hunter's creativity instantly.

Franklin quickly finds the chords to accompany the arpeggio Chad is playing as Chris sits and listens.

Hunter retrieves his pen and a small pad of paper from his pocket. Then, like magic, words begin to flow, and his fingertips start to race across the empty page.

"That's the gist of it," Chad says.

"Keep playing, Chad, keep playing. I hear it, I hear it," Hunter says with excitement. Julie enters the room and quietly watches as Hunter writes at a frantic pace. As he continues to write, Franklin and Chris add to Chad's musical arrangement and help develop the song.

To their amazement, Hunter begins to sing as if he had performed the song many times before. Julie watches and listens in the entryway, shaking her head in apparent disbelief.

### *That's Why I Love You*

*"If I know anything, we're like two birds on a wing.*
*You're the reason I sing, and that's why I love you.*
*If I stand or I fall, I fear nothing at all.*
*I sit and wait on your call.*
*That's why I love you. That's why I love you. That's why I love you.*

*Without you I couldn't be. You always help me to see.*
*You make up half of what's me, and that's why I love you.*
*When I hold you at night, and I am holding you tight,*
*I know that everything's right.*
*That's why I love you. That's why I love you. That's why I love you.*

*If you're the sea, I'm the shore, and where we meet, I want more.*
*You wash through all of my pores, and that's why I love you.*
*And if there's one thing I find, the smile in your eyes so kind.*
*You're always here on my mind,*
*And that's why I love you.*
*That's why I love you.*
*That's why I love you.*
*That's why I love you.*

"Hunter, that's absolutely beautiful," Julie says. She appears fascinated at how fast he completed the piece. She raises her narrow blonde eyebrows as she asks, "You just wrote that?" she asks. She opens her mouth as if taken entirely by surprise.

He blushes at the question. "Yes," he replies.

"You didn't write any of it before you came here today?"

"No," he says, shaking his head.

Julie mirrors him as he shakes his head. "How can you write that quickly?" she asks. She smiles as she stares at him, continuing to shake her head.

"I just sing what I feel, what I hear in my heart," Hunter replies rather quietly. He returns her stare, smiling at her more charmingly from the right side of his cheek than the other.

"It's perfect," Chris says. "Let's do it again. If you don't mind, I would like to record it. It is easier for me when I practice."

Hunter looks at him with a puzzled look. "It is always a good idea to get a raw recording, but where is your recorder?" he asks.

"Oh, I just use this pocket pen recorder when doing rough takes." He pulls the device out of his shirt pocket. "It's a simple tool, but you can catch the essence of what you are after for later reference. Sometimes you catch something so subtle it's worth revisiting. I use it all the time. The way you write songs so quickly, though, Hunter, we probably don't need it," he says.

Chris starts the recording device and sets it on the corner of the fireplace mantle.

"You never know when it could come in handy," Hunter says. "I have a program on my phone I occasionally use to catch raw ideas. I should use it more often."

Chad looks out the window toward Ithaca College. "Hey, tomorrow night is July fourth," he says with excitement. "It's the fireworks, and your backyard is the perfect spot to watch them. Maybe we can get that one guitar player from the Scale House up here and rip off a jam. Then afterward we can watch the fireworks. Your place is perfect to see them, Julie. What do you think?" he asks.

"Hey, that's a thought." She gleams at the idea. "Are you guys all into coming back tomorrow night?

"That would work for me," Franklin responds.

"Works for me too," Hunter says. A radiating smile overwhelms his face.

"Then it's a date," Julie says.

"Let's try that song again. Julie, you sing it this time," Hunter encourages. He hands Julie his lyrics pad.

"No, you sing it one more time for me, so I can hear it while I read the words. It will help me get a sense of how I should sing it."

"Alright," Hunter says. He quickly checks the tuning on his guitar. Chris counts out the metering, and the musicians play the song once again as the recorder continues to capture the evolving content.

# Chapter 12

## Scratch Fever

JENNY INSPECTS THE AREA outside her apartment on the Ithaca Commons. Suddenly she witnesses Hunter rounding the corner, accompanied by Julie and Chad. The three band members sit down at a table in the open-air café, not far from her. She reaches into her purse and retrieves her phone, shaking it as she looks into the screen.

"Hello, Krystal, how are you?" Oliver asks.

"Hi. I thought that you wanted me to use my alias," she whispers.

"Oh, right, hello Jenny."

"I am here on the Commons, and I'm within a few yards of Hunter. It looks like he's meeting a girl and another guy, and they're all sitting down at a table outside of Mercato's Café this very moment. What should I do?" she asks.

"Ah, yes, I see. A beautiful day down there, isn't it?"

"Yes, it's lovely," she replies quickly.

"Okay, I see the Universe Observation device shows that you have an Ally somewhere in the immediate area. Do you see what appears to be a homeless man anywhere around you, Jenny?" Oliver asks.

She surveys the immediate area. Her attention is quickly drawn to a disheveled man walking up the street and talking very loudly to people as he passes. She listens closely and can distinctly hear him reciting scripture. He is dressed in a dirty white shirt, and his baggy pants are more extensive than his frame. A white rope is tied through the loops holding his old grey corduroy pants around his waist. The man looks directly at Jenny then suddenly stops speaking. He fumbles through his pockets for something, appearing pleasantly surprised as he notices the angel apprentice.

"Yes, I see him now," she says as she smiles at him.

The vagrant pulls from his pocket a chain with a large silver cross dangling from it. He places it around his neck and reaches into his pocket again. He retrieves a small green book, and he rests upside a building as he begins to read in silence.

"He is reading a book, is he not?" Oliver questions.

"Yes, he is reading a book. A small green book," Jenny informs excitedly.

"Good. That is Raguel. He will likely begin walking while continuing to read out loud various scriptures. When he does, follow him. If he passes Hunter's table, take a seat as close to him as you possibly can, and just observe what occurs," Oliver says.

"Got it, Jenny replies, completely enthralled with the developing situation. She observes the available table next to Hunter and his party. She seems to mentally prepare herself for the encounter, taking a deep breath as if hoping her disguise will go unnoticed.

JULIE TAKES A SEAT next to Hunter. Her white sundress stands in stark contrast to the black outdoor café tables and chairs, naturally drawing attention to the beautiful college student. The delicate gold chain she wears perfectly positions a gold cross at the base of her neck. It sparkles in the early afternoon sunlight, drawing further attention to her. People that pass on the sidewalk quickly notice the innocently fashioned girl, for her smile alone is as warm as the early afternoon sunshine.

"I love this place. It so reminds me of Paris," Julie says.

"She's cultured, Chad. That's a great quality for a singer to have. Don't you think?" Hunter asks.

"Yes, I do," Chad replies. "I've never been there. What reminds you so much of Paris, Julie?" Chad asks.

"The ambiance, the outdoor cafés, the street vendors, and mimes. All of it, really," she replies with a smile.

"This guy Scratch should be along any minute. Do you two have any questions for him?" Hunter asks as he looks at the time on his cellphone.

"I just want to make sure that we can develop a good chemistry with him," Julie replies. Chad nods his head in agreement.

The Commons bustles with businessmen and women going about their daily affairs. A few street musicians play to the passing crowds. Suddenly Scratch appears before them. A guitar is slung over his back, and a cigarette dangles from his lips.

"Hey, how are you all doing?" he asks. He takes a last drag from his cigarette, then flicks it toward the street.

Julie glances to watch the cigarette bounce off the curb and into the street. She raises her eyebrows as she looks over to Hunter.

"Here he is. Have a seat," Hunter says to the musician. "Scratch, this is Julie, the singer I recently started working with, and this is Chad, one phenomenal keyboard player."

"Thanks, Hunter," Chad says. He smiles at the compliment.

"Nice looking package," Scratch replies. "People tend to hear with their eyes, so I'm sure you kids sound absolutely smashing."

"Hi. I have heard so much about you," Julie says.

Scratch removes the guitar from his shoulders and sits down next to her. "Oh yeah? I hope at least some of it was good," he replies.

She studies him as he gently leans his guitar against the table. She looks at his long well-manicured fingernails, and then his vintage black pinstriped vest. "They tell me you are one of the best," she says.

"Yeah. You mean there is someone out there equally as capable?" Scratch replies.

"I hope your attitude can keep up with your ego, Mr. Scratch," Julie says. She flips her hair behind her shoulder as she leans back into her chair.

"Oh touché, Miss Julie. I'm sorry. I'm used to playing with people who quickly cop attitudes. My apologies. I see that you folks are working as a team, though. Please forgive me," Scratch says.

RAGUEL POINTS HIS FINGER into the little green book of scriptures held within his palms. He begins to walk toward Julie and the others slowly. As he passes Jenny, he glances at her and nods. She begins to follow him, and she casually takes a seat at the table next to Hunter. Jenny starts to look through her purse as she watches Raguel out of the corner of her eye. He stops to lean against a parking meter, just over Scratch's shoulder.

"I think you'll be most impressed with his playing, Julie. He really is the most amazing guitar player I have ever heard in a live performance," Hunter says. He looks at Scratch and nods his head.

"Ah, you are too kind, mate," Scratch replies.

Raguel glances into his pocket Bible and begins to read out loud. "The thief comes only to steal and kill and destroy; I have come that they may have life and have it to the full. The one who does what is sinful is of the devil because the devil has been sinning from the beginning. The reason the Son of God appeared was to destroy the devil's work."

Scratch turns in his chair and speaks loudly enough for the hobo to hear. "Hey, why don't you go down to the ministry and get a job and a goddamn bath. It's a bloody weekday, man. It's not a bloody Sunday. Nobody wants to hear your Scripture recital today. Move on, man. I can smell your sorry arse from here."

Perhaps to draw attention away from what he is doing, Raguel turns, raising his left hand to his head while placing the little green book beneath his other hand, resting it on Jenny's table. "Be sober-minded; be watchful. Your adversary, the devil, prowls around like a roaring lion, seeking someone to devour." He slides the book into Jenny's lap as he continues to make a scene.

He steps away from Jenny's table and continues to speak, looking directly into Hunter's eyes. "For He will command His angels concerning you to guard you in all your ways." He grins with pleasure as he turns to face Scratch. "Thank you for the kind advice, sir. I will take leave of you and find a stream to bathe in, for I am now aware that my stench rivals only your breath," Raguel says. He begins to laugh as he turns and casually begins to walk away.

As the hobo retreats, Scratch watches him, nodding his head several times as he grins.

Julie looks at Scratch with a bit of sadness in her eyes. "There is a passage in the bible, Scratch, to not forget to show hospitality to strangers, for by so doing some people have shown hospitality to angels without knowing it."

"Do you believe in angels, Miss Julie?" he asks.

"Yes, I do, actually," she replies. She tightens her lips as she smiles at him.

"Well, if you do, then I do. To be honest, though, you look like an angel yourself, Miss Julie. And I'm willing to bet you sing like one as well," Scratch says.

"Thank you for the compliment," she replies.

"Wow," Chad says, "I haven't seen that guy before. We sure do attract all types to our little city, don't we?"

"I find him fascinating," Julie says. "It is such a rich community. The guy is probably a Cornell drop-out that couldn't express his thoughts. He probably holds the key to the universe or time-travel or something. I just love this town. You were just blessed, Mr. Scratch. You should be delighted. He just cited the Bible to you. Where else can you get that outside of, say, New York City or L.A.?"

"Scratch, please, Miss Julie, just call me Scratch. You obviously are a much better person than I am. I have traveled in the south where they do that, here I am, like it or not, instant sermon routine everywhere you go. If I wanted scripture, I only have to check into the nearest hotel, and, low-and-behold, there is Gideon, waiting in the room for me. But you are right. I should count my blessings because we're all here to discuss an audition for your band. Please forgive me of my outburst."

The waiter arrives and strikes a wooden match to light the candle at the center of the table. The smell of it lightly permeates the air as the waiter snuffs it out and retrieves his order tablet.

Julie looks up at the waiter. "Hi," he says. "I'm Randy. I will be serving you today. Can I start you, folks, off with a drink?" the waiter asks. He hands them all a menu then readies his order tablet.

"Iced tea and three lemons please," Julie says with a smile.

"Draft," Chad replies quickly.

"I'll have an Iced tea too, please," Hunter says.

"And you, sir?"

Scratch hands back the menu. "Yeah, no pub grub for me, mate, just a drink. However, I have yet to find a bar chef that knows it by name, so I will spell it out for you: An ounce of Gin, a half-ounce of Orange Grand Marnier, an ounce each of dry and sweet vermouth. Throw that in with an ounce of orange juice and a dash or two of Orange bitters over ice and shake the living hell out of it. Alright, mate?" He hands the man a $20 bill. "Get it right, and you can keep the change."

"Yes, sir, got it. Right away, sir. I will be right back," the waiter says. He turns from the table, quickly returning to the restaurant.

Julie grins, seeming to be impressed at Scratch's order. "Devil's Whiskers," she says confidently.

"Ah, you are a smart young lady, Miss Julie. Yes, that's precisely what it is. Very few people know that one by name. Are you a barmaid?" Scratch asks.

"No, my father orders that drink when he's in an excellent mood after completing a large business deal."

"Ah, I see where you get your good taste. I assume that your stunning beauty comes from your mum?"

Hunter looks up from his menu at Julie to witness her reaction to the compliment.

"You flatter me, Scratch. I trust your musical talent is as sharp as your praises," she says as she reaches for her water.

"Touché again, Miss Julie," he says as he reaches for another cigarette.

Hunter looks to Scratch as he begins to fill him in on some details of the developing band. "I have already conveyed that we kind of auditioned each other. It's now nothing much more than formalities and arranging a time to get together. With that in mind, the next logical thing to do is schedule a session where all of us pull together to write some fresh material and begin building a band."

"I like your mode of thinking, mate. I'm already working on some fresh material." He smiles at Julie as he reaches in his shirt pocket. "I brought along a sample MP3 of a song I wrote last night. I would like to see if you can work up some lyrics for it. Take this sound card and give it a quick listen when you get a moment. It's the only song on there. I hear something, like, really edgy. I hear something like, I don't know, maybe frustration meets angst, or someone really disliking this century. Know what I mean? Have a go at it, will you, lad?" Scratch asks as he hands the device to Hunter.

Julie squints as she looks at him, appearing perplexed by his suggestion.

"Sure," Hunter replies. He takes the storage device and looks at the end of it, noticing it will plug directly into his phone. He takes a moment to transfer the song file, retrieving his earbuds from his pocket and plugging them into the phone. He then begins to listen to the recording, handing the storage device back to Scratch.

The waiter arrives with their drinks, placing Scratch's down first. "Please let me know if that's to your liking, sir," the waiter says. He watches Scratch as he walks around the table, distributing the rest of the libations.

Scratch takes a sip and gives the waiter a thumbs up, "It's perfect, mate, keep the change."

Hunter compliments Scratch as he continues to listen to the song. "Nice," he says. He listens to the music as the waiter starts to take the group's order.

Julie informs the waiter of her selection, and she nudges Hunter to get his attention. "What do you want for lunch, Hunter?" she asks.

"Oh, sorry. Just a Tully burger and fries," he replies. He looks back into his phone and begins to type. The waiter notes the final selection and takes the order back into the café.

"So where are you from in England, Scratch?" Julie asks.

"Oh, a wonderful little place you've likely never heard of, I'm sure. I'm from a tiny town in Somerset known as Withypool," Scratch replies.

"Oh my God, I know exactly where that is," she says.

"You do, really? How in the hell do you know where Withypool is?" he asks.

"My father has taken me there many times as a child. That's near the Exmoor Nature preserve. There is an ancient bridge there called the Tar Steps. My father likes to fly fish there when he gets time. Yes, I know exactly where that is," she says. She begins to retrieve the lemons from her drink and squeezes them into her tea.

"You are well-traveled, Miss Julie. I have spent a lot of time at that very bridge myself. I, too, like to drown flies. Maybe I have seen your father fly fishing there."

"Maybe. We always went in the spring or early summer. The bridge is ancient. They say it's like 3000 years old. He likes to fish around that area."

"Oh, I would love to drive you through the neighborhood, Miss Julie," Scratch says. "Do you happen to fly fish as well?"

"No, I like to watch, though. It's relaxing," Julie replies.

"Well, maybe when we make it big, we can all go there together. Perhaps I can teach you to fly fish. Or maybe you can just watch, and I can slip you the trout when I land one, and help you wrestle it into the creel."

"Maybe," she says quickly. "Have you ever seen Satan there on the bridge, Scratch? I understand they call it the Devil's sunbathing rocks. What is the real story with the locals?" Julie asks as she laughs.

"You can laugh if you like, Miss Julie, but the locals there don't call it that for no reason. Next time you are there, be careful as you pass over that bridge. The Devil vowed that it is his and his alone. Things have been known to happen there. Be careful when you visit, lass."

"He can't hurt me," Julie says in defiance of the warning.

"No? And why is that?"

"Because I believe. That's why I wear this," Julie replies. She runs her finger across the golden cross on her chest.

"Yes, right, well, that might tend to keep the devil at bay, wouldn't it?" Scratch asks with a smirk. He takes his drink and leans back into his chair as he grins at the sight of the glittering jewelry.

"Done," Hunter says. He unplugs his earbuds, placing them back into his pocket. He quickly reads what he composed then hands his phone to Scratch for his perusal.

"There is no way could you have possibly written a song that fast," Scratch says. He takes the phone and begins to read the lyrics.

_Satellites_

*Get me out from this city. Get me out from this town.*
*Take me from this misery, and wrap me up in the clouds.*
*Get me away from that laptop. Keep me away from that cell.*
*Take me to where there's room for all,*
*for all who feel like me, if there's any left at all!*

*We live in a time, no time for Heaven.*
*We live in a time of Satellites.*
*These are the days long-gone soft-spoken.*
*These are the days that's just so right.*
*Ah ah. Ah ha.*

*I'd like to go into hiding. I'd simply like to escape.*
*With old and new worlds colliding, I feel I've been raped!*
*I feel dazed and confused, Lord. I feel tattered and torn.*
*Amused though, when my cell phone pops corn,*
*and my brain cells, too, if there's any left at all.*

*Governments they keep on falling. What can I do?*
*Corporations keep on calling me. I'm red, white, yet blue.*

*We live in a time, no time for Heaven.*
*We live in a time of Satellites.*
*These are the days long-gone soft-spoken.*
*These are the days that are just so right.*

*We live in a world too fast for changes.*
*We live by rich thieves with different rules.*
*We live in a frame that needs explaining.*
*We live in a Kingdom ruled by fools,*
*and their Satellites.*

*We live in a time, no time for Heaven.*
*We live in a time of Satellites.*
*These are the days that we're awoken.*
*These are the days that are just so tight.*

*Ah, the Satellites.*
*Ah-ha, there are Satellites.*
*Ah, the Satellites.*
*Ah-ha, their Satellites.*
*Ah, the Satellites.*
*Ah-ha, under Satellites.*
*Ah, the Satellites.*
*Ah-ha, the Goddamn Satellites!*

"Oh, you are just too good, mate. Can I get a copy of that sent to my phone?" Scratch asks. He hands Hunter back his phone.

"Sure, not a problem," Hunter replies. He takes the phone from him, opens his contacts, and forwards the document.

"So when is the first full get together of this band?" Scratch asks.

"We were hoping tonight we could all get together with our bass player and drummer. Oh, and here comes one of them right now," Julie says. She points to Chris as he approaches the café.

"Yeah, I'm free tonight. Count me in." Scratch replies. He reaches for his drink and looks to where Julie is directing his attention. "Well, that's a good sign. I have already had the pleasure to jam with him," he says.

JENNY OPENS THE LITTLE green bible Raguel gave to her and begins reading. She attempts to cover her face by raising her left hand over her eyes. Chris instantly recognizes her and appears more than happy to see her.

"Hey, Jenny, right?" Chris asks. "We meet again," he says excitedly.

Jenny looks up at him. "Oh my God, hey, you were up on campus the other day. I remember you. Yes, we meet again," she replies.

"Is anyone sitting here with you?" he asks.

"No, please, have a seat," she says. She takes a deep breath as Chris sits down.

The waiter comes to the table to take Jenny's order. He smiles, seeing a second patron join her. "Hi, my name is Randy, and I will be your waiter. Can I start you both off with a drink?"

"Just an Iced tea, please," she replies. Julie looks over and smiles at the girl.

Chris hands the waiter his credit card. "I've got that. I will have one as well, thanks," Chris replies.

"Right away," the waiter says. He takes the card and retreats into the café.

Chris looks at the book Jenny is holding. "What are you studying on campus?" he asks.

Jenny looks at the book. "Philosophy, and Religion. What do you study?"

"Music education."

"Oh. Are you in a band?" she asks.

"Actually, yes, that's why I'm here."

"Cool, maybe some time I can come to hang out and hear you guys play," she replies.

"For sure. I think we can arrange that." He looks into her eyes and smiles. "These folks here are in the band. Hey everybody, say hi to my new friend, Jenny," Chris says. The band members all say a quick hello to her, then turn their attention back to the details of the evening's get together.

"Chad and I are going to work off lunch and walk Treman Park if any of you would like to hike the gorge with us," Julie says.

"That would be great. I've lived here my whole life and still have not walked the entire park yet. I'm in. How about you, Scratch? Chris, Jenny, what do you think?" Hunter asks.

"Yeah and hell yeah," Chris replies. "Jenny, would you like to join us?"

"I would, but I don't have a car."

"I'll give you a ride. What do you say?" Chris asks.

"Sure, why not?" she replies.

"Scratch, are you in for a little physical exercise?" Hunter asks.

"Absolutely. I love the park, really. My car, though, is getting decked out today. I would also need a ride," he says.

"I can give you a ride. Not a problem," Hunter replies.

"Oh, lovely. I like to swim with my girls there, every chance we get. Yeah, let's do it," he says. He finishes his drink then lifts his empty glass to show the waiter.

Instantly responding to the heavy tipper, the waiter arrives at his side and takes his empty glass. "Same drink, sir?" he asks.

"You are a good man. Play your cards right, and you can work for me one day, mate. A little heavier on the gin this time, though, right? Need some energy to do a little hiking in a bit," Scratch says. He hands the waiter another $20 bill, and he rushes back into the café.

# Chapter 13

## The Melting of an Ice-Age

SCRATCH LEADS HUNTER INTO his apartment to pick up his equipment. As they enter, Hunter's eyes open wide in amazement. Aphrodite and Naamah, scantily clad in red and black lingerie, are lost in the exploration of each other on the couch.

"You two at it again? Naamah, we got to get you a bloody boyfriend, lass," Scratch says. He turns and taps Hunter on the shoulders. "It's like she sucks the bloody life right out of my girl. Would you take her, lad?"

"Go away, Scratch," Naamah says. She laughs, unhindered by the interruption. "You can stay if you want to, though, Hunter." She continues to look at Hunter as the two girls begin to roll their tongues together.

"Well, there you go, mate. She won't let me kiss her, but Aphrodite loves letting her attempt to convert her into a bloody lesbian. Have at them if you please, mate. I'll grab my guitar case and my amp and be right back. Careful of that one, though. I'm warning you." He points to Naamah as he cautions, leaving Hunter alone with the two of them.

Hunter leans against the door jamb and lets out a short little laugh.

Naamah rests her head on Aphrodite's chest. She smiles at Hunter as she continues to caress Aphrodite.

"Want to join us, Hunter?" Naamah asks. "I promise it will be fun," she says.

Hunter's heart must surely race like wildfire across a drought-stricken plain. His eyes dilate, and he opens his mouth as if amazed by the thought of the erotic suggestion. He notices that Aphrodite's hands are bound to her neck with a long black-satin scarf. Naamah runs her hands up and down Aphrodite's long silky legs, caressing her friend with slow, gentle strokes. "Scratch likes to watch, and Aphrodite tastes like a lollypop. Sure you don't want to join us?" Naamah asks again.

"I don't like spectators," he replies. He raises his eyebrows with a grin as he continues to look at the half-naked girls.

"Too bad, she really likes threesomes," she replies.

"Listen to you. You are a walking nymphomaniac," Aphrodite replies.

"Maybe some other time," Hunter says. He shakes his head as he continues to watch.

Scratch makes his way back into the room with a small amplifier and case for his folk guitar. "I'll be back later tonight, ladies. Carry on. Hunter, would you be so kind as to grab that guitar there by the sofa and the door?"

As the two leave the apartment, Hunter shakes his head in disbelief. "You have quite the arrangement with those two, Scratch," Hunter says. He appears physically restricted as he begins to walk.

"I love it when they tease each other. They end up making me walk just like you seem to be walking right at the moment, mate," he replies. "I don't know what she does, but Naamah makes Aphrodite boff like a wild little bitch. She won't let me bang her, though, the little tart. It's depressing. She must have a tongue a mile goddamn long because Aphrodite screams like she's on electroshock therapy. Oh, I just love it so. It makes me wanker feel like it's about to bloody explode. Know what I mean?"

"Yes, I think I do." Hunter opens the tailgate placing the guitar in the truck's bed, and retrieves Scratch's other guitar from the cab, placing it in the empty case.

"Yeah, I see you do." He laughs as he looks down at Hunter's bulging pants. Scratch sets his amplifier down and closes the tailgate. "It's a great arrangement, really. I was surprised she invited you into the mix, though. I thought she was a complete Todger Dodger, but she just revealed that she's apparently an experienced switch-hitter. You should take her up on that. I'm willing to bet it would be the ride of your life if she doesn't suck the goddamn life right out of you and spit you out like pomace." Scratch laughs as they both get into the truck.

"Yeah, she probably would. She's one good-looking girl, that's for sure. Come on, let's roll," Hunter replies. He starts the truck and waits for Scratch to close the door.

"So what's your deal, mate? Are you trying to get a leg over on little Miss Julie, or is she open game?" Scratch asks. He reaches for a cigarette, placing it between his lips.

"A leg over? I'm not sure what that means," Hunter says. He looks at Scratch, raising one eyebrow in curiosity as he begins to drive off.

"You yanks, totally crack me up sometimes, really. You know, like snog her the hard way. Give her a long and serious Aussie kiss. Know what I mean?"

"No, actually, I have no idea what you are saying. I guess you lend a lot of credence to Winston Churchill's statement that the American and British people are 'two nations divided by a common language.' It's funny to hear you talk. It certainly is a lesson on culture. It's one part puzzle and one part comedy." Hunter looks over at the guitar player and laughs.

"Right. Well, I guess I'm asking if you're trying to Roger that. I'd Roger that, if it wouldn't like stomp on your feelings and all," Scratch says. He rolls down the window and lights his cigarette. "Oh, shite," he says. "I didn't think to ask you if you mind if I smoke in your buggy. Do you mind, mate?"

"No, go ahead. It's not a problem."

"Yeah, so you know, she is one hell of a pretty looking little girl with perfect Belisha Beacons just beaming away."

"Are you asking me if I want to date her?"

"No, I'm asking you to go beat the goddamn bishop. Yeah, I guess that's how you Yanks politely put it. Are you looking to date her, mate, or what?" he asks.

"I am not sure that's a good idea, dating the singer. I just want to take a shot at the big leagues, and she is what I consider a great performer," he replies.

"She sure is pretty. I will say that much. I bet she can be taught to perform real proper-like. You know what tends to happen more often than not is that once female singers make it big, they ultimately stray to the men with more money. The rest of their band has a propensity to drift into the 'where the hell are they now' files. Slipping her the old bell end now would likely mean that you have much less of a chance of that happening, you know? If you were trying to date her, that is. Stuff that little muff, and your heart won't be broken. Use your head, mate. Both of them, actually. Know what I mean?" he asks.

"Barely," Hunter replies.

"Well, there you have it, then," Scratch replies. He looks out the window at the rolling hills that surround the city. As they arrive at the park's entrance, Scratch, ever watchful of pretty and unsuspecting prey, begins to eagle-eye Jenny, who awaits with Chris and the rest of the group at a picnic table. "She's a nice little tart as well, don't you think?"

"Yes, a most kind and petite little frame. Yes, sir, that she is," Hunter replies in a mock English accent. He looks over at Scratch as he parks the truck.

"Oh, that was good, mate. Got a little English in you, do ya? Yeah, she truly is beautiful, basking there in the sun like a bloody little flower child," Scratch says.

"Yes. There is something about her. She's not just beautiful outside but seems even more beautiful inside," Hunter says in agreement.

"They're all pink inside, mate. That's what truly matters. This town really has some nice-looking felines in it. I must admit. I think if we were to make it big, it would be really hard to call anywhere else home," Scratch says. He lowers his shades, openly eyeing Jenny with a lustful stare.

Julie smiles as Hunter and Scratch take a seat at the table. "I have so wanted to do this since coming here to Ithaca. Is everybody ready?" she asks in her usual joyful manner.

"Wait, I have just one question. I thought we were walking the park, right?" Scratch asks.

Julie looks at him, somewhat confused. "We are. That's what we're doing as soon as you get your backside up off that bench," she replies.

"No, I think you have it backward, Miss Julie," Scratch says. He shakes his head gently in disagreement. "If we start here, then we have to walk up the hill and then back down."

"Okay. I'm thinking you have some sort of point there, Scratch," she says. She puts her hands on her hips as if waiting impatiently for the guitar player to reveal something to her.

"I thought we were walking down from the top of the mountain. Walking up the trail and back down will take the better part of the day. If we leave a car here and drive to the top, then the trail will only take about two hours for us to walk. That way, we won't be, how do you Yanks say it, all tuckered out for jamming tonight?"

"I do, Scratch. That's why we're taking the shuttle," she replies. She smiles as she cocks her head.

"Hunter, look at that, would ya? We got ourselves a singer with a great voice, smashing good looks, and has the brains to lead this here band. Great minds think alike, Miss Julie, cheers. I better grab the 6-string. Creativity is like lightning. You never know when it might strike."

Scratch takes his folk guitar from the back of the truck as Hunter places the remaining equipment inside the cab. "You'll be a love, and lock that, won't you mate?" Scratch asks Hunter.

"Sure, but do you think someone will mess with a country boy's truck out here in the country, especially with a Pittsburgh Steeler sticker in the back window?" he asks.

"Well, I don't know, but I don't want them stealing my Les Paul."

"Good point," Hunter replies. He reaches into his pocket, retrieving his keys, and locks the vehicle with the keyless device.


THE SHUTTLE COMES TO a stop at the old Grist Mill at the top of the park. Scratch smiles as he steps off the bus and looks down into the waterfall. Two large rainbow trout lay in the back of the pool, keeping a steady pace with the upland stream's gentle current. "Look at those two beauties, would ya." he says to Hunter. Scratch points to the pool below the mill.

"Yes, I see them. They've been there for about the last two years. Throw a line in there, and they disappear underneath that ledge," Hunter replies. He points toward the waterfall that cascades over the shale and sandstone formation.

"Yeah, you've fished them before I take it?" Scratch asks.

"Yes. I've fished here at the top of the park for years. The biggest ones are at the bottom, where the other waters meet this creek, so I prefer to fish there," he says.

The crew walks along the stone path as they begin their descent down through the gorge. The canyon's timelessness and beauty place them in a state of silent awe as they marvel at the creation carved out from the retreat of the last Ice Age.

"Wow," Julie whispers in fascination. "This is so amazing. That has to be a hundred-foot drop-off," she says. She grabs Hunter's arm in nervous response. The rest of the group pause as they round the gorge trail's corner, which leads them into the large natural amphitheater.

"Close. It's actually 115 feet. It's called Lucifer Falls," Hunter informs.

"It takes my breath away," Julie revels with joy as she stands and absorbs the view down the mountainside. The canyon's bottleneck creates a wind tunnel, and Julie's hair blows on the rising current. Her eyes are as wide as a child's on Christmas Day, and she shakes her head at the majestic sight. Hunter studies her closely as if wanting to kiss her.

"If you want to take a break, we can swim at the bottom, if you like," Hunter says quietly.

"I just want to stand here a moment and take it all in," she replies, marveling at God's creation.

"Me too." Hunter sighs with a smile as he focuses exclusively on Julie.

"I wonder why they call it Lucifer Falls?" Julie asks. She stands near the edge of the drop-off, clutching Hunter's arm more tightly. "It is just so beautiful."

"Nihasa," Scratch whispers onto the wind, just loud enough for Hunter to hear. The look of extreme pleasure overwhelms his face. He lowers his shades to completely take in and admire the view of the dangerous landscape.

"Nihasa?" Hunter asks. He turns to look at him out of curiosity.

"Yeah, Nihasa. Iroquois for the Devil. Fitting really. It was named so, well before the Français and Yankee traders that came to the area. That would be one hell of a nasty fall if you were caught upstream in the current and swept over its side. Don't you think?" Scratch asks as he pushes back his sunglasses to shield his eyes from the sun.

"Yes, I guess it would. All the times I fished here, I never once got even remotely close to the top of these falls. For that very reason."

"That must mean you have some respect for the Devil, mate."

"Perhaps, but it certainly meant that I didn't want to meet him anytime soon, that's for damn sure." Hunter laughs as he looks at Scratch.

"You'd probably get along quite well with him, really."

"I would prefer not to meet him." Hunter continues to laugh.

The group continues to make their way down the trail to the large natural pool at the base of the drop-off. Julie holds Hunter's arm the entire descent, clinging to his arm like a child looking for security, and he places his hand over hers, letting her know she is safe.

At the base of the waterfall, Hunter watches as Julie begins to tease him. She wiggles her hips as she looks at him and unbuttons her jeans. She smiles as she takes them off, revealing her yellow bikini bottoms. She then takes off her black tee-shirt, holding it against her matching yellow top as she looks at him again. She places her clothing by her shoulder bag, and she stretches out her arm to remove her gold and silver Cartier watch, placing it inside the bag. The rest of the group takes the liberty of wading into the park's cool, clear waters, and Julie turns to join them.

"This is truly the spot of inspiration that I was hoping for, Hunter," Scratch says. He sits on a step, lustfully watching the two girls in the water. "What do you think of this progression, lad?" he asks. He begins to strum his guitar.

Hunter, who appears to be adrift in some carnal thoughts of his own, listens intently as the guitar player begins to play his piece. As he listens, he watches Julie play around with the group in a friendly water fight. They each cup their hands and snap them on the surface of the water as they attempt to splash one another.

The music Scratch begins to play instantly seems to command Hunter's full attention. "Hey, I really like that," he says. He retrieves his notepad and starts to write, constantly glancing back at Julie then back to his notepad. Suddenly, Hunter begins to sing out loud as Scratch continues to play.

*Never Let Go*

*"Never let go. Never ever tell me so.*
*I'll never let the keys to your heart slip out of my pocket.*
*Never say goodbye, and if you do, don't tell me why.*
*I couldn't stand the weight from the pain which that would put me*
*under.*

*Where do you go when I'm wanting you?*
*Where do you stay, because I'm wanting to.*
*I'll meet you all the way. I just wanted to say,*

*These times are not meant to last.*
*I'm falling in way too fast. I need you.*
*There is something I need to show.*
*My heart it hides here below and waiting*
*for you.*

*Never let go. Never ever tell me so.*
*I'll never let the keys to your heart slip out of my pocket.*
*Never say goodbye. And if you do, don't tell me why.*
*I couldn't stand the weight from the pain*
*that it would put me under.*

*What will you say when the time is right?*
*You can call on me any day or night.*
*I'll meet you all the way. I just wanted to say.*

*Where does the wind go that blows through your hair?*
*I may never know, but I can meet you there.*
*I'll meet you all the way if you'd like it that way."*

"I would like to know just how in the bloody hell you can do that so goddamn quickly. It's like you've been given a real gift only reserved for, like, chosen ones. Are you a chosen one, Hunter?" Scratch asks with curiosity.

"You mean by God or something?"

"Yes, by God," Scratch says. He lifts his hands above his head as he looks toward the heavens. "Are you one of his favorite mortals? He has them, you know." He looks at Hunter closely, as if prodding for his spiritual beliefs.

"I don't know about that. I like to think that He smiles upon me more often than not. It's probably more than I appreciate sometimes. I like to think I'm a good person. I believe in Christ if that helps you. Chosen, though, is a considerable stretch there, Scratch. The Universe is pretty vast. I don't know that God meddles in what we do," Hunter says.

"Right. Well, you sure are good at what you do, lad. I wish I had your abilities. Then I wouldn't need you—no offense, mate. I can only play this here guitar. I can't sing to save my arse. And I sure as hell don't have your dashing good looks. Yeah, you have been blessed, that's for damn sure." Scratch reaches to tune a string as the others finish their swim.

Chris walks over to retrieve his beach towel from the rocky ledge. "Is that a new song, Hunter?"

"Yes. We just wrote it," he replies. Hunter reaches over to bump knuckles with Scratch.

"I love it. I say let's work on it this evening," Julie suggests. She uses only her hands to whisk the water off her body, then retrieves her watch from her shoulder bag. "We better be going if we want some time to play before the fireworks. I still have to stop at the store."

The group agrees, and they make their way down through the canyon.


UPON ARRIVAL AT JULIE'S house, they discover Franklin is waiting patiently in the driveway. The group makes their way into the back yard. Julie invites Jenny into the apartment, and they start making up some salads as the others gather around the grill. The boys start the barbeque and begin to bond over a few beers as they talk about the band's direction.

Julie's two roommates arrive home, and Julie greets them as they enter the kitchen. "Hey, you two, meet Jenny," she says, pointing to her new friend.

"Pleased you meet you both," Jenny greets them as she cuts some carrots on the countertop.

"Hi. I'm Zoey," the first roommate replies as she sits down at the kitchen table. She immediately immerses herself in the digital world of her cell phone.

"Hello, Jenny," LaShonda says. A genuine smile accompanies her greeting. She quickly turns her attention to Julie. "Are you guys going to play some music tonight, or are you just going to watch the fireworks?" she asks.

"Both," Julie replies.

"Oh, I can't wait, girl," she says as she answers an incoming call, then turns to leave the room.

"I am going to change, Jenny. There is soda in the fridge if you want one. I'll be right back."

"Okay," she replies. She retrieves a can from the fridge and joins Zoey at the table.

A few moments later, Julie returns. Her red summer dress and matching Mansur Gavriel ballerina shoes elicits a smile of approval from both Zoey and Jenny.

The repercussion of a test firework rocks the windows of the Victorian house. The report roars like a cannon across the countryside, startling the unsuspecting girls. Zoey and Julie both let out a quick scream to the sudden shockwave.

"Hell yeah," Scratch cries out with great enthusiasm at the unexpected display. The boys laugh at his excitement. Julie comes to the door with a plate of burgers, and Chad takes them from her to the grilling station.

The group gravitates toward the picnic table as Julie and Jenny begin to bring more food out from the kitchen. Chad finishes cooking the burgers and serves them to the hungry party. They all chat as friends usually do, speaking of nothing in particular as they enjoy their evening meal.

"Thank you for dinner, Miss Julie. That was wonderful," Scratch says. "If you lads and Miss Julie are ready, then why don't we go see if we can come up with some ear candy together?"

"Great idea," Julie replies. She rises from her seat, and the band follows her into the practice room. There they begin to experiment with an array of different musical ideas. The band works until sunset, creating some fresh material.

"The fireworks will be starting soon. Let's stop right here on a high note and celebrate," Julie suggests. The band watches her reach into the cooler and take a beer from its icy depths. "Don't be shy, boys," she says. She steps out onto the patio and joins the other girls in the garden.

"You guys sound really good, Julie. Was that all of your band's music?" Zoey asks.

"Yes. That last one Hunter and Scratch wrote just this afternoon in the park."

LaShonda lays her hand on top of Julie's. "That Hunter is a handsome boy. You two look perfect together when you stand there playing side-by-side. You both complement each other so well," she says.

"Yes, you sure do. Don't you think so, Jenny?" Zoey asks.

"Yes, I do. Do you see how he looks at you?" Jenny asks Julie.

"Kind of," Julie replies. She scrunches her eyes as if in a state of reflection.

"He likes you, girl," LaShonda says.

"He lights up when you are around. It's like he gives off a glow of happiness or something," Jenny reassures her new friend.

"Huh," Julie says. She appears pleased by her friends' observations. A curious look overwhelms her face as she glances at the practice room.

"Don't tell us you haven't thought about it, Julie," Zoey says.

Julie looks back at Zoey. "He is a handsome man, isn't he?" she asks. She raises her eyebrows as she smiles.

"Uh, yeah. I told you that before," Zoey replies.

"Uh-huh," LaShonda says. She nods in agreement.

"You really think he is interested in me?" she asks. She looks back again at the practice room. Taking a strand of her hair, she begins to twirl it around her finger.

"Girl, if you can't see it, then you are blind as a bat," LaShonda says. "You are only the most beautiful girl in this whole damn town."

"Not as pretty as you, my love," Julie says. She bats her eyes at her roommate.

LaShonda smiles at Julie, appearing flattered by the compliment. "Thank you, my dear," she says.

"Why don't you just kiss him and get it over with, because here he comes right now," Zoey says. She laughs as she smiles at Hunter.

Julie stops twirling her hair and sits back in the lawn chair. She straightens her dress over the top of her knees just as Hunter joins the crowd. He sits down next to Julie as he smiles at the other three girls, who all are looking at him.

"Thank you," he says to Julie. "I haven't played with a full group in so long I had forgotten how much I miss it all. We're going to have a lot of fun together."

"Promise?" Julie asks. She turns, resting her elbow on the arm of her chair and chin in the palm of her hand.

"I promise," he says. He nods his head as he looks at her.

"I hope so," she replies. She nods her head in unison with him, mirroring her songwriter.

Hunter looks back to the house, watching the remaining musicians come onto the patio. Chad plunges his hand in the cooler for a beer as Scratch wraps his arms around Chris and Franklin's shoulders. Hunter and Julie both listen to the discussion.

"I want both of you two to know something," Scratch says. "I have played with many great rhythm sections, from London to Liverpool, and from Boston down to Birmingham. But the two of you are the most smoking rhythm section I have ever had the pleasure to play with. And I want you to know it is my pleasure writing songs with you lads."

"Thank you, Scratch," Franklin says.

"I truly believe that what I hear evolving out of this project is some truly unique, melodic, and outright magical music. Cheers to every one of you," Scratch says. He raises his bottle as he looks directly at Julie and Hunter.

"Cheers to you as well, Scratch," Julie replies.

Within minutes the fireworks begin. Julie watches Hunter in the flickering light. He looks at her, and she curls her finger as she leans toward his ear. "I'm already having a lot of fun," she whispers.

# Chapter 14

## Halloween with Marilyn

THE SUMMER GIVES WAY TO FALL, and the band begins recording some of the material for their debut album. As October ends, Julie and her roommates decide to celebrate. Together, they concoct a theme for their All Hallows' Eve celebration. Julie drives to Hunter's house to break the good news to him. She takes a bag from her car and carries it to Hunter's apartment. She calls him as she walks down the hallway, then knocks on his door.

Hunter answers the incoming call, "Hello."

"Hi," she says.

"Hey, what's going on?" he asks. As he opens the door, he looks at her standing there and begins to laugh.

"I was just wondering what you are doing," she says into her phone.

"Oh, you goofball. Come on in." He holds open the door, immediately noticing the brown paper shopping bag in her possession. He looks at it with curiosity.

"What are you doing for Halloween, Hunter?" she asks. "I need a designated driver for my posse and me," she says. She flutters her eyes to make it impossible for him to say no. She walks over to the kitchen table and sets the bag down.

"Did it occur to you that I might want to have a designated driver myself?"

"Oh…well…too bad for you. The posse nominated you. It was a unanimous vote. Congratulations, you won. So it's a done deal. I need you to also dress up as a character from a movie," she says. She slides the bag across the table to him.

Hunter looks at her with a pleasant smile as he takes the sack and peers in at its contents. "A character from a movie?" he asks.

"Yes, a man in a very famous movie."

"Okay," he replies cautiously. He reaches into the bag and pulls out a hat, placing it on top of his head. "Do you want some coffee?" he asks as he continues to look into the bag.

"No thanks. I can't stay long."

"So you want me to dress up as a character in a movie." He pulls out a pair of tan pants, a suit coat, and a bowtie.

"Yes, I'm sure you know it. Everybody is familiar with it," she replies. She lifts the right side of her cheek as she smiles as if she has something devious on her mind. "Would like me you take you to see it?"

"Well, let me think for one moment. Yes, actually that's a good idea. If I'm going to dress up as a character, I should see what he looks like. So, yes, you have to take me to the movie."

"Well, you are in luck. I have to see it again myself for some pointers anyway."

"Alright, so when are we going?" he asks. He begins to place the garments back into the bag.

"Tonight."

"Tonight? Just like that? What if I had something planned?"

"Then you'll cancel it for me, just like that, won't you?" she asks. Again, she bats her eyes.

"If I had something planned, then yes, I sure would."

"I knew I could count on you. You're a doll."

"Where is it showing?" he asks.

"At Fall Creek pictures."

"Alright, but since you asked me out, then you have to pick me up."

"Not a problem. Just be ready by six o'clock. And don't be late. I have to go. See you at six. Oh, and you need to pick up a pair of brown dress shoes," she says. She pulls her sunglasses down over her eyes as she turns to leave. She opens the door and looks at him over her sunglasses. "And don't be late."

"Okay, Okay," Hunter replies.

HUNTER IS WAITING ON the porch when Julie arrives. He walks down the pathway to meet her and climbs into her white SUV. Julie greets him as he gets into the vehicle.

"I just noticed after all these months that your license plate holder says, Cornell. I thought you go to school at Ithaca College. What's up with that?" he asks.

"My mom and daddy are Cornell Alums. My daddy put them on there."

"I see. What does he do?" he asks.

"He is a copyright attorney. So is my mother. They wanted me to go to Cornell to get my law degree. I think they were a little disappointed that I wanted to study music," she says. She engages the vehicle and begins to drive toward the theatre.

"Parents shouldn't pick their children's professions. It makes for unhappy adults when they grow up."

"Wow, that's exactly how I feel," she says. She smiles as she looks over at him.

"I would rather die broke and happy rather than rich and unfulfilled."

"I would have thought that they'd be happy I'm following somewhat in their footsteps. They represent some famous musical stars."

"Really? Who?" he asks. He looks over at her, clearly interested in her statement.

"I'm not allowed to tell you that, Hunter, but I think you can help me make them happy with the band. They certainly will help us, too. They will really like the music we're creating."

"I understand. I will do my best. You can count on that."

"I know you will." She looks over at him again and smiles. "I have heard some local people say that you are the happiest person they have ever known. It's amazing how many people will never find happiness. What is your secret?" she asks.

"Finding value, I guess. Finding value in everything I do. So many people think it's about getting a job and gaining money. Then they spend it before they even get it by acquiring stuff on credit. Then they have to work harder to pay for it, never finding happiness at all, it seems. I see it all the time with my friends."

"Me too. My parents want me to be successful, and they probably think that being an attorney offers everything they want for my success," she concludes.

"You're doing the right thing. You are seeking something you love, something that's in your heart. That's positive energy. That, I think, is the key to life," Hunter replies.

"I think you're right." She glances at him quickly and smiles again as she continues to navigate the streets of the city.

The two enter the foyer of the movie theatre, and Julie purchases the tickets for the show. Hunter springs for some popcorn and a couple of sodas, and they make their way into the theatre. Julie opens the door to the darkened room, immediately turning into the back row. She leads Hunter to the middle of the row and lays her coat across the back of the red velvet movie chair. "I like to sit as far back as I can when I see a movie," she says. She sits down, then reaches to take the popcorn from his hands.

"Oh yeah, why is that?" he asks, handing her the container.

"Just in case I want to suck face and not draw a crowd," she replies with a smile in her eyes. She tosses a piece of popcorn into her mouth.

"I see." Hunter blushes as he takes a seat next to her.

He pops a straw into a cup and offers her the drink. "Thank you," she says. She reaches for some more popcorn as the lights in the theatre dim. The movie begins, and the cast of characters seem to come to life on the screen.

"Oh, it's Marilyn Monroe. I've always wanted to watch one of her movies," Hunter exclaims.

"Uh, yeah. It's probably her most famous movie of all."

"Why is that?" he asks.

"You'll see in a bit," she replies. As the movie plays out, the two watch Marilyn Monroe's larger-than-life presence. "This is my favorite part," she whispers into Hunter's ear. Hunter places his arm around her, and she immediately rests her head on his shoulder.

Captivated by the movie star, he breaks the silence. "She sure was beautiful," he declares.

"Yes, she sure was."

Hunter's jaw drops as Marilyn's timeless and most memorable onscreen moment occurs. "Wow," he murmurs. His eyes open wide at the sight of her perfectly sculpted legs. Julie turns her head to look at Hunter, and he senses her movement. He turns his head, and they stare deeply into each other's eyes. Without saying a word, they begin to kiss.

As the movie ends, they leave the theatre hand-in-hand, and Julie drives Hunter to his apartment. "I had a wonderful time. Thank you," he confesses. "That was the one movie I always wanted to see. Thank you again."

"I would let you ask me in, but I still have to do some studying for a test tomorrow," she says. She looks at him as if she's ready for another kiss.

"They make you take tests on Halloween? Isn't that like sacrilegious or something?"

"Yes, they make us take tests, and it is going to be a tough one. For professors, it is just another day. There is something you can do for me, though, that would help me on the test."

"Anything, name it," Hunter says. He edges closer to her.

"Kiss me one more time," she suggests. She throws her arms over his shoulders, and he gladly obliges. "See you tomorrow… my place?" she asks in between kisses.

"I wouldn't miss it for the world," he whispers back.

"Good night, Hunter," she says softly.

"Good night, Julie. See you tomorrow." He gives her one last kiss and exits the vehicle, seeming thrilled at how perfect the night is ending.

THE FOLLOWING EVENING Hunter arrives at Julie's apartment. Julie's two roommates and another girl are already there in the living room, and they greet Hunter upon his arrival. The girls laugh and fawn over Hunter in his 1950's wardrobe that Julie had so meticulously picked out for him.

Dani, Julie's friend, looks him over carefully. "He sure does have everything down to a tee, doesn't he?" she asks.

"His hair is the only thing out of place. We should cut it to reflect the 1950's pre-Elvis era hairstyle," LaShonda suggests, taking off her glasses. She walks around Hunter to thoroughly analyze him.

Hunter resists the idea. "Yeah, uh, no. That's not going to happen."

"He is absolutely adorable," LaShonda declares.

Zoey provides her opinion to the masquerade. "I think he's purely dreamy."

"Don't you dare cut his hair," Julie shouts out. "We can live with long hair with his costume for one night." She comes to the top of the stairs. Knowing she has everyone's undivided attention, she begins to speak like Marilyn. "Do you know anyone who will escort me to the Oscars? I hate to go out alone." Everyone looks up in amazement at the stunning likeness of Marilyn Monroe.

Hunter looks up at her. "Oh, my God… Wow! You look simply amazing, Miss Monroe."

Julie continues in character, mimicking Marilyn's soft, sultry, and sexy voice, "Do you like my dress? I wore it just for you." She walks elegantly down the staircase, holding the railing with every step.

"Uh-huh," Hunter replies. He looks as if in a trance, nodding ever so subtly.

"No one can touch you, girl," LaShonda declares. She reaches over to primp some of Julie's hair.

"Thank you," she replies.

"Why don't we grab something to eat at the Sunset Grill?" Zoey suggests.

LaShonda supports her roommate's plan. "Oh, I think that's a great idea. I'm with her. Then afterward, Hunter can drive us down the hill and drop us off on the Commons while he parks the car," she says.

"That's a swell idea," Julie says, still using Marilyn's voice. The gang laughs at Julie's perfect impersonation. They leave the apartment, and Hunter drives them to the quaint little eatery overlooking the city.

As the evening progresses, the girls sit and chat about their studies, their hopeful careers, and Marilyn, her movies, and her lifestyle. Hunter sits quietly, watching Julie in the flickering candlelight while she converses. Hunter is the perfect escort, sitting patiently and only speaking when asked a question. While the girls chat, he jots down many notes on their conversation about Marilyn.

"I heard that she was secretly a lesbian," Zoey says.

"No," Dani replies. "No way. Really?"

"Yes. She was rumored to have affairs with several leading stars," Zoey continues.

"Really?" Julie asks. "You can't be serious. I didn't even know that."

"Oh yeah. Sex was like ice cream to her, so the saying goes. She probably liked women more than men, given how incorrigible some of them were to her. Given that, she was likely a full Lipstick Lesbian," Zoey says.

"I never heard that. Who did she make love to? I'm so curious," Julie asks.

"You're curious, or you're *curious*?" LaShonda questions jokingly.

"Funny. Only for you, my love," Julie softly replies in her Marilyn's voice. She rubs LaShonda's hand, then raises her glass of wine. She flirts with her lips as she places the glass to her mouth and winks at her roommate lovingly.

Hunter's eyes open wide. He smiles at Julie in apparent admiration of her charm.

"So who did she play scissors with? Come on," Dani asks.

"Her teacher, Barbara Stanwyck, Marlena Dietrich, Liz Taylor, Joan Crawford. Even the Wizard of Oz star, what was her name?" Zoey pauses for a moment to think.

Dani helps to finish her sentence, "Judy Garland?"

"Yes. Thank you, Judy Garland," Zoey says.

"Well, I never knew any of this. I just like her movies," Julie replies.

The girls talk over Marilyn Monroe's various exploits and her celluloid moments for nearly an hour. Throughout the conversation, Julie never neglects Hunter. She subtly flirts with him. He looks at her, almost expressionless, as she silently runs her foot up the back of his leg, as she bats her eyes at him in the candlelight.

As midnight arrives, Hunter drives the girls back to Julie's apartment. The girls are highly intoxicated, and he escorts them safely in from the cool autumn air. LaShonda quickly bids everyone good night and makes her way to her bedroom. Zoey stumbles her way to the bathroom bracing the walls as she struggles. Dani looks at Hunter and incoherently mentions breakfast as she collapses on the couch.

He looks at Julie for clarification of what her friend just said. "Did she just ask me to make her breakfast?" Hunter asks.

She laughs as she begins to lose her balance, and Hunter catches her as she falls in his arms. "I thought she said, 'you can take advantage of me now if you want to,'" she replies. He laughs along with her, for she is far too intoxicated to engage in such activity.

"How about a rain check on that, Miss Monroe, and I will just help you to your room," he says as he holds her.

"Okay, that's a good idea," she says as she continues to laugh.

He lifts her into his arms and carries her to her room. He places her onto the bed, removes her shoes, and gently pulls the covers over her.

She is barely able to look at him through her glazed-over eyes. "You are a perfect gentleman. You promised not to drink, and you didn't." She pulls the covers underneath her chin, smiles, and closes her eyes.

He kisses her gently on the lips. "Goodnight, Miss Monroe."

"Good night," she replies. He watches her for a moment as she quickly drifts off to sleep.

HUNTER LEAVES JULIE'S apartment and drives back home. While on the way home, he begins to whistle a melody. Arriving at his apartment, he sits down with his notebook and transforms the piece into a new song.

*Marilyn*

*How can I love this girl, we've never met?*
*Beyond the curtain and her cigarette.*
*No other woman turns more head around.*
*She doesn't even need to make a sound. Marilyn.*
*I like to kiss her when I fantasize. Get lost forever in her deep*
*blue eyes.*
*Pleasant distraction is her disguise.*
*The perfect woman with the perfect thighs,*
*Marilyn, Marilyn, Marilyn, Marilyn.*
*A perfect woman, yes, a perfect mess.*
*Sultry woman in red shoes and dress.*
*Most like her dressed in pink and glittering.*
*I just like the way she moves and sings.*
*She has a smile so pure time can't erase.*
*And how my heart it beats to see her face.*
*Some took her picture on the open end. I'd have bought her*
*Diamonds because they're girl's best friend.*
*Marilyn, Marilyn, Marilyn.*
*I'd have held her close so gently, my Misfit.*
*I love the way that words slip off her lips.*
*I love her barrel, her locks, and stock.*
*I'd go to see her, I just wouldn't knock.*
*I know her habits. Yes, I love them all.*
*She's just a Bombshell. She's a Fireball.*
*Most think she's pretty, yet some may not.*
*As for me, well, I just 'Like it Hot.'*

*Marilyn.*
*She's just so pretty, you know it's true.*
*The time that separates us makes me blue.*
*For 50 years or more, this love's accrued.*
*And I'd done any bloody thing for you,*
*Marilyn.*
*Joan, and Liz, Barbara, Marlene too,*
*behind closed doors, lost in those private rooms.*
*It's not just men that wished to see her bend.*
*Oh, to have been the grate on Lexington.*
*So fitting she stuck to the Silver Screen.*
*I even love her as Miss Norma Jean.*
*Millions still love her, and it's understood.*
*She's still the talk of girls in Hollywood.*
*Marilyn.*
*Marilyn, Marilyn.*
*Why do I love you, Marilyn?*
*Marilyn.*
*I can't*
*Love you,*
*Marilyn.*

"It's a show tune," he says to himself. "I just wrote a show tune." He reclines on the couch as he rereads the song in its entirety.

# Chapter 15

## Burning Young Hearts

HUNTER AWAKENS THE NEXT MORNING to the sound of his cell phone ringing. He grabs his neck as if cramped from sleeping on the couch all night. It slows his attempt at reaching it as he winches in pain.

Retrieving the phone, he notices it is Julie calling him. "Hello, Miss Monroe. And how are you this fine and beautiful morning?" he asks.

"Not so good. What are you doing right now?"

"And why is it not so good? Are you feeling a little sluggish, Marilyn?"

"Yes, I am. I need a favor." Her voice conveys she has a hangover.

"What kind of favor are you looking for, Miss Monroe?" Hunter asks.

"Stop. I don't feel good. I need something to eat. Would you be a love and come make us all breakfast?"

"Sure, anything you wish. I'll be right over."

"You are a doll," she says. He listens to her begin to moan as she ends the call.

He arrives at Julie's apartment to find the girls huddled underneath various blankets scattered throughout the living room. Each of them appears to be attempting to drink a cup of coffee. All are present from the night before, except for LaShonda.

As Hunter closes the door, he looks at Zoey in the recliner. Her long face and baggy eyes suggest that she may have expatriated her libations from the night before. "Good morning, sunshine," Hunter greets her in a chipper tone.

She looks up at him from underneath her blanket. "Are you making us breakfast?" she asks as she leans her head back into the recliner.

"Sure," he says. He looks at her with amusement at her discomfort, "but don't you want another beer first?"

Zoey looks at him with dread and leaps from her cover as she races off toward the bathroom.

"That was just wrong of you," Dani says. She raises her hands to her mouth. Hunter laughs lightly underneath his breath.

"You better start cooking something, or she is going to hurt you when she gets back," Julie says. She is barely audible beneath the cover of her dark blue bedroom comforter.

"Judging by the sound coming from the bathroom right now, that could be awhile. So what do you party animals want for breakfast?" Hunter asks. He begins to walk toward the kitchen, laughing as he shakes his head.

Julie musters up some strength to fully speak her wishes, "Omelets and toast. Dry toast!"

Hunter continues to laugh under his breath as he looks into the refrigerator for provisions. In little time he has a full production of comfort food coming off from the grill, and he delivers breakfast plates to the three over-imbibers. As he hands the last dish to Zoey, she looks at him with contempt. Returning to the kitchen, he creates an omelet for himself. He turns to sit at the table as LaShonda enters the kitchen.

"Oh, you are a catch," she says. She takes the plate from his hands and sits down at the table. She appears in much better shape than the other three girls in the living room. "Do you do windows, too?" she asks.

"Yes, whatever you need," he replies. Hunter shakes his head and prepares another omelet for himself. LaShonda finishes her meal and checks on the others, who are slowly making a half-hearted attempt to introduce the food to their stomachs.

"I have to go up to the Law School. Does anyone need to go up to the Cornell campus?" she asks. With no response from the girls, she makes her way back to the kitchen and places the plate in the dishwasher. She looks out the window and notices that snow begins to fall from the November sky. "Oh my God, it's snowing," she announces.

"No, no, no, I'm so not ready for snow," Zoey complains. She grasps her head as she begins to moan.

Julie looks at Hunter in disbelief. "Is she serious?" she asks.

He gazes out the window detecting the wintry precipitation, and nods to her, confirming the squall.

Dani joins in on the grievance by slowly shaking her head in disgust. "Julie, take me to the islands with you on Thanksgiving break," she says.

Hunter looks over at Julie, waiting for her to respond. With no response, he finally asks, "You're going to the islands?"

"No," she replies.

"But she just said you're going to the islands on Thanksgiving."

"Well, she's wrong."

"I just heard her. She said you're going to the islands on Thanksgiving break."

"We're going to the islands on Thanksgiving break. You are going to meet my parents. We leave in three weeks."

"Oh. I see. And you were going to tell me that when?" Hunter asks. He smiles, looking as if he is pleasantly surprised.

"Last night, actually, I just forgot."

"I've never been to the islands before. What island are we going to?" he asks with excitement.

"The Bahamas. My parents have a beach house there. We go every year. This year you're going," Julie says. She takes another sip of coffee and looks at him, managing a subdued smile.

"I see. Well, I guess I have no choice." He pulls his baseball cap down as he grins behind his hand.

THREE WEEKS PASS BY, and just as Julie promised, the two arrive in Nassau. Julie and Hunter exit the plane, bombarded by a Bahamian sun. Hunter pulls his sunglasses down over his eyes as he steps onto the tarmac. The intensity of the sun and heat cause him to stop and take a deep breath. A light breeze gently sways the Palm trees just beyond the terminal. He stares for a moment at them, admiring his first glimpse of the tropics. As they enter the airport, Julie quickly spots her mother.

"Hi, dear, how was the flight?" her mother asks. She kisses Julie on the cheek as she looks Hunter over. She smiles slightly, appearing pleased at the sight of Julie's handsome-looking boyfriend.

"It was fine. Hunter has never flown before. He got a little nervous when we hit a little turbulence. Fortunately, Mom, he doesn't have to change his pants."

"Julie, stop talking like your father. Hello Hunter," she says.

"Hi, Mrs. Christianson. I've been so looking forward to meeting you."

"Well, we have heard so much about you and delighted you could make it," she says as she continues to inspect Hunter.

"Mom, where is daddy?" Julie asks.

"Where do you think he is? He's golfing with some clients. You know the deal," she replies. As they begin to walk, she wedges herself between Julie and Hunter, taking both of them by their arms.

"He didn't put up too much fuss about me bringing Hunter along, did he?"

"No. I told him after several strawberry daiquiris. He's fine. He's looking forward to meeting him," she says. She looks at Hunter, smiling again as if assuring Hunter she approves of him.

They retrieve the luggage and make their way to an awaiting vehicle. Hunter observes another hint of Julie's family wealth as a chauffeur takes their baggage. Hunter admires the silver Mercedes they are about to get into as Julie and her mother continue to talk.

As they arrive at the beach house, Hunter attempts to take his luggage. Julie shakes her head, indicating it is the chauffeur's job. Surprised, he looks at Julie, quickly tensing his lips like he has done something wrong. Casually, he turns, opening his eyes very wide at the sight of Julie's home. The tan two-story house is large, appearing almost like a Spanish castle. He looks up at its roofline and cocks his head as he examines the red roof tiles. "Good God," he says to himself. The Hibiscus that line the walkway draws his attention as they enter the luxurious home.

"Hunter probably wants to get freshened up from the flight and get into a pair of shorts. Sydney, would you show Hunter to his room?" Mrs. Christianson asks.

"Yes, ma'am. This way, Mr. Watkins," he says. Julie smiles at Hunter as he follows Sydney up the stairway.

"Why is there netting around the bed?" Hunter asks.

"Have you never been to the islands, mon?" he asks. He walks over to the dresser and places Hunter's luggage down.

"No, I haven't," he replies.

"It's so you don't get bit by da mosquitoes at night."

Hunter nods his head. "I see," he replies.

"The bathroom is right through dat other door," he says. He points across the room. "If you need anything, mon, don't hesitate to ask." The chauffeur turns to leave as Hunter attempts to hand him a tip.

"Oh, thank you, but you don't have to tip me, mon. Thanks just da same, though. I work for the Christianson's, so you don't have to do dat, mon." He smiles as he shuts the door.

Hunter shrugs his shoulders and tosses the money on the bed. He changes into a pair of blue shorts and a matching sports shirt then joins Julie and her mother back downstairs.

"Julie, be a love and run to the market for me, would you please?" Julie's mother asks.

"Sure, Mom. I was going to take Hunter for a walk through the market anyway."

"Here is a list. And make sure the mangos are ripe and that the cilantro is fresh."

"I will," Julie says. She looks at Hunter and smiles. "I was going to wear the same outfit. Come on. I will show you the living room while I change."

The two head off to the market hand-in-hand. Hunter seems fascinated by all the sights and sounds of his new surroundings. The market bustles with natives and tourists, all of them interacting in the timeless act of commerce. Hunter pays close attention to a calypso song that is being played by some street musicians on the steel drums.

"Catchy song. That's fascinating," he says to Julie. He watches the musicians play on the steel drums. "What a beautiful sound. It has a certain magic to it, doesn't it?" he asks.

"You've never heard steel drums before?"

"Once, a long, long time ago. I'm sure I listened to that song before. It sounds hauntingly familiar."

"It's called 'Yellow Bird'," she says.

"'Yellow Bird.' Yes, I think that was the song's name. My parents used to play that for me."

"It's an old Haitian song, but it's played throughout the islands," Julie replies.

"So it has words?"

"Wait," Julie says. She takes Hunter's hand, pulling him close as she throws her arms over his shoulders. She leads him as she begins to dance with him in the street. Softly she begins to sing him the song.

A small crowd that has gathered begins to clap at the two lover's classy public display. As the song ends, Hunter smiles as Julie laughs with pleasure. He looks her in the eyes as if hoping the moment will never end.

The two of them begin to walk away as one of the drummers yells to Hunter, "Kiss da girl, mon." Needing no further encouragement, he responds, pulling Julie back in close, obeying the simple instruction as he kisses her in the midday sun. Some of the tourists witnessing the event begin to cheer and clap. Hunter smiles and reaches into his pocket, placing some money into the musician's collection hat. Slowly he and Julie start to stroll down the street as the band begins to play the 'Jamaican Farewell.'

"You two look so purdy together for true, hey," a young island girl says to Julie and Hunter.

Julie smiles at the vendor as she begins to inspect some of the fruit at the girl's stand. Hunter also looks at the girl, appearing taken by her beauty.

"Thank you. You have a beautiful island," he says.

"True, true for true. Can I get you an' your lady friend a glass of Switcha?"

"Yes," Julie answers.

As the attendant begins to pour the drinks, she gazes across the street. A smile overwhelms her face. Hunter notices the attendant is subtly flirting with a boy across the market.

The boy stands out in appearance, wearing long red shorts and a clean white muscle shirt. Hunter watches him as he waits for the beverages. As he does, he notices that the boy begins to dance, holding his right arm up into the air and his left arm out as if pretending to dance with the girl. The island girl shakes her head as she hands Hunter the two drinks.

Hunter gives her some money as he takes the two glasses from her, and she promptly returns his change. "Wow. Outstanding," Hunter says after taking a sip. "Switcha. You must make this with limes." He looks back at the vendor for verification.

"Yah, for true," she replies.

"What a great drink. I have never had this before," he says. He hands Julie her glass.

"I take it that you like it?" Julie asks.

"Yes, it really quenches your thirst. I can't believe it isn't as popular as lemonade," he says.

Julie picks out several mangos and sets them aside, then begins to pick through the cilantro. "I thought you would like that," Julie says. She hands the mangos and cilantro to the girl. The vendor bags the produce and rings up the sale.

"Tanks. Come again soon," the girl says.

As they begin to walk away, Hunter watches the boy approach the fruit stand. He listens as the boy begins to speak with the attendant.

"What da wybe is?"

"Een nothin," the island girl replies.

Hunter appears perplexed by the phrase.

"My darling, won't you see me tonight?" the boy asks.

"For true dear, meet me here at seven, for true," the girl says.

"Julie, what does 'what da wybe is' mean?" Hunter asks.

"It's small talk. Like saying, 'Hey, what's up?' Where did you hear that phrase?"

"A boy just ran over to the girl where we bought the fruit. I heard him say that as we were turning to walk away. You must not have heard him."

"They have a lot of phrases that take a while to understand. We can go back now. You do want to go to the beach, don't you?"

"Yeah, for true, for true," he says.

Julie laughs. "I gun tell you something, come here, boy," she says in her best Bahamian accent. "I ben watchin' you, for true. I kiss you, for true, for true." She wraps her arms around Hunter and gives him a soft and steamy kiss.

As they arrive back at the entryway of the house, Julie's father pulls into the driveway.

"How's my little girl?" he asks. He gets out of his sports car and opens his arms, expecting a proper greeting.

"Hi, Daddy," she says. She squeezes him tightly as she hugs him, and the two of them rock back and forth together for a moment. Her excitement makes it clearly evident that she deeply loves her father with all her heart.

"How is school going?" her father asks.

"Excellent. Straight A's again." She smiles proudly, placing her hands on her hips and holding her head high as if posing for a picture.

"That's my girl. And this must be Hunter," he says. He extends his hand for the introduction.

"Yes," Julie says. She steps out from between the two.

"Pleased to meet you, sir," Hunter says. The two shake hands as Julie's father looks over his daughter's new love.

"Do you golf, son?" he asks with a grin.

"Yes, sir. Very poorly, in fact."

"Good, maybe we can get you out this week." He pats Hunter on the back as he escorts the two young lovers into the luxurious home.

"Hi, sweetheart," Mr. Christianson says as he kisses his wife. He immediately reaches into the refrigerator and retrieves two beers. "Hunter, do you want one?" he asks.

"Oh, no, thank you, sir. But thank you anyway."

"You must not have heard me correctly, Hunter. I asked if you wanted an ice-cold refreshing beer?" The older man grins, holding two bottles in his hand as he attempts to change Hunter's mind.

"Why, yes, sir, I would love one. Thank you very much." Hunter laughs as he throws a smile on his face for the patriarch.

"I knew Julie would only date a brilliant guy. Good answer, my friend," Mr. Christianson says. He hands Hunter the bottle, then takes a seat at the kitchen table. "Welcome to the Bahamas, Hunter. Is this your first time in the islands?" he asks. He retrieves a phone from his white checkered golf pants, setting it down next to his beer.

"Yes, sir. It is," Hunter replies. He takes a seat across from Julie's father at the table.

"You are going to love it. There are so many things to see and do here on the islands. Do you fish?" he asks.

"That I do, sir, yes. I fish for trout mostly, when I get time," Hunter replies. He nods with a look of confidence.

"Well, then I get to take you out on the boat at least one day to round up some dinner. Julie likes to play Captain, so we'll bring the girls along. Sound like a plan?" he asks.

"Sounds like a great plan, sir," Hunter replies.

The phone begins to ring and vibrate on the table. Mr. Christianson looks at the caller ID on the display screen. "Oh, I have to take that. Hunter, if you'll excuse me for a bit," he says. He rises from his chair and answers the call as he walks out of the room.

Julie watches her father go into his study. "If you don't want that beer, Hunter, you don't have to drink it," Julie says.

"I'm good," he says. He raises it and winks at her, then takes a healthy swig.

"What's for dinner, mom?" Julie asks. She retrieves the cilantro and begins to rinse it in the sink.

"Jerk chicken, rice, and a Key Lime pie for dessert. Do you like Key Lime pie, Hunter?" Mrs. Christianson asks.

"Well, I like Switcha, if it's anything like that. But to be honest, Mrs. Christianson, I haven't ever had it," he replies.

"He'll like it, mom," Julie says. She puts the mangos, and the cilantro on the countertop then goes under the counter for a cutting board.

"You don't have to cut those up, dear. Take Hunter to the beach before dinner. I'm sure he would like to take a swim, don't you, Hunter?"

"Yes, ma'am. I do."

"Okay, Mom. We'll be back in a couple of hours." She grabs a tube of cocoa butter and an oversized beach towel from the linen closet. She kisses Hunter as she hands the towel to him. "Come on. I want to show you something beautiful," she says. She leads Hunter through the living room and out the back door.

They walk down a long path through large Palm trees and Caribbean pines. As they arrive at the seashore, Hunter looks out over the horizon, appearing fascinated by the ocean's vastness and the big blue sky. He shakes his head as Julie takes off her tee-shirt and shorts then hands them to Hunter. His eyes open wide at the sight of her hot pink bikini that barely covers her body.

"Close your eyes," she says to him. Hunter does as he is told, and Julie steps behind him. She grabs the bottom of his shorts, and pulls them down to his ankles, and immediately runs toward the sea. Completely caught off guard, Hunter starts to chase after her, falling face-first onto the hot white sand.

As he struggles, Julie splashes into the water and turns to look at him. She laughs as he gains his composure. As he does, he races toward her in the surf. He quickly chases her down and catches her. He throws her over his shoulder and marches into the surf as she begins to struggle in his grasp.

"No," Julie screams. She kicks her legs helplessly as he flips her into his arms.

"Do you believe?" he asks. He begins to baptize the girl, dunking her beneath the waves.

"No," she screams some more as he pulls her back above the waterline. He plunges her head into the clear blue water, quickly raising her back up so she can catch her breath.

"Do you believe?" he asks. Again he dunks her. He repeats the maneuver several times, each time asking if she believes.

"Yes," she finally says.

He drops her, feet first into the water, holding her in his arms. They stand face-to-face, kissing as if they both have just entered into paradise.

"I could stay here forever, girl," he says.

"It's hard to do a band in the Bahamas, but we could spend the winters here," she suggests. She rests her head against his chest as she hugs him. She looks out over the ocean as she smiles.

They make their way back onto the beach. Julie spreads the towel out and lays down on it. Hunter sits down beside her. He looks around, scanning the beach and the few other tourists who bask along the shore.

"Be a dear and rub this on me, please," Julie says. She hands him the tube of cocoa butter as she rolls onto her stomach and unties her top.

Hunter obeys as he drops to his knees. He straddles her legs as he places a liberal amount of the fragrant lotion into his hands. Julie pulls her hair off her shoulders, signaling to him to start on her neck. She rests her head on her arms and closes her eyes. Hunter begins to massage the girl, working his way down her back. Julie smiles as Hunter rubs the lotion on her skin. He grins as he slips his hand underneath her bikini.

"I don't think you need to apply that under there, Hunter," Julie says. She laughs at his prank. "But you can do my legs now."

"Oh, sorry," he says. He laughs as he finishes putting the lotion on her. He sits down on the towel and looks back out over the ocean, wiping the excess butter on his face.

While Julie basks in the sun, he scans the beach, watching the waves gently roll ashore. His peripheral vision catches a glimpse of a girl and several boys walking on the shoreline. They race around the girl, throwing her a Frisbee. As she comes into full view, Hunter sees that it is the young island girl from the fruit stand. He notices that none of the boys is the one she made a date with at the market.

"That little heartbreaker," Hunter says quietly beneath his breath. He watches her closely as she splashes in and out of the surf.

"Julie?"

"What?" she asks.

"I'm going over to that vending stand and get a water. Do you want one?"

"Yes, please."

"I'll be right back."

"Don't get lost," she says.

"How do you get lost on an Island?" he asks.

"Most people are lost, Hunter."

"Great point. I promise you I won't get lost."

He parallels the group playing on the shore. He continues to watch the beautiful girl as he approaches the vending stand. A group of street musicians playing near an outdoor café distract him. The music appears to captivate him enough to look away from the girl. He looks over at the musicians and begins to walk to the tempo of their beat. Arriving at the vending stand, he glances back at the girl. As he does, she disappears, walking through a small stand of brush and Mango trees.

"Hey, Chief, welcome to the Bahamas. How it go?" the attendant asks.

"Oh hey, thank you. Good. Two waters, please."

"She a fine-looking girl, mon, dat for true. She got lots of man friends, though," the merchant says as he reaches into an ice chest.

"What's that?" Hunter asks.

"Da girl you been watchin' on da beach der, mon. She be on da beach all the time, ya know. She is a looker, mon, isn't she?" he asks. Hunter pays the vendor and takes the bottles.

"You are a wise and observant man," Hunter says. He looks at the vendor as he grins.

"Dey be liming on da beach every day with her, mon. She be with child before she hit twenty playing with dat many boys, for true. She sure is a sweet fa so sight doe, but the sea en' got no back door for her, mon. Dat for true."

"Lucky boys. Lucky boys, indeed. Have a good day, my friend," Hunter replies.

"You too, mon," the Bahamian says. He smiles as he places the currency into his register.

The street musicians continue to play at the café and distract him once again. He bounces in his step to the ensemble's island beat as he makes his way back to Julie.

"Here is your water. Do you have a pad of paper in your purse?" he asks. He sits down beside her on the beach towel and hands her the water bottle.

"Yes, I think so. Why?" Julie asks.

"I have a song in my head."

She reaches into her purse, retrieves a paper tablet and pen, and hands it to him.

"What does 'the sea en' got no back door' mean?"

"Where did you hear that?" Julie asks. She takes a sip of the water as she looks at him with curiosity.

"The man at the stand over there." Hunter nods his head toward the vendor.

"It means that sometimes you are in a situation that there is absolutely no way out of."

"I see. What does 'liming' mean?"

"'Liming' means to gather a crowd. What were you two talking about that there is no way out of?"

"The vendor and I both watched that young girl from the fruit stand playing on the beach with several other boys. They disappeared behind that brush over there that leads into that lagoon. He thinks she'll be pregnant before she's twenty. I think he means that if she is not careful, she'll be in a situation that she can't get out of."

"I see. Well, at least she is doing it right, with several boys at a time."

"Julie!" he says. "Oh my God, I can't believe you just said that."

"Relax, mon, een nothin. Write me a song. You are on vacation, mon." She takes another drink from the bottle then lays her head back down nonchalantly.

Hunter laughs at Julie then shakes his head, looking back toward the sea. He pauses for a moment then begins to write.

### She Won't Wait for You

*She has a face that cries out to his burning young heart,*
*and when he sees her he hopes to say something that's smart.*
*She has a smile that's as wide and as big as the tide.*
*He has a crush on, and he knows that he cannot hide.*

*He says, 'My Darling, My Darling, tonight, won't you see me tonight?'*
*'For true dear at seven, meet me here at seven, all right?'*

*But the sea en' got no back door, so off to the shore.*
*To fetch all the nets to collect as his chores.*
*It's late when he finish, no boss man in sight.*
*And so there's no money to spend out tonight,*
*and she won't wait for you.*

*No, she won't wait for you. No, she won't wait for you.*
*There's nothing you can do,*
*and she won't wait for you.*
*No, no, she won't wait for you!*

*The sun it escorts her as she makes her way across the sand.*
*The waves tumble over to grace her and augment her tan.*
*To lime all the others, they gather for sweet fa so sight.*
*So many fine options to greet her in this evening's light.*

*Oh, but you'd better hurry, or the others will score.*
*Time does not care if you see her no more.*
*The last thing you want is them with her beneath the moon,*
*down on the beach where the brush meets the lagoon.*
*She won't wait for you.*

*No, she won't wait for you. No, she won't wait for you.*
*There's nothing you can do,*
*and she won't wait for you.*
*No, no, she won't wait for you!*

"Can I read it?" Julie asks, noticing that he has finished writing.

"Sure," he replies, handing it over to her as he steals another glimpse of her mostly exposed flesh.

"You amaze me. You just simply amaze me." She rolls onto her side to take another drink of water.

Hunter grins as he catches his first glimpse of her exposed breasts. Julie smiles, seeing he is captivated by their exposure. "See something you like, Mr. Watkins?" she asks. Quickly she lays back down on the towel, biting her lip as she looks at him.

"Why, whatever do you mean?" he asks. He laughs, playing dumb to her question.

"Play your cards right tonight, and maybe you can personally have a private chat with them."

"I like to chat. I love good stimulating conversation. It's what the world needs more of."

"Yeah? And how long can you carry on a stimulating conversation, boy?"

"Boy? Guess maybe we will have to see about that, won't we?"

"Maybe. The moon is out tonight. Maybe we can take a walk, then talk."

"I would like that. I would like that very much."

"Well, then we should head back in a bit because you, white boy, are not going to do any talking if you continue to bake in the sun. Come over here and kiss me, and tie my top," she says. Hunter reaches over to tie her straps. As he finishes tying the knot, she rolls over, curling her finger to her lips. She puts her arms over his shoulders as he moves in for the kiss.

JULIE'S FATHER TALKS with Hunter all through dinner about business, fishing, and golf. He listens in fascination to all of his tall tales and laughs at his jokes. Julie smiles at her mom as if knowing her father truly likes Hunter.

"Hunter promised me a moonlight walk, daddy. You can speak with him more in the morning, but it's my turn now," she says.

"You two have an enjoyable walk, dear. Your father is slurring his speech, so it's time for him to go night-night, or he'll miss his tee-time in the morning."

"Oh my, it's already nine o'clock, right. Can't miss that," he says. Mr. Christianson rises from the table and finishes his glass of wine. "Good night, kids. Don't let the sand fleas get you as you two roll in the surf," he says. He kisses Julie on the head.

"Daddy," Julie replies, "I'm not stupid enough to be on the bottom. Good night, Mom. Good night, Daddy."

"Julie. Stop talking like your father. Goodnight, Hunter," her mother says.

The two lovers kick off their shoes on the patio as Julie takes a clean beach towel from the closet. She wraps the linen over her shoulders, and they begin to walk back down the path to the beach.

"My parents like you a lot, Hunter," she says.

"Oh. And how do you know that so quickly?"

"Because if they didn't, there is no way daddy would let you walk me on the beach alone at night," she says.

"I see. I like your parents, too. I learned a lot from your father in just those last couple of hours. He is a really good guy."

"He probably sees in you the son he always wanted. He wouldn't have given you that much time if he didn't really like you."

"And your mom is one beautiful lady. She is a straight shooter, isn't she?" he asks.

"Yes, she is. My daddy is a pushover, but not my mom. They make a good legal team, though. Daddy is really good at signing clients. But if they have to go to court, it's my mom people have to worry about."

"So the moral of the story is don't make her mad?"

Julie stops and laughs as she looks at him. "That's right. But they will represent what we're doing, so I don't think you have to worry too much about that."

Julie spreads the towel out onto the sand. She sits down on the cloth and removes her ponytail holder allowing her hair to fall onto her shoulders. The moonlight twinkles in her eyes and gleams off of her silky-smooth legs. She places her face in her hands and rests her arms on her knees as she stares out at the sea. Hunter sits down beside her, and she leans into him, resting her head on his shoulder. Hunter closes his eyes and listens for a moment to the sound of the waves.

"This is my favorite place to dream," she says.

"I can see why."

"I sat here many times at night, alone, and just wondered." She sighs as she continues to look out over the ocean.

"What did you wonder about?" he asks.

"Lots of things. What I would become? Where I would go to school? Who I would fall in love with?"

"Sounds like something most young girls probably go through."

"Yes, I'm sure it is."

"I have a similar place that I go to," he says.

"I figured you did. You are too talented, especially in your writing, not to have a place like this. Can I ask you something, Hunter?"

"You can ask me anything you want, any time you want."

"What is your ultimate dream?"

"Well, I have always struggled to try and do something with my music. I guess I would like to make it big somehow. But I don't know that it is so important anymore."

"Oh, and why is that?" she asks.

"Because I met you."

She smiles as she looks at him. "You don't want to make it big anymore?"

"I want to be with you. Everything else is just not as important," he says.

"Maybe you can have both," she replies.

He turns his head and looks into her into eyes. "Does that mean I can really kiss you now?" he asks.

"Uh-huh," she replies softly.

Hunter places his hand on her face as the two begin to kiss. They wrap themselves in each other's arms as Hunter slowly begins to undress her. Their fingers gently caress each other and wander beneath the light of the moon.

# Chapter 16

## The Rat in Strategy

THE TWO ARRIVE BACK IN THE Finger Lakes and quickly fall into their regular routines. Julie and her friends once again utilize Hunter's chauffeur service, and he takes them out on a warm December evening to their favorite night club. Hunter talks with some acquaintances as the girls dance the night away.

Julie hears one of her favorite contemporary dance songs and races to Hunter. She grabs him by the arm and drags him out onto the dance floor. Equally enamored with the tune, Julie's posse spins Hunter around, each taking their turn grinding into him as they all sing along to the latest international dance hit.

*Twisting*

*Society seems broken, with so many downtrodden.*
*Not really sure how this whole thing started.*
*Avarice intentions and corporate profits?*
*Everything is fine, says the Orange-headed prophets!*
*Each new generation knows just what to do.*

*Twisting, yes, twisting, out on the dance floor glistening and twisting.*
*Twisting the night away.*

*Oil is burning. Forests keep falling.*
*A fragile ecosystem we keep mauling.*
*Populations, heat, and the tide are rising.*
*Is that really so surprising?*
*Your generation has a plan for you.*

*You're twisting, you're twisting, out on the dance floor glistening.*
*Just twisting. Twisting the night away.*
*You're twisting, they're twisting.*
*All the world just keeps kissing and twisting.*
*Twisting the night away.*

*Who cares of tasks as the ages pass, when all that lasts is the end?*
*But you might find as you grind that it seems so sublime*
*on a floor that's shined for twisting.*

*Oceans are collapsing, while scales are striding.*
*Each day it seems that it's all colliding.*
*Through the spiral of time, we know just what to do.*

*Yes, twisting, we're twisting. I don't think we're really listening,*
*twisting the night away.*
*We're twisting, and missing, out on the dance floor kissing and twisting.*
*Twisting the night away.*
*Twisting, yes, twisting. The planet screams while it's hissing and twisting.*
*Nobody dares at all.*
*We're twisting, yes, twisting. The world seems to be listing and twisting.*
*We have no cares at all.*

*Twisting, they're twisting. It's so easy. Just keep resisting and twisting.*
*Twisting the night away.*
*We're twisting, insisting, most of the world is just subsisting and twisting.*
*Who cares if we might fall?*
*Oh, twisting, yes, twisting. Help we might get to enlisting,*
*but we're twisting, twisting the night away.*
*It looks like I'm twisting with you.*


In their dizzied state of intoxication, Hunter and the girls are unaware they are being very closely watched. Scratch, Aphrodite, and Naamah secretly observe the group from the upper loft of the bar. They monitor the group as they search for any clue as to how to steal their souls.

"It is going to be hard to pull him away from her, you know. Look at how he ogles over her," Aphrodite says.

"He's whipped and probably hasn't even tasted her insides yet," Naamah replies.

"The spell of true love, possibly?" Aphrodite asks. She looks at Naamah for her opinion.

"I'll take bullshit for a thousand, Alex. Really?" Scratch says. He seems to fume as he spews forth a toxic tirade. "Don't give me that true goddamn love crap. He's a bloody male. Males like to free their goddamn willies, especially on pretty little vixens like you two. True love. Really?"

"It happens, Scratch," Aphrodite says. She playfully runs her finger on the inside of Naamah's leg.

"True love? Oh, that just bloody disgusts me. The very idea makes me want to vomit," he replies. He shakes his head as he watches Julie on the dance floor.

"Well, what is your assessment then?" Naamah asks.

"If someone is stepping on your goddamn toes causing you a great deal of pain, right, whose fault is that? Theirs? Or yours for not yelling 'ouch?' Now listen, I'm yelling bloody goddamn 'ouch' here. Do you know what I mean? It's time to put the goddamn rat back in goddamn strategy. It's time, Naamah, or both of you two if need be, to be a good goddamn rat. I got a lot invested in trying to steal their worthless little souls. The more that little bitch gets closer to him, the harder it becomes. She's got a golden bloody cross in between those pretty little tits of hers, ya? She is a true believer and off-limits. I can't touch that, and neither can either one of you two. She is a praying type. I can smell it. Mess with her, and the next thing you know, I've got a hornet's nest of God's angels lurking about. I want you to quit screwing around about it. Do you understand me?

"I think so," Naamah replies. She subtly raises an eyebrow and laughs.

"Now, I don't care if you tag him, and I don't care if you both have to bloody tag him. I want his goddamn soul, and the others if possible, and I'm getting a little bit goddamn pissy about it. I want you to do your goddamn job, Naamah. Now take that perfectly shaved little pussy of yours over to his flat, and you slip into his dreams. Then bang the living crap out of him. Make him want you so goddamn bad he'll bang her one last time then dump her like the sludge that she is, all right? You do that in the spirit form, and the little wanker will come begging for you to do it again and again in the bloody flesh. Then you can suck the life out of him all you bloody want. All right?

"My pleasure, boss," she replies. She gracefully finishes her drink as Aphrodite continues to caress the inside of her leg.

"Oh, and another thing while you're at it. Find out if that bongo boy is a bloody butt-snorkeler. He's been courting some tight ass bloody little flower child, and he hasn't even laid a goddamn hand on her yet. Find out if he likes the baloney pony, or he's just bloody slow about it. The goddamn little girl is screaming out, 'bang me, bang me now' and he's like Tweedle Dee and Tweedle Dum's goddamn love child.

"As you wish, boss," she says. Paying more attention to Aphrodite's caress than to Scratch, she lays her hand across her girlfriend's, leading it farther up her legs.

"Yeah? As I wish, eh? Then why won't you bang me? I wish that all the time and you don't bloody bang me."

"I'm not supposed to bang the boss. That's Aphrodite's job," she replies. Naamah looks encouragingly into Aphrodite's eyes, whose fingers are beginning to explore beneath her mini shirt.

"Hey, would you pay attention to me when I'm speaking? We live to break the bloody rules every goddamn day, and you are going to get bloody proper on me? Unbelievable, your ethics just disgusts me. Just bloody go. Do you hear me?"

"I will do my very best and then some, boss," she replies. She leans over and gives Aphrodite a kiss on the lips.

"Yeah, we'll see about that. Now go get to it."

Naamah rises from the table and leaves with a look of excitement about her new assignment.

Aphrodite watches Naamah disappear into the shadows of the crowded room. "You were a little harsh on her, weren't you?"

"No. Harsh is what I'm going to be on you in just a little bit." He grins as he reaches for his drink.

"Oh, you're such a bad boy." She laughs as she begins to rub his leg.

"Yeah. I'm bad! I'm really, really bad." He laughs, turning his attention back to the dance floor.

NAAMAH BRIEFLY WATCHES the lover's dance, then turns to leave the bar. The moonlight aids her search as she uses her powers and a keen sense of smell to find her way to Hunter's apartment door. She turns the knob only to find it locked. Unhindered, she transforms into her powerful spirit form. Passing through the door, she quickly finds her way into Hunter's bedroom.

An hour passes, and Hunter arrives, unaware of the presence of the succubus. She watches from the shadows, observing that he does not appear intoxicated. "Oh, Hunter, you are making this so easy. She begins to cast her spell to the unaware quarry. "Get in here. I want you now," she seductively whispers.

He looks around as if puzzled, shaking his head to his faint perception of the incantation. He retrieves his notepad from the table as he sits down on the couch. He takes a pen and begins to write. As he does, Naamah appears to grow somewhat impatient.

She cups her hands around her mouth. "Come to me, Hunter. I need you now," she whispers again. Hunter looks into his bedroom and shakes his head one more time. His determination to write seems to frustrate her. Invisible to Hunter, she rises from the bed and walks to the couch, looking down on him as she begins to read his prose.

She can see that he is performing a free-flow writing process whereby he jots down a myriad of thoughts. "Rendezvous at Treman Mill," she quietly reads out loud as she sits down beside him. Naamah rests her head on his shoulders as she watches him reveal his innermost thoughts. Her smirk grows as he enables her to tie these very thoughts into her demonic trap.

Hunter finishes writing, and Naamah follows him into the bedroom. She watches as he removes his clothes, and she slips onto the bed, propping her head on her hand on top of a pillow. As she watches him, she begins to caress herself, gently gliding her hand from her breast to her legs and back again. Hunter lays down, falling fast asleep.

Influenced by his notes of the Park, he begins to dream, utterly unaware of Naamah's presence. His dream takes him back to the water's edge below the 1800's era grist mill that sits at the top of Treman park. Steam rises from the stream, creating a fog throughout the entire area of his dream. Naamah slips into his dream and watches him from the mill's loading dock. He searches the rocky ledges of the waters for trout, oblivious the other hunter has prepared an ambush for him just inside the mill's receiving room.

She sits down at the top of the stairs and lays a strand of her long red hair across her breast. To lure his full attention, she leans against the railing, positioning her burgundy satin negligee to reveal her matching bra and panties. She loosens the knot of her magic rope, which holds the nightgown around her perfectly shaped hips, making it easy for him to undress her when the time is right.

Next, Naamah reaches for her locket dangling below her neck. She presses a tiny release button several times that delivers a potent dose of Dark Desire Dust into the palm of her hand. The powerful dust will assure that Hunter will remain locked in the dream for hours. With the dust in her hands, she begins to take command of his dream with the theatrics refined over the last thousand years.

"Hunter, please help me. I fell, and I think I broke my leg," she says to him. Hunter abandons his search of the pool, looking up at her stroking her perfectly sculpted leg. Instantly he is at the top of the stairs, lusting over the beautiful girl who looks at him with tear-filled eyes. "Help me, Hunter," she says. A tear gently rolls down her face. He looks over the deceivingly helpless girl.

"What do you want me to do?" he asks in a daze. He begins to look over Naamah's body, and his eyes dilate from the power of lustful desire. The visual of her wardrobe further entices him into her trap.

"Hurry. Lift me up and take me inside. I have to lay down. Please hurry, Hunter, I'm in so much pain," she says. "Take me through that door. I need to lay down," she says as she pulls her red hair off her breasts and looks at him with a look of distress.

He lifts her into his arms without hesitation. As he does, she sprinkles the Dark Desire Dust over his head. The satin helps his hand to glide effortlessly across her back as he lifts her. He carries her into the dimly lit mill. The room receives only a faint hint of light through a dirt-covered window that directly casts its rays onto the red satin sheets of an antique canopy bed.

She caresses him on the neck. "Lay me down, Hunter," she whispers into his ear. He does as she asks, now wholly caught in her web of deceit. "My leg, Hunter. Rub my leg. You need to tell me it's not broken," she continues to whisper. She curls her right leg away from her left, exposing her inner thighs. Again he does as she suggests as her demonic mastery continues to manipulate him.

"I need you, Hunter. Untie the rope around my hips. It's hurting me, too," she says. She moans as she turns her head, exposing her alabaster neck.

Again, he does just as she instructs. As he unties the loosely secured obstacle, the front of her nightgown falls gently down across her side like leaves falling to the forest floor. She lays back, open and exposed. "My ribs, Hunter, rub my ribs. They hurt too," she says softly. She playfully bites her lip as she places her hand on top of his. She moves his hand across her side, directing it toward her breast.

Naamah leans back onto the pillows and twirls her finger around on her lips. Hunter watches as she places her finger inside her mouth and gently begins to roll her tongue around it. She begins to rub her breasts, lowering her right hand from her lips down across her stomach. His eyes open wide as her fingers disappear beneath her satin panties. She pulls her hand off her breasts and motions with her index finger to come to her lips, and he obeys without hesitation. The two begin to kiss in a sensual exchange. As they do, she pulls his hand underneath her panties.

She whispers as she looks into his eyes, "Now, Hunter. Take me. Make love to me now." Hunter momentarily pulls from her kiss to better position himself in between her long silky legs. The succubus wraps her magic rope around his neck, helping to assure that he remains locked in the dream.

HUNTER AWAKENS IN THE morning, still suffering from the effects of the Dark Desire Dust. He rolls over in his bed and immediately reaches for her, only to find she is not there. He looks around, seeming confused, and stares into the mirror. He looks at himself with a degree of suspicion, as if trying to recollect the events that occurred in his sleep.

# Chapter 17

## Bewildered and Bewitched

MONDAY MORNING ARRIVES, and Nick enters Hunter's apartment to pick him up for work. He looks closely at Hunter as he hands him a coffee. Hunter is exhausted, and Nick quickly notices.

"You weren't up late drinking all weekend again, were you, old boy? You look like you've been run over by a freight train."

"I didn't sleep well at all, no," Hunter replies. He places the coffee on the counter and retrieves his work jacket. Sluggishly, he follows Nick to the truck to begin the new work week. Nick looks over and laughs as Hunter struggles to stay awake. "Wake up, we got work to do," he says.

"Thanks for the coffee, Nick. I'm beat," Hunter says. He takes a sip from the caffeinated brew.

"So you did it, didn't you?" he asks.

"Did what?"

"Spent the entire weekend rolling around like little bunnies with Julie, didn't you?

"I have a problem, Nick."

"What, she's a nympho, and you can't keep up with her? I can take her off your hands if you can't handle it, old boy."

"I think I'm falling in love."

"She is a good girl, Hunter. That's what is supposed to happen when you meet a girl like Julie."

"Yeah, but…"

"Yeah, but what? She has, in a matter of months, brought you out of that shell you were in. I remember that day at the bar when you first met her. The girl is beautiful, funny, and talented. What do you mean, yeah, but?"

"I want to bang the piss out of that Naamah chick," Hunter says in an elevated tone.

"One of your guitar player's girlfriends?" Nick asks. "Oh, not sure that's a good idea, buddy. Be careful on that one. That girl will chew you up and spit you out." He looks at Hunter like he has lost his mind.

"I know, but that's what seems so appealing. It's not his girlfriend, either. The other redhead is," Hunter says. He takes another sip of coffee, starring forward with a look of concern.

"That girl wants to take you for a ride, my friend, but with her whips and chains. I don't know about that one, definitely not a good idea. Julie won't take you for a ride, though. She will, however, help take you around the world with what you two are building together. What the hell has gotten into you?" he asks.

"I'm not sure. It's like she hit me with a ton of bricks." He glances over at Nick and shakes his head.

"I can't tell you what to do, Hunter. But if it were me, I wouldn't even think of leaving Julie. She is so beautiful. I don't see how you could take your eyes off her."

"I know, you're right. It's just Naamah has some serious electrical sexuality."

"I can see that. But Julie is smart, pure in heart, and so drop-dead beautiful. You would be a fool to let her go for any other woman, Hunter. You are so lucky. It's not funny. I can't believe that Julie wants your scrawny little ass. I hope you make the right choice, old boy."

"I can't stop thinking about either one of them. It's like my mind is weighing its options, locked in some sort of combat."

"I only see one wise option. So, what do you think about Julie?"

"Everything. Anything. I think about making love to her, and I think about living life with her. I, damn, I can't believe I'm saying this, but I wonder what our kids will look like."

"Well, hopefully, they come out looking like her and not you. But what do you think about this other girl? Nick asks.

"Sex. Sex with whipped cream, or ice cream, or both. I think about screwing her until she says 'stop,' and hope that she doesn't say 'stop.' I think about banging her on a dance floor, then I think about banging her in her dress up against a wall," Hunter says. He rubs his eyes then looks over again at Nick.

"Okay, all right, I get the point."

"No, you don't. I think about banging her on a boat or on a picnic table. I think about banging her in the back of a car or on the forest floor."

"Wow. You might need some help, old boy."

"Yes, I do. That's why I'm asking you. What the hell am I supposed to do about it?"

"Well, you are a writer. Write about it."

"It's like she has some sort of spell on me or something, I don't know."

"Do you believe in witchcraft, Hunter?"

"I don't know, man. I just can't seem to do anything without her being around every corner of my every goddamn thought."

"Lust will do that to you, Hunter. But you didn't describe lust about Julie. You described a woman that you likely have an opportunity to spend a great life with. One people would envy. Do you know how few people there are that ever get to enjoy that type of bond?"

"No, I don't."

"On paper, you just spelled out your best decision. Pursuing this other girl will likely not only break Julie's heart but your own as well. I will assure you that if you act on this Naamah girl that you will lose Julie. Eventually, you'll realize the mistake and want and need her back. Julie is one class act, Hunter, and if you blow that, you likely won't get a second chance. Just saying."

"I could not live with that."

"And there you go," Nick responds.

"Yeah, there I go. Thanks. Maybe if I wax one off while thinking about her, it will help get rid of the problem."

"May I ask why all of a sudden you are lusting after this girl?"

"I had a rather lucid dream. It was outright peculiar. It lasted all night, it seems."

"I see. And in this dream, I take it you had your way with her. Is that right?" he asks.

Hunter's eyes open wide as he looks at Nick. "It is more like she had her way with me."

"Oh, that's not good." Nick looks at him with concern. "Have you ever heard of a succubus, Hunter?

"A what-you-bus?" he asks. He looks at Nick, perplexed by the word.

"A succubus. It's a demon that preys on men in their sleep. She could be a succubus. Waxing one off, as you so eloquently put it, would only make you want her that much more. If you pay full attention to Julie, you won't need this other girl. However, you might want to start asking God for some help on this one. Prayers certainly are a good idea, assuming you believe," Nick says.

"Yes, of course, I believe. I actually prayed for an Angel to come into my life. Next thing I know, there was Julie."

"Well, if God sent Julie to you, I want to know every word you said in that prayer, old boy. But as far as these dreams go, if they continue, then I want you to know it may require we find a few people to come together and pray."

"Yeah, you're probably right."

"Let me tell you one thing, so there is no uncertainty. If you slip off into a daydream about this other girl on a job site and start looking at my ass like it's hers, I will pop you so hard you never will think about another woman again.

Hunter looks at him in disgust. "You can count on the fact I will never look at your ass, Nick. Your face is bad enough."

# Chapter 18

## The Show Must Go On

SPRING ARRIVES, AND THE BAND GATHERS at Taughannock Falls State Park for their first outdoor concert of the year. Hunter pays the attendant at the gate, and he looks over to see the others awaiting his arrival at a picnic table near the pier. He parks his truck and places his phone on the dashboard. As he joins the others, he instantly takes notice of Julie's sexy black shapewear dress.

"Hi," Julie says. She kisses him as he comes close to her side.

"You look spectacular. Can I take you home tonight?" he whispers in her ear.

"Maybe. We'll see," she says. She wrinkles her nose at him in a playful manner.

Hunter sits beside Scratch on top of the table. "I thought we could do a quick acoustic run-through of 'Take Me Home to Mama.' I worked out a new guitar lead for it," Scratch says. He looks to Hunter for a response.

"That's fine. No time like the present. Let's do it right now, unplugged," he says.

Hunter and Scratch begin to play their guitars as Julie sings along.

## Take Me Home to Mama

*"I should have shared more of the sunshine,*
*should have laughed more in the rain.*
*I should have realized how my soul shined.*
*Without you there's just pain.*
*We met as total strangers.*
*Two kind hearts spinning 'round.*
*Within there lies the danger*
*of a heart cast to the ground.*

*So if you want to leave, then just leave.*
*There's just one thing before you go.*

*Take me, take me home to Mama.*
*Lay me where the sun sets with a view.*
*Take me home to Mama,*
*because I won't know what to do,*
*if ever I lose you*

*Within your eyes I saw it,*
*and I opened up my door.*
*Then as quick as you came through it,*
*you wanted something more.*

*How I'll miss the nights of pure pleasure,*
*just memories that I'll keep.*
*One more chance, oh, how I'd treasure*
*all your kisses, oh, so sweet.*

*So if you want to leave, then just leave.*
*There's just one thing before you go.*

*Take me, take me home to Mama.*
*Lay me where the sun sets with a view.*
*Take me home to Mama,*
*because I won't know what to do,*
*if ever I lose you."*

"Nice," Franklin says to Julie.

"Thank you, Franklin," she replies. She sits down beside him as he begins to play a catchy musical pattern on his bass guitar. Chris joins in, tapping his drumsticks on the table. Julie moves her shoulders in sync to the catchy dance beat that the two are creating.

Hunter's phone rings, distracting his attention from the others. He hands his 12-string to Chad and races to his truck to intercept the call. He retrieves his phone and looks at the phone display with concern. "Hello," he says.

"Hunter, this is Mrs. Rogers."

"Hi, Mrs. Rogers, is everything all right?" he asks. Hunter appears alarmed in receiving a call from his best friend's mother.

"No," she replies. She begins to cry uncontrollably, and Hunter's eyes open wide at her response.

"Mrs. Rogers, what's wrong? Is Johnny all right?" he asks.

Barely able to speak through her tears, she informs him of the terrible news. "No. No, he's not. Johnny was killed last night by a roadside bomb," she says. "The Chaplain and Major were just here. He's gone, Hunter."

In shock, Hunter leans against his truck and slides down the side. Julie notices and runs to his side. The rest of the band also take notice and follow Julie.

"No, no, please say it isn't so," Hunter says. The look of dread overwhelms his face. Tears instantly begin to swell in his eyes.

"I know how close you two were. He was so looking forward to coming home and seeing you," she says.

"Oh my God, I'm so sorry, Mrs. Rogers. I don't know what to do," he replies. Tears continue to swell in his eyes and begin to run down his face.

"They're bringing him home tomorrow. I would like you to be here, Hunter."

"I will. I will be there, Mrs. Rogers," he says. In vain, he wipes away his tears, only to find more quickly take their place.

"Thank you," she says. She ends the call, and Hunter looks up at Julie.

"What's wrong," she asks.

"It's Johnny. He was killed last night in Iraq by a bomb."

"Your best friend? Oh no," Julie says. She places her hand over her mouth as the rest of the band comes to Hunter's side.

"What is it?" Chad asks Julie.

"It's his friend Johnny. He was killed," she replies. She sits beside Hunter and comforts him, cradling him in her arms.

"Wasn't he coming home in just a few more days?" Chad asks.

"Yes," she replies.

"Do you think he'll be all right to play?" Chris quietly asks Scratch.

"Yeah, it's going to be tough on him, but the show must go on mate," Scratch whispers back to him. Chris nods his head in agreement.

Hunter hangs his head in his hands. Julie looks at the rest of the band. She shakes her head and glances over at the crowd forming around the bandstand.

"I'm really sorry, Hunter. I know how good of a friend he was to you. I am so deeply sorry," she whispers in his ear. She holds him as he begins to cry uncontrollably. Julie looks at the rest of the band helplessly.

"Do you want me to cancel tonight's show?" Julie asks.

"No. We worked too hard to get here," he somehow manages to talk through his moment of grief. "Friends will want to know anyway. We have to play." Hunter begins to stand, his eyes completely filled with tears. Julie and Franklin help him to his feet.

"Hunter, if you want to cancel tonight, I'm sure the park director would understand," Franklin says.

"No. Johnny wouldn't want that," Hunter says. "He would be pissed if I didn't play tonight. Can you guys go set up for me, please? I need to walk around a few minutes alone," Hunter says.

"Do you want me to come with you, Hunter?" Julie asks.

He shakes his head. "No, I just need to be alone for a few minutes."

He walks toward the shore of the lake, sitting down at the water's edge. The waves roll onto the beach, gentle in their rhythm. He closes his eyes and quietly begins to pray. "Dear Father in Heaven, Johnny was a good man. Please watch over his wife and his family. Comfort them and let Your spirit wash over them. Amen."

He opens his eyes and looks up at the sky. "This sure isn't easy, Father. I guess sometimes life works out that way. I sure could use your help, though, if you are not too busy," he says. He looks back down at the shore, shaking his head. He watches the waves as they break.

I've heard wise men say," he says. He stares blankly at the waves crashing on the shore. "Sometimes it works that way." He reaches into his pants pocket and retrieves his notebook.

Nick approaches, just as Hunter begins to write something down. Sensing that something is wrong, he asks him, "Hey, are you all right, buddy?" Hunter takes a moment to explain, and Nick instantly becomes saddened by the disturbing news.

"My God, man, you have to play tonight. Are you going to be able to pull yourself together in time?"

"I have no choice, Nick. You know we have a lot of people coming. The show must go on. I always thought that was a cliché, but now I know it's not. Johnny wouldn't want us to cancel it."

"You're a good man, Hunter. I don't know how you do it," his boss says. He shakes his head as he looks at Hunter.

Unable to jot down much more than a few words, Hunter places the lyric sheet back into his pocket. He and Nick begin to walk toward the soundstage.

"Really sorry to hear about your friend, mate," Scratch says. "Why don't we open with 'Cry Myself to Sleep.' It'll be therapeutic for you, know what I mean? I'll make you feel real swell, mate, and I'll just burn the guitar lead in your friend's honor."

"You know what, Scratch, that's a great idea. You all right with that, Julie?" Hunter asks.

"Yes, of course," she replies.

"Hey everybody, the first song is 'Cry Myself to Sleep." The other members nod their heads in agreement.

As the sun begins to set, the emcee begins to announce the evening's program. "Ladies and gentlemen, welcome to the first show of our summer concert series. This summer, we are pleased to have a lot of great acts lined up for your enjoyment. It might still be officially spring, but tonight we are proud to start our summer series with a local band that's starting to gain a lot of attention. We have had many email requests over the winter months, and we're delighted to start tonight with the most requested band. So without further ado, ladies and gentlemen, please help me welcome to the Taughannock Falls summer stage the New York Satellites."

The band members wave as they take their places on the stage. Scratch pats Hunter on the back as he plugs in his guitar. Julie lifts her arms as she steps up to the microphone, encouraging the crowd to cheer, and they respond accordingly. Chris looks to Hunter and taps out the four-count to begin the song.

### Cry Myself to Sleep

*"I fell in love so naturally. Why he's gone now, I just can't see.*
*You know I don't like what he's done to me.*
*Broke my heart, and left me cold. Now I sit here all alone,*
*and wonder if I will ever see him again.*
*I don't know. I don't know. Won't you tell me where did he go?*
*Now that's what I try to see.*
*I still care. I still care. Won't you tell me he'll always be there?*
*Now I cry myself to sleep.*

*Now I think that they're all the same. Breaking hearts can be a lethal game.*
*Someone tell me does he really have no shame?*
*Put them on a carousel. Throw your pennies down a wishing well.*
*And I hate this feeling, because I feel like Hell!*

*I don't know. I don't know. Won't you tell me where did he go?*
*That's what I try to see.*
*I still care. I still care. Won't you tell me he'll always be there?*
*Now I cry myself to sleep.*

*Wasted days and sleepless nights. How I wish that I still held him tight.*
*And if time heals all wounds, I'll be all right.*
*I don't know. I don't know. Won't you tell me where did he go?*
*Now that's what I try to see.*
*I still care. I still care. Won't you tell me he'll always be there?*
*Now I cry myself to sleep. I Cry myself to sleep."*

Julie's dynamic vocal performance coupled with Scratch's blistering guitar lead greatly pleases the crowd, and the fans erupt in a roar of applause. The crowd's enthusiasm appears to affect Hunter significantly, and he smiles at his fellow bandmates as they finish the piece. Perhaps inspired by Hunter's terrible circumstance, Julie and the rest of the band deliver a brilliant and unforgettable performance.

# Chapter 19

## Not Jane Too

HUNTER RISES THE NEXT MORNING. He starts the coffee machine then steps into the shower. As the water washes over him, he begins to sing. "I've heard wise men say sometimes it works that way. When it works that way, I'm calling." As he sings, he starts to add more words to the new song. "I have to write that down," he says to himself. He turns off the shower and dries himself off, throwing the towel over the shower curtain. He exits the bathroom, unaware that Julie, Nick, and Chad had let themselves into his apartment.

They watch from the sofa as he steps into the hallway, naked and unaware of the company. "Nice ass," Julie says.

"Hey," he yells out, startled by the intrusion. He looks at them with contempt, then marches into his bedroom. The three home invaders begin to laugh.

Nick puts his coffee on the end table and begins to clap. "Water shrinkage," he says.

"I heard that, dickhead," Hunter yells.

Julie taps Nick on the arm. "Told you he was a Diva," she replies. Her response causes him to struggle for breath as he continues to laugh.

Hunter quickly puts on a pair of Levi's and a black Steelers T-shirt, retrieves a pair of socks, and steps out of the bedroom. The three once again applaud, eliciting a sinister look from Hunter.

"I always thought you were a bit of a Diva, and now I know I wasn't far off," Nick continues to joke, wiping tears from his eyes.

"Yeah, that's funny," Hunter replies.

"There's always Botox," Julie says. Hunter looks at her as he takes a seat to put on his socks.

"Yeah, that's pretty funny too. Haha," Hunter says.

"We thought it would be a good idea for all of us to go over to the Rogers' house together. What do you think?" Julie asks.

"Yes, that's a good idea. It may help Mr. and Mrs. Rogers find some sort of peace," Hunter replies. He pulls on his socks and then puts on his sneakers. "Let me get a quick cup of coffee. Then we can go."

I already got you one," Julie says. She smiles as she hands Hunter the cup.


JULIE AND HUNTER ARRIVE at the Rogers' home followed by Chad and Nick in their separate vehicles. Hunter leads them into the kitchen, where Johnny's older brother, Rick, greets them. Hunter looks into the living room and observes a pastor comforting a distraught and broken-hearted mother. Mrs. Rogers, however, doesn't notice Hunter and his friends.

"I'm so very sorry, Rick," Hunter quietly says. He gives him a sincere hug. Nick, Chad, and Julie remain respectfully quiet.

"Thanks, Hunter. I know how close you two were. Unfortunately, the news is now much worse than it was last night."

"What do you mean?" he asks. His eyes open wide, anxious to hear his response.

"Well, last night, Johnny's wife brought their daughter to spend the night. She told mom that she wanted to be alone and go through some pictures she had. She asked that mom pick her up in the morning. She had no idea."

"What you mean she had no idea? No idea about what?" Hunter asks quietly. He looks back into the living room.

Rick's eyes begin to swell with tears. Somehow, he manages to convey the tragic news. "Mom found her this morning on her bed. It appears that she ate a bottle of sedatives." He pauses as he looks at Hunter. "She's gone. Dad is down at the morgue now with my wife getting her transferred to the funeral home." He looks over at his mother as he sighs, clearly struggling not to break down.

"Oh my God," Julie says. She quickly covers her mouth with her hands. Her eyes fill with a look of horror.

Hunter's eyes fill with sadness. "No, no, oh Rick, no," he replies. "I'm so sorry, I am so very sorry," he says.

"I know, Hunter," he replies.

"I think it would be best if we come back later," Hunter suggests.

"Yes, that's probably a good idea. Mom is in no shape to talk at the moment, and Dad is just devastated," Rick replies. He sniffles as he wipes his eyes with a tissue.

Chad looks at Nick and nods toward the door. Nick acknowledges, and the two step outside.

"Rick, if there is anything I can do, let me know," Hunter says.

"I will, Hunter, I definitely will," Rick replies.

Hunter takes Julie's hand and turns toward the door.

"That poor family," Julie says. She pulls the door shut as Chad and Nick shake their heads.

"I can come back with you two later if you want," Nick says. "Say the word, Hunter."

"I appreciate that," he replies.

Hunter, I didn't know Johnny as well as you did, but I will come back with you if you want. Though it is probably better to wait until tomorrow," Nick suggests.

"I think you're right. I will call you in the morning," he says.

Chad and Nick step off the porch and begin to walk toward their vehicles. As they do, Hunter turns to Julie and wraps his arms around her. "Why do things like this have to happen?" he asks. He begins to cry on Julie's shoulder.

"I don't know, Hunter, I just don't know." She looks out at Nick and Chad as they get into their vehicles. Chad looks up at her as he opens his door, slowly shaking his head.

Julie continues to hold on to Hunter, running her fingers through his curly brown hair. "This is all so very sad. I feel so bad for that family," she says.

"I know, and there's nothing I can do about it. That's what really sucks." Hunter breaks away from the embrace, taking a seat on top of the porch steps. A blank stare overwhelms his face as he looks off into the distance. He wipes his eyes then takes a deep breath.

Julie sits down beside him. "I've never had a tragedy like this happen to me," she says. She leans her head on his shoulder and begins to rub her hand up and down on his back. "Hunter, do you ever meditate?"

"No, not really. Why?" he asks.

"When things happen to me, I like to find a place I can go, a tranquil place. I go there, and I sit. I don't talk. I don't speak. I just meditate. They say it is essential to lead a quality life."

"That sounds like it would be good for your mind."

"Well, it is, as well as for your soul," she replies.

"So when you need some quiet place to go, where do you go, the library?"

"Anywhere that puts me in a state of tranquility. Preferably a place where you can feel the sun's rays," she says. She closes her eyes, and he looks at her longingly. Her long blonde hair glistens in the sunlight, contrasting against her dark purple Blouson top.

"Your hair smells like Jasmine, and being with you warms my heart. That's all the meditation I need." He looks at her, submitting his first genuine smile of the day. "But if I were to go to someplace to do that, it would be Connecticut Hill," he says. He looks off toward the hills in the distance.

"Where is Connecticut Hill?"

"There." He leans closer to her as he points to a distant mountain. "It's where I go when I need a place to get my mind off things. It's a large tract of New York State forest," he says.

Julie laughs. "That's what meditating is, silly. It gets your mind off of things."

"Well, why didn't you say so? The place is, well, it's like being lost in time. It's like my idea of heaven. I was thinking about going up there this afternoon."

"I will make a deal with you." She cocks her head to the side as she smiles. The sun reflects off of her diamond in the middle of the golden cross on her neck.

"Yeah, what's that?" he asks. He looks down at the cross as it glitters in the sunshine.

"If you take me with you, I will teach you how to meditate." She puts her hands on his knee, batting her eyes as she awaits his response.

He lays his hand across the top of hers. "Deal. You have yourself a date, Miss Christianson," he replies in a melancholy voice.

"I have nothing to do today. Why don't we go right now? What do you say?"

"Sure. Sounds good. Let's go," he replies.

The two exchange a brief kiss and walk to Hunter's truck. He starts the engine and begins to drive her to the remote and pristine area. As the highway rises up the mountainside, Julie marvels out over the breathtaking view of the valley below.

"When I first heard about you, I did not figure you as a truck guy," Julie says. She surveys the landscape of the rolling hills.

"No? Why?" Hunter asks.

"Because I pegged you as a Diva."

"Yeah? You're funny. That's me, and this is my truck. Would you like to see my panties and my microphone now?" he asks.

"Tell me about Connecticut Hill, Hunter. Why is it such a special place to you?"

"It is home. It's my backyard that I like to get lost in. It's where my heart goes. It is where my mind stays, or at least a piece of it, anyway. I guess it's where I go to think about my future and whether there is a God."

"Do you believe in God, Hunter?"

"Yes, I guess I do. It's just so hard to believe that one man, or one being, has such power to create everything. Do you believe in God, Julie?" he asks.

"Yes. I do," she replies. Again she looks out over the valley below.

Hunter turns off from the highway and onto a seasonal dirt road. "Hold on," he says. He places the vehicle into 4-wheel drive. Julie watches with a bit of concern as they drive up the rutted and treacherous path. Before long, they arrive at the top of the mountain, deep within the heart of the Connecticut Hill Wildlife Management Area.

Julie reads a state forest designation sign tacked to a large hemlock tree. She looks at the large tree in awe of its majesty and grandeur. "Are we there yet?" she asks.

"Yes, we are," he replies. He parks the truck and walks around to Julie's door. "We're in the middle of about 12,000 undisturbed acres of forest. Come on," he says. He takes her hand, helping her down from the vehicle. He walks her down a scenic dirt road, and the two take a seat on top of a picnic table that sits beside a large beaver pond. A warm breeze blows across its waters. Large trees line the water's edge. Their leaves gently sway as if dancing to the rhythm of the gentle wind.

"This is absolutely magnificent, Hunter. It's simply beautiful," she says. "I can see why you come here. You are so extremely fortunate to have a place like this. It's so quiet and peaceful." She looks around like a child at Christmas time. She closes her eyes for a moment as if imprinting the sight in her memory.

"I wish I could stay here forever with you. So what about this meditation thing. What do we do?" he asks.

Julie opens her eyes. "Well, the first thing you have to do is get comfortable where you are sitting."

"I'm pretty comfortable right here with you," he replies.

She smiles at the compliment as she stands and faces him on the bench. "Okay, so what you have to do is lay your arms down over your legs. Let your hands find their center where the thumbs and your fingers touch one another. And sit perfectly erect." Julie talks very softly, coaxing him into a trance-like state. "Now you want to close your eyes." She lays her hands upon his forehead. Gently she begins to glide her fingers down over his eyelids. "Good, Hunter, good. Now all you have to do is let go of all thoughts," she continues speaking softly.

"I don't think I can do that, Julie," he whispers with a smirk.

"Yes, you can. Just concentrate. Concentrate on the center of your mind."

"But I can't, Julie. I really can't."

"Why not?" she asks softly.

"Because I have to pee," he whispers back.

"Oh, my God, why didn't you say something before we started?"

"Because your voice is so relaxing. I'll be right back," he says. He leaps from the table and races behind a large hickory tree.

As he returns, Julie shakes her head as she smiles. "You're an idiot, but I love you," she says. She wraps her arms around him, taking a moment to kiss. "Are you good with the body functions now?"

"Yes, ma'am," he says. He looks down at her shirt as he strokes the side of her breast. "But I bet I could really concentrate on this meditation thing if maybe we lay down for a while beneath a shady tree." He opens his eyes as he raises his dark brown eyebrows.

"Maybe later. Right now, let's just try this again," Julie replies. She pulls his hand down off her breast and sits down on the bench, tapping her hand on the table for him to sit beside her. He obliges, and she begins to coach him once again softly. "Now, close your eyes. Put your hands on your lap with your fingers touching each other. No peeking. Enjoy the warmth of the sun on your body. Think no thoughts. Think in your mind of nothing. Think of nothing at all."

"What if I have a thought?" he asks.

"Just let it go. Just wrap the thought in a balloon in your mind and let it float off and away."

Hunter nods as he closes his eyes. The two sit motionless for more than twenty minutes, basking in the sunshine. Finally breaking the silence, Julie opens her eyes and whispers to Hunter, "Did you do it? Were you able to sit without any thoughts?"

"No, not really." He opens his eyes and looks at her. "I tried, but it didn't work. However, I did find it is a great technique for writing a song," Hunter replies. He reaches into his blue fleece jacket, pulling from it his pen and notepad. He places the notebook on the table and quickly begins to write. Julie watches in fascination. As Hunter finishes, he sighs as he puts the pen back in his pocket.

"You never cease to amaze me. May I read it?" she asks.

"Sure, here," he says. He hands her the pad. She takes it and begins to read.

## Calling

*Johnny's an American son, and so well loved by everyone.*
*Heading off to a foreign shore for another senseless war.*
*Janey is scared half to death.*
*She loves that boy with every passing breath.*
*She works two jobs to make sense of this so well thought out mess.*

*I've heard wise men say sometimes it works that way.*
*When it works that way, I'm calling.*

*An M-16 is his new toy.*
*Lock-n-load and Rock-n-Roll, let's Rock and Roll.*
*The 4$^{th}$ ID is his Band of Brothers.*
*Janey writes him every day. He means to write in his own way.*
*He never heard of Tikrit before all this trouble.*

*I've heard wise men say sometimes it works that way.*
*When it works that way, I'm calling.*
*When it's all too much. When I need your touch.*
*When it's all too much, I'm calling.*

*I've got a weary heart.*
*I've got an open mind.*
*Can we make a new start?*
*I think it's just about time!*

*Johnny never had a chance. An IED was his last dance.*
*Laid there crying out for home and mother.*

*Janey got the news and cried, and so well thought out her suicide.*
*She took their baby girl to Johnny's Mother.*
*She rushed home to an Oxy Co.*
*Downed the bottle with a Jack and Coke.*
*She laid herself on the bed for Johnny's mother to find.*

*I've heard wise men say it shouldn't work that way.*
*When it works that way, I'm calling, calling.*
*When it's all too much. When I need your touch*
*When it's all too much, I'm calling, calling, you!*
*I'm calling you. Calling. I'm calling you.*

She finishes reading the prose, leans over, and kisses him on the cheek. "Wow, you heard all this in your head while you were meditating?"

"Yes," he replies.

"The words, how do you hear them?" she asks.

"Sometimes I hear a chorus. Sometimes, words come to me that start telling a story, and I have to follow them to see where they lead. The goal is to let whatever I hear progress until it is ingrained. Sometimes I hear just a melody. If I hum it long enough, or if I lay back and listen to it in my head, words usually start associating with the melody." As he finishes explaining the process, he looks at her, raising his eyebrows as he tightens his lips.

"Huh, and that's all there is to it?" she asks.

"Well, then the real work begins. You have to find the chords to what you are hearing. Then you have to work out several parts. After that, you have to let the band make it better. A team needs to play with it and make it their own."

"Hunter."

"Yes."

"I love you," she says. She looks at him as she takes his hand and leans toward his lips.

"I love you too," he replies just as she delivers a kiss to him.

# Chapter 20

## Pushing Buttons

OLIVER SITS DOWN TO READ THE latest data report from the Universe Observation device. His attention is immediately drawn to the Angel Communication program. He places a call to Krystal by tapping her Angel Identity Icon on the screen. Her real-time image instantly appears on the Angel Interface screen.

"Hello," she says.

"Hello, Krystal, I mean hello, Jenny. How are things down there?" he asks.

"Hi, Oliver. Everything is fine. Do you have something for me to do?"

"Yes, I do. The Universe Observation device indicates that you need to contact Hunter's drummer friend once again, Chris. It's been a few months. Do you remember him?"

"Oh yes, of course. I remember him. He's really cute."

"The device indicates that you need to make contact and begin hanging out with him much more often than you have up to this point. Your assignment has now evolved with more finite details. How would you like to learn the finer art of being a percussionist, in addition to your other studies?"

"That sounds exciting," she replies.

"Good, because you now have the skills of an advanced percussionist, and you are to enroll in an elective course at Ithaca College. He is listed as a student advisor, so that should aid you in discussions with him. It is suggested that you seek his advice on various techniques whereby the probability exists he will ask you to come to his practices more often."

"I will head up to the college right away," she says.

"Be sure to take advantage of his tutoring hours. You are to seek his help as much as possible. It will get you closer to Hunter, Julie, and the others. You are to keep this relationship strictly platonic. Those are all the details that I have for you at the moment."

"All right, I got it. Is there anything else, Oliver?"

"No, there are no other details at the moment. Just keep in mind that your assignment is to watch over the band and quietly observe whatever Scratch is up to and report if necessary. Only attempt to interfere by throwing one of the nuts you have if you think it absolutely necessary. Try and get as close as possible to Chris so that you are invited more often wherever he goes. All right?" he asks.

Drake listens from across the room to ensure Oliver has not forgotten any of the details.

"Will do, Oliver," she replies.

Drake looks over his assistant's shoulder at the finer details on the display of the device. He reminds her, "And don't forget to avoid consuming ice cream."

"Hi, Drake. I know, no ice cream. I remember," she says.

"What I can see that Oliver cannot see is that the probabilities calculator is working overtime. My advice is to be ever cautious and vigilant to the ways of Scratch and his nasty little vixens. If you are perplexed by any situation that you are in, don't hesitate to call. There also is a text option on your device if you feel you cannot speak. Good luck, Jenny," Drake says. He looks back into his hand-held device as he begins to walk away.

"Didn't I tell you about the text option?" Oliver asks.

"No, but I saw the feature," she replies.

"Oh, good. Drake gets a little upset if I don't get things to his liking. I figured you would make full use of the communicator," he says.

"I thought it might come in handy. Did you want me to send a test message to you now, Oliver?" she asks.

"Oh, yes, we should have done that in the beginning. Yes. Please do," he replies. He begins to monitor the text section of his command station screen. "Oh, there you are, you are good. I got it." He sighs with relief, seeing her fast response. "Okay, I will leave you to your assignment. And don't have too much fun. Remember to stay diligent." He looks over to see Drake enter the Hallway of Eternity. He looks back to the screen and whispers, "Well, have a little fun."

THE BAND GATHERS FOR a writing session at Alex's guest house on the lake. Scratch begins warming up, playing a new guitar riff. Hunter looks over, cocking his head.

"What is that?" Hunter asks.

"I don't know, something I ripped off from some shit-stomping little Telecaster-twanging country music wanker. I think he spent the bulk of his time wallowing in cow dung, really. Kind of catchy, though, I guess. Why, you hearing something to accompany it?" Scratch asks.

Julie's affection for the musical progression is clearly evident, and she cozies up next to Hunter as she listens. "I like it."

"Yeah, you like it, do you, Miss Julie? Well then, let's write something to it," he replies.

Hunter reaches over to the computer and instantly begins typing. "Stop playing for a minute or two."

"Country music is so bloody predictable. Know what I mean?" Scratch asks. "It's like one stupid bass line will cover half of the entire industry's biggest hits. Mind-numbing wankers who buy the shit really, but I think that no one ever went broke underestimating the intelligence of the American public."

"Wow," Chris says. He shakes his head at the cruelty of the statement. Hunter laughs as Julie slaps him across the arm.

147

"That wasn't very nice, Scratch," Julie says. She gives him a stern look, not appearing amused by the criticism.

"It's true, you know. Think about everything they write. Most of it is so blatantly stupid that you'd like to club the author to death for writing it in the first bloody place. Or it's so repetitive and redundant that all you need know consists of either, like, your lady is leaving you, or your lady is leaving you and banging your best mate. Or that your dog up and bloody died. Sometimes, they write some intricate plots. You know, like, you lose your house because your lady left you, and then discover you're being fired because you took a day off to bawl your bloody eyes out because you had to bury your dog. I don't know how people can listen to it willingly, without vomiting all over themselves, really."

"Well, you could say it a whole lot nicer than that, Scratch. We plan on target marketing those country music fans with some of our cross-over material." Julie turns and slaps Hunter again for continuing to laugh at Scratch's blatantly offensive comments. "And you better start writing something," she says to Hunter.

"Yes, ma'am," Hunter replies. He looks over at the others struggling to hold their laughter for fear of Julie turning her anger on them.

"I bet that you would have a whole different attitude if you were playing in one of those stupid country music groups and making it big, Scratch," Julie says.

"Sorry, Miss Julie. Please excuse my tongue. But I would rather shove a cork up my arse and shit through my teeth than have to play those predictable and uncreative orchestrations all night long. The only one who ever had any talent was Johnny Cash, and that's because he really lived through the pain he was writing about. It's a drag, a real drag playing that Hillbilly Honky-tonk wanker music. But you're right, and I will play whatever you want me to play if it helps us make it big. You tell me what you want, and I can play it."

"I want you to play what you were just playing," Julie says. She looks at him with a degree of contempt.

"Miss Julie, if you want me to play Honky-tonk trash, I'll play Honky-tonk trash. If you want me to play Chicken Pickin,' I'll give you Chicken

Pickin' until the bloody cows come home and fling their crap all over the inside of the barn. If you want me to lay on stage and roll around playing my rusty trombone, I'll do it. Whatever you need, Miss Julie. Just say the word. I'm here for ya, love."

"Thank you. That's just what I want to hear. And start writing and stop laughing, damn it," she scolds Hunter once again, then storms into the kitchen.

Scratch turns to Franklin and Chad. "You know why pigs roll around in their feces, don't you? It's so they can plug their ears with their own shit, so they don't have to listen to the real filth called modern country music that farmer John plays on the radio around the goddamn clock inside the bloody barn."

"I heard that," Julie yells. "You better start playing something, Scratch."

"Just keep playing that turn-around, Scratch, or she's going to get really pissed," Hunter advises.

The core of the band begins to follow Scratch as he begins to play the catchy progression. Hunter continues to write as the others develop the essence of the song. Hunter prints the document and places it on the music stand. Julie takes a cup from the microwave and drops a tea bag into the water. A smile returns to her face as Hunter begins to sing the lyrics to the new song.

*Diamonds and Fire*

*"Every bit of sundown she can draw right out of me.*
*Every little whisper sounds like one great mystery.*
*Oh, child, slow down. You're growing way too fast.*
*Beauty has grown out of a long-lost innocent past.*

*She don't need Daddy's money. She has plenty of her own.*
*She has a thousand numbers programmed in her Android telephone.*
*He wants her, she wants her, and maybe you want her too.*
*She'll be the judge of just who she'll Rendezvous.*

*She likes the weight of her diamonds and fire.*
*Her heart at the moment is not tethered by wire.*
*The boys like the way that she walks when she moves.*
*Most just don't know what to do,*
*and you can be stealing her heart.*

*If you want to love her and she turns away, make sure you follow.*
*She once had a lover, but he went astray. Her heart is now hollow,*
*and maybe waiting for you*

*She likes the weight of her diamonds and fire.*
*Her heart at the moment is not tethered by wire.*
*The boys like the way that she talks when she moves.*
*Most just don't know what to do.*

*Hope is the one thing that's first on her mind.*
*Love is the one thing she's hoping to find.*
*Love is the one thing that's common with you.*
*Tell her. You'll know what to do,*
*and you can be stealing her heart."*

Julie claps as the band finishes. She walks over to Hunter's music stand and snatches the lyric sheet. "Now see, Scratch, that's what happens when you try and be creative. You end up writing something that can make people happy. I love it." She steps up to the microphone. "Great job, everyone. Now let me try it. From the top, boys, let's do it again."

# Chapter 21

## While the Cat's Away

JULIE BEGINS TO SHOW HER TRUE COLORS, directing the musicians between each take to perform specific techniques that help develop the new song's dynamics. The band plays it several more times for Julie, tailoring it to her liking. An hour passes by as she challenges the musicians like a conductor until she is satisfied with what she hears. Finally, she suggests that the band take a break, and Hunter, Chris, and Scratch step out of the cottage to enjoy some of the sunshine.

"I can't believe that song came together that quickly," Chris exclaims.

"We've got a little magic going on. That's an expected outcome when you develop chemistry," Scratch replies.

Julie steps out onto the patio and looks at Hunter as she pulls her sunglasses over her eyes. "Franklin, Chad, and I are going to run downtown to the store. Do you guys need anything?" she asks.

"I'm good," Hunter says. He picks up a small flat rock and skips it across the lake.

"Would you be a love and grab me a box of fags?" Scratch asks. He reaches into his jeans for some cash.

"I didn't know you were gay," Chris says jokingly.

"Yeah, I am, mate. Only because I have seen your mum naked, and it forever tied my penis into a bloody pretzel," Scratch responds.

"Cigarettes are bad for you, Scratch, but if it helps keep your mouth shut, how many cartons would you like?" Julie asks.

"Just a pack. Thank you, Miss Julie," he says. He laughs at her joke as he hands her a $20 bill.

"We will be back in a bit," she says. She takes the money from Scratch, placing it in the pocket of her black Adidas jogging pants.

Chris sits down on a chaise lounge. He eases the recliner back and looks out at the lake. Scratch retrieves his folk guitar and brings it out on the patio. He checks the tuning and begins to play. A warm breeze steadily begins to blow in from the south.

"Ah, there is a nice Georgia wind blowing. Do you smell it, lads?" Scratch asks. He raises his nose to the air, looking much like a wolf sensing the wind.

"No, not really. We're kind of a long way from Georgia, Scratch," Chris says.

"You have to get in touch with your senses, mate. The wind can tell you a lot about things if you listen real closely," he says.

"Maybe. I guess it has to blow in from somewhere." Chris taps his drumsticks on his lawn chair's fabric to the progression Scratch is playing on the guitar.

Scratch watches Julie and the others drive off. He places the guitar gently against the rock wall and stretches his arms up toward the sky. "You lads mind if I smoke?" he asks. He reaches into his pocket and retrieves a metal matchstick holder.

Hunter laughs as he skips another rock. "Since when do you ask?"

"I just thought I'd be proper," he replies.

"It's your lungs," Hunter says. He takes a seat by Chris and closes his eyes as he begins to relax. Chris watches as Scratch pulls out a hand-rolled cigarette. Scratch strikes a match across the rock wall and lights the smoke. Chris looks at him with suspicion in smelling the piney aroma.

"What the hell are you smoking?" Chris asks.

"A Wazzgiblet," Scratch says. He steps onto the dock and looks down into the water.

Hunter opens his eyes. "A what?" he asks.

"An herbal jazz cigarette. Know what I mean?"

"No, I don't know what you mean. What the hell is an herbal jazz cigarette?" Hunter asks.

"I think it's what the English call a joint," Chris says.

"Jesus, you're smoking marijuana," Hunter shouts. His look of alarm seems to amuse the guitar player.

"Relax, mate, quiet down. You don't need to bring Jesus into this. He'll only try to get me to put the damn thing out," Scratch replies.

"That stuff is illegal, Scratch. Alex would get pissed if he saw that," Hunter says.

"No, not at all. Where do you think I got it from? Don't be a din. He keeps a stash at the studio all the time for musicians like me. Didn't you know that?"

Hunter seems to realize the ordeal is not worth arguing over. "No, I didn't. It sure does have an interesting smell. I will give you that."

"I take it you don't partake?" Scratch asks. He steps back off from the dock as he takes another drag.

"No, I don't. Never have," Hunter informs.

"Are you serious?" Chris asks.

"Yes, I'm serious."

"Oh, we got ourselves a virgin on our hands," Scratch exclaims.

"I would've thought you smoked marijuana, Hunter," Chris says.

"No, I really never have. I watched a friend's brother get mixed up on drugs, so I just never hung out with people that did it. Some musicians I've played with offered it to me before, but I never took them up on trying the stuff."

"Well, here is your chance, mate," Scratch says. He tempts Hunter, handing him the joint.

"No. I'm good," Hunter replies.

"Chris?" Scratch asks. He holds the joint out for him to take.

"Sure, why not? I like to get creative when I smoke." Chris takes the joint, carefully inhaling the drug. As he does, he gags slightly on the smoke. Hunter watches curiously.

"I must admit that stuff really does smell good. It's like a fragrant pine or almost a fruity smell," Hunter says.

"Oh man, it's the fruitiest. Adam would not have gone for the apple had he had this stuff," Scratch says.

"Adam would have been too busy for it being tempted by a naked woman," Chris chimes in as he releases his hit.

"What do you know?" Scratch asks.

"I know a lot, what do you know?" Chris replies.

"I know a lot more about it than you think, mate," Scratch says in a serious tone.

"What is getting high really like, anyway?" Hunter asks. "I don't think I would like it."

"Man, it's like the whole universe opens up to be received by your mind. It's like, everything is cool and magnificent, and all things are in order all at once, know what I mean?" Scratch replies.

"Everything tends to be completely funny, Hunter," Chris adds. He looks at Hunter as he inhales another toke.

"Yeah, that's it, everything tends to be really funny," Scratch says. He takes the joint from Chris and offers it again to Hunter.

Hunter stares at it. The smell of the marijuana lofts about the area. "What the hell? What do I do?"

"Well, you take it in real easy like, not too much since you've never smoked it before. Just get a little bit in your lungs," Scratch says. He smiles as Hunter takes the joint.

Hunter waves it under his nose. He looks at Chris with a bit of apprehension as he holds it to his lips.

"That's it, now inhale just a little bit." Scratch smiles with the reassurance of an experienced salesman as Hunter does as instructed. "Good, now hold it in as long as you can, yeah, then let it out," Scratch says. He takes the joint out of Hunter's fingers.

Hunter releases the smoke. Only a trace vapor trail exits from his mouth.

"There you go, mate. You took your first hit. You won't feel anything, so don't expect it."

"No, why not?" Hunter asks.

"You really need to take two or three hits before you begin to feel any effect," Chris interjects. "It seems like pretty good stuff, so I wouldn't take many more than that."

"Yeah, he's right, you know," Scratch says. He hands the joint back to the novice. Hunter takes it and inhales too large of a hit. He attempts to hold it in his lungs, but the smoke overwhelms him, and he begins to cough uncontrollably. He bends over in order to try and catch his breath, dropping the joint in the process. Scratch picks it up and begins to laugh at him while patting him on the back. "Not that much, mate. The stuff expands in your lungs, man."

Hunter gasps as he struggles to catch his breath as he responds, "Thanks for telling me that."

"You better stop on that one, Hunter, or Julie might know you are stoned," Chris says.

"Yeah, there is an idea," he replies.

"You all right, mate?" Scratch asks.

"Yeah, I'm good." As he begins to catch his breath, he stands up.

"You sure? Might want to sit back down a bit, lad," Scratch says. He grins as he looks at Hunter.

"Yeah, you might be right," Hunter says. He sits back down, coughing as he struggles to catch his breath.

Scratch watches him while picking up his guitar. He begins to play once again as Hunter and Chris sit and listen. "That's 'Bach's Minuet.' I love that piece," Chris says.

Scratch acknowledges with a nod and a grin. As Scratch finishes playing the piece, Chris claps with approval.

"Amazing," Hunter says. "It's like, uhm, it's like, uhm."

"It's like, uhm, it's like you're stoned, mate," Scratch replies. He places the guitar back in its case.

"Yeah, that must be it," Hunter replies.

"Let's go get a beer," Scratch says. The three of them make their way into the kitchen.

"What do you think about Naamah and Aphrodite running our media blitz? Naamah is doing a spectacular job building my own personal website. I think she would do an excellent job for us. What do you think, lads?"

"She's got my vote," Chris says supportively. "I don't know much about her, but a girl that good looking, all you have to do is put her picture on the site, and it will sell."

"She is all that, isn't she?" Hunter asks.

"Well, think it over. She is a great saleswoman, and she knows how to gain attention," he says. He opens the refrigerator door and retrieves a beer for each of them. "Cheers," he says. He raises his bottle into the air.

"We should write something," Chris says. He opens his beer, looking at the other two for input on his suggestion.

"Yeah, what a great idea," Hunter replies. He squints as he looks at Chris.

Scratch walks over to the piano. The guitar player briefly demonstrates his ability as he breaks into Beethoven's 'Fur Elise.'

"Man, you rule," Hunter says.

Scratch finishes playing the piece and immediately begins to play a completely different arrangement. They both listen closely, mesmerized by the music.

"We need a real catchy 'Crown the King' type of song. Do you know what I mean? A 'play it real safe' type song," Scratch says. He plays a few bars of the music then stops to look at his two stoned band members. "You know, like a discovering your own potential, or do it your way type of stuff."

Hunter looks lost in his thought as well as confused. "You mean like, uhm, you like, uhm. No, I don't know what you mean," he replies.

"My God, man, talking to you is like aiding and abetting a known felon! What I mean is like, stretch the truth a bit and like, you know, elect the President."

Chris looks on, equally confused in his marijuana tizzy. He finds his way to his drums as he listens to Scratch.

"You Yanks really are slow sometimes, I swear to God. What I'm sayin' is like hitchhike underneath the big top and like liquidate the inventory. Real manual labor type stuff, man."

"Oh, like a working-class song?" Hunter asks.

"Yeah, a working-class song, like, you know, empower yourself and exercise your rights. Raining on your own parade is like par for the learning curve, know what I mean? Get out there in life and like, you know, start dancing in the dragon's fiery breath type of song." Scratch starts to play the progression again from the beginning.

"Oh, I like that," Hunter says. He laughs as he looks at Chris.

"Yeah, I bet you do. Climb that tree of enlightenment of yours, mate. Roll it off the lot for me. Don't let us down now. I know you got it in you. Let it out." Scratch laughs at his bandmate's state of ignorance as he plays.

"What's the theme you want. What is it about?" Hunter asks.

"Really. I mean, like really?" Scratch stops playing. "I've been telling you all along what it's about. I just don't think you're really listening. It's like feeling your way around and canning the vandal type stuff, you know what I'm saying?"

"Can the vandal." Hunter looks over at Chris, appearing confused about what Scratch is saying.

"You're a bloody Din. Are you stoned or just plain stupid, lad? I'm talking about playing peek-a-boo. Clearing the snorkel, bleedin' the weed, burpin' the baby, a little bit of wrist aerobics. Come on, man, do I got to spell it out for you?"

"What? Wrist aerobics? What the hell is wrist aerobics?" Hunter asks.

"I mean like hitchhike to heaven or, better yet, cuddle the kielbasa. You follow me now, mate?"

Hunter's jaw drops, and his eyes open wide as he shakes his head. "You are one sick son of a bitch, Scratch," Hunter says.

"Thank you. I try not to disappoint."

"Is he talking about what I think he is talking about?" Chris asks.

"I think so," Hunter replies. He nods his head in verification.

Chris begins to laugh. The contagiousness of his laughter seems to cause Hunter to do the same. Scratch looks at the two stoned messes and shakes his head as he continues to play the new composition.

As Hunter catches his breath, he listens to what Scratch is playing. Chris picks up the drumsticks and begins to accompany Scratch. Hunter opens a new document on the computer and spends a few minutes writing some lyrics to the musical piece.

"I got it," he says. He prints the document, then walks over to the piano. "Play it again."

Scratch and Chris do as Hunter asks and begin to play the song once again. Hunter picks up his guitar and quickly finds the proper musical key as he begins to sing.

### Cyber Girl

*"He keeps one eye open all the time. She's cutting with a sharper mind. She never has a broken heart. He found her just by clicking Start.*

*He chanced upon her late one night, while the Wi-Fi took him for a ride. He chanced upon her in the dark while surfing out through Data Park. I, Yi-Yi-Wi-Fi, Cyber Girl.*

*And so he sent a message through. She'll talk to me, she'll talk to you, and she always looks her best. She marks up sex in Hypertext. I, Yi-Yi-Wi-Fi, a Cyber Girl.*

*Her lingerie will fascinate, and her seductive voice will stimulate. She licks upon a lollipop, then hides it in a private spot. I, Yi-Yi-Wi-Fi, a Cyber Girl. I, Yi-Yi-Wi-Fi, it's a Cyber Girl. She gives new meaning to a hard drive.*

*How can it be, she's so alive.*
*All for $19.95,*
*and she has many friends there too.*
*There is nothing they won't do.*

*She's oiled up, and slippery. She has girlfriends, toys, machinery.*
*Yes she really gets around, but faithful while his zipper's down.*
*I, Yi-Yi-Wi-Fi, another Cyber Girl.*
*I, Yi-Yi-Wi-Fi, and another Cyber Girl."*

# Chapter 22

## The Hope Within a Rainbow

"YES, HELLO AGAIN, OLIVER," Jenny says as she answers the incoming call.

"Hello Krystal, I mean Jenny. There is an indication that you need to go immediately to Wegmans grocery store, strike up a conversation with Julie, and tag along with her for the rest of the day," he says.

"Okay. And what am I supposed to do?"

"I'm not rightly sure yet. It is often up to the angel on assignment to ascertain that answer, so trust your instincts and stay on high alert. I suggest grabbing a small cart at the store and casually bump into her to start a conversation."

"I understand. Then just tell her I'm on a mission from Heaven, and I need to hang out?"

"No, I wouldn't do that."

"Oliver."

"Yes, Jenny."

"I was kidding."

"Oh, haha, I forgot you have a sense of humor. Anyway, something calls for your attention. You have all the devices that Drake and I gave to you on your person, correct?"

"Yes, Oliver."

"Good. If I see something important, then I will ring you. Likewise, if you need me," Oliver says.


IT DOESN'T TAKE LONG for Jenny to find Julie inside the grocery store. She follows along, waiting for just the right moment. Julie finally steps in front of Jenny's cart, and Jenny lightly bumps into her. "Oh, I'm so sorry. I hope I didn't hurt you," she says.

"Oh no, it's my fault, I stepped right in front of you. I'm fine," Julie says. Instantly she recognizes Jenny.

"Hey, I know you. I watched the fireworks at your house. How have you been?" Jenny asks.

"Hi, yes, Jenny, right?" Julie asks. "Good, thank you," she replies.

Chad and Franklin turn, also recognizing her. "Oh, hey, hi," Chad says.

"Hey, girl. How have you been?" Franklin asks.

"Good, thank you. How is Chris? I haven't seen him in a while," Jenny asks.

"We're taking a break from practice to grab some stuff for dinner. Did you want to come along with us and hang? Chris is there right now if you wanted to see him. You are certainly welcome to come with us if you'd like," Julie says. She smiles as she offers Jenny the chance to join them.

"You know what? Sure, I didn't have anything planned for tonight. Why not? I can do my shopping later."

"Good. We're just picking up a few things. Then we can go."

Julie drives them all back to the lake house. As they exit the vehicle, the sound of thunder rumbles across the landscape, foretelling the approach of a fast-moving storm. Chad looks up to notice the clouds moving in from the north, darkening the bright blue sky. Julie enters the cottage and places her purse and the bag of groceries on the counter. Franklin, Chad, and Jenny follow behind her. The three musicians in the living room are unaware they have returned.

"That must be a new song," Franklin says. He looks at Julie as they listen to the music. Julie smiles as Hunter begins to sing the new piece.

"Yes, it certainly sounds like a new song," she replies. Julie begins placing the provisions into the refrigerator. "That is new. It sounds like they were busy little beavers while we were out," Julie says.

Franklin takes the potatoes and begins to rinse them in the sink as Chad begins to look through the cabinets. Julie's smile fades as she listens closely to the words. Chad retrieves a large pot, appearing dumbfounded by what Hunter is singing. Jenny peaks around the corner of the kitchen into the practice area of the living room. She looks at Hunter, appearing surprised by the lyrics he is singing.

Chad sets the pot down on the counter next to Franklin then turns to Julie. "Did he just say she licks upon a lollipop then hides it in a private spot?" Chad asks.

"Yes! He did," Julie replies. A distinct tone of disgust swells within her voice. Jenny places her hand over her mouth as she, too, realizes the meaning of the dirty little song.

Chad lets out a quick laugh. Julie looks at him with a distinct hint of anger and disapproval in her expression.

"Bravo, bravo," Scratch responds as they finish the song. "It's bloody brilliant, mate. I love it. I love it. I absolutely love it."

Julie steps into the practice area. "Hunter, can I speak with you a moment?" she asks.

"Hey," he says. He places the guitar in its case as Chad, Franklin, and Jenny enter the living room.

"Oh my God, hi," Chris says with excitement upon seeing Jenny.

"Hi," she replies. She watches Hunter as he steps into the kitchen to speak with Julie.

"Walk with me, Hunter," Julie says. They both step out onto the porch, and Hunter closes the door behind them. She spins around and points at him. "What the hell was that filth you were just singing?"

"It's a new song we just wrote. Why?" he asks.

"Oh, I don't know, maybe it was the 'she marks up sex in hypertext' part or maybe the 'oiled up and slippery part.' Either way, it's dirty. What the hell has gotten into you?"

"Julie, it's just a song that Scratch asked me to write words to."

"I can't sing that kind of song, Hunter."

"It's Rock and Roll, Julie."

"No, it's dirty. And I won't sing it." Suspiciously, she looks at Hunter's eyes. "And why are your eyes so red, Hunter?" she asks. She looks closer, noticing they are glassy and bloodshot.

"Julie, come on."

"Come on, nothing. Why are your eyes so red? Did you smoke weed while I was gone? You look like you smoked marijuana. Did you?" she asks. Her lips tighten, and her eyebrows drop as she interrogates Hunter.

"Yes, I just tried it for the first time."

"I see. Hunter, I refuse to be around drugs. I think you need to take a good look at yourself. We can't be together if you are going to use them. I am going to take the night off so you can think about what is more important to you."

"Okay, I get it. You know I will do anything to be with you. I didn't know you were that adamant about it. But you don't have to take the night off. You just bought dinner for everyone. Please don't leave."

She reaches into her pocket and pulls out her car keys. "I'm not hungry. You guys go ahead. Can you see to it that Jenny gets back downtown?"

"Yes. I am sure Chris will take her. One of us will anyway. Julie, please don't go."

"No. I'm mad at you, and I can't work when I'm mad. I will call you tomorrow." She exits the cottage and gets into her SUV.

Hunter watches as she starts her vehicle and proceeds up the driveway. "Nice going, Hunter," he says to himself. He drops his head as he turns to go back into the cottage.

Chad steps out of the house. "Did she just leave?" he asks.

"Yes," Hunter replies.

"She didn't like the song so much that she had to leave? That doesn't seem like Julie. Something must be bothering her."

"Well, I probably shouldn't have smoked the marijuana earlier."

"Oh, yeah, she doesn't like being around any drugs. I'm surprised you didn't know that," Chad says.

"It's not something we talked about in all the times we've been together."

"She'll come around. She has invested too much of her time into this project. We'll just call it an early night. But the potatoes are on now, so we may as well have dinner. And the song you guys just wrote, I think it's a hit, Hunter. I really like it," Chad reassures.

"Julie sure doesn't like it." Hunter looks at Chad as if ashamed.

Scratch turns off his pocket recorder and sets his beer down on the counter. He starts to turn toward the door then stops for a moment, looking back at the purse on the counter next to his beer. He steps out onto the patio. "You all right, mate?" he asks.

"Yeah, fine, Scratch. Thanks," Hunter replies.

Hunter and Chad go back inside, and Scratch follows, closing the door behind him. An air of uneasiness quickly fills the room. Chris, Franklin, and Jenny look at Hunter as he walks into the living room.

"Is there a problem?" Scratch quietly asks Chad.

"Well, Julie is taking the rest of the night off."

"I see. And what is Miss Julie's problem?" Scratch asks. He looks over at her purse once again.

"I don't think she approved of the new song or Hunter being high."

"Right, well, she is in a rock and roll band," Scratch replies.

"I know," Chad says. He reaches into the refrigerator. "Need a beer, Scratch?" he asks.

"No, not right this moment, I have one. Thank you, though," he replies.

As Chad reaches into the refrigerator, Scratch smirks. He retrieves his beer from the counter, looking down at Julie's purse.

Scratch enters the living room, taking a seat on the couch, in between Chris and Hunter. He taps Hunter on the shoulder. "I want you to know that you are one amazing songwriter. I understand Julie left because she is mad at you. Is that right?"

"Yes, you could say that," Hunter replies.

Chris quickly turns his head toward Hunter. "Julie left?" he asks.

"Yes. She's mad I smoked a joint."

"I see," Chris replies.

"I don't think she liked the song very much either," Hunter says.

"She might not like the song, but her reaction means you're definitely onto something," Scratch says. "The worst thing we can do now is stop working on that song. Hell, you can sing it if she doesn't want to. But that song is a winner. I know you probably want to bag it for the day, and that's understandable, but we need to be right back here tomorrow working on material. Especially that song. You know what I mean?" He lights a cigarette as he waits for an answer.

"Yes, I know. I'm just kind of bummed right at the moment," Hunter replies.

The sound of thunder rumbles across Cayuga Lake like a cannonade. The sky quickly turns dark and ominous.

Franklin walks to the picture window to look at the sky. "I am thinking grilling steaks is not going to happen tonight, boys," he says. Chad joins him to look at the developing storm.

"We could just save the steaks for tomorrow night. Besides, there are a couple of bands playing downtown I would like to see tonight. Do you all want just to call it a night and meet back here tomorrow?" Chris asks.

"Great idea. Let's go," Franklin says.

"Hunter, you game? Or did you want to run through some stuff without Julie?" Chad asks.

"No, go ahead. You guys have fun." Hunter replies. He goes to the kitchen and grabs a beer from the fridge, then sits down on a stool at the counter.

"Scratch, do you want to come with us?" Chris asks.

"No, I'm good. I want to hang with Hunter. Go listen to our competition, lads."

Franklin looks at the pot on the stove. "You want me to shut the potatoes off, Hunter?"

"Yeah, that's a good idea. I can put them in the fridge when they cool down," Hunter says.

Hunter turns on the stool to look out at the lake as Chris, Chad, and Jenny also enter the kitchen.

Chris taps Hunter on the shoulder. "We're going to go the Boatyard Grill if you and Scratch change your mind," he says.

"Okay, maybe we will come down in a bit," Hunter replies. He pulls his writing pad from his pocket, setting it down on the counter. He stares blankly at it as the others begin to walk out.

Jenny frowns as she looks at Hunter. "Are you all right, Hunter?" she asks.

"Yeah, I'm fine, thanks. You guys go. Have a good night," he says.

"Okay," she replies. She follows Chris to his car.

A moment later, Chad comes back into the kitchen. "Scratch, can you move your car for me?" he asks.

Scratch fidgets with a text message as he answers, "Yeah, give me one second, and I'll be right there."

"Thanks," Chad replies.

Scratch looks at Hunter as he moves toward the door. "You all right, mate?" he asks.

"Yeah, I'll be fine."

"I'll move my car and be right back."

Hunter nods his head. He looks up from his writing tablet and gazes out at the white caps on the lake. Scratch returns a moment later, disrupting his thoughts.

"Why do women act so unpredictably, Scratch?" he asks.

"Ah, it's the nature of the beast, mate. The best time to boink them is when they come around again after throwing their little tirades, really."

The storm outside suddenly releases its full fury. Down from the sky, a torrent of rain begins to fall. The wind begins to roar, bending the trees like blades of grass. A lightning strike touches the hillside across the lake, instantly accompanied by a clap of thunder. The cottage shakes from the violent repercussion.

"Yeah! Hell, yeah!" Scratch revels in approval as he watches the atmospheric assault. He opens the fridge, retrieving another beer, and looks down at what

Hunter is writing on the notepad. Hunter looks up at him as Scratch lights another joint. He takes a drag then hands it to Hunter. "Come on, lad. She's not coming back tonight," he says.

"No. That got me in trouble."

"Look, you probably won't ever do this shit again, and it's not like you are going to get yelled at again tonight either. Come on. You wrote a very cool song earlier when you smoked just a little bit. Run with it."

"It did make writing that song easy."

"Then imagine what a little more will do. We can write another great song together. Come on with ya."

Hunter stares at the offer a moment. "Give me the damn thing," Hunter says. He takes the joint, then pauses.

"Remember, not too much. I'm not giving you mouth-to-mouth resuscitation if you start gagging again. I'll just let you flop around like a bloody trout on the goddamn beach."

Hunter takes a hit from the joint then hands it back. "No, go ahead, take a couple drags, mate. Get good and ripped. Let's see how well your mind works when you are really chased. That song you wrote an hour ago, you were only mildly stoned. I bet you can come up with some spacey material if you're all flame-broiled. Relax. Forget about Miss Cranky Bottoms and let your mind find a really creative corner. Know what I mean?"

Hunter shrugs his shoulders and continues to smoke the joint. "It tastes exceptionally good with this beer," he declares. He takes several more tokes then hands the joint back to Scratch.

"Had enough, have ya?" Scratch says. He laughs as he takes the joint, turning his attention to the ongoing storm.

"Yeah, I think so." Hunter replies.

Scratch's phone begins to ring, and he takes the incoming call as he walks down the hallway to the bathroom. Hunter looks out the window. The storm shows signs that it may be short-lived. The hillside across the lake becomes partially illuminated with the summer sun.

The shifting beams of sunlight outside catch Hunter's attention, and he turns to the window. A spectacular rainbow suddenly appears before his eyes. It graces the opposing shore with its sparkling array of colors. It seems to captivate Hunter as his eyes fill with the look of wonderment. He looks closely at the space around the rainbow. It seems to radiate in the air as it glows, and he squints his eyes as he focuses on it, captivated by its magic. He places his beer on the end table and the pad of paper on the arm of the couch. The natural phenomenon's beauty seems to spark a degree of creativity, and he begins to write.

*Rainbow Preamble*

*The grey in the sky seems to clash with blue.*
*It leaves a hole in the middle where the light still shines through.*
*A pillar of light dares to cut through it all.*
*It seems to hold up the sky so that it shall not fall.*
*You're like the light that I search for by day.*
*You lift me up in a nurturing way.*
*Grey clouds, like rage, shroud you from sight.*
*Grey clouds are no sage as I search for the light.*
*The white ones above them seem to laugh at their plight.*
*Their view is much better, and why they seem right.*
*The colors between them scatter off of the clouds.*
*From the matter of grey, it can't stop that now.*
*The rain brought by grey, its purpose to cleanse,*
*is commanded by the sun from the heat it will dispense.*

*So the grey serves a purpose in a darkening day,*
*but it won't stay too long, quickly passing its way.*
*For again the sky opens, its white clouds like arms,*
*it welcomes with pleasure in its passionate charm.*
*And there in the middle where the sun shines on through.*
*Its hope and its warmth remind me of you.*
*As the grey passes, there is an arch in its tow,*

*and the promise of you in a gleaming rainbow.*
*Raised by the wind and watched by the stars,*
*never anchored in place, and that's who you are.*
*One day at a time, with tomorrow in sight.*
*Angels, they know that our flight is a fight.*

*Like a Rainbow*

*I should call you, but I need more than a chat.*
*I've fallen in love with you, and I need more than that.*
*I've never been anything out of the blue.*
*You are the one thing that I am wanting in you.*

*You are the soul that I see in your eyes.*
*So close should I kiss you that I know it is why.*
*Our tongues, when they dance, so perfect and relaxed.*
*Senses enhanced from each other's soft step.*

*Oh, you're like a rainbow*
*that warms me through colors just after rain.*
*Just out of reach, you're a prize worth more than Gold.*
*I feel you racing all through my veins,*
*and my heart says go, and my heart says go.*
*Go try to find you, a certainty that I know.*
*And my heart says go... go past the Rainbow's end.*

*You are magic, a product of light from the sun.*
*In your reflection, I see you're the only one.*
*Your refraction disperses hope all around.*
*You speak volumes, yet you make not a sound.*

*And if you wear Satin, I'll caress you so slow.*

*Where I will kiss you, only we need to know.*
*We'll fall down, as lovers, caught in each other's web.*
*In and out, we will stroll with the flow and the ebb.*

*Oh, you're like a rainbow,*
*that warms me through colors just after pain.*
*Just out of reach, you're a prize worth more than gold.*
*I feel you racing all through my veins.*
*And my heart says go, and my heart says go.*
*Go try to find you, a certainty that I know.*
*And my heart says go... go past the Rainbow's end.*

# Chapter 23

## The Pounce of the Fox

SCRATCH COMES BACK INTO THE LIVING room, interrupting Hunter's concentration. "Hey, mate, you don't mind if my girls come over and like, you know, enjoy the view, do ya?" he asks.

"I'm sorry, did you say something?" Hunter asks. He shakes his head as if he were lost in another world.

"Oh, you're ripped, mate. I asked you if you mind if my lady friends come over and hang out with us."

"Lady friends. What lady friends?" Hunter asks.

"Aphrodite and Naamah. You met them several times. I hate to disappoint them and all. Do you mind if they come over?"

"No, not at all. You can bring anyone you want over here," Hunter replies.

"Well, good, because I see they're here now. Hey, look at all those words on that pad already, would you? You continue to impress me. You wrote all that in just the last ten minutes while I was on the phone?"

"Yes," he replies.

"Amazing, really. All right, I'll be right back," he says. He steps outside to greet his company.

Hunter looks out at the lake. He can hear another, more violent storm approaching from the north where the previous storm originated. In spite of this, he turns his attention back to his notes and picks up where he left off. He rereads his words as Scratch talks to his two guests in the kitchen. Hunter pays little mind to them as he refines his prose.

"Ladies, I'm sure you remember Mr. Hunter Watkins," Scratch says. He escorts the two girls into the living room. The click of their high heels upon the tile floor forces Hunter to turn his head.

"Hi, Hunter," Aphrodite says.

"Hi, how have you been?" he asks. He can't help but notice her voluptuous curves showcased in a tight-fitting black dress.

Naamah follows close behind her friend. "Hi, Hunter. I am so excited to see you again," she says.

"Hi, how have you been?" he asks.

"Good," she replies. She walks to the picture window; her short candy apple red dress elegantly graces her perfectly sculpted body. She glances back at Hunter with a suggestive smile.

Scratch makes his way toward the bar. "You ladies need a drink?" he asks.

"Uh, yeah," Aphrodite replies. She turns away from the view of the lake to follow Scratch.

"Naamah, what would you like, lass?" he asks.

"Wine, please."

Scratch steps behind the bar. "Any particular kind, doll?"

"Red Cat if you have it, but if not, any wine is fine," she replies. She looks back at Hunter with her seductive blue eyes. "What are you drinking, Hunter?" she asks.

"I'm not certain. Beer, I seem to recollect."

"You don't know?" she asks. She laughs at him as she smiles.

"Well, I..."

"Did Scratch get you stoned? Tell me he has some left. He did, didn't he? I am so dying to catch a buzz," she says.

"Well, I'm not certain, really." He turns his attention back to his notepad.

The girl takes a seat on the couch next to Hunter. Her perfume seems to capture his attention.

"Wow, what are you wearing?" he asks.

"Oh, do you like it? It's a Lost in Love A-line dress. She crosses her legs as she smiles at him.

"Yes, I… I do, but I meant your perfume." He smiles back at her as he looks at her long slender legs.

"Oh, it's called Pure Poison by Christian Dior," she replies.

"It's really nice."

"Thank you, and what are you writing today?" she asks.

"A song."

"I figured that, silly. What's it about?" she asks. She pulls her hair back over her shoulders as she looks at his writing pad.

"It's about turmoil and seeking peace."

"Scratch says that you are the most amazing songwriter he has ever worked with. You truly are gifted, aren't you, Hunter? Are you going to be rich and famous?" she asks.

"I don't know about that. We'll see."

Aphrodite hands Naamah her glass of wine and sits down beside her. She places her right hand on Naamah's knee and gently begins to caress.

"Where is the rest of the band, Hunter?" Aphrodite asks.

"They left for the evening."

"Ahhh, we were so hoping to hear you play tonight," Naamah says. She looks at Hunter, displaying a childlike pout.

"We're going to play, all right. Right after we break out a little joystick for the two of you," Scratch says. He reaches for his matchstick holder, retrieving another joint.

"I love joysticks," Aphrodite jokes. A big grin adorns her face as she looks at Naamah. She raises her eyebrows up and down, eliciting a laugh between the two vixens.

"Behave," Scratch says. "Don't go scaring off our superstar. It's not the double-headed type." He shakes his finger at the two girls, playfully scolding them both.

"Here, mate. Have some wine. It's better for you than beer. It helps your heart keep up with strenuous situations when they arise," Scratch says. He hands the glass to Hunter.

"Oh, thanks." Hunter takes it without regard to mixing the grape and the grain. He immediately begins to drink from the glass. Naamah raises her glass for a toast, and Hunter taps his glass to hers.

Scratch hands the joint and lighter to Naamah. She passes her glass to Hunter to hold for her, and she lights it. Ecstasy seems to engulf her face as she tilts her head back. She exhales the intoxicant as she hands it off to Aphrodite. She looks at Hunter as she takes her drink back. "Thank you," she says.

Aphrodite also takes a hit then gently taps Naamah's arm. She places the lit end inside her mouth and begins to blow smoke to Naamah. She responds by placing her lips on Aphrodite's, inhaling the smoke. Hunter watches in fascination.

Scratch stands beside the couch and taps Hunter on the shoulder. "Aren't they something?" he asks.

Hunter looks at him, nodding his head.

Aphrodite takes the joint from her mouth and holds it up for Scratch to take. He walks over and then performs the same maneuver for her as she did to Naamah. Scratch takes the joint from his mouth and hands it to Hunter. "I'm not going to shotgun you, mate," he says.

"I will," Naamah announces.

She passes her drink to Aphrodite, then takes the joint. As she puts it into her mouth, she rolls her left leg over onto Hunter's lap. Her dress lifts higher, exposing more of her flesh as she moves, and he looks down at her thighs. She places both hands upon his face as she lays her lips gently onto Hunter's and begins to blow smoke into his mouth. He lays his hands on her waist and inhales. Naamah drops her right hand to Hunter's chest, playfully digging her nails into his flesh.

Scratch and Aphrodite begin to laugh as Julie, Chris, and Jenny enter the kitchen. They immediately cease in their laughter as Julie watches with fire in her eyes through the serving station window. Naamah releases Hunter from her grip and takes the joint from her mouth. As Hunter exhales her gift, he notices Scratch and Aphrodite looking into the kitchen at a jury looking on in judgment.

Julie picks up her purse from the counter. "Really?" she retorts. Chris and Jenny remain motionless, appearing shocked and speechless. They begin to shake their heads in disbelief as Julie storms out of the cottage.

"Oh man, is she pissed now," Scratch quietly says. He looks at Hunter like a condemned man who is ready for the gallows. Aphrodite starts to laugh but holds it in, placing her hand in front of her mouth. Naamah stands up and puts the joint into the ashtray Scratch is holding, and she subtly displays a malicious grin.

Hunter leaps from the couch and runs to the door just as Julie reaches her car. In a desperate plea, he yells out, "Wait."

"Stay away from me. I hate you. I don't ever want to see you again, Hunter." Julie slams her car door and drives off.

Hunter frowns at the sight of his love racing out of his life. "Dear Father, what have I just done?" he asks. He walks back into the kitchen, appearing ashamed, defeated, and dejected. He hangs his head as Chris and Jenny look at him, clearly disappointed.

"Dude, I got her to come back to get her purse and take you out to see a band. She felt bad about going off on you. She was coming back to apologize. She admitted she overreacted. What in God's name were you thinking?"

"I guess I wasn't," he says solemnly.

Jenny watches Scratch and the girls in the living room, noticing they are quietly laughing with one another. She reaches into the white satin pouch inside her purse, retrieving the walnut, and clutches it tightly in her hand.

"Well, you really went and did it now. You can pretty much assure that little instance drove her away for good. Come on, Jenny. Hunter here has some real soul searching to do," he says. Chris shakes his head as he turns toward the door.

Hunter sits down in a chair at the kitchen table. He rests his head in his hands, appearing to sink into despair. Jenny looks at him with pity. She begins to follow

Chris out the door, pausing momentarily. "Do not have sex with those women tonight, Hunter," she whispers, much too softly for his conscientious mind to hear. She tosses the walnut onto his back. Light immediately scatters in all directions, then quickly dissipates. She shakes her head as she closes the door. "Please, Father, protect him," Jenny whispers, then turns to follow Chris to the car.

Scratch comes into the kitchen with Hunter's glass of wine in hand. Hunter stands and leans up against the countertop, staring at the floor.

"Right. Well, I guess that about spells it out that we are now officially a four-piece band, mate," Scratch says. He leans against the counter, handing Hunter his wine.

He takes the glass and shakes his head.

"Listen. If there is one thing I know, mate, it's that women get turned on by seeing their man with another woman. And yeah, you know, most of them get really pissed off about it and all. But what goes on in their mind is they question themselves as to how it is likely their fault. And that thought, yeah, always permeates their thinking. Sooner or later, they submit to the notion that they did something wrong and want to make it better. They blame themselves, and then eventually they ask for your forgiveness in one way or another."

Hunter listens as he looks up at Scratch. He takes a deep breath then drops his head again, staring blankly at the floor.

"Mate, it usually leads them to be much more savage in bed, and the sex becomes much more amazing. They usually want to try and please you in hopes that they're doing it right, so you won't have to leave them again."

"That all sounds good in theory," Hunter struggles to speak.

"Come on, mate, forget about it. What's done is done. I got two crazy women here, right now, that don't get all wrinkled about things and are here to party a little bit. Let's not let them down, lad. We'll party for a bit, then I'll cook those steaks up, and we'll just chill out here all evening. What do you say? Come on, let's go see what the two little bombshells are up to." He pats Hunter on the shoulder, and Hunter follows him back into the living room.

They find Aphrodite and Naamah lost in a kiss at the picture window. With their wine glasses in hand behind each other's back, they explore the outside of each other's thigh with their free hand. Though clearly tormented by his lapse in judgment, Hunter manages a sedated smile in noticing the affectionate embrace of the two redheaded nymphomaniacs.

# Chapter 24

## Admission and Suspicion

THE NEXT MORNING JULIE CRIES into her pillow. LaShonda comforts her roommate as Zoey comes into Julie's room, alarmed by the sound of her distress. Unaware of the previous evening's events, she gasps at the disturbing news LaShonda conveys to her.

"He did what?" Zoey asks.

"You heard me," LaShonda says quietly. She runs her hand through Julie's hair as Zoey joins her roommates on Julie's bed.

"That son of a bitch," Zoey replies. She pushes her reading glasses back onto the bridge of her nose.

"That boy has broken her heart like no other boy has ever broken a heart before," LaShonda says to Zoey.

"No way. I will so punch him right in the nose," Zoey replies. Her response sounds completely passive and non-threatening.

"Her mother and father are coming into town today, and they were going to take the two of them out to lunch. You and I are going instead because that boy isn't getting anywhere near this child," LaShonda says in no uncertain terms. She looks out the window. "What time are your parents due to arrive, girlfriend?" she softly asks.

"Any time now," Julie replies. She rolls onto her back and stares at the ceiling. "You'll both come with me then?" Julie asks.

"Of course. We're always here for you," Zoey replies. She takes Julie's hand to help try and ease her pain.

"Oh Lord, there is a black limousine pulling up to the house. Julie, do your parents have a limousine?" LaShonda asks.

"Yes. Don't tell them about Hunter. They're excited about the band, and I want to tell them in my own time," Julie says. She sits up and looks out the window. Zoey pulls a fresh tissue from the box and hands it to her.

"Whatever you think, girl," LaShonda replies.

The girls grab their belongings and greet the chauffeur as he opens the limousine door.

"Thank you, Sydney," Julie says.

Julie slides across the seat, making room for her roommates to sit comfortably next to her.

"Hi, Dear," Julie's mother says.

As cheerfully as she can, Julie greets her parents. She kisses her mother on the cheek. "Hi, mom. Hi, Daddy," she says. Immersed in a business call, her father waves at her from the front seat. While her father tends to his phone call, Julie introduces her two roommates to her mother.

"Where do you want to go for lunch, dear?" Mrs. Christianson asks.

"Take us to the Boatyard Grill at the end of Taughannock Boulevard, Sydney," Julie instructs the family's driver.

"Oh yes. I know right where that is," he replies. He tips his hat as he looks at her in the rearview mirror. Within minutes the limousine arrives at the destination. Julie and her entourage enter the restaurant and are seated near the fireplace, overlooking the lake.

"Where is Hunter?" Julie's mother asks. LaShonda and Zoey look at Julie, uncertain as to how their friend will answer.

"He has made some poor choices, mom. I don't think we will be seeing him anymore."

"Oh. What about the music? I thought you have been recording and getting ready for us to handle the copyright stage. You aren't just going to walk away from all that work and let him own it, are you?" Mr. Christianson asks.

"He wrote all of the material, Daddy."

"He didn't hit you, did he?" he asks with concern.

"No, he just made a couple of poor choices, Daddy," she replies. She takes a deep breath as if relieved she has broken the news.

"Well, what did he do that was so bad?" he continues to question.

"I caught him smoking."

"You caught him smoking? Smoking what?" he asks.

"He was stoned, Daddy. He was high on marijuana."

Mrs. Christianson joins in on the cross-examination. "He was smoking marijuana?"

"Yes."

Julie's parents look at each other and begin to laugh.

"What's so funny," Julie asks. She appears irritated by their insensitivity. LaShonda and Zoey listen in suspense.

"Well, that happened to us when we were your age, dear," Julie's mother says. She taps her husband on the hand. "Isn't that right?" she asks. Her husband smiles as he looks at his daughter.

"You caught Daddy smoking?" Julie asks. She looks at her father, confused by the revelation.

Her parents begin to laugh slightly harder.

Sensing more to their story, LaShonda asks, "you caught her, didn't you, Mr. C?"

"Yes, actually," he replies. "I was absolutely furious."

Zoey joins in the questioning. "So what happened?" she asks.

"I told him that I smoke it on occasion and that if he didn't like it, then go date his right hand," Mrs. Christianson replies.

"Oh, my God, I don't believe I am hearing this," Julie says. Her mouth drops in disbelief.

"You have gotten this far in college and not smoked marijuana yet? I am proud of you, Julie," Mr. Christianson says.

"At least you grew out of it, right, Mrs. C?" Zoey asks. She pushes her glasses back up onto the bridge of her nose.

"Oh, God no. Are you serious? With the stresses of today's world, I have to have several bags kicking around the house and in my purse at all times."

"I don't believe I am hearing this. I don't believe I am hearing this," Julie says. She shakes her head in a state of denial.

"Well, dear, you can ignore it if you choose, but don't spend the rest of your life dating your right hand either. Don't throw away a great relationship over something so exceedingly small. Julie, my dear, times are changing."

LaShonda laughs, and Zoey nudges her in the leg in an attempt to silence her.

"You don't smoke the stuff, too, do you, Daddy?"

"I refuse to answer that question and invoke my Fifth Amendment rights," he replies. Quickly he picks up the menu and begins to look it over.

"I don't believe I am hearing this. I don't believe I am hearing this. You are both attorneys. You could lose your license if you were caught." Julie shakes her head and looks away from the table.

"Who cares? Screw the legal system. The stuff was outlawed by greedy rich people who bought crooked politicians, nothing more. And it continues to be outlawed because of weasel politicians that take Big Pharma bribes. They're nothing more than corporate prostitutes working for blow job money. They keep it outlawed, while many of them hide in their closets and smoke in secret, the fucking little cretins," Mrs. Christian says.

"Mother!" Julie replies.

"Julie, my dear, we have made so much money that the Bar Association can shove the license up their legal ass. Oh, Julie, don't be a prude. It's marijuana. It is a simple weed. You do more damage to yourself drinking at your sorority parties than you do smoking it. Lighten up, sweetheart. Besides, they're now legalizing it all over the country. That should've been done a long time ago."

"What are you really feeling, darling?" Mr. Christian asks. He looks up from the menu with a grin.

Her mother retrieves her eyeglasses from her purse and begins to look over the menu. "We are off this afternoon to LaGuardia to catch a flight to England. Your father has some work to do, and I have some holiday shopping to do. Is there anything you want from Europe, dear?"

"Chocolates, she wants chocolates," Zoey says excitedly. The others look at her and laugh. Appearing to sense the awkwardness of her request, she slumps back into her chair. "I thought you said the other day that you wanted chocolates, didn't you?" she quietly asks Julie. "I just didn't want you to forget telling them," she sheepishly says. She pushes her glasses back up onto her nose and casually begins to look over the menu.

"Yes, mom, some chocolates would be nice," Julie says. She takes the menu into her hands, staring at Zoey for a moment before looking over the list.

The group continues to converse while they eat their lunch. As they await the bill, LaShonda looks up and notices Scratch enter the establishment. "Julie, your guitar player just walked in," she whispers. She watches him like a hawk, and Julie casually looks over at the bar just as Scratch notices her.

"Miss Julie, hello," he says from the bar.

"Hello, Scratch," she replies.

"Is everything thing all right? You left in such terrible haste last night."

"I wonder why." Julie appears to struggle as she smiles.

Mr. Christianson looks on with curiosity. His eyes shift from watching his daughter to watching her acquaintance.

"I think you should know that my girls weren't molesting your boy," he says. He looks over at Julie's party, paying particular attention to Julie's beautiful mother.

"Yes. Thank you, Scratch," she says. She turns her attention to LaShonda and Zoey. She looks at them with her brows raised, as if asking for help to save her from the uncomfortable encounter.

"Will you be at practice tonight?" Scratch asks.

"No, I don't think so. I think Mr. Watkins has a great deal of growing up to do," she replies. She looks at Scratch as if she has had enough of the conversation.

"Right, well, that's not my business. I believe what is between you two should be resolved there on a personal level. I also believe that professionals should keep their personal feelings at bay. Know what I mean?"

"Yes, thank you."

"He is right, Julie," her father says. "I take it this is one of your co-writers?"

"Yes, it is, daddy. This is Scratch, the guitar player."

"Pleasure to meet you," her father says.

"Oh, this here is your dad, Miss Julie?" Scratch asks. He steps over to the table to shake her father's hand. "Hello, sir. I'm pleased to meet you. Then this, Miss Julie, clearly must be your sister then. Is that right?" he says. His flattery elicits a smile from Mrs. Christianson.

"Yes, I am, Mr. Scratch," she replies.

"You can call me Nick, ma'am."

"Do you have a last name, Nick?" she asks.

"Pocker, ma'am. Nick Pocker."

"Well, Mr. Pocker, we hope to hear your work real soon," Mrs. Christianson says. She continues to smile as if relishing the compliment.

"And so do I, ma'am. So do I."

Mr. Christianson signs the bill for the waiter, then retrieves his phone from his jacket. He quickly types something then places it back inside his pocket.

"Have a good day, Scratch," Julie says. She rises from her seat, attempting to move the group along.

"You as well, Miss Julie. It was a pleasure to meet you, folks. I'm sure we'll meet again."

"You too, sir," Mr. Christianson replies. As he begins to escort the girls out of the restaurant, he takes one last look back at the musician.

At the airport terminal, Mr. Christianson enters more data on his phone. He turns to his daughter as he places it back into his jacket. "There is something that bothers me about your guitar player, Julie. I am not sure what it is, but if you decide to keep playing in that band, I advise exercising a great deal of caution with him. You may want to keep an ear out for someone a little closer to your age bracket from the Cornell or Ithaca College music community. There is just something about him that I do not trust. Just be careful with him, kid," he says.

"Flight 1010 to New York City LaGuardia now boarding at Gate 7," the airport broadcaster announces the Christianson's flight.

"I will, daddy," she replies. "I am not sure what I want to do just yet."

"Well, you and Hunter should try to work things out, dear. Give me a kiss. We have to go," Mrs. Christianson says.

Julie kisses her mother as she hugs her. "Have fun, mom," she says. She turns to her father, hugging him with all her heart. "Goodbye, Daddy." Tears begin to swell in her eyes as she holds him.

"LaShonda, Zoey, keep an eye on her for us, or I will give those chocolates to an orphanage or a charity," Mrs. Christianson instructs. She shuts off her phone and places it in her into her purse. "Now, both of you, come here and give me a hug," she says.

"You can count on us, Mrs. Christianson," Zoey replies. She and LaShonda do as they were told, simultaneously wrapping their arms around Julie's mother.

# Chapter 25

## Yet Another Attack

JENNY TAKES A SEAT AT AN OUTDOOR CAFÉ. She orders an iced tea and begins to read from the little green bible Raguel had given her. She looks up every few minutes, watching the pedestrians go about their evening routine. The waitress brings her drink and then retreats into the café just as her phone begins to ring.

She looks at the Icon on the display as she answers, "Hello, Oliver."

"Good evening, Krystal, I mean, Jenny. Oh dear, please forgive me. I will get it down sooner or later. Please excuse me. I always seem to look at the angel's name first, instead of the alias," Oliver says.

Jenny laughs, reassuring him, "I know what you mean, Oliver. It's all right. You have a difficult job."

"Oh, thank you. Yes, I do. It looks like we will need you to rendezvous with Chris again. The Universal Observation Device is showing some warning signs over Hunter's apartment complex. It suggests that you should visit him before 9:00 p.m. tonight."

"Okay, what are the instructions?" she asks.

"The Probabilities Calculator suggests that you utilize an excuse that you wish to arrange an interview for a paper you are writing. It suggests that you interview Chris first, then suggest to him that you interview Hunter as well."

"All right, Oliver, but I have another question."

"What is that, my dear?"

"Just in case Chris asks, what is the topic of this interview?"

"Oh, good point, Agent Jenny. Let's look. Ah, yes, here it is. It states that you should use the topic of a music entrepren—oh dear, I can't pronounce it," he says.

"Entrepreneur, Oliver?" she asks.

"Yes, that's it. However, you just said that word."

"Music entrepreneur. I got it. Is there anything else?" Jenny asks.

"I don't think so, but let me look. Oh, yes, actually there is. You should ask to interview him based on his experience as a local musician trying to make money in the music industry. From there, you can ask an array of issues like marketing, if need be. Or you can ask him about the writing process. Use your adaptive angelic skills. Sometimes the excuse you need for the interview is not nearly as important as being at the right place at the right time," he says.

"All right, thank you," she replies.

"You're welcome, my dear. Talk to you soon. Oh, and Chris is just around the corner and walking your way."

"Oh. You make this pretty easy, Oliver. Thank you."

"Remember, no ice cream."

"I won't," she replies. She hangs up the phone and looks up to see Chris coming into view.


HUNTER DECIDES TO DRINK the evening away. He drives to the Southside Liquor Store to purchase some spirits. Raguel is walking on the street outside of the liquor store. As Hunter approaches the store, the vagrant begins broadcasting the gospel.

"The Lord is close to the brokenhearted and saves those who are crushed in spirit."

"Thank you. I needed that," Hunter says. He walks by the hobo and enters the establishment.

"Is he bothering you?" the store manager asks. She looks outside at the downtrodden man, appearing disturbed by his presence.

"No. He's not bothering me. Poor guy has nothing but hope in the afterlife."

"Can I help you?" she asks.

"Sure, it all started when I was a little kid," Hunter says.

"I am not sure I have that much time this evening," she replies.

"Where can I find Mr. Daniels?"

"Mr. Daniels? There is no Mr. Daniels that works here."

"To drink," he says.

"Oh, you're funny. It's right there." She points down the central aisle.

He walks down the aisle, glancing over the assorted sizes. He secures a liter bottle and proceeds back to the counter.

"That was quick," the manager says.

"Yes, I know," Hunter replies. He reaches into his pocket and pulls out some money. He pays the merchant and exits the store without haste. "Have a nice night," he says. As he leaves the store, Raguel begins to speak to him.

"Come to me, all you who are weary and burdened, and I will give you rest. Matthew 11:28. But as for you, be strong and do not give up, for your work will be rewarded," the hobo says.

"Thank you. I will keep that in mind," Hunter replies. He hands the man a ten-dollar bill. "Here, go get yourself something to eat, my friend."

"Thank you, my brother. You are a blessed man. Peace be with you," Raguel says. He opens his arm, raising his hands to the sky. Hunter gets into his truck, watching the man. He listens to him give thanks to the Father.

Hunter places the bottle in the passenger seat. "Looks like me and you tonight, Jack," he says as he begins to drive off. At the stoplight, he looks at his phone. "Not sure I will ever be rewarded for my work if she doesn't call, Jack," he says. He looks at the bottle. "Maybe I should call her."

A minute later, he arrives at his apartment. He takes the bottle and makes his way inside, throwing the keys onto the table. He winces as he takes the first swallow directly from the bottle then sits down on his couch, placing the whiskey on the end table. He then rolls over and retrieves the writing pad from his back pocket, looking down for a moment at the blank page.

He stares back at the bottle. "Yup, it's just you and me, buddy. What you got to say about that?" He shakes his head as he frowns. "So this is what I have done. I am sitting here, drinking Jack alone," he says to the bottle.

The statement appears to spark a measure of creativity within him. He reaches for a pen on the end table and begins to write. Two hours pass, and by the time he finishes writing, he is severely intoxicated.

### *Jack Tonight*

*One Wish, one night, I should have held onto you tight.*
*Instead, I'm sitting here, drinking Jack alone.*
*It's late, and I might still hold you tonight.*
*But I'm still sitting here, drinking Jack alone.*

*It's too late, but I should try to call you.*
*It's just fate, I guess I'm a sentimental fool.*

*If you would try, come look me in the eye,*
*and tell me that you don't love me anymore.*
*Then I won't fight. I'd simply say goodbye,*
*and I would sit back down to drink my Jack alone.*

*It's so late, but I should try to call you.*
*It's just fate. I'm always just a fool.*

*It's been so long, and I'm not having fun.*
*Do you miss me like I am missing you tonight?*
*I understand if you might kiss another man.*
*So I confine myself to drinking Jack alone.*

The Angle of the Angels

*It's been so long since you have called me darling.*
*It's been so long, and nothing's quite the same.*
*Without you, girl it doesn't matter anymore.*

*I cry, you know, because I do hate to see you go.*
*Could we maybe give it just another try?*
*If you say no and that you don't think it's so.*
*Then I will fall asleep drinking Jack alone.*
*I'm Jackin' It, baby.*

A knock at the door catches Hunter off guard. He looks up, informing the unknown guest, "It's open."

Naamah opens the door. "Hi, stranger. What are you doing tonight?" she asks. She folds her arms and crosses her legs as she leans against the door jam.

"Writing, that's about it."

"I have a problem and thought only you could help me," she says.

His attention quickly turns away from his work. His eyes open wide at the sight of the vixen, clad in a black satin miniskirt and red blouse.

"Well, I certainly can try. I always give everything my absolute best effort. Come on in," he says.

"I was hoping that you would say something like that," she replies. She steps into the apartment and turns to close the door.

"I am just finishing writing another song, Naamah. Have a seat and tell me about your problem."

The succubus seizes the offer and joins him on the couch, placing her legs onto the coffee table, crossing them precisely as he has.

"You're drinking alone?" she questions.

"Yes, I'm afraid so."

"Nobody should drink alone. It's much more fun to share, don't you think?"

"Well, yes. Yes, I do," he agrees. He hands her the bottle, grinning as he nods to her.

She playfully licks the port of the bottle as she looks at him with her inviting blue eyes. Leaning her head back, she takes a healthy swallow, revealing a thin silver necklace wrapped around her neck. A small silver locket further draws Hunter's attention, nestled in the middle of her chest.

"Easy, Naamah. You don't want to kill it in the first couple minutes."

"No, I don't," she says. "I prefer the slow kill. It's much more fun that way." She takes another drink then hands the bottle back to him. "How did you know Jack was my favorite anyway? It makes me feel so warm inside." She laughs as she pulls her finger in between her breasts and down the center of her abdomen. "Know what I mean?" she asks. She begins to twirl her left index finger around on her satin blouse. Hunter watches her subtle maneuver as he takes a large swallow from the bottle, then places it back on the table.

"Yes. I think I do," he replies.

"What are you writing about tonight, Hunter?" she asks.

"Well, that there bottle of Mr. Daniels, ma'am," he replies in a southern dialect.

She laughs at him as she smiles. "You are an actor as well as a musician. You are going to make it so big when your recordings are finished. I can see it all happening right before my very eyes," she says.

"I'm not so sure."

"Why not? You can sing, you can play, and you can act as well. You have almost everything you need," Naamah reassures.

"Yeah, well, don't forget luck. You need a lot of luck in this business."

"I think, Hunter, that luck is more of a planned event than it is just a happenstance. Can I read your new song?" she asks. She grins and moves closer to him.

"I guess so," he replies. He hands her the notepad, then looks away as he retrieves the bottle with his other hand.

As he does, she takes her locket and pushes the small lever to release the Dark Desire Dust into her palm. As he turns his attention back to the girl, she ignores taking the book from him, opting to move even closer to his side. She looks at him, taking his hand as he holds the pad, resting it on her leg as she reads. She smiles at him as she simultaneously moves her hand around his shoulder. She sprinkles the dust over the back of his head in the process.

He smiles at her as she begins to run her finger along his neck.

She starts to read the lyrics. "Wow, Hunter," she says softly. "I wish I had your talents." She lifts her eyes from the page to meet his. Her soft voice seems to lock him into a trancelike state, and he falls deeper into her trap. Though unsuccessful in seducing him at the lake house the night before, she now has him exactly where she wants: spellbound, intoxicated, and alone.

"Why?" he asks. He looks closely at her ruby red lips as she speaks.

"Because then I could play with you. Do you want to play with me, Hunter?" she asks in a whisper. She closes the short distance to deliver her poisonous kiss.

He silently nods his head in acceptance of her attack. The perfection of her kiss seems to render him helpless to her powers. She lifts her left hand to the side of his face, caressing it with her palm.

Gently, she pulls Hunter as she begins to lean backward, slowly falling to the arm of the sofa. He follows her, appearing not to want to break free from the bond of her lips as she takes his hand and guides it to her breast.

Naamah swirls her tongue inside his lips as she runs her fingers across the side of his chest. She reaches down his side, tucking her hand beneath his shirt and stroking his flesh. He moves his hand down her satin clad body and in between her legs.

"Deeper," she whispers with pleasure as she begins to grind to his rhythm. Lost in the foreplay, Hunter does as she commands. Naamah places her left hand into the mix, joining Hunter's hand in the exploration.

"He opens his eyes and pulls his hand out from beneath her skirt. I will be right back," he says. He attempts to rise from the couch, but she pulls him back to her lips.

"Where are you going? Don't leave me," she says.

"I have to go to the bathroom first. I will be right back." He manages to stand and begins to make his way across the room. The alcohol levies its full effect, and his attempt to make his way to the bathroom fails. He trips, slamming face-first into the door jamb, then falling to the floor, cradling his face from the sting of his stupidity.

"Ahhh," he cries out.

Naamah sits up to look at him. "Are you all right?" she asks. She shakes her head.

"Yeah, I'm good," Hunter replies. He checks his nose to make sure it's not broken.

"Are you sure you don't need help?"

"No, no, I'm all right."

The loss of horizontal hold is not the only problem he faces. As he struggles from the pain of his physics lesson, he finishes his trek to the toilet. There he immediately begins to disgorge his evening's liquid meal.

"Really," Naamah whispers. She shakes her head, appearing frustrated by his clumsiness.

Chris and Jenny arrive at Hunter's door, alarmed by the sound of Hunter's porcelain pillow serenade. They look at each other, puzzled and perplexed.

"What the hell?" Chris asks. He opens the door, and the two enter the apartment. Startled, Naamah quickly straightens her blouse and crosses her legs.

Jenny notices the vixen and looks at her like a cat that has cornered a mouse. Chris also sees Naamah and begins to confront her, "What are you doing here?"

"Are you writing a book?" she nicely asks.

"Whatever," he replies. He looks down at Hunter, hanging onto the toilet for dear life. Unhappy at the sight, he shakes his head in disapproval. "Hunter, what the hell am I going to do with you, man?" Chris asks.

"Ohh," he moans. "Shoot me. Just shoot me."

"You reek of alcohol, you stupid son-of-a-bitch. Tickle your throat, goddamn it, and get that shit out of you. Man are you a dumbass," Chris yells at him, shaking his head as he looks back at Jenny. "Would you go into his kitchen and make him a pot of coffee, please?" he asks.

"Sure," she replies.

Hunter does as he is told, sticking his finger into his mouth, expatriating what little is in his stomach. Naamah rises from the couch and walks over to the bathroom door. "I don't think he'll be at practice tomorrow," she says. She shakes her head as she looks down on him.

"I'll drag the little son-of-a-bitch to practice. How long has he been drinking?" he asks.

"Most of the evening, I suspect. I just got here a few minutes ago."

"You shouldn't mix business and pleasure, Naamah. If you are going to run our media, it is not a clever idea to fraternize off hours. Especially since it already caused a great deal of uncertainty with the band yesterday."

"We were just talking," she replies.

He looks down at her skimpy attire as he confronts her. "Dressed like that? Really?" he asks.

"We were strategizing how he could get Julie back. Yesterday, I was just blowing smoke to him, and you all rushed to judgment that something was going on. It wasn't. We were just partying. I know he's with Julie. Or was, anyway."

Chris looks at her with a hint of suspicion but doesn't dispute her version of the events. He turns his focus back to his inebriated band member. "You done yet, pukey boy? Come on. Get that shit out of you. Hurry the hell up," he continues to yell.

"Yeah. I'm good," Hunter moans as he attempts to stand.

"Give me a hand getting the idiot to the kitchen, please," he says. Chris pulls the drunkard to his feet, and the two of them escort him to the kitchen table. Hunter moans as he sits in a chair.

"Serves you right. What the hell is wrong with you? You need to get your shit together, Hunter," Chris scolds.

"I feel like shit," he says. He drops his face into his hands.

"You should feel like shit. I'm only going to tell you this one time, Hunter. I refuse to play with a drunk. You need to focus, man, and get it together. We have something so close to making it big, and you have your head so far up your ass, I swear that you need a snorkel. If I see you like this again, I am going to drown your ass in that toilet. Do you hear me?" Hunter acknowledges with a nod as he continues to hold his head in his hands.

"Goodnight, Hunter. Thanks for the talk," Naamah says. Hunter fails to respond to the girl, preoccupied in his precarious position.

"Have a good night, Naamah," Jenny says. She smiles in watching her leave the apartment, appearing to relish her little victory over the powerful demon.

# Chapter 26

## The Triumph of the Trout

"DAMN IT," MR. CHRISTIANSON CURSES as his phone slips from his hands. It bounces off the stairwell and falls onto the hotel lobby floor. The front desk clerk steps out from behind his station and picks up the damaged phone.

"Careful, sir, the glass screen is severely shattered," he informs. He hands it to him, appearing sympathetic in his mannerism.

Mr. Christianson carefully takes the device. "Shit," he says.

The clerk steps back behind the front desk. "Terribly sorry about the phone, sir. I can place a complimentary call for you if you would like."

"Yes, let's do that. I need to call New York."

"Not a problem, Sir. Step right up here to the desk, and I will dial the number for you."

"Thank you. Do you have a scrap piece of paper that I can write down the number on?"

"Here you are, sir," the clerk replies. He hands him a small notepad. Mr. Christianson writes the number down and passes it back to the clerk.

The clerk takes the note and dials the number. As it begins to ring, he passes the phone off. "Here you are, sir." The clerk sits down and begins to look at his computer screen.

Julie looks at the incoming call. "Hello."

"Hi, kid," he replies. A hint of concern hangs in his voice.

"Hi, Daddy. What's up? Is everything all right?"

"No. Well, I am not sure. Julie listen. I did some research on that guitar player of yours. If he is who I think he is, then he is an international scumbag. Nick Pocker is named as a plaintiff in over thirty-three copyright disputes on this side of the Atlantic alone. It appears as if there may be about that many lawsuits in the states as well. If you care at all about the music that you have been working on and about Hunter, then you owe it to him and yourself to be incredibly careful with this guitar player. He could be the guy that I am researching."

"I knew I had a bad feeling about him," she replies. Her eyes blaze with suspicion.

"I am not 100 percent positive yet. I could be wrong. I am waiting for a fellow attorney to get back to me with a picture of him. If it is him, then he probably has been secretly recording your sessions. Doing so will give him a live recording and the crux of the song idea. That is enough to register a copyright. So if it is him, then he is almost certainly attempting to steal everything you and Hunter have been creating. It is my belief that he is."

"Well, how soon will you know?"

"I should hear back from my friend by tomorrow afternoon. It would be best to have Hunter send me all the material as soon as possible so that I can protect it for him. Send me any and all material that either of you have typed, written, or recorded. Okay, kid?"

"Okay, daddy. I guess I will try to talk with him."

"That would be my immediate advice. If Hunter has any questions, then he can call me. Oh, and another thing."

"Yes. What is it, daddy?"

"Do you love him?"

"I don't know. I am so mad at him right now. I just don't know."

"Well, I can tell that he is a good man, Julie. If he's just smoking pot, don't be so hard on him."

"Okay, daddy. I love you."

"Love you too, kid. I have to go. Your mom and I are wrapping up this contract today, so I can get up to Withypool to do some trout fishing tomorrow morning."

"Have fun. And be careful. Don't make mom a nervous wreck by slipping on the rocks and hurting yourself like you did when I was little."

"I will try not to. I love you, kid. Goodbye," he says.

"I love you too, Daddy, bye."

Mr. Christianson hands the phone back to the clerk, reaches into his pants pocket, and hands the young man a tip. "Thanks, my friend. Now, do you have a casket for my poor dead phone?"

"No, sir, but I can find you a small bag to contain it in if you would like."

"Yes. That would be good."

"Not a problem, sir. I will locate one for you. Would you like to leave it here, or shall I have the bag sent to your room?"

"Yes, please, place it in the bag and have it sent to my room," he replies. He turns away from the desk and begins to proceed up the staircase.

The clerk picks up his phone and calls housekeeping. "Yes, I need a small bag brought to the front desk and then taken up to room 616. Thank you." The clerk sneers at Mr. Christianson as he ascends the staircase and disappears. The clerk retrieves his personal cell phone from the inside of his jacket and calls a preprogrammed number.

"Hello, Mr. Pocker, it's Nigel Struthers from The Ritz Hotel in London. How are you today, sir? Good, thank you. I thought you would like to know that there is a guest at the hotel who was just on the telephone. He was speaking with someone there in the United States. It seems that he has been researching you, sir. He informed the party about your musical lawsuits here in the UK. Yes, sir, he called the party by name. Julie, sir. No, sir, he is not here all week. He is checking out tomorrow morning. He said something to the effect that he was going fishing around the Withypool area. Yes, sir, I do have a room available for you this evening. Would you like me to make the reservation? Very good, sir. Yes, sir, I will keep you posted if anything changes. I am here until 11 pm tonight, our time, should you need me for anything else. Thank you, sir. I look forward to your arrival then. Have a safe flight."


SCRATCH HANGS UP the phone. "Girls, I have to go to England," he informs his two vixens. He looks at them and grins as they touch and kiss each other on the couch.

"I want to go," Aphrodite pouts as Naamah nibbles at her neck.

"No. You two need to stay here and mind the store. Besides, it looks like Naamah is about to take you for a ride around the world anyway. I have some things that need attending. I'll be back soon enough," he says. He exits the apartment and drives off without haste.

As he pulls into Hunter's driveway, Scratch checks his watch. Unaware of his guitar player's arrival, Hunter props the hallway door open to allow a breeze through the apartment. He glances at the piano. Sitting down, he begins to leaf through various piano pieces. He begins to talk to himself. "Sonata 16 in C, that should do it." He opens the page and begins to perform the timeless piece.

As he plays, Scratch silently appears in the doorway. "Mozart! I bloody love Mozart!" he declares. Startled, Hunter immediately ceases his recital.

"You son of a bitch. Where the hell did you come from?"

Scratch opens his eyes wide and sports his devilish grin. "I am much like the wind. You'll never know where from or why it blows. How it comes, or where it goes. All that is certain, only I need to know!" He twirls his hands around his head in a dramatic fashion as he begins to laugh.

"You scared the shit out of me," Hunter yells at him.

"I'm sorry about that, mate. Well, no, actually, I'm not. I do get a bit of a laugh out of startling people, really. But I will compliment you on tackling the ultimate master. Did you know Mozart considered that a beginner's piece?" he asks.

"No, I didn't," Hunter replies. "If this is a beginner piece, then he expected a lot out of a student. What are you doing here? I didn't think you did mornings, Scratch."

"Yeah, well, I got some business back home to attend to. I was just popping by to see if you would like to join me for a couple days while I deal with some issues back home?"

"In England?" Hunter asks. He looks at Scratch for clarification.

"Yeah, to jolly old England. I could show you around the sights while we're there. We can grab some pub grub, then round us up a glass and a lass for our hands. It'll maybe give you some new creative energy and some culture. It'll be good for you, lad. What do you say? Do you want to come along?"

"On a plane?"

"No, on a bicycle. We'll head up to Montreal for the night and bang some crazy Canadian girls. Then in the morning, we'll head over to Greenland and take a bloody Ferry. Yes, on a goddamn plane, don't be a din!" Scratch shakes his head in disbelief at Hunter's question.

"I just flew with Julie. I wasn't really fond of the process. I prefer to drive."

"Oh, that's precious. You like driving, do ya? Well, we can't drive to the goddamn UK from the United States, now can we?" he asks. His elevated voice highlights his level of frustration.

"I really don't like to fly, Scratch. I'm not a fan whatsoever."

"Well, what the hell are you going to do, mate, if we make it big and have like a twenty-city tour?"

"Well, then we get what I have always wanted, a tour bus. And besides, I seek fame for the fortune, not fortune for the fame. So if we get to that stage, then we will have enough fortune for a tour bus," Hunter replies. He smiles as if happy with the thought.

"A tour bus? Right. What do you plan on doing if we get booked in Europe? Does this bloody bus of yours float?" Scratch asks.

"Don't they have boats?"

"Boats? Yeah, they got boats! It only takes a bloody week one way, you know! You really are a din sometimes, aren't you?"

"I'm not sure what that means, but if the plane goes down, I am toast. If the boat goes down, I can swim. And besides that, they have casinos on boats, don't they?" Hunter asks.

"Yeah, I guess they do, and loose-fitting showgirls as well, I suppose," he replies. He stops for a moment, appearing to think about the idea.

"Well, since life is a gamble anyway, then I would rather gamble on the boat, taking my time getting there and enjoying life while having some fun on the way."

Scratch changes his tone to a less confrontational demeanor. "All right, it's hard to argue with that logic. Maybe you are a genius," he says.

"There you go," Hunter replies.

"I do have to go. You coming or not? My treat. All-expense paid, mate. Come on with ya. It will get your mind off things."

"Thanks, but I'll pass. When will you be back?" Hunter asks.

"All right then. I'll be back Monday. You'll arrange a practice for next week, won't you?"

"Yes."

"All right, I got to go. Oh, and as you go back to that Sonata, try playing it blindfolded, yeah? I find it really helps you to own the song and the instrument at the same time."

Scratch disappears from the entryway. Hunter shakes his head at the disturbance and goes back to tackle the ivory. He pauses a moment, then closes his eyes as he begins to play the sonata from the beginning.

DARKENING SKIES LOOM heavily over Withypool as the Christianson's helicopter approaches the Crown Hotel Exmoor. "Looks like heavy rain is in store, sir. I'm not so sure it will be good fishing for you," the pilot warns as he begins his descent onto the green.

"Are you kidding? When the water dirties is the best time to float a fly. Those big ones come out from underneath the ledges and feed in the back of the pool. It is the most perfect of days," Mr. Christianson says.

The pilot lands the helicopter in the park across the street from the hotel. "Right, sir, not much of a trout fisherman. It makes a great deal of sense, though. Good luck," the pilot replies.

Mr. Christianson and his wife take their overnight bags and duck to escape the danger of the helicopter's rotor blades. An attentive hotel worker rushes to greet them, and he takes their bags as the helicopter lifts off and departs.

"Morning, ma'am. Morning, sir. I hope you both had a nice flight. We don't get many people flying in like that. Seems like a terrific way to go," the bellhop says. He offers Mrs. Christianson his arm and escorts them both into the hotel lobby.

A portly front desk clerk joyfully welcomes the couple as they come into the hotel. "Well, Mr. and Mrs. Christianson, hello. Welcome back to the Crown Hotel. So wonderful to see you both once again."

"Hello, Mr. Cradock, how have you been?" Mr. Christianson asks. He steps up to the front desk to shake the clerk's hand.

"And Mrs. Christianson, you grow more beautiful every time I have the pleasure to see you. How have you both been?" he asks.

"You are too kind, Mr. Cradock. Very good, thank you," she replies.

"I have you both down for one, possibly two nights, is that correct?"

"Yes. That's correct. I was looking to get a ride this morning out to Withypool. A local shop owner should have delivered a fly-fishing rod, waders, and some tackle for me. Did it arrive?" Mr. Christianson asks.

"Oh yes, sir, they certainly did. We have a car waiting to take you to your stalking grounds as soon as you are ready. It's a great choice in timing with the rain coming if I do say so myself. You will likely enjoy some added advantage with the murky waters that will certainly occur later this morning," Cradock says.

"Then grab your waders, Mr. Cradock, and let's go."

"Ah, duty calls, unfortunately, sir, or I would certainly take you up on that. Thank you for the offer, though. Perhaps next time," Cradock replies.

"Carpe diem, Mr. Cradock, carpe diem," Mr. Christianson says.

"Good point, sir. I will just need a quick imprint of your credit card if you don't mind." Mr. Christianson reaches into his wallet and hands the clerk his card. "You both will be dining with us tonight, I trust?" Cradock asks.

"Oh, yes, Mr. Cradock, we certainly will," Mrs. Christianson replies.

"Splendid, ma'am, I will make a reservation for you. Did you have a time preference?"

She looks at her watch. "Six o'clock will be fine. That will give me time to do a little shopping and still take in an afternoon nap. The flight over here has simply taken the life out of me."

"Yes, ma'am, 6:00 p.m. it is. If you both are ready, we will show you to your room."

"Thank you, Mr. Cradock. I will be ready in about ten minutes or so."

"Best of luck in your expedition. Mr. Fisher will drive you out to the river when you are ready," Cradock replies.

The bellhop places their baggage on a bellman cart and guides them to their suite. He informs them about the various amenities, and Mr. Christianson hands him a rather large tip.

"Thank you, sir," he says with great excitement at the sight of the generous gift. "If there is anything you need at all, sir, let me know, and I shall run it right up to you."

"Thank you," Mr. Christianson replies. He escorts the boy to the door and closes it as he leaves.

"Now don't you be all day out there," Mrs. Christianson says. She walks into the bathroom and begins to draw a bath.

"I won't, dear. It will just be a few hours. The flight took a lot of me. I am pretty tired and could take a long nap myself."

"Well, if you are tired, be careful. You know how dangerous that river can be."

He steps into the bathroom and kisses his wife. "I will. I'll see you in a while. Love you," he says.

A torrential rain begins to fall across the land. It beats against the windshield, forcing the driver to slow his approach to the flowing waters of the River Barle.

"No offense, sir, but I've heard you Americans are half crazy. This weather is not fit for man nor beast. Nor does it look like it's going to let up any time soon. Are you certain you want me to leave you out here?" Mr. Fisher asks.

"I am sure. Pick me up at 2 p.m., right here. I'll be fine. I'm going to catch the big one today for sure."

"I understand, sir, but here is my cell phone number should you change your mind, just in case." The chauffeur hands him his card.

"Thank you," Mr. Christianson says as he gives the driver a tip. He exits the car, quickly pulling the hood over his head.

At the river's edge, he secures the waders to his belt. As he works his way into the river, he looks up ahead and finds pleasure at the sight of the Devil's sunbathing rocks. He halts his progression to focus his attention on the river's turn just below the ancient bridge.

The sudden appearance of a dorsal fin in the back of the pool brings a smile to his face. He edges up to within casting distance. There is a slight discoloration to the river, and the trout fans gently in the back of the pool. He looks closely at the water in an apparent attempt to choose the proper fly for the line.

"Wet fly or dry fly?" he quietly questions himself. He glances up the river again to see that the fish is still swaying gently in the rising current.

"Dry fly," he whispers as he watches the fish pierce the surface of the water as it feeds.

He looks at the assortment of flies and wisely chooses a Royal Coachman. He ties the line to the fly and begins to work the pole, swinging the rod back and forth. His first cast falls just behind the fish and drifts back downstream. He pulls out several feet of line as he continues to swing the rod through the air, placing the fly out in front of the trout. It drifts directly toward the unsuspecting quarry. The trout's nose breaks the surface as it arrives. As planned, the trout takes the artificial bait. Mr. Christianson sets the hook, and the fight begins.

The trout's survival instinct takes over, and it darts toward the cover of the overhanging brush along the river bank. He steers it away from the bank and the submerged root system. The creature darts throughout the pool in a desperate attempt to free itself. The reel whines in a high-pitch, much to the angler's delight. The trout's weight and its spirit work together as a worthy adversary as it begins to splash upstream. Quickly it changes its course and races past the angler as he reels in the slack. The yellow and orange markings shine through the shadow of the murky water as it heads downstream. Mr. Christianson reacts, knowing the physics of the fight is now in the trout's favor.

"No, you don't. No, you don't," he yells out. The line peels from the reel as the trout gains distance from the would-be captor. As the fish enters the rapids, it turns sideways then lunges with the current, quickly snapping the line.

"Damn it," he shouts. He shakes his head then begins to laugh out loud.

A sudden voice cries out. "Guess that's why they call it fishing."

Startled, Mr. Christianson looks around the banks of the Barle. "What?" he asks, as he spots a hooded figure in the tree line.

"I said I guess that's why they call it fishing," the hooded man shouts from the bank.

"Yes, that's a good assessment. Did you see it? It was a lunker," he replies. He struggles to see the man's face, hidden beneath the hood of his rain gear.

"Yeah, I saw it. Been watching him for a long time. He's been under that bank off and on for the last several years."

"Well, he'll be back again," Mr. Christianson replies. He reaches for the box of flies and begins to look for one similar to what he just lost.

"Were you using a dry fly?"

"Yes, yes I was."

"Well, the river is rising pretty quickly. You may want to use a colorful wet fly now."

"Yeah, thanks for the tip. For the moment, I will stick with what just worked," Mr. Christianson replies. He takes out another and begins to tie it.

The man on the bank lays both his hands onto a large basswood tree, closes his eyes, and begins to chant softly. "Raging fire and eye of the storm, release the rain and change banks form. Where Linden's root and truth be told, shall free its grip from this earth and stone. Fall this tree on the mortal's head and pin in the current until he's dead." He opens his eyes as he finishes his incantation, "from within the clouds where ions spike, RELEASE HERE NOW A LIGHTNING STRIKE!"

An immediate destructive force of energy is released from the sky, striking the ancient tree. The instantaneous flash of lightning and roar of thunder causes Mr. Christianson to react in fright. The lighting strike splits the tree in half, pulling some of the river bank with it as it tumbles. Mr. Christianson watches helplessly as the treetop comes crashing down on him. The other half of the tree remains standing as if in defiance of the Devil and his spell.

Instantly he is pinned in the current, and he struggles to lift his head above the rising waterline. His right arm is crushed and wedged between the treetop and the river bed. "Help, help me, help!" he screams out in pain and fear.

Scratch enters the waters of the Barle. He snaps a dead branch from the tree and pulls the hood from the top of his head. "It looks like you need a set of gills, old man." He laughs at Mr. Christianson's predicament. He places the branch in the water and leans on it as the attorney struggles to break free.

"Help me!" Mr. Christianson continues to scream. The more he does, the more Scratch seems to find a perverse pleasure in his victim's plight.

"Yeah, you want help, do ya? Sure, mate, I'll help you," he says. "I'm going to help you by comforting that poor soon-to-be-grieving little widow of yours. Then I'm going to bang her over and over again in drunken and drug-crazed stupors."

Mr. Christianson quickly begins to lose strength. He desperately stretches out his arm in hopes of aid from the Wicked One. His eyes open wide in panic as he struggles to lift his head above the rising water.

"They say, old man, that death by drowning is the ultimate way to go. So before you go, I just want you to know that while I continue to bang your wife, I'm also going to pump the living shit out of that little daughter of yours. As I do, I am going to smack her tight little ass as I make her scream out the right answer to who her real goddamn daddy is. Tell Saint Pete not to wait up for me."

Scratch places the fork of the branch under his victim's chin, submerging his head beneath the current. Mr. Christianson expends his last ounce of energy, trying to remove it from his neck with his free hand. Scratch leans heavily on top of the stick, ensuring the death that he has conjured. As Mr. Christianson expires, Scratch wades back to the riverbank and casts the rod downstream. He looks back at the scene with an evil grin, then vanishes into the dense mist of the English countryside.

## Chapter 27

### Hell Gives Up a Hag Stone

"GOOD AFTERNOON, THE CROWN HOTEL. This is Mr. Cradock," he says in answering the phone call. "How may I help you?"

"Mr. Cradock, it's Mr. Fisher. I am here to pick up Mr. Christianson at the designated rendezvous site, but I do not see him. What should I do, sir? He's well over twenty minutes overdue from when he instructed me to pick him up."

"Well, we can't leave him there, can we? Has the rain let up enough to take a quick look for him?

"No, sir, it is still an incessant downpour at the moment."

"Right, well, you're going to have to take a look for him just the same, Mr. Fisher. You dropped him off below the Tarr Steps, didn't you? Cradock asks.

"Yes, sir. He was going to work his way upstream. I dropped him off about a half kilometer below the bridge. I am at the Tarr Steps now."

"Well then, take a quick walk upstream along the riverbank. That's likely the direction he headed. I am certain from past experiences that he can't be too far."

"Okay, sir, I will do that," Mr. Fisher replies. He glances toward the river in hopes of seeing the guest. The chauffer reluctantly leaves the comfort of the car. "Crazy goddamn Americans," he says out loud. "Stupid bastards would catch a bloody death of the cold for the sake of a stupid trout. Crazy goddamn Americans!"

He makes his way along the Tarr Steps path, noticing the freshly fallen tree laying in the river. Through the twisted biomass, he discovers in horror the lifeless body pinned beneath the murky current. "Mr. Christianson. Mr. Christianson," he shouts in vain. It appears certain the man has succumbed to the river, and he races back to the car to call for help.

Within minutes the police and emergency technicians arrive. The effort to retrieve the dead man is cumbersome. The current is swift, and the large tree requires a chainsaw to free the body. A policeman stands on the riverbank, watching the emergency worker's progress, as the Chief Inspector arrives on the scene. The constable gains the Inspector's attention, pointing to where the lightning hit the tree.

"Inspector White, look at this, would ya?" the constable asks. He draws the attention of the Inspector to the side of the tree that remains standing. He points out where the lightning has burnt a mark in the wood. "It looks like the bloody Devil with his pitchfork dancing around a fire, doesn't it?"

The Inspector looks on with alarm and concern at the charred scar. "Tells me the Devil was here. I hate this place. It gives me the bloody willies every time I am out here." A hint of fear looms within his eyes.

"They don't say it's the Devil's bridge for no reason. Oh, and look at that. The tree kicked up a large hag stone when it fell over. Do you see it exposed in the bank there, sir?" The constable directs the Inspector's attention to the uprooted earth.

"Yeah, I see it. I'm telling you this place is possessed. I'd prefer they just pull the poor bloke out of the water so I can get the hell out of here. It just feels like evil is lurking about every tree and every goddamn shrub."

"Makes sense, given the ancient folklore."

"Yeah, I know. Leave it to some crazy Yank to want to come out here in the middle of the pouring goddamn rain and test the old tales. Some of them got more money than common sense, know what I mean? What the bloody hell was he doing out here?" the Inspector asks.

"Trout fishing, sir," his subordinate replies.

"For God sakes, there's not a fish in the world worth bloody dying for. You can go down to the market and get a bloody fish. Here I am getting soaked because some crazy goddamn Yank couldn't divert his cranium from his goddamn rectum long enough to see its bloody pouring rain."

"I hope he believed in Christ Almighty because it sure looks like the devil tried to drag him straight into bloody hell," the constable says.

"Well, it sure looks at very least like he pissed him off a bit anyway," the Inspector replies. He nods to his subordinate to focus his attention on the river.

A rescue worker who has secured Mr. Christianson's wallet wades across the Barle and climbs the bank to the awaiting police. "Think you are waiting for this for your report, Inspector." The technician hands the belongings of the deceased to the Inspector.

He begins to leaf through the wallet for the dead man's credentials. "Thank you. How much longer do you think you'll be?" he asks.

"It'll only be a few more minutes, sir. Did you want to wade over to the scene to have a look at him?"

"A tree fell on him, didn't it?" the Inspector asks. He looks at the technician for verification.

"Yeah. Pinned him in the water and drowned him real quick like," the technician replies.

"Right. Then it's not a bloody crime scene, is it?" he asks rhetorically. "Take him to the morgue when you free him. We have to go to the hotel and inform his wife. Carry on," he says. He turns and hurries back to the patrol car.

At the hotel, Mr. Cradock waits for the Inspector to break the horrible news to Mrs. Christianson. As the police arrive, Mr. Cradock nods to the Tea Room table, where she sits patiently, quietly reading a book.

"Inspector White, Constable Hayes. Sorry to drag you both away from your regular duties," Cradock whispers to them.

"This is part of our duties, Mr. Cradock. It's not a problem. It's sad, but it's not a problem," Inspector White assures as he notices the attractive widow sitting all alone.

"Right this way," Mr. Cradock says as he leads them both to her table. With a heavy heart, he interrupts the unaware widow. "Excuse me, Mrs. Christianson." She looks up to see Mr. Cradock and the two policemen. "Inspector White here, ma'am, would like to have a word with you if you don't mind." He steps around behind her as she looks at the Policemen. She immediately grows concerned as she looks at the men's faces.

"Oh my God, what is it?" she asks with alarm.

"Ma'am, I am afraid I have some terrible news for you. Is your husband John Edward Christianson?"

"Yes," she says timidly. She places the book into her lap as she looks up at him.

"Well, ma'am, I am afraid there has been a terrible accident. A tree has fallen on your husband, ma'am. I am incredibly saddened to have to inform you that your husband has died due to the accident. I am so very sorry, but he's gone. I so hate to have to inform you of this, ma'am," the Inspector speaks as gently as he can. He looks at her in pity.

"No," she cries, "No, it can't be. No, no, no."

Mr. Cradock sits down next to her and lays his hand on her back to comfort her. She turns and falls immediately into his arms, burrowing into his chest. He begins to hug her, gently swaying her back and forth in his arms.

"I am very sorry, ma'am," the Inspector says once again. "She will need to come to identify the body when she is able, Mr. Cradock," he quietly informs the innkeeper. "Here is my card, ma'am. If you need anything, anything at all, please don't hesitate to call me. My sincere condolences, Mrs. Christianson." The Inspector lays his card on the table and shakes his head.

The head groundskeeper nods from behind the front desk as the two policemen turn to leave the establishment. Mr. Cradock motions to him to come over to the table. "Go get Mrs. Shopshire from housekeeping," he whispers.

"I must get some things in order," Mrs. Christianson laments. Slowly she lifts her head out of Cradock's comforting embrace. "How will I tell my daughter? She loved her father so very much."

"I can call her for you if you would like, ma'am," Cradock offers.

"No, I have to call her. She is going to be devastated. She is going to be absolutely devastated." She breaks down once again and continues to sob into the Innkeeper's chest.

"You wanted to see me, Mr. Cradock?" Mrs. Shopshire asks as she approaches the table.

"Help me get Mrs. Christianson to her room, please."

"Yes, sir, of course," she says.

"I want you to stay with her the rest of the evening. See to it that she is not left alone. News like this is terrible enough, let alone being 3,000 miles away from home with no family nearby. We will take her in the morning to identify her husband," he whispers to Mrs. Shopshire.

"No. I want to go see him now. Can you please just take me there now, Mr. Cradock?" she asks.

"Yes, ma'am, of course. I will have the chauffeur take you immediately." Mr. Cradock looks toward the front desk. "Mr. Fisher, would you bring the car around for us, please."

"Yes, sir, right away." His assistant acknowledges the request and hurries off to the garage.

"Can I get you another cup of tea, Mrs. Christianson, or something from your room for the drive?" the housekeeper asks.

"My coat, please. It's laying across the bed," she replies. She looks out the window as if searching for a lost part of her soul. Sadness swells in her eyes. Several guests dining in the hotel suddenly speak in hushed conversations.

The housekeeper returns with the jacket. She notices the car pulls up in front of the hotel. "The car is out front now, sir," she says. Cradock looks up to see Mr. Fisher enter the hotel, nodding to him that the vehicle is ready.

"Thank you. If you are ready, Mrs. Christianson, then Mrs. Shopshire will escort you now," Cradock says to the widow.

"Mr. Cradock, would you please escort me as well? I feel so faint and would feel more comfortable if you would come with me," she pleads.

Cradock looks to Mrs. Shopshire. The housekeeper shrugs her shoulders as if there is no way they can disappoint the grieving lady. Cradock looks back with a look of surrender to the request. "Sure, Mrs. Christianson, I will escort you."

Cradock looks at Mr. Fisher and motions with his hand to come to the table. "Mr. Fisher, can you handle the phones and front desk while I'm gone," Cradock asks.

"Yes, sir. Will do, sir," he replies.

Cradock helps Mrs. Christianson and Mrs. Shopshire into the back of the car. As he begins to drive, Mrs. Christianson reaches into her purse and retrieves her cell phone. She calls her daughter as she looks off into the distance of the English countryside.


JULIE'S PHONE SITS on top of a book in the living room. Zoey looks over at it as it begins to ring. "Julie, your phone is ringing," she yells down the hallway to her roommate.

"Grab it, would you please?"

"Hello. Oh, hi, Mrs. Christianson, how are you? Yes, Julie is here. Hold on one second. She's coming right now." Zoey looks at Julie with concern. "It's your mother. She sounds really sad." She hands the phone to her roommate. Zoey stands close by, appearing to sense that something is not well.

"Hi, mom. What's up?" Julie asks. "Oh my God, no! No," she shrieks. "Daddy. Oh no, mom. Oh my God. No." She begins to cry, overwhelmed by the shock of the tragic news. She listens to the explanation her mother conveys of the event. Zoey looks on in apprehension as she moves closer to her friend.

"Yes. Okay. Yes, I will be there, mom. Let me know what time the flight is. I love you too," she replies. She looks at Zoey as tears begin to race down her face. "My daddy's gone," she cries.

"Oh my God," Zoey gasps. She instantly begins to cry as well, wrapping her arms around her grief-stricken roommate.


THE PUBLIC ADDRESS SYSTEM announces the incoming flight throughout the terminal, "American Flight 3121 from Heathrow Airport London now arriving at Concourse D gate D3. American Flight 3121 from Heathrow Airport London now arriving at Concourse D gate D3." Julie looks out the window at the plane. She closes her eyes for a moment as if in a state of meditation.

Julie's mother appears on the passenger boarding bridge, and the girl's rise to greet her. She instantly embraces her mother. LaShonda and Zoey look on, as tears well in their eyes.

LaShonda ushers them over to a row of seats, out of the way of the other passengers exiting the plane. Her keen observational skills force her to take notice that Scratch is also deboarding from the same flight. She taps Julie on her arm. "What was he doing on the same plane?" she asks. Scratch hurries away down the hallway, disappearing into an endless sea of passengers.

Julie looks up at her friend. "What?" she asks.

"What was he doing on the same flight?" LaShonda points to where she just saw Scratch exit the plane.

"Who?" Julie asks.

"Your guitar player. He just came down that landing and walked down the hallway."

"Are you sure?" Julie looks over to where her roommate is pointing.

"Am I sure? Yes, I'm sure."

"I don't know," Julie replies. She continues to cradle her mom while looking down the hallway.

# Chapter 28

## The Sting of the Pain

ZOEY PLACES A SECRET CALL TO HUNTER and informs him of Julie's father. He listens to her tear-filled explanation. He opens the tailgate to his truck to sit down, clearly overwhelmed by the tragic news. He thanks her for the information, and he ends the call. Nick arrives at the job site, and he immediately explains the situation to his boss.

"You need to go see her, Hunter. Do you want me to go over with you?" Nick asks.

"No, I'm not sure I should even go. I doubt she'll even see me."

"Yeah, you should go. If you're going to get back with her, you should try to speak to her. It may be your best chance. Take the rest of the day off. Get out of here."

"She said she never wants to see me again. She won't even take my calls."

"Hunter, the girl is hurting. She is probably crushed right down to her very soul. If there is anything you can do, you need to avail yourself to her right now. If she wants you back, showing her you are there for her will go a long way. She probably needs you now more than ever."

"You sure, Nick? We have a lot of work to do."

"Yes, go." He is stern in his command as he points toward the road.

"All right, all right, I'll go," he replies.

Hunter shuts the tailgate then drives off toward Julie's apartment. LaShonda opens the door as Hunter is about to knock.

"What do you want?" LaShonda asks.

"I heard about Julie's father. I wanted to give her my condolences. He was a good man, and I admired him very much."

Zoey joins her roommate at the entryway. LaShonda looks at her as if seeking direction. Zoey nods in silence to let him in.

LaShonda throws a sideways smile on her face as she lets Hunter in. "Come in," she says. Zoey relinquishes a slight smile as well as if knowing Hunter is doing the right thing.

"Will you go let her know he is here and see if she'll come down here, please?" LaShonda asks. Zoey nods her head and proceeds up the stairs.

"Sit down," LaShonda says. Hunter quickly complies. "You know you hurt her really bad, Hunter," she says quietly.

"Yes, I made a terrible mistake."

"That girl loved you with all her heart. Well, maybe you'll get lucky, and she'll want to talk to you. But if I say it's time for you to leave, don't make me say it a second time. Do you understand me?" she asks.

"Yes, ma'am," Hunter replies.

Julie and Zoey come down the stairs, hand-in-hand.

"Yes?" Julie asks. She is visibly exhausted, appearing to have cried her heart out over the last several days.

"Hi," he says to her. "I wanted to say how sorry I am about your father. I know how much he meant to you, and I wanted you to know just how sorry I am to hear about him passing away. I really enjoyed meeting him and thought he was a great man. I wish I had a magic wand to make everything better for you, Julie. But I don't, so all I can do is give my most sincere condolence."

"Thank you," she replies. Tears begin to swell in her eyes.

"Do you need anything, anything at all? Say it, and I will make it happen."

"No, Hunter. Thank you. But right now, I want to be alone. Maybe one day we can talk again, but I just need to be alone." Julie turns and walks back upstairs with Zoey.

LaShonda turns to him with tears in her eyes. "You have to go now, Hunter," she says softly. She opens the door.

"Yes, ma'am," he replies. He climbs into his truck and looks up at Julie's bedroom window. He shakes his head and begins to drive off. He finds his way to Stewart Park. Unable to rectify the nightmare he created, he looks out over the lake and begins to cry. Despite the emotional pain, he retrieves his writing pad and slowly begins to pen his feelings.

*What Are You Going Through*

*Must be your demons catching up to you.*
*Must be the season. That's the reason.*
*It must be you're going through Hell.*
*I've been there, yes, I know it well.*
*It's the only way to get to Heaven.*

*You say what you say, then you turn and walk away.*
*Hey, little child, what are you going through?*
*There must be a way, but every time you turn away.*
*Hey, little child, what are you going through?*

*Tell me are you getting all you planned for,*
*or have you even planned at all?*
*If you think the world owes you a living,*
*well it does, but it starts by giving.*
*It's the only way you get to Heaven.*

*You say what you say, then you turn and walk away.*
*Hey, little child, what are you going through?*

*There must be a way, but every time you turn away.*
*Hey little child what are you going through?*

*Don't you want coverage on your back door?*
*Do you care anymore at all?*
*You can control world,*
*if you only understood.*

*You say what you say, then you turn and walk away.*
*Hey, little child, what are you going through?*
*There must be a way, but you seem to have gone astray.*
*Hey, little child, what are you going through?*
*Hey, little child.*

# Chapter 29

## The Critique of the Critic

HUNTER PROPS THE APARTMENT DOOR OPEN. A glimmer of hope lifts his spirit as he looks to his cell phone, noticing that Julie is calling. Quickly he answers her call.

"Hello."

"Hi," Julie says. She sniffles, and her voice is weak.

"Hi."

"I want to talk," she says.

"Perfect."

"No, Hunter, nothing is perfect. You hurt me. You hurt me very badly."

"I didn't mean to hurt you, Julie. You know that. I never wish to hurt anyone. I would never willingly hurt you."

"Well, you did."

"I can make it up to you if you let me."

"I'm not so sure."

"I can't change that nightmare. I can only try to make it up to you."

"Did you have sex with her, Hunter?" Julie asks.

"No," he quickly replies. "That would have violated all of our trust."

"Then why were you kissing her?"

"I wasn't. She was blowing smoke to me through the joint that was in her mouth."

"If you're lying to me, Hunter, I will find out."

"Julie, I didn't sleep with her. I would never do that to you."

"You better not be lying."

"I swear, I didn't."

"Does she still come over to practice?"

"No. We haven't practiced at all since you left. I don't want to do this without you. I wish you would come back and give me a second chance."

"Well, you should've thought about that before you went and lost your stupid mind smoking that crap."

"I know. You're right. And I'm sorry. I promise it won't ever happen again."

"It better not. Who had it, Scratch?"

"Yes."

"What made you want to be a pothead?"

"I don't want to be a pothead. I guess the smell and curiosity tempted me."

"Are you still smoking it?"

"No."

"I want to believe you're not lying to me."

"Julie, I would never lie to you. You brought me into your life. And I can't imagine life now without you. And every moment I spend with you, I can't get enough. I have fallen in love with you, Julie. Then this whole stupid incident happened. And I am madder at myself than you are, trust me.

"Oh, I doubt that," she says.

"I am. And I can't make that up to you until you let me. And I will. I promise. I made a mistake, and I am asking for your forgiveness." Hunter's voice drops as he adds, "And I want to be with you every day of my life."

"I have to go now," Julie says through her tears.

"I love you, Julie."

"I have to go, Hunter." She abruptly hangs up the phone.

Hunter realizes she is gone. "Goddamn it!" he yells in anger.

Scratch stands in the doorway. "You, uh, still trying to mend that relationship with Miss Julie, are you?" he asks.

Hunter is startled, unaware of his presence. "Where the hell did you come from?"

"Well, some say from a jackal, actually, but I was simply coming over to drag your little ass out to grab a cocktail or two this evening." He laughs as he enters the apartment.

"You sneaky little son of a bitch, you scared the hell out of me."

"Yeah. You got some hell in you, do ya? Good. Come on, lad, let's go raise some of it. There are girls all over the bloody Commons. They're all half-naked as they loiter about in the warm spring air. They've all got that stupid little deer-in-the-headlights look going on like prey species normally do. There's so many of them, lad, and so terribly little time. Come on with ya, let's go."

"I am not really feeling it tonight."

"Naamah is down there. I know you like that," he says. He winks at Hunter with an exaggerated expression.

Scratch's English charm appears to make it hard for Hunter to stay mad at him as he shakes his head at the guitar player and lets out a laugh. "Ha. You idiot, that's what got me into this stupid mess in the first place."

"Oh, come on, man, the girl is a walking sex goddess. Any one of a thousand men would give their left testicle to be with that. Aphrodite says Naamah is the best-goddamn sex she's ever had in her life. If that girl can make Aphrodite satisfied for days, imagine what she can do for you, mate. Come on, man. Live like you're going to die tomorrow, that's what I always say."

"Yeah. No. Not interested. Besides, I have a song I'm working on."

Scratch shakes his head. "Wow. I set you up for the time of your life with a bloody goddamn bombshell, and you would rather stay with one little inexperienced girl. Well, I guess you are a better man than I am, mate," he says.

"I don't know that I am a better man. But I do know that Julie is all that to me and more," Hunter replies.

"Yeah, well guess if that's your final answer, then that's your final answer. All right then, sing that song for me there, choir boy, and we'll write it down right now, together, come on. I will help you find just the right chords for it. Then we can go out have a drink, while you ponder your next move with Miss Julie. Deal? Scratch asks. He extends his hand to shake.

"You buying?" Hunter asks.

"Yeah, mate. I'm buying."

"All right," he replies. He shakes his guitar player's hand in agreement. "The 12-string probably needs tuning. Go ahead and grab that tuner on the table while I jot down the words." Hunter flips his notebook to a blank piece of paper.

Scratch secures the guitar and touches it lightly, strumming the harmonics. "I love your 12-string, mate. It's still in tune. It has such a rich and deep sound. Play your cards right, and I might let you sell this to me," he says. He runs through an Algerian Scale in several different positions on the neck, testing its intonation.

"I don't buy tools to sell them," Hunter replies.

Scratch watches Hunter as he begins to write down some lyrics. He grins as he casually engages his recorder in his pocket. Hunter begins to hum a melody as he reads his hastily written words. Scratch picks up on the melody and mimics it perfectly on the guitar.

Hunter looks up. "Hey, that's it. You even have the right key," he says.

"Yeah, you know, I do this for a living."

Hunter steps over to the piano and begins to play. Scratch wastes no time in finding chord variations to flesh out the song. As if they both had played it many times before, the two seasoned musicians hammer out the details, and Hunter begins to sing the new piece.

*Want You to Know*

*"If I had a chance to run away,*
*would you ask for me, girl, to simply stay?*
*Because I would, that's all you'd have to say.*

*If I had a heart that's broken down,*
*Would you smile at me and still come around?*
*And lift me up in your kind-heart way.*

*Sometimes it's all just too complex.*
*Sometimes we're all too circumspect.*

*I'm standing here, and I am all alone,*
*and I want you to know, I want you to know that I need you*
*A life built around this bloody phone*
*is no way to go, is no way to go, and I need you now.*
*I'm crying, and I'm trying,*
*you should know, and*
*I need you to know, I want you.*

*Sometimes it's all just too complex!*
*Sometimes we're all too circumspect!*
*My thoughts you help me to collect.*
*You help me find my redirect.*

*And if I wear some thorny crown,*
*would you kindly help me get it down?*
*You are the color to me when I'm feeling gray.*

*I'm waiting here, and, no, I'm not a stone,*
*and I want you to know, I want you to know I need you,*
*and I need you. I need you."*

"Well," Hunter asks, "should I keep my day job?"

"Yeah, it's all right. You have a propensity to write a lot of warm fuzzy positive stuff that certainly can find a market. Me, I like darker stuff, really, but yeah, you know, there you have it. It's good."

He doubtfully looks at Scratch. "I guess that's a compliment."

"I like how you write when it comes from such furious, almost chaotic, creativity. You continue to amaze me, really. I just need to get you to look at things more from a Rock and Roll perspective. No offense, mate, but it seems like a lot of what you write is a lot of bubble gum. And it's erudite and brilliant cherry-flavored bubble gum. But you should write some darker stuff, too, you know?

Hunter listens with interest to the critique. "You think so?" he asks.

"Yeah, people out there want to hear uplifting stuff, but there are so many more out there that are pissed off and angry. And they don't want to see other people in a state of happy-go-lucky or warm-and-goddamn-fuzzy. They want to stay angry. Mainly because they don't know what happiness is, so they respond to the negative mental reinforcement. They're angry, and they want to stay in that state of mind. If you tap into that anger, that frustration, that angst that exists, that's what makes for some great bloody songs. You know what I mean?" Scratch asks. He reaches into his pocket for a cigarette as he waits for a response.

"Tell me, how many of these people, in their state of, what did you say, angst? How many of them, being so pissed off, will take the time to listen to us, let alone buy a song or our album?"

"Hard to say, really." Scratch appears to ponder the question as he lights a smoke.

"I kind of look at writing like this. The big guy upstairs gave me, for whatever reason, a talent or two. And songs come to me very quickly. Rarely are they negative songs. Who am I to question it?"

"Yeah, you said something like that before. Like you receive this magical beam that He throws them to you with, and that's how you do it, right?" Scratch rolls his fingers around his head in a mocking fashion.

"Yeah, it's kind of like that," Hunter replies.

"Well, then maybe, just maybe, you have to try writing another way. Like, you know, do what they call free association. Pick a topic of, like, a woe in the world and sit down and write out whatever comes to your mind."

"Now that's interesting. I have heard of that technique."

"Yeah, I think if you purposefully write about a dark subject, it will likely come out as brilliant Rock-and-Roll commentary. Then we can reach into the F minor or F# minor keys that really give a gloomy dark feel. If we do that, you'll develop a whole new angle and a new set of fans. And it will make you better as a writer, and us as a band. Just ask yourself, how often have you practiced those two musical keys?"

"Good point. I haven't much."

"Right, I mean, if this thing takes off, you'll want to be a voice of like social or environmental justice and change, won't you? I'll work with you. I'll help you see the dark side of this overcrowded and over-complicated goddamn planet," Scratch says. "Come on, lad, let's go now and look at some half naked-women and grab a few pints."

"You say you want darkness, yet you want to go out in the light. That makes you a walking contradiction in terms, Scratch, but you said you were buying, so let's go," Hunter replies. He puts his writing pad in his pocket as he follows Scratch out the door.

# Chapter 30

## A Walk in the Park

THE FIRST SATURDAY OF JUNE ARRIVES, and Nick finds Hunter sound asleep on his couch. A smirk comes across his face at the opportunity to playfully torment his sleeping friend. Nick takes a seat in the recliner. "Wakey, wakey," he says in an Australian accent. He picks up one of Hunter's outdoor magazines, glancing over the pictures. Hunter lifts his baseball cap off the brim of his nose and peers over across the room. He takes a deep breath and stretches his arms.

"How long have you been here?" he asks.

"Long enough to take your credit card out of your wallet and order us a breakfast pizza."

"You didn't," Hunter says. He looks to make sure that it is still laying on the table where he left it, then pulls his cap back down over his eyes.

"No, but I will if you want. What are your plans for today, Diva boy?"

"Don't tell me you have a side job. I don't feel like working today," Hunter replies.

"No. It's Saturday. You know I don't want to work, let alone on a Saturday."

"You want something. You don't normally bother me on Saturdays if you don't have something to do."

"I thought I would drag your ass down to the park. There is a Scottish fest going on today. Lots of pretty girls down there. And men in kilts, if you like."

"You go play with men in skirts. You probably have a few in your closet, you goddamn pervert."

"Ha, no, I am more of a German and English half breed. I would rather have some tea and crumpets now, then in the evening go suck down some beer and wiener-schnitzel with a pretty young fräulein."

"Actually, you are a wiener-schnitzel."

"Ouch, now that hurt. Come on, get cleaned up and wash that stink off of you while I sit here and read your wildlife pornography."

"Wildlife pornography? You are whacked, man. It's a hunting tactics magazine. You wouldn't understand. You better stick with your fun with farm animals website. They're much easier for you to catch, you friggin' pervert."

"Ha, that's good. Now go get showered, man. Hurry up."

"I don't know. I was thinking about scouting a stand of woods today, up on Connecticut Hill."

"Julie is down there," he sings.

"How do you know that?"

"I just saw her, that beautiful goddess she hangs out with and the four-eyed flakey one. They were all driving into the park."

Hunter smiles and laughs at his description of Zoey. "She's a nice flake."

"And an attractive one at that. If I didn't like her one friend, I would attempt to take her out. I always love the librarian look."

"You are a frigging dog, man. First of all, LaShonda would eat you alive."

"That's what I am hoping for, come on. Move!"

And second of all, Zoey has way too much class even to be seen with a schmuck like you. I don't know, Nick. I really don't think she wants to talk to me. I would be wasting my time. I screwed up, and I am just going to have to live with it."

"I thought you were a fighter, old boy. You are nothing but half-a-sissy. Get your ass moving. It's Saturday. No rain in sight. It's a beautiful day, and they have food and women all over down there.

"I am kind of hungry."

"Good. Let's go then. If she doesn't want to talk to you, then speak to some other women. Get her jealous. Use your head. She'll come around. It's the one signal that you have to send to her. There are hundreds of women down there right now that you can flirt with. Come on, buddy. Don't retreat. Do what General George S. Patton would do."

"What's that?"

"Attack, attack, attack!"

"Huh. That's good advice, I guess. And it is kind of how I look at things."

"Now you're coming around. Let's go, Diva!"

"I'm not a Diva."

"You aren't fooling anyone. You're a Diva, don't kid yourself. We'll get you in some kilts this afternoon, and you can start singing some Aretha."

Hunter rises from the couch as Nick turns his attention back into the magazine. He takes a pillow and flings it at the magazine, smashing Nick in the face.

"You are going to pay for that," Nick threatens.

Hunter takes off his shirt and enters the bathroom. Nick slips into the bathroom and dumps a pot of cold water over the curtain and onto Hunter's head as he washes.

"Ahhh, you son-of-a-bitch," Hunter shrieks. Nick runs from the bathroom, sensing imminent retaliation. "You even shriek like a Diva." He laughs as he flees.

The two drive to the park where the Scottish Fest is being held. Nick, always aware of his surroundings, quickly pulls his vehicle into a freshly vacated spot. The two of them exit the truck and begin their walk in the park.

"You can pay me back later, buddy." Nick nudges him with his elbow. Julie and her roommates bask in the sun at a picnic table. Nick and Hunter's path will lead them directly toward the group.

"Oh, my God, it's Hunter Watkins," a pretty brunette girl says to her friend. The girl glows with excitement as she grabs her friend's hand. The other girl, unaware of Hunter's popularity, looks at her friend with curiosity.

Nick shakes his head, having informed Hunter that something like this would likely occur. He waves at LaShonda, who looks over in hearing Hunter's name. She waves back at Nick and smiles, then turns to whisper to Julie.

"Can I have your autograph, Hunter?" the girl asks.

"Sure. No problem," he replies. The girl reaches into her purse and retrieves a permanent marker, and hands it to him.

"Do you have something to write on?" Hunter asks.

"My shirt," she replies. She grabs the side of her shirt, stretching the fabric across her breasts.

"Okay," Hunter says. He signs his name as he laughs.

"Are you playing today?" she asks.

"No, not today. Sorry."

"Too bad. I love your music. I hear you have a new band. When are you playing next?"

"Soon," he replies.

"Thank you," she says. "I look forward to hearing you." She flicks her hair and smiles, and the two girls continue on their way.

"Oh, Julie saw that and then turned around in disgust. If that didn't make her jealous, nothing will. You'll be back with her in no time," Nick says. The two continue to walk on their intercept course toward Julie and her friends.

"Hi. How are you?" Hunter stops to question Julie. Zoey and LaShonda look on, uncertain how Julie will respond.

Julie turns to him with a forced smile. "Fine," she replies. Her terse response contradicts the positive statement. Hunter notices the dark circles that shroud her eyes. It appears she has slept very little since he saw her last.

"Can we talk?" Hunter asks.

"We just did. You have a lot of fans here, though, like the two bimbos that wanted you to fondle them. I would think you should be wandering around with them promoting yourself. So with that in mind, have a good day," Julie replies. Her contemptuous smile illustrates her lack of willingness to talk.

"Are you going to stay mad at me forever?" he asks. Zoey and LaShonda look at Nick and subtly shake their heads.

"I don't know, Hunter. Right now, I want to take in some fresh air and hang with my friends. So if you'll excuse me," she says. She stands up and begins to walk away. LaShonda looks at Nick with obvious disappointment. The two girls join Julie as she walks toward the lake. LaShonda looks back at Nick and shrugs her shoulder.

"Come on, buddy. She'll come around. Let's go get something to eat."

"I don't know, Nick. She sure is an unhappy girl."

"You tried your best, and you definitely made her a little jealous. You can't force her to talk, but you did your best. Psychologically speaking, the signal you just sent was enormously powerful. You had a pretty little girl flirting with you, and you brushed her off. She clearly saw that. But you immediately showed that you would rather talk to her."

"You think so?"

"Yes. I think so. Think of it as planting a seed. It's going to sprout, and it will grow. She'll call you when she's ready to talk to you, my friend, so forget about it. Come on, man, let's go get a hot sausage."

"Yeah, that sounds good. Sometimes, Nick, well, more like once in a great while, you do make some sense."

The wafting smell of meat cooking over fire leads them directly into the sausage vendor's line. They pay for their sandwiches and take their meal to a table near the boathouse. Nick wastes no time as he quickly gobbles down his first sandwich and starts on his second.

"You, uh, ever come up for air there, Nick?" Hunter asks.

Nick laughs just as his phone begins to ring. "Shit," he mumbles through a mouthful of food, and he hurries to clear his pallet.

"What?" Hunter asks.

"I was supposed to stop on the way here and give an estimate. Hello, Mrs. Wright. Yes, sorry I am running late, but I am almost there. About ten more minutes, yes, ma'am. See you there."

"Nice going there, Nick."

"This will take me about half an hour. Do you want to come with me or wait here?'

"I'll wait here. I'm feeling a song coming on," Hunter says. He reaches for his pad of paper. "Mrs. Wright, isn't she that cougar you were warning me about last week?"

"Yes. I am hoping she really wants an estimate and not a full-blown service call. If I am not back in half an hour, then I will be back when she releases her claws."

"You idiot. Go," Hunter says.

Nick wanders off out of sight. No sooner does he vacate the area; Hunter begins to write.

### Don't You Run Away

*You're your own brand. You're like quicksand,*
*you suck me in, then pull me deeper.*
*You're like a summer's breeze. You warm me when I'm freezing.*
*Basking in your glow, I'm cleaner.*

*Now, don't you run away.*
*No, don't you run away.*
*The things you say today, they just blow my blues away.*
*No, don't you run away.*

*You lift me up. You calm my nerves. You glance my way,*
*and I draw nearer.*
*You're more grand than the sky,*
*I can't take my eyes off of you.*
*If you whisper, then I will hear you.*

*Now, don't you run away.*
*No, don't you run away.*
*The things you say today, they just blow my blues away.*
*No, don't you run away.*

*Something's happening, and it's been so long.*
*You set the motion and the moment.*
*The stars must be aligning. You've set my soul to shining.*
*I get lost without your kisses, so don't you run away.*

*I close my eyes, there you are and still in sight.*
*It doesn't get much clearer.*
*A moth caught in your flame, burning up who is to blame?*
*From your fire, I am set free…*

*Now, don't you run away.*
*No, don't you run away.*
*The things you say today, they just blow my blues away.*
*No, don't you run away.*

# Chapter 31

## The Mending at Mercato's

LASHONDA PEEKS HER HEAD INTO Julie's room. "Summer classes started two weeks ago. Are you not going to school again today?"

"No. Not today," Julie replies. She takes a deep sigh and looks down as if in shame.

Zoey also peeks in. She looks at LaShonda and shakes her head in frustration. The two girls enter the room and sit on the side of the bed.

"Julie, you can't keep missing classes. We know you are hurting, but you need to get up and go to school today. You have to either go to your classes or withdraw, Julie. Otherwise, it's going to affect your GPA. Come on now. We'll help you. It'll be all right. But you have to get up and move around a little bit, girl," LaShonda encourages as she rubs her back.

Julie turns her head into her pillow and softly begins to cry. Zoey turns to LaShonda with a look of helplessness. LaShonda shakes her head, appearing uncertain how to nudge Julie out of her state of pain.

"I'll go tomorrow," Julie says. "Professor Pistorovski and the Dean's Office both called me yesterday. They want to meet with me no later than Thursday."

232

She sniffles as she raises her head. "Will you come with me? I think he is going to yell at me for missing so many classes."

"Yes, I'll go with you," Zoey replies. She nods her head as she pushes her glasses back up onto the bridge of her nose. "I have to have him critique a project for me anyway. And we call him Professor Pissed-her-off-ski. He always seems so very angry." Her attempt to make Julie laugh fails to elicit even a smile.

Julie rises reluctantly from her bed and makes her way to the bathroom.

The girls follow her out of the room. Zoey turns to LaShonda, motioning for her to walk down the hallway so that Julie cannot hear. "Should we try to get her back with Hunter? I know he has called her many times. When she sees the call from him, she begins to cry. It must mean she wants him back, don't you think?" Zoey asks.

"It has to. I guess getting them to talk would be the first step. How can we get them to do that?"

Zoey looks toward the bathroom. "I don't know, but you heard her mother. Don't throw away a great relationship over something so small."

"I was looking at her when her mom said that. Her mom was right about smoking pot. It's not such a big deal. The look she had was as like she made a huge mistake with Hunter," LaShonda replies.

"When I get back from my morning class, I will try to get into her head. Now that we're able to get her up and around, I'll get her talking. See if she is going to stick out her classes and what she feels about Hunter," Zoey says. "I will go make something to eat. See if you can't get her to come down and join us."

"Good idea," LaShonda replies.

Zoey gets up from the table, placing her dishes in the sink as Julie finally joins her and LaShonda in the kitchen. She pours Julie a glass of orange juice and sets it in front of her. "Do you want some toast with your omelet, Julie?" Zoey asks.

"No, I'm not hungry," she replies.

Zoey smiles at her as she takes a plate from the cupboard and a clean fork from the drawer. She serves Julie the dish she made, setting it next to the glass of orange juice.

"Well, you will eat that for us, won't you?" LaShonda asks. She rubs Julie's forearm as she smiles at her roommate.

She nods her head as she looks down at her plate. She lifts the fork, taking a small bite of her food.

"We have to leave in a few minutes. Don't you go back to bed, Julie. We'll be back after our morning class," LaShonda says.

"I won't. I was going to call mom and talk for a while."

"Good. We will see you in a while then. You ready, Zoey?" LaShonda asks.

"Yes, I am. See you in a bit, Julie," Zoey says.

On the way to campus, LaShonda detours into the parking lot of her favorite coffee shop. She looks in the rearview mirror, taking a moment to apply her lipstick.

"I'll buy coffee if you run in and get them while I work on this paper," Zoey says. She hands LaShonda some money.

"Deal," LaShonda agrees. "Café latte, right."

"Please," Zoey replies.

She takes the money and makes her way inside. As she waits in line, she begins texting, oblivious to the morning hustle going on around her.

"Hi, LaShonda," Hunter says.

LaShonda turns to notice Hunter and Nick in line behind her. "Hi, Hunter. How have things been going?" she asks. She glances at Nick and smiles at him.

"I'm doing all right. How is Julie doing? I've called her several times and left messages, but she's only returned one of my calls."

"You know she is going through a lot with the loss of her father. And with whatever happened between you two sure didn't help."

"No, it didn't. I wish I had a do-over, LaShonda. I really do love her, and I miss her, and I don't know what to do."

"I know you do. You know what? Let me talk to Zoey. Maybe we can come up with a plan. Here, take my phone and call your number, so I have it," she says. She hands him the phone as she glances again at Nick.

Hunter gives her phone back as his begins to ring. LaShonda quickly saves his contact information. "Great, I got it. Now, if I call you and tell you to meet me someplace, you have to drop what you are doing and meet me there. Can you do that?" she asks.

"Yes. I understand. I won't let you down," Hunter replies.

"What can I get you?" the clerk asks. LaShonda steps up to the counter and orders two café lattes. Nick places down a $20 bill. "I've got those," he informs the clerk. LaShonda turns and smiles at him once again. "Thank you. I don't think I ever caught your name, did I?" she pleasantly asks. She steps to the side as she waits for her drinks.

"I'm Nick Kincade," he says. "And I would love to help you get them back together. It would be my pleasure."

"Nice to meet you, Nick. I will keep that in mind. Maybe I will see you around with him," she replies.

"Maybe. Or maybe I can give you my number if you would like, just in case you need extra help," he suggests.

"Now that's a promising idea. What is it?" she asks. Nick promptly hands her a business card.

Hunter shakes his head at Nick's forwardness as he steps to the counter. He laughs as he orders two coffees.

"Thank you. I might take you up on that offer. We'll see. Thanks again," she says. She takes the two lattes from the clerk. Nick watches her, looking her up and down as she walks away. Before exiting the café, she looks back at him as she leans into the door. She smiles again, appearing to encourage his attention. She hands Zoey her coffee as she gets in the car and shares what just happened on their way to school.

As they return from their classes, Julie is working in the living room. She appears frustrated and discouraged as she attempts to read her coursework.

"Have you been studying?" Zoey asks.

"Yes. Trying anyway." She sighs, dropping her arms onto her book, then resting her head in her palms.

"Maybe it's time you take a break. I will fix us something for lunch," LaShonda says to her. She proceeds into the kitchen as Zoey sits down beside Julie.

"So Julie, what are you going to do about the music you recorded with Hunter? You said, before his bonehead maneuver, that there were a few songs you recorded. Are you going to get copies so we can hear them or what?" Zoey asks.

"I don't know." She begins to cry. Zoey looks to LaShonda as if she had done something wrong. LaShonda looks on, nodding her head in approval of the questioning.

Zoey puts her arm around Julie, and she turns into Zoey's shoulder as she continues to weep. "I don't know. I just wish he hadn't done those things. I miss him so very much," she declares through her tears.

The words seem to be precisely what the two roommates were hoping to hear. LaShonda gives Zoey a thumbs-up for extracting the encouraging words from their grieving friend.


HUNTER AND NICK PICK UP their tools as they finish work. "Load those excess materials in the back of my truck, will you, old boy? I have to go check the plumbing." He turns to go to the restroom.

"On it," Hunter replies as he begins rounding up the spare lumber.

As Nick opens the bathroom door, his phone begins to ring. He notices the icon on the display and grins. "Hello, Nick Kincade," he says.

"Hi, Nick. It's LaShonda Moraise. How are you?"

"I was good, but now I am even better. How are you?"

"Oh, I'm all right. You said I could call you. Am I catching you at an inconvenient time?"

"No, no, not at all. Your timing is impeccable. I'm just finishing work. What's on your mind?"

"Zoey and I are going to take Julie out to dinner tonight at Mercato's. We're hoping to get her back together with Hunter. I was wondering if I could get you to help us as you suggested. If you didn't have plans, that is. I thought maybe you might somehow be able to get him there, and we could work together on this. What do you say? Are you busy?"

"I love Mercato's. Yes, I can get him there. If I have to club him in the back of the head with a two by four, I will get him there. What time are you thinking?"

"Zoey is making the reservations for 6:30. So you will come?"

"I wouldn't miss it. I look forward to helping you. The boy has been pretty bummed out lately. So yes, we will definitely see you there," he says.

"Good. We will make a separate reservation for you. That way, it will seem like a total surprise to both Julie and Hunter. Our reservation is for a party of five, but there will be just the three of us. Your table will be right across the aisle so that it will seem totally random. If it feels right, we will ask you both to join us. Sound like a plan?"

"It sounds like a perfect plan. I can't wait," he replies.

"Thank you. I owe you one."

"I wasn't looking at it that way, but I will let you owe me one if you want."

"I'm sure we can figure that out later. I'll see you tonight then. Bye," LaShonda says.

SEVERAL HOURS LATER, LaShonda, and Zoey escort Julie to the restaurant. Its inconspicuous façade contradicts the warm and inviting atmosphere that awaits just inside the establishment's doors.

Raguel leans against the brick building, talking loudly to anyone who can hear. As the girls approach the entrance, he looks directly at the three young ladies as he recites some scripture. "Get rid of all bitterness, rage, and anger, brawling and slander, along with every form of malice. Be kind and compassionate to one another, forgiving each other, just as in Christ, God forgave you."

LaShonda and Zoey smile at the unkempt man, yet his words seem to resonate with Julie. She reaches into her purse and hands the man some money as she enters the restaurant.

"Thank you, my child. May God smile on you," he says, and he bows as the girls enter the restaurant.

As the door closes, Raguel looks around with a bit of suspicion. He takes his staff and circles it around in front of the doorway. "You cannot harm them. The Spirit protects them. You hear me, Satan? You have no power here. Pestilence be gone!" he decrees as he begins to walk off.

"Hi, what can I get you?" the bartender asks.

Zoey pushes her glasses back up onto the bridge of her nose. "I'll have a Screwdriver," she says.

"Whiskey and ginger," LaShonda informs the barkeep. She turns to Julie, "What do you want, girlfriend?"

"Just an iced tea and three lemons, please," she says, her voice soft and her eyes downcast.

"Will you be dining with us this evening?" the hostess asks.

"Yes, the Zoey Arroyo party. I think I spoke with you when I made the reservation this afternoon?" She winks, having recruited the hostess as a co-conspirator to accommodate the party and the predetermined seating arrangements.

"Oh, yes," the waitress says. She winks back at her. "Your table is ready. I will bring you your drinks. Right this way, please."

The waitress escorts them down the narrow passage to the back of the eatery. LaShonda moves to the booth closest to the back wall to watch for Hunter and Nick. Zoey takes the other booth seat by the north wall. The waitress directs Julie to a chair, forcing her to sit with her back to any guests that arrive.

"Your waiter will be right with you. I highly suggest any of the dinner specials he'll tell you about tonight. They're all simply to die for," the hostess boosts. "I'll be right back with your drinks."

"Thank you," Zoey replies. The girls begin to look over the menu while LaShonda casually scans for her accomplice to arrive with Hunter.

"Nothing is sounding particularly good to me. I guess I am not very hungry," Julie says. The lack of energy in her voice seems to alarm LaShonda.

"Girl, you have hardly eaten all week. You have to eat something, dear. You like the Marsala, don't you?" LaShonda asks.

"I guess so," she replies. She smiles with her lips, but her eyes betray the falsity.

"Iced tea?" the waitress asks as she looks at Julie.

"Yes, thank you."

"Screwdriver," the waitress says. Zoey reaches over to assist her.

"Whiskey and ginger," the waitress says. She hands LaShonda her drink.

"Can I get you anything else before your waiter comes?"

"No. I think we're good for the moment, thank you," Zoey replies.

LaShonda observes Hunter and Nick enter the restaurant. Nick scans the area, quickly making eye contact with her. She immediately begins to act surprised.

"Don't look now, Julie, but Hunter and his friend are here, and it looks like they're going to be seated right next to us," LaShonda quietly says across the candlelight.

Julie's eyes open wide as she looks at her roommate. "Are you serious?" she asks.

"Hello," LaShonda says as the waitress escorts them to their table.

Hunter's eyes also open wide. "Hi," he replies, completely caught off guard. He quickly looks at Julie, pausing as he stares at her beauty augmented by the candlelight. "Hi, Julie," Hunter says. She looks up at him with a subdued smile.

"Hi," she calmly replies.

"If I am bothering you, we can go somewhere else," Hunter says.

"No, it's okay," she says. Her slight smile is suddenly more genuine upon seeing him.

Zoey reaches over and grabs her hand in support. Julie responds by returning the grasp. She leans over and whispers into Julie's ear, "Do you mind if they join us?"

She looks at Zoey, then nods her head. "All right," she replies.

"Why don't you both join us? There is plenty of room here," Zoey says to Hunter.

"Is that all right, Julie?" he asks.

She takes a deep breath then looks at him longingly. She nods her head to him and manages another subdued little smile.

The waitress smiles and pulls the seat out for Hunter. Nick pats him on the back then takes the booth seat next to LaShonda. "Can I get you both a drink," she asks.

"Iced tea, please," Hunter says.

"I'll have a fourteen," Nick replies.

The waitress looks at him curiously. "I have never heard of that one. What is it?" she asks.

"It simply a seven and seven," he replies with a grin on his face.

"Okay then," the waitress replies. She laughs, and it helps the others at the table to do the same.

Hunter looks at Julie. "How have you been?" he asks.

"All right, I guess."

"How is your mom doing? Is she okay?"

She nods her head as she speaks. "She's doing ok. It's hard for her right now."

"I miss you," he whispers to her.

Julie looks at him. She smiles ever so slightly as she whispers back. "We can talk about that later. Right now, we're having dinner. What would you like to order?" she asks. She hands him the menu.

"Thank you. I'm not sure yet, but can I tell you something?" he quietly asks.

"What?" she whispers.

"You look very beautiful tonight."

"Thank you," she says. The others take notice as she blushes.

While they dine, the group listens to Nick tell some tall tales. Even Julie manages to find a few laughs at his stories. The dinner goes a long way toward helping to repair the damaged relationship.

Julie leans over and whispers again to Hunter. "We have to be going. I have a lot of things to do. If you call me tomorrow, we can talk some more."

"I will. I promise."

"I have a lot of homework to make up. Are we ready?" Julie asks. LaShonda agrees as she reaches for the check to pay the bill.

"I've got that," Nick insists. He briefly places his hand over LaShonda's to take the receipt.

"Are you sure?" she asks.

"My treat. I had a great time. Thank you. Maybe we can do this again sometime soon?" he says.

"Maybe." She smiles as she surrenders the bill.

The party exits the restaurant and say their goodbyes.

"I'll talk to you tomorrow," Hunter says to Julie.

She nods, and the girls proceed to the parking garage. They are all unaware that Scratch and his girls watch them from the bar across the street.

"Not good, Naamah. I bloody hate it when they smile like that. I am beginning to think your powers are becoming outdated."

"My powers only grow stronger with every passing century."

"Well, look at them, would ya? They're leaving with that look that I hate so very much. It's like they're all warm-and-goddamn-fuzzy. I hate warm-and-goddamn-fuzzy. That leads to the bloody alter and the most stupid two words that two people can possibly say to one another. What the bloody hell! I thought you were winning this war, Naamah. Why does it look like they're getting back together? Next thing you know, they will be getting married. I don't think you're working hard on this one. I really don't." Scratch scolds.

"Well, it's not like I can visit him every night, silly."

"I'm not silly, goddamn it! I'm the bloody goddamn Devil. And why *can't* you, I ask?"

She smiles as she confronts him. "You are silly. Have you ever looked at my schedule that you so freely imprint your requests on?" she asks.

He watches the party on the sidewalk begin to go their separate ways. "No, I don't believe I have. And what bloody difference does that make?" he asks.

"You have me visiting half of the perverted professors in this town alone and screwing each one of them in their dreams. Do you have any idea of the planning that takes? That's not even mentioning all the big cities outside this quiet little town. I think I need a vacation, to be honest."

Aphrodite listens as she runs her finger along the outside of Naamah's thigh, excited at how tactfully she handles their hot-headed boss.

"A vacation? A vacation? Are you serious? There are over eight billion people on this overcrowded planet, all waiting to spend eternity with us, and you want to take a bloody vacation. You're killing me, Naamah. You're really killing me."

# Chapter 32

## It's All Too Much

THE NEXT DAY JULIE ATTEMPTS TO GET back into a regular routine. She sits on the couch, examining the material that she must complete to salvage the semester. The enormity of the task must seem overwhelming to her as she breaks down once again. Zoey notices her crying as she gets ready for her classes.

"What's wrong?" Zoey asks.

"It's all too much. I'm too far behind, and I can't concentrate and… and, I'm lonely." She sniffles as she tries to catch her breath in between the tears.

Zoey sits down beside her. "Can I give you a hug?" she asks. Julie nods and falls into her arms. They cry together as LaShonda enters the room. Without hesitation, she sits down on the other side of Julie, wrapping her arms around her.

"What's wrong, girlfriend?" she asks, whispering into Julie's ear.

"I can't do it. I am too far behind."

"What did the Dean say? Didn't he say you have until Monday next week to withdraw?" LaShonda asks. Zoey nods her head in verification. "You need some time, girl. It's Okay. Everybody needs some time once in a while. It will be all right."

"Are… you… sure?" she whimpers, trying to catch her breath.

"I'm sure. I want you to forget about it. We will take you up to campus and explain to the Dean that you need the rest of the semester off. Why don't you go back and lay down in your room to rest a bit? We will take you up to withdraw when we get back this afternoon. Take that load off your mind. Okay?"

"Okay," she replies. She puts her book on the coffee table and walks back into her bedroom. Zoey and LaShonda remain on the couch, wiping their tears.

"We have to do something. But what can we do?" Zoey asks.

"Well, she was fine last night when Hunter was around. First time I have seen that girl smile in weeks. That boy is our best hope to get her back on her feet. Know what I'm saying?"

"Agreed. You want me to call him?" Zoey asks.

"Will you? I have to finish getting ready for class. See if he can come over this morning."

"Yeah, me too. He's probably working, though," Zoey says.

"See what you can do. If I have to, I will call his boss," she replies.

"I'll call him right now," she says.

Within a few minutes, Hunter knocks on the door, and Zoey lets him in.

"Where is she?" he asks.

"She's upstairs sleeping, and she's really starting to worry us," Zoey replies.

"Me, too," he says.

"She has to come out of it. Do you think you can get her to school today, Hunter? Zoey asks. She closes the door, and they join LaShonda in the kitchen.

"Well, she is talking to me now. I'll see if I can bring her around. Don't you worry about that," he replies.

"She has to withdraw from the summer semester. We were planning on taking her up to school this afternoon. If you can get her up and around, that would be great. It will take a lot off her mind that she won't have to think and worry about," LaShonda says.

"I took the day off so I can run her around if that's what needs to happen. It won't be a problem."

"Thank you, Hunter. Come on, Zoey, we're late," LaShonda says.

Zoey follows her roommate toward the door. "Have a good day, Hunter. We'll be back around noon."

"See you then," he replies.

As the two girls leave, he walks up the stairs and taps on Julie's door jam. "Hi," he says as she opens her eyes. She smiles upon seeing him. "Are you getting up?"

"Yes, I have to. I have to withdraw from school. I am just too far behind." She sits up and leans against the headboard, cradling her head in her hands as she frowns at the thought.

"Well, that's understandable. You have had a terrible loss," he says. He enters the room, sitting down on her bed. "Sometimes, you have to slow down in life and reflect before you can ever move forward. You sound like you are down on yourself about it. Don't be. Life's too short to get down on yourself."

"I guess you are right."

"It's okay to take time for yourself. Come on. Let's get you around," he says. He holds his hand out to her, and she takes it. He stands up and pulls her into his arms.

Immediately she hugs him, resting her head on his chest. She appears to find peace in his embrace as he gently presses her head against his body.

"Professor Bowman is going to be mad at me."

"Yeah? Why?"

"Because it's his last semester, and he has helped me through several classes. He has grand expectations for me."

"Here, maybe this will help. I thought you could use this," he says. He pulls a petite white tea rose from his pocket and hands it to her. She smiles as he gives her the gift.

"It's a tea rose. Thank you. My father loved them. He planted them all around the house in. He would pick them all the time for me and my mom."

Julie begins to shed a tear and then another. Hunter holds her as she cries into his chest. He cradles her more tightly in his arms and begins to rock her back and forth like a child.

"Why, why, why? Why did he have to go out in a lightning storm? Why? I want my daddy back. I just want my daddy back." She begins to cry like a baby, and her tears are testimony to her state of grief.

"It's okay, Julie. It's okay," he whispers.

He manages to get her dressed, but no closer to the door than the living room couch. There, they sit and talk about her father for several hours. The conversation seems to wear her out, and she rests her head on his lap, falling fast asleep.

Zoey finally returns home from her morning class. Hunter lifts his finger to his mouth as she enters. "Shhh," he softly says. Zoey nods in acknowledgment. She quietly places her books on the coffee table and sits down next to Hunter.

"She cried herself back to sleep, didn't she?" she quietly asks. Hunter nods his head.

"You have to get her back up on her feet, Hunter," she says.

"I will," he replies in a whisper.

"I'm going to the kitchen. Do you need anything?" she asks.

"No. Well, actually yes, a pad of paper and a pen if you can find one," he says.

Zoey reaches into her purse and hands him a small writing pad. She then retrieves a pen, hesitating before she hands it to him. "Julie gave me this. You will give it back to me when you are done, or I will find you." She hands him the pen, then begins to shake her finger at him. "I hope that I am being very clear with you that I want it back."

Hunter looks at her with his eyes wide open and nods his head. "Yes, ma'am, I understand." He carefully takes the Montblanc Rollerball from her, examining it in his hand. She pushes her glasses back up and turns toward the kitchen. He watches her for a moment, then looks at the pen, balancing it in his hand. Appearing impressed, he says very quietly, "Nice." He positions the pad on the arm of the couch and begins to write.

*Baby Blue*

*Hey, what's your name? Tell me all you know. I'll do the same.*
*Shy, are you shy? Do you know that you have caught my eye?*
*Fears, do you have fears? Perhaps they hide beyond,*
*just behind those tears.*
*Dream, do you dream? Or are they all just nightmares*
*where you sit and scream?*
*Oh, tell me do. Baby blue. Baby blue.*

*Hide. Where do you hide? Is it somewhere deep or in plain sight?*
*Love, do you know love? For you are the only one*
*that I am dreaming of.*
*Oh, tell me, Baby blue. Baby blue.*

*I want to hold you, but I don't know your name.*
*How Can I tell you? Do you think we're all the same?*
*Baby blue*

*How can I tell you with a teardrop in your eye?*
*How can I love you? Please open your disguise… for me.*
*Baby blue. Baby blue. Baby blue. Baby blue.*

*Tight, does someone hold you tight?*
*Wish I may, wish I might.*
*Lost, are you lost? Do you crash throughout the shadows*
*on a ship that's tossed?*
*Oh, tell me, Baby blue. Baby blue.*
*Tell me, baby blue.*

*I want to love you. I want to wrap my arms around you.*
*I have to tell you. I want to build my world around you,*

*Baby blue.*

*Do you... do you need someone?*
*And can I be the one?*
*Love, how do I win your love?*
*Now it's only you I'm dreaming of!*

*How do I tell you, with a teardrop in your eye?*
*How do I see you beyond your disguise? Tell me,*
*Baby blue. Baby blue.*

"Are you sure you need this pen back, Zoey? I think it's defective." Hunter holds up the pen as Zoey looks into the living room. She rises from the table and comes over to retrieve it.

"You are a smart man, Hunter. You would be defective if I didn't get it back," she says in a monotone voice. She looks down at Julie. "You need to wake her up and get her to school to withdraw."

Hunter looks at the time on his phone. "I will give her about another five minutes."

Zoey nods as she turns back to the kitchen.

# Chapter 33

## Closure on Connecticut Hill

JULIE AWAKENS AND STROKES HUNTER'S flannel shirt like a security blanket. She looks up at him as she manages a genuine smile.

"Are you getting up so I can take you to school?"

"I just want to lay here a while. Can you just hold me?"

"I have been holding you." Hunter reaches over and grabs a pillow. "Now, you are going to get up. Now! Or the beatings will begin until morale improves. Get up."

"Hunter."

"Get up." Hunter gently lifts her head off his lap and stands, walloping the girl across her thigh with the pillow.

"Hunter," she whines. She curls tightly into a fetal position.

He hits her again, and she lets out a laugh. "Hunter Watkins," she screams. Zoey looks in from the kitchen. Julie shields her head as he delivers yet another blow. Zoey watches the commotion in a state of relief and laughs, hearing Julie do the same.

"All right, I'm getting up," she declares. Zoey continues to laugh at Hunter's unconventional motivational methodology. Hunter gets her moving and, in little time, drives her to Ithaca College to withdraw from her classes.

"We have to go see Professor Bowman before we go," she says, appearing as if a great weight has been lifted from her shoulders. "I have to let him know I'm taking the semester off. If I don't personally tell him, he'll ... oh my God, there he is. Professor Bowman. Hi!" Julie yells, attempting to gain the attention of the professor. He turns to see who is calling out his name.

"Julie. Hello. How have you been?" the professor asks. "We have been missing you in class."

"I'm sorry. I had some things happen, and I just haven't been myself," she says, lowering her head.

"The Dean informed me about your father. I understand exactly why you have not been around. It has to be very hard dealing with such a loss. Julie, you are young. A loss like that warrants taking some time off from school. Go up to the Registrar and take the rest of the semester off if you haven't already."

"I just withdrew a few minutes ago, professor."

"Good. School will still be here in a few months. This way, your GPA doesn't suffer. It is the right thing to do. A major loss like you are going through needs time for the brain to heal. And I know your roommates are a good support network for you. I take it this is also someone in your support network?" The professor asks as he looks at Hunter.

"Yes, sir." Hunter reaches out to shake his hand.

"I had the pleasure of hearing you both perform out at Taughannock Park. You two together on stage not only have great appeal, but you also have some particularly wonderful music. Am I to understand you write most of the material yourself?" the professor asks.

"Yes, sir. For the most part, I do."

"Well, you both need to collaborate. Julie has shared some wonderful works with me. Julie, one of the best things you can do right now is to go and channel your thoughts from what has happened. Take this time off and utilize it wisely as a way to write about what you feel. It will help your mind relieve itself of the pain you surely must be going through. Trust me. It will get you back on track and ready to attack the next semester with a new-found passion."

"But you are retiring. You won't be here next semester. And I will miss you." Tears swell in her eyes.

"Julie, you can bounce your material off me any time. I am retiring. I'm not dying. I will still be in Ithaca. Come on now. It will be all right. I would love to have you meet me for a coffee or something and look over anything you might be working on."

"Do you think I could have a hug?" she asks.

"You bet you can have a hug, my friend," the professor says without hesitation as he opens his arms.

"Now listen, go. Go right now. Take your friend here and go down to the park or somewhere special where your mind is at ease. Take your writing tablet and write down all your feelings about what you are going through. Do you remember the free association writing exercises we did last semester, Julie?"

"Yes, sir. I remember." She retrieves a tissue from her pocket and dabs the tears from her eyes.

"Great. Go down to the park, or find a place where you'll not be disturbed and treat yourself to a session this afternoon. Write about your father. Write about what he meant to you and how you loved him. Trust me, Julie, it will help bring peace back into your life."

"Thank you, Professor."

"All right. I have a faculty meeting to go to. I will see you soon. And I look forward to catching some more of your shows."

"Pleasure meeting you, sir. Have a great day," Hunter replies.

"Bye now." The professor turns and continues down the hallway toward the student center.

"He seems like a pretty nice guy."

"Yes, he is," she says.

"Can you explain free association writing to me?" Hunter asks.

"It's just a way to force your mind to throw out all that it is thinking about," she explains.

Hunter pulls her in close as they begin to walk. "Why don't we go to the park, as the professor suggested? It's a beautiful day. Maybe we could write something together like he just said. Or maybe I can watch as you do this free association exercise thing. What do you think?"

Julie nods her head. "Can we go back to that place you took me on Connecticut Hill? I really liked it there."

"Yes. Absolutely," Hunter replies. He kisses her on the cheek and begins to escort her back to his truck.


THE SOUND OF CIVILIZATION is absent in the depths of the forest as they walk to the beaver pond. They take a seat at the picnic table that they visited before.

"I am supposed to be alone with my thoughts to do this, so when I begin, you can't say a word, okay?" Julie asks.

"I won't make a sound," Hunter replies.

She looks at him nervously. "Promise?"

"I promise. Not a sound."

Julie takes her writing tablet from her purse and leans up against Hunter's side. He sits in silence just as he promised, appearing to take in only the scents, sights, and sounds of the timberland. While she begins to write, he closes his eyes as if practicing the meditation technique she had taught him.


*Hey Dad*

*Hey Dad, I'm missing you. I know that you wouldn't want me to.*
*You gave your life all for God and country.*
*You taught me the love for everything.*
*Do you have wings? I'd bet my life.*

*For you, I always was the right time.*
*Because of you, there're tears in my eyes.*
*All because I miss your love.*

*Hey Dad, I'm missing you. I loved you more than you ever knew.*
*Your guiding hand, so greatly missed right here now.*
*Guess that I'll carry on somehow.*
*Thanks for your love. Thanks for your smile.*

*For you, I always was the right time.*
*Because of you, there're tears in my eyes.*
*Love like yours is not lost in time.*

*And when I see you next time.*
*And when the seasons are gone.*
*And when I feel you next time, as we walk along.*
*We will plant a garden.*
*And it will grow forever strong.*
*And we can live the promise and bask in the sun.*
*There will be no more crying.*
*There will be no more pain or no wrongs.*
*And there will be a next time that moves us along.*

*Hey Dad, I still love you. Hard to think that you're gone so soon.*
*So many things I'd like to say*
*of how I will cherish every day we had.*
*Should I find wings, I'll be by your side.*

Julie breaks from her task. "I think that's what I want to say." She lays the tablet down for him to read. He smiles at her as he reads the poem.

"Wow," Hunter replies. He sets the pad down on the table. "That is truly a special piece, Julie. There is no doubt you loved him very much."

Julie falls into his open arms, hugging him as tightly as she can. She looks down at the tablet as he returns her embrace. A sense of closure appears to come over her as she whispers the words, "Goodbye, daddy."

# Chapter 34

## Southside with the Angels

HUNTER ARRIVES HOME FROM WORK the next day, and he props open the door just as his phone begins to ring. He notices Zoey's icon on the screen and answers the call.

"Hello," he says.

'Hi, Hunter. It's Zoey."

"Hi, Zoey. How are you today?"

"I'm all right, but I'm still a little concerned."

"Yeah. What are you concerned about?"

"I am still concerned about Julie. She seems like she is getting better. It really helped you spending the day with her yesterday. But I think she misses being with you as much as she misses being in the band. I know she needs you more. After you left yesterday, she sat and just stared off out the window like some heavily sedated patient in a psych ward."

"Not good."

"No, it's not good. I know she would start feeling a lot better if you would come around even more, so I have a plan."

"Another plan. Good. What is it?"

"There is this community festival that we went to last year with LaShonda."

"Okay, I'm with you so far."

"It's on the south side of town, and it's called the Southside Fest. It is a day-long event that raises money for kids while celebrating the community. It's like a fair with all sorts of games for kids and a fashion show for the youth. They can win prizes, and there is food from, like, heaven!"

"Food? Do tell."

"Yeah, food. Really great food. We help get the talent show off for the kids then we sit and eat all day long. It's so good. Anyway, LaShonda and I were hoping you could come with us. It will be fun."

"Zoey, I will do whatever it takes to get her feeling better and back on her feet. Tell me what to do, and I will be there."

"Great, it's this Saturday. Do you know where the bridge is on Cayuga Street, two blocks down from the police station?"

"Ha, well, considering I can see that very bridge from my apartment, yes, I do."

"Oh, cool. I did not know that. Okay, we will meet you there. Be on that bridge at 11 a.m."

"So all three of you are my date. Great, it's a date, Zoey."

"I knew I could count on you, Hunter. I'll see you then. Ciao for now."

"Okay, bye, Zoey." Hunter hangs up the phone and sets it on the table.

Chris suddenly appears in Hunter's doorway. "Hey, what's going on? When are we practicing again?"

"I thought I heard you coming up the stairs. Yeah, that's a great question."

"Have you talked to Julie? It seems that since she left, everything is on hold. Chad and Franklin want to know when we're getting together again? Well, I would like to know as well. We aren't going to bag this thing, are we?"

Hunter lets out a huge sigh. "No, we can't let it die. It has come so far. I hate setbacks, and that would be a serious setback," Hunter replies.

"The best way to deal with setbacks is to fall forward, isn't it?" Chris asks.

"Yes, I guess it is. I think Julie is starting to come around, but we better start practicing again without her, at least until she is ready. Let's shoot for tomorrow night. Can you call everyone for me?"

"Yes, I will. Scratch popped by this afternoon, and he suggested that I shove a cattle prod up your ass to get you moving. I think he's getting antsy to play out."

"Yeah, I bet he is. So, yeah, let's do it tomorrow night at six at the lake house," Hunter says. A distinct degree of enthusiasm resonates in his voice.

"What are you doing the next day? Saturday, there is a festival over at the Southside Center."

"I was just told about that. Zoey called me and wants me to escort her, LaShonda, and Julie to it. So I intend to attend."

"Cool. You'll love it. I went last year. I ended up eating so much food that I had to go home and sleep it off."

"Sounds like a good plan. I look forward to it," Hunter replies.


SATURDAY ARRIVES, AND Hunter takes his time making himself presentable. As the hour of the rendezvous approaches, he walks down the stairs and into the late morning sunshine. His neighbor, who regularly sells freshly cut flowers, is out tending to his garden.

"Sure is a beautiful garden, mister," Hunter says to the older gentleman. He stops to admire the flowers, paying particular attention to the freshly blooming hibiscus. "I think it is the most magnificent in all the entire city."

"Thank you. Getting hard any more to keep up with it and all," the old man replies.

"Do you have any flowers for sale today?" Hunter asks.

"I always have some flowers for sale. What kind do you want? I have lots of Iris today. I have the purple ones there, and some yellow and white one's outback."

"How about the hibiscus?"

"Oh, them there are not for sale. Them there is momma's prize possession. You'd done get me in a whole lot of trouble cutting any of them off. I can't do that," he replies. He pulls out a handkerchief and rubs the back of his neck.

Hunter looks at the three most perfectly blooming flowers and reaches into his pocket to grab his wallet. "I will give you twenty dollars apiece for three of them," he says. He pulls out some money, holding it out for him to take.

"Which ones you want?" the man asks. He takes the money, then looks up to his kitchen window. He slips the money into his pocket, quickly turning his attention back to Hunter.

"Those two smaller yellow ones and that larger red one, please."

"Must be a fine, fine lady to pay that kind of money, son. Treat her well now, you hear?" the old man says. "That way, you'll be needing more flowers. Then you can come treat me right again in order to treat her right some more." The old man puffs out a laugh as he reaches into his pants and retrieves a small pocket knife. He carefully cuts the flowers at the base of their stem and hands them one by one to Hunter. "You come back anytime, son."

"Will do, sir. Thank you," Hunter says. He proceeds to the bridge as planned and unbuttons both of his cuffs. He gently tucks the two yellow flowers under his right sleeve and buttons the cuff. Carefully, he positions the stems for easy retrieval from their hiding spot. He then places the red flower under his left sleeve the same way as the other two, dropping his arms to his side to assure they don't fall out.

He grins as he looks up to see Julie and her roommates come into view. As the girls greet him, he yells, "Stop, LaShonda! Don't move." He reaches behind her ear and pulls out both the yellow flowers, handing one to her and the other to Zoey.

"Awww," the two simultaneously coo.

"Hi," he smiles as he greets Julie. "Don't move," he says softly. He reaches behind her ear, pulling out the red flower, displaying it before her eyes.

Zoey had taken the time to create a waterfall braid for Julie, and Hunter tucks the flower in one of the ropes. It complements her white Martinique Dress, and the flower makes her look like a fairy tale princess.

"Can I have a hug?" Hunter asks as he opens his arms. Julie immediately falls into them, and Hunter holds her tightly.

He escorts the three girls through the fairgrounds, where they run into Chris and Jenny. The group wanders around together, enjoying the atmosphere of the carnival.

"Don't look now, but that girl that Julie hates is heading right this way,"

Zoey whispers to LaShonda. They both watch Julie's smile disappear when she sees Scratch and the two beautiful redheads.

"Well, hello, Miss Julie. So nice to see you out and about today. You look like a princess, just in case you were not aware," Scratch says. Aphrodite and Naamah look on, appearing uninterested in Scratch's compliment.

"Thank you, Scratch," Julie replies.

"Love the flower. It is such an exquisite touch. I take it you and Hunter have worked things out?" he asks. Naamah looks at Julie with an artificial smile.

"Yes," she says. She glances at both Naamah and Aphrodite. "Yes, in fact, we have."

"Oh, goodie. That's great," Scratch says. "I am really sorry to hear about your father, Miss Julie. My utmost condolences."

"Thank you." She folds her arms as she looks across the fairgrounds.

"Does this mean, Hunter, that Miss Julie will be joining us back at practice soon?" he asks.

"We haven't gotten that far yet. Julie has a lot on her mind at the moment. When she thinks she's ready, we'll see."

JENNY RETRIEVES HER phone and quickly dispatches a text message to Oliver. 'Help, please,' is instantaneously displayed on the text monitor that Oliver is manning.

"That's odd," Oliver says.

"What is it now?" Drake asks. He looks over at Oliver's data station.

"Jenny texted for help. It is the first time she has sent a text," Oliver replies.

"I see. I will bring her up on the main screen, Oliver." The two angels watch the developing situation unfold. "It's him again. I knew he would not let up. He is trying to upset Julie," Drake says.

"What do we do, Drake?"

"Get him away from them is what you do. Julie is vulnerable. Get him and those two evil mistresses away from them now."

"How do I do that, Drake?"

"You get him off his game," he replies.

"Oh. All right." Oliver looks back at his station controls on the viewing screen's taskbar. Drake watches on with a little concern. "Uhm, how do I do that, Drake?" Oliver asks.

"Why don't you send Raguel a message? He makes the wicked one very uneasy," he suggests.

"Hey, that's a great idea," Oliver says. Acting on the suggestion, he quickly dispatches an urgent text to Raguel. Within seconds, Drake and Oliver observe a hue coming onto the screen. "That must be him," Oliver says.

"Yes, it is," Drake replies. He pats Oliver on the shoulder.

Raguel walks down the street directly toward Scratch and his temptresses. He approaches from behind as he begins to recite scripture. Scratch and his two vixens turn their heads as they hear their nemesis's words. "You believe that there is one God. Good! Even the demons believe that and shudder," Raguel speaks loudly for all to hear.

Aphrodite and Naamah yield a look of concern, not wanting to confront a man who is citing scripture. Jenny, however, seems to rejoice in observing Scratch and his demons' uneasiness.

Raguel looks directly at Julie. "Finally, be strong in the Lord and in his mighty power. Put on the full armor of God so that you can take your stand against the devil's schemes."

"How did those scriptures work out for you there, homeless man?" Scratch asks. "You ought to ask God for a job and some goddamn deodorant, you bloody little vagrant. This here is a block party, not a platform for your bloody scriptures. Have a little common sense, man, and move along."

Julie's eyes open wide as she glares at Scratch, "That's enough! Common sense, like common courtesy, isn't so common anymore, Scratch. That man is down on his luck and still has faith in God. So you stop it right now!"

"Right. I'm sorry, Miss Julie. We'll just ignore the tramp. Sorry," Scratch replies.

She reaches into her purse and hands some money to the hobo as she looks at Scratch in disgust. Raguel takes the offering, bowing before her as he takes the gift.

"Ah, thank you, my lady. Zephaniah 3:17 states for the Lord your God is living among you. He is a mighty savior. He will take delight in you with gladness. With his love, He will calm all your fears. He will rejoice over you with joyful songs." Raguel begins to walk backward and raises his hands toward the sky. "John 4:4. Ye are of God, little children, and have overcome them: because greater is He that is in you, than he that is in the world."

Scratch scowls with a look of contempt.

Chris attempts to change the subject as the hobo walks away. "Right, well, I smell sausage. You guys hungry?" he asks.

"You have a great sense of smell, Chris, so your job is to lead us to it," Hunter replies.

"You kids, go get your sandwiches. The girls and I are heading over to the Commons for a cuppa. I'm buying if any of you would like to join us."

"A cuppa. What is a cuppa?" Chris asks.

"A cuppa tea then maybe a gin chaser. I don't know yet. Maybe some Island Rum. We'll see. Miss Julie, again it was a pleasure to see you out and about. Have a wonderful day," Scratch says as he turns away.

Hunter reaches into his pocket and hands Chris a $100 bill. "Julie and I will grab that picnic table over in the shade," he says. "My treat. Take the girls over and buy everyone lunch, would you?" he asks.

Chris looks over his shoulder, watching Scratch leave. He takes the money from Hunter as he smiles. "Yes. Right. Well. Indeed. Smashing idea. Be right back, old chum," he says in an English accent.

Hunter and Julie find an open picnic table. As they sit down, he takes the opportunity to whisper in her ear, "You're the reason I sing, and that's why I love you." She turns to look into his eyes.

"I love you, too," she says like a scared little girl.

"Would it be too soon to ask you for a kiss?"

Julie shakes her head *no* and she slowly closes her eyes. Hunter places his hands upon her face and kisses her. She smiles ever so slightly as he takes her hand.

"Do you like Scratch as a person?" Julie asks.

Hunter looks at her, perplexed. "Sometimes, I don't know. Why?"

"He just is such a cold individual."

"Yeah. I imagine he has had a pretty hard life."

"Well, do you think he would change if your band makes it big?"

"I was kind of hoping you might start to think about referring to it again as *our* band."

Sadness flashes through Julie's eyes and across her face.

"What's wrong, kid?" Hunter asks.

"I just get a bad feeling about him. I find myself praying that he wasn't in the picture."

Hunter sighs. "He's not easily replaced, Julie. The guy knows the guitar. Do you know anyone on campus as good?"

"No. Unfortunately, I don't. I know he is a great guitar player. I just don't think he is a great human being."

Hunter sighs again. "What do you want me to do?"

"I don't know. I just pray someone would come along who is better."

"Well, Scratch knows musical theory like the back of his hands. He certainly has his shortcomings but finding an even more brilliant guitar player is a challenging task at best. Your happiness is more important, though. Why don't you start looking a little closer in that music school of yours? Maybe someone is there you don't know about and the right piece to our puzzle. I know Scratch does tend to irritate, and with that in mind, he is a bit toxic."

"A bit toxic? Lemons are a bit toxic. He is the full-blown vat of acid," she says with the hint of a smile.

Hunter laughs at her remark. "Well, if you have been praying, then pray a little harder. The bottom line is this. I love you and will do anything to make you happy. Just don't force me to shoot the horse in the back forty and have to walk to town hoping a new horse is there to buy. Do you know what I mean? At least let me ride the horse into town before I shoot him."

"I won't make you shoot him, Hunter. I'd rather pull the trigger myself."

"That's the spirit. I love you." He kisses her again. "Will you come back to the band?"

"We'll see." She smiles a little more at the thought. "What do you really know about him? Do you know anything about his past?" Julie asks.

"No. That I do not." Hunter smiles as Chris, and the girls return with a tray loaded with food and drinks.

"Auntie LaShonda," a little girl shrieks from the crowd. She rushes up to the bench, and the child leaps into her arms. Her wide eyes and youthful exuberance distract the two lovers from their conversation as she captivates the attention of everyone seated at the table.

"What are you doing, girlfriend?" LaShonda asks her little niece.

"I'm going to be in a fashion show," she declares with excitement. "Mommy made me this dress."

"Oh, look at you," LaShonda says. She grabs the child and gives her a big hug. "Twirl around for everyone to see," she tells her. She takes the child's fingers, spinning her like a ballerina. "You go," LaShonda says with delight.

LaShonda's sister approaches, following the little girl to the table. "Hi," her sister says.

"Hi," LaShonda replies.

"That dress is simply adorable," Zoey says to her sister. She pushes her glasses up as she looks at the child.

"Thank you. She is entered into the show today. It's going to be her first walk down the catwalk," the mother replies.

"You're going to walk down the catwalk?" Zoey asks the little girl.

"Yes. I'm going to fling my bling and dominate this thing," the child replies. The group all laugh at the girl's catchy phrase and her undeniable spirit.

"You be nice about it if you win," her aunt advises. "You hear me?"

"Uh-huh." The little girl nods her head, looking down as if being scolded.

"And if another girl wins, you go up and congratulate her."

"Okay, Aunt LaShonda."

LaShonda looks suspiciously at her sister. "You pregnant again?" she asks.

Her sister's smile reveals the hope and warmth of an expecting mother.

"Girl, you are going to have ten kids before you are thirty years old if you don't slow down."

"No, I won't. But you are going to be an Auntie again."

LaShonda looks to her little niece with a wide smile. "You're going to have a brother or sister, girlfriend. You excited?" she asks the child.

"Sure am!"

"Are you going to share all the toys you got?" she asks her niece.

"No way. He can go get his own toys. Auntie LaShonda, are you going to be a judge at the show for me?"

"That wouldn't be fair, darling. That would be a conflict of interest."

"What's that?" she asks.

"It's a way of being sneaky. Like when you are up snooping around at Christmas time."

The child lowers her head as her mom stares with a look of suspicion.

"I ain't snoopin' around at Christmas time," the child says. Her mannerism suggests quite the contrary as the child breaks eye contact and looks down at her shoes.

"Uh-huh," her mother replies.

"Well, if I were a judge, it would be like stacking the deck in your favor. That would not be right."

"What's wrong with that?" the child asks.

"When you grow up, and the law finds you to have a conflict of interest, you can go to jail for it."

The child looks up with widened eyes. "You do?" she asks.

Zoey joins in the conversation, supporting her roommate's lesson. "Yes, ma'am, you do," she says.

"I could go to jail if Aunt LaShonda sits on the judge's panel?" the little girl asks Zoey.

"Well, you might not, but your auntie would possibly come under a whole lot of trouble if people found out about her conflict of interest," Zoey replies.

The little girl looks with fear to her aunt, trying to make sense of the concept. "She could go to jail then?" the child asks.

"Yes, then the police would have to take her away. We don't want that to happen, do we?" Zoey asks in a warm and sensitive voice.

"No, ma'am." The child shakes her head at the thought.

"Good, because we sure don't want that either," Zoey replies.

"Can you be a judge?" the child asks Zoey.

Zoey smiles at the little girl. "Well, I could because I am not related to you, but I would have to be an impartial Judge. And I would be impartial. Even though I know you, I could still be an impartial judge. I would vote for the absolute best presentation, even if that means that one of your friends has a better package."

"Impartial?" The child looks at her, confused by the unfamiliar word.

"Yes, impartial. It means to treat everybody equally," Zoey replies.

"You mean that you might vote for someone else, not me?"

"Yes, if they have a better presentation than yours, I would have to vote for them."

"Then where do I find someone not impartial?" the child asks. Laughter erupts once again at the table of friends.

"Child, you aren't listening to what Miss Zoey is saying. You need to play fair. If you are second best, you learn from it and make your next attempt better. You understand me?" LaShonda asks.

"Yes, I understand." She looks down again at her feet.

"We have to go. They want her there before 11:30 to register," LaShonda's sister says.

"Bye, Auntie LaShonda," the girl says with excitement.

"Bye, my dear. Give me a hug and a kiss," she says. She opens her arms, and the child obliges.

"That child is simply adorable," Julie says in affection.

They watch the child walk away with her mother, and the group continues with their conversations. The girls talk about school, professors, and their struggles. Chris joins in on the girl's conversation as Hunter takes out his pad and begins to write.


_A Southside Serenade_

_Come to me on the wind. If I could just see you again._
_Sometimes you're the song that you will sing,_
_and it's a Southside Serenade._

*If I could see all the way,*
*always know that there's no shame.*
*It is just life's game it seems to play*
*to the Southside Serenade*

*They might sing it over there, but while you and I are near,*
*let's gather closer, get over here.*
*We'll sing a Southside Serenade.*

*In the end, if I should find you,*
*I'll cradle you. You cradle me.*
*We can both try just to fight it,*
*I'll cradle you. You cradle me*

*Hope is always around the corner.*
*That is how we all should live.*
*To a sphere there are no borders.*
*If you should ask, I'll try to give.*

*Sometimes you lose, sometimes you win.*
*It's just a sign of the times we're in.*
*But you can't start, 'till you begin.*
*Sing the Southside Serenade.*

*I can see, by and by. Along this weary road, I'll try,*
*just to find a nice place to die, singing a Southside Serenade.*

*There are always things we never know,*
*always colder than the snow.*
*Maybe we'll find someplace to go and sing our Southside Serenade.*

*If your heart is there behind you, on a road that never mends.*
*Then that's the choice that will define you.*
*I'll cradle you. You cradle me.*

*And if you choose hope to refine you,*
*then my help I will always lend.*
*Then that's how I will define you.*
*I'll cradle you. You cradle me.*

# Chapter 35

## If Your Heart is Pure

HUNTER AND JULIE FULLY REKINDLE THEIR relationship and make up for the lost time. Their commitment to each other leads to them spending every available moment together. They manage to find a little downtime one lazy afternoon. Hunter holds Julie as they snuggle together on the couch, watching a music documentary.

"Promise me something." She rolls over in his arms and looks at him.

"Anything that keeps that smile on your pretty face," he replies.

"Promise me that you will never leave me."

"Okay, I promise. I will never leave you."

Julie places her hands behind Hunter's head, pulling him into her smooth, soft lips. "This is your lucky day, Hunter Watkins," she says. He looks at her with curiosity as she raises her eyebrows, grinning on only one side of her face.

"Yeah? Why is that?" he asks.

"Because nobody's here, and I am going to take advantage of you." She stands up and begins to walk to her room. She removes her tank top as she climbs the stairs. She looks over her shoulder at him, curling her finger for him to follow.

"Oh," Hunter says with surprise. "I guess it is." He follows her without hesitation, watching her every move.

She turns to face him at her bedroom doorway, untying the string to her sweatpants as he draws ever closer. She steps out of them as they fall to the floor. He quickly removes his t-shirt, and they kiss as she leads him into her room. They fall onto the bed, exploring each other slowly and sensually, as lovers do. Amid their arousal, Julie rolls on top of Hunter, pushing him onto his back. He lays his hands on her hips as she guides him inside.

When they finish making love, Julie pulls his arm over her as they cuddle. She holds his hand close to her chest as he kisses her neck, relaxing for several minutes in the serenity of the moment. "I love you," he whispers. She smiles as she kisses his hand, whispering back to him the same.

"Okay, I want some ice cream now," Julie says. She leaps from the bed and begins to rummage through her chest of drawers.

"Then let's go get ice cream." He laughs as she looks through her clothes. She retrieves a matching set of undergarments and quickly puts them on.

She looks at him a moment, appearing suspended in thought. "Actually, I want lunch first, then some ice cream," she says. He shakes his head as she turns back to her dresser, watching her as she puts on her Ithaca College sweatshirt.

"Lunch it is," he replies. He lays there, continuing to marvel at her as she jumps into her jeans. He smiles as she lays on the bed, wrestling them over her hips. "Are you coming ... boy?" she asks.

"I just did, twice. Third time's always a charm, though," he replies. His eyes seem to sparkle as he looks at her. He rises from the bed. Taking her into his arms, he kisses her once again.

"Get dressed, and we'll go," she says. She kisses him once more, then turns away, walking across the hallway and into the bathroom.

The two make their way to the Ithaca Commons, taking a seat in the sun at the Mahogany Grill. "Can I start you both off with a drink?" the waitress asks. She hands them a menu and retrieves her pad.

"Two iced teas, three lemons in both, if you would, please," Hunter says.

"Sure, I'll be right back," she says.

Julie lifts her sunglasses to look over the menu, then notices out of the corner of her eye the hobo who recites the scripture. He steps up onto the elevated gazebo. She puts her menu down and listens as he begins his sermon.

"Who can find a virtuous woman? For her price is far above rubies. He who finds a wife finds what is good and receives favor from the lord," Raguel shouts out. "Therefore, I tell you, whatever you ask for in prayer, believe that you have received it, and it will be yours."

Julie studies Hunter, watching his reaction to the street preacher's biblical professing. He tilts his head slightly, and his eyes squint as if perplexed by the hobo's statements. She smiles as if adoring his youthful look of concentration.

"What's the matter?" she asks.

"If I asked you to marry me, would you?"

"Hunter." She smiles with surprise.

"Would you?"

"You don't ask a girl for the answer to that question before you ever ask it."

"Would you?"

"I think you know the answer, Hunter."

"I thought I lost you. I don't ever want to feel that way again," he says. He lays his hand across hers.

"Neither do I," Julie replies. She smiles at him as he squeezes her hand.

The hobo catches Julie's eye as he vacates his elevated platform. He begins to walk along the sidewalk toward the couple, preaching as he waves his hands toward the Heavens. "John 14:27 tells us 'Peace I leave with you. Let not your hearts be troubled, neither let them be afraid.'"

He continues to look directly at Julie as he speaks. She smiles and reaches into her pocket.

"What are you doing?" Hunter asks.

"Here," she says. She hands the hobo some money. "And thank you, I really appreciate your sermons."

"Thank you once again, my lady," he replies. He begins speaking directly to Hunter, "Treat her well, my son. Treat her well. May you both have a blessed day." He waves his hands around them.

"You too," Julie says as the drifter wanders off.

"That's some odd shit," Hunter says.

"Hunter, the man is down on his luck. He is probably homeless."

"What I mean is, it's as if he always seems to know exactly what is on my mind. It's like he has some sort of connection to what I am thinking. I find him fascinating, really," Hunter confesses.

"Well, he speaks the word of God. What do you expect? We're all connected. Jesus said that, 'the Kingdom of God is within you.'"

"That makes a lot of sense. I guess I don't think about God enough." Hunter glances back toward the vagrant as he disappears around the corner.

"When you think about God, what goes through your mind?" Julie asks.

"Well, it is like you just said, there seems to be a connection to him. I guess I hear the right from the wrong in my mind. That's probably him, I guess. There has to be something greater than us all to have created the heavens and Earth. And it makes sense that we're all connected in that way. So I certainly believe in God. Because of that, I believe in the man named Jesus."

"Did your parents ever take you to church?" she asks.

"No. They never did. They both believe deeply in God, though. However, my father sees religion as man-made, and he believes that religion uses rhetoric as weapons against people in some instances. He wanted me to develop into a free-thinker, and if that leads me to God, then that leads me to God."

"Why does he think they use it as a weapon?"

"That's a good question. Look at Ireland. You have a country made up mostly of Christians. For years Protestants pitted themselves against Catholics. Though the conflict was mostly political, Christians killed fellow Christians. Thou shall not kill, right? How many have died for their sect Christianity that is supposed to operate in the name of Jesus Christ?"

"A lot, I guess." Her voice seems saddened as she responds.

"What about you? Did you go to church growing up?" he asks.

"Yes. My parents took me to church every week until they got so busy that it became infrequent. As I grew older, Daddy began traveling all over the world, and mom immersed herself in work as well. We slowly stopped going by the time I entered high school."

"So why don't you continue to go since you've been here at school?" Hunter asks.

"Well, I am extremely busy on Sundays. My classes require a lot of time. I usually practice, study, write papers, or prep for tests all week long."

"But you are supposed to rest on Sundays. With that statement, I question, when will you get time to go to church?"

"I like to think that when life becomes a little less hectic."

"Does it ever become less hectic, Julie? You just said your parents' lives got hectic, didn't you?"

"Yes, I guess I did say that, didn't I?"

"If there is one thing I have learned, it's that you have to appreciate every day you are given and give thanks to God for every day you get. That much I try to do. That does not require religion. It does require faith in God and Jesus. You have to have faith in a higher being or power greater than yourself. It's so extra special that subscribing to religion means you allow other men to help form your viewpoint of what it's all about, instead of the scriptures themselves.

"But the scriptures can be confusing. That's why you should go to church so that elders can help with your understanding of God."

"I can tell I have not read as much of the Bible as you have, but I do believe. I think that's an essential thing if you are a Christian. You have to believe in Jesus and accept him as your savior, for He was so in touch with something so grand that He could do amazing things. That was the embodiment of God, and the testimony of Jesus creates faith for all of us."

"But the scriptures say to come together and rejoice. One verse says something like, 'For where two or three gather in my name, there I am with them.' Part of the purpose of the church is about having relationships with the people."

"Perfect, so aren't you and I talking about Him now, and don't you and I have a relationship?" he counters.

"Yes, that's true." She looks at him as if having an epiphany.

"So He is here. That did not require a church, did it?" Hunter asks.

"Well, no, but I bet that's how a church comes together. Two people in a community likely talk and decide to found one, I would imagine."

"Maybe, but the first thing you need is faith. Without it, those two people would never erect a church. There is nothing wrong with gathering at a church, don't get me wrong. The hard part is to find one where you feel that you fit in. You and I sit here and speak of the truth about God and the path to him through Jesus without the intrusion of religion, and He is here. And it is pure, and it is good, isn't it?"

"Yes, I guess it is. I guess you're right. I never thought about it that way," she replies.

"Do you know what is really interesting?"

"What?" she asks.

"Some churches are worried that they may have to shut their doors. Yet I read an article that about seventy-five percent of Americans say they try and talk to God."

"Really." She tilts her head sideways in curiosity.

"Really. And even more fascinating is that about thirty percent of them say that he answers them."

"That's fascinating."

"So you see, the church must do much more to attract people back, and the first way to do that is to provide activities for young people like us. Our generation believes every bit as much as other generations that there is a God. We just don't seem to go to church. But if churches catered more to us, then we would likely start attending services."

"I can't believe that you don't go to college. You have such a unique way of describing things. You should be a professor, Hunter."

"Well, maybe one day I will go to school. Right now, I want to take a chance on the music we're writing. I almost gave up on that dream. I was thinking about going to college, but it seemed that God wanted me to write again when you came along. Why? I don't know, but I immerse myself into doing this because He brought you into my life. So that is my studies at the moment. I feel that's my current direction given by God to go forth and spread a positive message to a world that is so terribly mixed up, confused, and in need of hope," he says.

"I am thinking about what you said. When I drive into town from New York City, there is a beautiful little church, just before Ithaca College. I keep telling myself that one Sunday, I am going to go there for service. Will you go with me next Sunday, if I make time?" She reaches out, touching his hand while batting her eyes.

"Is it an old 1800's era church with a big steeple?" he asks.

"Yes. It looks like something on a Christmas postcard. It is so pretty. Will you take me?"

"I know right where it is. I sometimes hunt up that way, not very far from there. I would be honored to go with you for my first church attendance, mainly because it is likely God telling you to take me there. You've got a date, Miss Christianson," he says. He leans over to kiss her, and she leans in, meeting him halfway.

The waitress returns with their libations. "Are you ready to order, or do you need a few more minutes?" she asks as she places their tea in front of them.

"I will have a Reuben," Julie says as she hands the menu back to the girl.

"Oh, that sounds good. Me too, please," Hunter says.

"I will put this right in for you. It will be about ten minutes," the waitress replies. They hand her the menus, and she turns back into the café.

"I have to use the ladies' room. I'll be right back," Julie says. She takes her purse from her lap and sets it in her chair as she rises from the table. Hunter watches her follow the waitress into the restaurant as he retrieves his pen and paper and begins to write.

_A Girl Like You_

_I can't wait until eternity ends for another like you._
_I've never had any better friend to compare them to you._

*There's nothing quite like an infinite sky.*
*That's what I see when I look into your eyes, and it's nice.*
*It seems so right, with a girl like you.*

*I would walk to the rainbow's end, around a mountain or two.*
*I would sail across the seven seas for just one rendezvous.*
*I get lost when I look into your eyes.*
*I'm not afraid, though, because it seems so nice. It seems so right.*
*With a girl like you. With a girl like you.*

*Because you're magic, and you're magical. Don't ever stray too far.*
*You're magic, you're magical, and I wonder who you are.*

*I can be all you want me to be if you want me to be.*
*I can see all you want me to see if you'll show it to me.*
*I fall in love as I look into your eyes.*
*So not afraid, though, because it seems so right. It seems so right.*
*With a girl like you. With a girl like you. With a girl like you*

# Chapter 36

## A Dear Old Friend

"OH, GOODIE, THE LATEST UPDATES are ready," Drake says to Oliver. Oliver smiles at Drake's state of happiness.

"Updates. Updates for what, Drake?" he asks.

"The updates that will make our life easier here at the Command Center. I have to go to the main computer room and restart everything. I'll be back in a few minutes," Drake says. He punches some information into his hand-held device as he leaves the room.

Oliver sits patiently watching the screen when it suddenly goes blank. As he waits, he turns in his chair to look down the Hallway of Eternity. Perplexed, he observes the sight and sound of a bouncing golf ball coming down the Hallway of Eternity straight toward him. The ball begins to lose its momentum and rolls into the control room, resting against the base of his chair. Oliver studies it and shakes his head at the oddity. He looks back down the hallway. His eyes open wide as he notices God and his caddy approach.

"Hello, Oliver. How are you today, my good man? Did you, by chance, see a golf ball come through here?" God asks. Oliver quickly stands up, thunderstruck at the sight of the Almighty, who seldom comes by the office.

"I'm good, Father. Thank you. "Yes, Father. It's right here." Oliver points to the ball.

"I know, Oliver. I was just toying with you," God replies. He laughs as he taps Oliver on the back.

Hobbs walks up to Oliver to assess the lie of the ball. "You might want to take the stroke on this one, Sir. I see no way to get a good swing at it where it rests up against the chair pedestal."

"Hmm," God says, appearing to ponder His options. As He stands looking, the computer reboots. It begins to broadcast music, signifying that the updates are complete. God looks up with a look of great delight.

"Oh, it is Bach's 'Jesu, Joy of Man's Desiring.' I love that one. It's a catchy little tune, isn't it, Hobbs?" he asks. He begins to conduct a pretend orchestra while the song plays out. Oliver and Hobbs both smile as they watch their boss.

"Yes, Sir. Yes, Sir, it is," Hobbs replies.

"Why is it doing that, Oliver?" God asks as he sits down to take a closer look at the data that races across the screen.

"Drake is performing some updates, Sir," he informs the All-Knowing. The Bach piece ends, and a gold cross flashes across the display.

"And why is it doing that?" he points as He winks at Hobbs.

"Good question, Father. Let's look." Oliver assesses the new computer platform that Drake has just installed. "Ah, it says in the fine print, Sir, to touch the cross icon on the screen."

"Oh. I Love it. Do you know what that will do?" God asks. Hobbs smiles as he looks over at God.

"Well, I suspect it will tell us if you touch it."

"Oh, may I please? I don't want to distract you from your duties," God says politely.

"I'm quite sure it won't be a problem, Sir. Please, be my guest."

"Oh, this is so exciting. Okay, if you insist. Ah, wait a minute. Drake won't get upset, will he? He kind of worries me sometimes. I think the job tends to stress him out more than I wish for him. Fortunately, you will come to be a great help to him, Oliver."

"I'm pretty sure he'll be fine with it, Sir. Nothing he can't fix while you finish your game."

"I have full faith he sure can, Oliver," God replies. "Okay, good, all right then, here we go." God carefully touches the screen, and a new command appears. "It says, 'to initiate a random act of kindness, touch here.'"

"Ah, there it is, Sir. Yes. If you touch it again, you will send the first suggestion to a mortal we are monitoring, to purchase a golden cross as a gift."

"Excellent. Let's do it! Ha." He laughs as He touches the screen. "I did it. I just did a good deed then, didn't I?" He looks at Oliver with excitement.

"Yes, indeed, you just did a good deed, Father," Oliver replies.

"Well, then, there you have it," He says. "Hobbs, doesn't that mean I can forego the penalty stroke and place the ball back into the fairway in exchange for doing a good deed?"

"I think we can substitute that as grounds for a Mulligan, yes, Sir," Hobbs replies.

"Excellent." He grabs Oliver by the shoulders. "Carry on, my good man. Keep up the excellent work, Oliver." He smiles and turns back to his caddy. "Grab that ball and wipe it down, will you please, Hobbs? Check it over to make sure it's not nicked. I find it hard to think that I sliced the ball that bad. I never slice," He says. He turns back to Oliver. "Have a blessed day, Oliver."

"Thank you, Sir," Oliver replies. He looks in awe as God and Hobbs disappear back down the hallway.

Oliver turns his attention to the computer and notices Julie in full view on the screen just as she enters a jewelry store.

"That one," she directs the salesman with her finger. "The gold necklace and cross with the diamond in the center."

"Oh, nice choice," the salesman compliments her. He pulls it from beneath the glass and hands it to her for inspection.

"It's lovely. Yes, I'll take it," she says. She smiles as she hands it back to the clerk and reaches for her credit card.

HUNTER IS WAITING FOR Julie on the porch when she arrives to escort him to rehearsal. She places the necklace into her hand as he approaches the vehicle. Hunter opens the back door, putting his guitar inside the SUV, then opens the passenger door.

"I got you something," she says.

"What?" he asks. He closes the door then looks over at her.

"This." She smiles as she reaches around his neck with the open chain and latches it, admiring the jewelry's glitter in the evening sunlight.

"It's a cross. Thank you. I have always meant to get one. It's perfect." He leans over and kisses her.

"I thought we should match when we're on stage."

"Yes, we should."

She begins to drive out of the parking lot. "Do you have everything?" she asks.

Hunter hesitates at the question and reaches into his pocket, displaying a look of bewilderment. "Good question," he replies. He starts to ferret through his pants pockets.

"What are you doing?" she asks.

"I thought I had a guitar pick, but I guess I don't."

"Do you want me to stop at the music store?"

"Yes, actually, that would be great."

"Which one?"

"The one on Adams Street. That's the closest one."

The two enter the music store hand-in-hand. In the process of paying, he and Julie notice the sound of musical perfection beginning to stream from the back of the room. Upon closer inspection, Hunter laughs, noticing that the music being performed is by an old friend he has not seen in several years. He grins like a wolf as he looks at Julie. She smiles with curiosity in observing his excitement. Hunter waves his hand for her to follow him.

"It's Pachelbel's Canon in D. That's one of my most favorite songs," she whispers. The musician plays with the perfection of a master, and the melody seems to please Julie, and she closes her eyes as she listens. Hunter claps as the guitar player finishes the classical piece. The musician looks up, unaware and surprised that someone has been listening. "Hunter? Hey man, how have you been?" the player asks. He stands to greet Hunter, shaking his hand in the process.

"I see that you learned a thing or two about a thing or two on classical music. That was beautiful, my friend. Where did you go to music school, Boston, wasn't it?" Hunter inquires.

"Yes, Berklee College of Music. I just graduated. I'm hanging out at the folks' house until something happens. What about you? What's up with your music? Are you still playing?"

"Yes, actually, this is Julie, our lead singer. Julie, this is Billy. We played together in a couple of bands when we were teenagers."

"Hi. I love that piece you were playing. 'Canon in D' is one of my favorites.

"Hey, you have great taste. It's mine too," Billy replies.

"I have friends who are learning that very piece," she says.

"Oh, do you go to Ithaca College?" Billy asks.

"Yes. I am a voice major," she replies.

"Oh, cool. I would love to hear you guys perform. Don't need a guitar player, do you?" he asks.

"Ah, Billy, it's Rock and Roll. You never know from one day to the next," Hunter replies.

"Keep me in mind if you do. I have student loans about to start, so I would like to find something on the side. They needed someone here to give lessons." He notices some customers coming into the store. "And I think this little guy coming in the door right now is who I'm supposed to meet. Give me a call later on, and we can go grab a drink and a pizza."

"I will do that. Maybe you can come out and jam for a few hours for the fun of it," Hunter suggests.

"For sure. Give me a call. I am available pretty much every night." The two quickly exchange phone numbers, and the guitar player turns to greet his new protégé.

Julie looks over at Hunter as she begins to drive off. "He is really good," she says.

"Yes, I heard that." Hunter nods his head as he smiles.

"I take that back. He is outstanding."

"Yes, I agree."

"Hunter, what do you think about replacing Scratch with your friend?"

"I knew you were going to ask that. As I said before, Scratch is an amazing guitar player, Julie. They don't come along like that every day, but we can audition him if you would like."

"Yes, I would like that. Your friend there is a much better player. I have heard professors who can't play that piece as well as he just did."

"We don't know if he could cover everything that Scratch does. That's a serious leap of faith to think he can, based on hearing just one piece, don't you think?"

"Not really. Did you observe how he played that piece? He didn't make one mistake, yet he never looked down at the fretboard. He knows it so well he just kept reading the music. Didn't you notice that?" she asks.

"No. I just noticed his perfection," he replies.

"He probably sleeps with a guitar. I hear a lot of gifted musicians every day. Not one of them has anything on your friend back there."

"Huh, he didn't look down, did he?" he replies.

"No, he didn't. What is even more impressive is that he didn't tap out the metering to it. I did, and he held perfect timing. He is every bit as good as Scratch. I think he is better. He's also younger and a lot better looking. That would help us market the band better," she pleads to his intellect, glancing at him as she drives.

"Okay, I will arrange a session with him. Classical music is one thing, but Rock and Roll, and its sounds effects, are quite another. Let's see what he can do."

"Who is your greatest idol, Hunter? I know it's not any recent modern star. Who is your ultimate idol?" she asks.

"John Lennon," he replies without hesitation.

"John Lennon. That's right. You don't have a picture in your room of anyone else. Why did you put a picture of John Lennon in your room?"

"I don't know. What does that have to do with anything?" he asks. He looks at her, appearing confused by the question.

"It has to do with affirmation. You put it on your wall to remind yourself of what you want in life. You see it, and you try to replicate it because you love what they stood for. It wasn't by chance you put it there. Your mind chose that representation because you love the Beatles. Don't you?" she asks.

"Yes, you know I do."

"Yes, I do know. You love their music. You love their movies. You love their message of peace, love, and hope. And so you put it there in your room. You see it when you wake up. You see it when you go to bed. You constantly bombard your mind with your greatest idol in hopes of finding a piece of his success one day. That's why it's there, for affirmation."

"Okay, maybe, Miss Freud, you are right. So what? What does that have to do with anything we're talking about?" he asks.

"Well, I studied the Beatles in a music appreciation class. The professor went a little further behind the scenes of their story. They fired Pete Best, a guy who gave the Beatles his all, in order to make it big. So tell me, what did your idol say about the replacement of Pete Best?"

"He said that Pete was a better drummer, but Ringo was a better Beatle."

"That's right. So they replaced the drummer in order to make it big?" she asks. A grin slowly comes over her face.

"I guess they did," he says. He squints his eyes and looks at her as if he has just been outsmarted.

"So maybe you should think about replacing Scratch with Bill, regardless, even if he isn't quite as good. Myself, I think he's better, and I certainly like him better."

"Scratch bothers you that much?"

"Yes, he does. He's rude, obnoxious, vulgar, and there is just something about him I don't trust," she replies. Julie's eyes narrow, and she shakes her head as she responds.

"I see." Hunter takes a deep breath.

"I was hoping it would resolve itself. But it hasn't, and he is the one who broke out the drugs and got you stoned. If he wasn't around, I doubt you would have done that."

"No, probably not."

"If you want to make it big, sometimes you have to do things that you don't want to do, Hunter. John Lennon didn't want to get rid of Pete Best. It's almost as if I can see us making it, but Scratch isn't in the picture."

"If you feel that strongly then I guess we should. I will ask Bill if he can commit to our project, but we need to handle this carefully."


OLIVER TOUCHES THE Severe Alert icon on the main control console in Heaven. A Red warning alert displays Hunter and Julie on the viewing screen and Chris in a side window. He listens in on the conversation as the two lovers drive closer to their destination. He instinctively reaches over, touching the icon to contact Jenny.

"Hello," Jenny says as she answers the call.

"Hello Krystal, I mean, hello, Jenny," Oliver replies.

She laughs at his absent-mindedness. "Hello, Oliver."

"It looks like we will need you to rendezvous with Chris again. The Universal Observation Device is showing some warning signs over the lake house. It appears it is time to pay them a visit tonight. Chris will be coming into your area momentarily. He's probably going to that little bagel shop near you on the Commons before he heads to practice. You need to be part of his evening's plans and tag along with him," Oliver advises.

"Okay. I think I see him walking down the hill from Ithaca College right now."

"You still have the bag of nuts Drake gave to you, correct?" Oliver asks.

"Yes. I used one on Hunter, but I still have two left," she replies.

"Good. It appears that Julie will be returning to the group tonight. You need to monitor the situation closely. When warnings show up like this on the main counsel, there is the distinct probability you may need to use one of the remaining nuts in your arsenal, so be ready," Oliver informs the angel.

"I will do my best."

"Of course you will. That's what secret angel agents on assignment do. Good luck," Oliver says. He terminates the communication, and Jenny begins to look around. She can see an empty table, and she positions herself in a café chair in Chris's oncoming path.

Chris smiles when he notices Jenny, and he walks with a quicker step to greet her. "Hey, girl, what are you doing?" he asks.

"Oh, hi Chris. How are you?" she replies. "I'm just sitting here soaking up some sun and debating what I'm going to do with the rest of this beautiful evening," she replies.

"Do you want to come along with me? I am going to grab a quick bite to eat, then head to practice out at the lake."

"Oh, that's a thought. Sure, why not?" she says excitedly.

"Well, let's go," he replies. He extends his hand to help her from her seat.

When Chris and Jenny arrive at the cottage, they find Chad, Franklin, and Scratch waiting on the patio. Chris notices that Scratch is smoking a joint. "Scratch, it may be a good idea to put that stuff away tonight. Julie is returning, and we all now know she does not like to be around it," Chris says in an amiable tone.

"Are you kidding me? Do you have a ball-peen hammer, because I would like to smack it on my bloody head? I thought she bloody quit! I thought we were going to do this without the little tart. Excuse my mouth, lass," he says to Jenny. She looks at him without expression.

"Well, Hunter and Julie are working things out. And I think it's safe to say that we all want her back in the band," Chad replies.

"Oh, I'm sorry. I thought we were focusing on him being the lead singer now, and everything was starting to sound phenomenal. Now we have to change everything back again. But if you boys want her back, then we bring her back," Scratch says.

Scratch, just chill, alright? She is the one who got this whole thing rolling. Not to mention it's what Hunter and the rest of us want, come on, man," Chris says.

"Yeah, well there you have it. Guess I will go practice and get ready for her Royal Highness," he says. He turns to go into the lake house. Franklin sits shaking his head, quietly playing scales on his unplugged bass guitar.

"I didn't think he would be like that about it," Chad says to Franklin.

"The dude can put off some seriously bad vibes," Franklin replies. He continues to shake his head. Hunter and Julie arrive as Scratch pierces the warm evening's air with a progression of dark sounding music scales.

"Great to see you, Julie," Chad says. He rises from the beach chair and gives her a big hug. "I am so glad you're back."

"Thank you," she replies.

"Wow, listen to those licks he is playing in the minor keys," Hunter says.

"It sounds like the devil's music," Julie replies.

"I think he met up with the Devil. He is in rare form tonight," Chris says.

"Really, why do you say that?" Hunter asks.

Chris hesitates as he looks at Julie. "I don't think he's thrilled that Julie is returning. When I told him, he asked if I had a ball-peen hammer so he could smack his bloody head with it," he informs.

"I wonder what his goddamn problem is." Hunter is visibly agitated by the revelation, and he looks at Chris with the eyes of an eagle. He enters the house and sets his guitar case down in the practice area. He watches Scratch as the guitarist plays a sweeping array of notes. Scratch briefly looks at Hunter as he increases the tempo with every measure he plays, shredding the progression with precision and fury.

"Nice. It's a bit loud, though, don't you think?" Hunter yells to him.

"What?" Scratch responds as he looks up again from his guitar. The cross that Hunter now wears proudly upon his chest catches Scratch's attention. He grins as he looks at it.

"Cool progression. It's a bit loud, don't you think?" Hunter yells a little louder.

Scratch stops playing and places his guitar on the stand. He reaches for his cigarette pack and takes out a smoke. "Rock and Roll is at its absolute best when it's loud and obnoxious. It's just part of the territory, really. Do you know what I mean?" he asks.

"Yeah, but there comes the point at which the pleasure oversteps the threshold of pain. I think you were standing on that line, Scratch," Hunter replies. "Oh, and from now on, smoke the cigarettes outside, please." Hunter turns to retrieve a guitar chord from his case.

"Yes, right well, there you have it. So I see Miss Julie is back. Does that mean you're bangin' her again, and we will have her gracing the microphone with her presence?"

"Hey, man, come on. Have a little class, all right?" Hunter looks at him like a wolf, ready for confrontation. He grits his teeth, and his eyes glare at the guitar player.

"Class. You want me to have a little class? Right. I thought we agreed to move on without her and that you would be our shining little star. Didn't we spend the last month rearranging all our material to promote you, or did I bloody miss something?"

"Scratch, she is a far better singer than I am, certainly far better looking. We worked things out. I would think you would be happy about that. Come on. This is a team effort to try and go somewhere."

"Yeah, I'm sorry mate, I just don't like wasting time, is all. And I guess if I had the chance to bend that pretty and petite little thing over regularly, I would be her little doggy boy, too. Hell, I'd sit wherever she goddamn told me to."

Hunter throws the guitar chord down by his amp and addresses Scratch's insults. "Hey man, what is your problem? I don't appreciate you talking about her like that, all right? She is a lady. She's not one of those little redheaded bimbos of yours," Hunter remarks.

"Ahhh, that's it. You don't like the thought of someone else bending her over, do ya? Yeah, that's it. Well, maybe that's just what she needs then is a good hard bend her over, and smack that tight little ass until she squeals like a goddamn little pig," Scratch replies.

Hunter takes a deep breath and turns to retrieve his guitar chord. Scratch edges into his personal space, pushing the limit of Hunter's patience. He warns his guitar player, "Scratch, don't get in my face. You don't ever want to go down that road."

"Yeah, you're right, mate, the only thing I want going down is that sweet little tart of yours on me bloody wanker. I'll give her the jewelry she really wants."

"If you don't get out of my face, Scratch, I am going to beat your sorry ass. I'm warning you right now. Why don't you take the night off? Go home, Scratch." Hunter stares him down, appearing more than ready to back up his promise.

"You, hah! Beat my ass?" Scratch laughs tauntingly. "I was the Liverpool boxing champ three years running, you little wanker. The only thing you could beat, mate, is your goddamn meat." Scratch is unrepentant, as he refuses to back out of Hunter's space.

Hearing the argument develop, the rest of the band begins to file into the room. Jenny lags behind them, watching through the serving station window. A look of concern envelopes her face as she listens to the tense situation that is developing. Jenny reaches for the white pouch inside her purse and retrieves the acorn that Drake had given her. With Scratch's back to her, she readies it in her hand.

Scratch puts the cigarette in his mouth and lights it, defying what Hunter had just told him. He takes a long drag off the cigarette, smiling in a snide and disrespectful manner. "Besides, I bet you hit like a little a bloody girl," he says in an attempt to taunt Hunter.

The angle of the angel is perfect, for no one can see her throw the acorn at Scratch's back. An array of light immediately scatters in all directions as the acorn finds its target. The Heavenly power held within the acorn stuns him just as Hunter swings at Scratch's outstretched jaw, momentarily frozen in time. The blow levels him as it jars his head across his right shoulder. Hunter instantly follows through with a powerful left hook to Scratch's nose. The guitar player stands only a moment as his eyes turn toward the heavens. He falls backward, and his head bounces as it strikes the ceramic tile floor.

Chris, Franklin, and Chad rush across the room to Hunter's side, attempting to break up what has already ended. Knocked out cold, Scratch twitches violently on the floor. Franklin moves quickly to check his vitals. Julie and Jenny place their hands over their mouths, Julie in shock and Jenny silently laughing in amusement.

"You, uh, got any new guitar players in mind, there, Hunter? I don't think he's going to want to come around and play with us much anymore," Franklin says. He looks up from the floor with a distinct grin on his face.

"Ask the son of a bitch if that was the hardest a little girl has ever hit his sorry ass," Hunter says in defiance. With his fist still clenched in rage and ready to distribute more cowboy diplomacy, Chris taps him on the shoulder, motioning him outside.

"I will definitely do that, Hunter, just as soon as he wakes up," Franklin replies. Hunter turns and walks with Chris to the beach. Julie and Jenny quickly follow, leaving Franklin and Chad to oversee Scratch's awakening.

"Did you have to hit him?" Julie asks.

"He deserved it. I refuse to listen to what he was saying about you. He's done. Chris, would you help that piece of shit with his gear to his car, please?" Hunter asks.

"Yes, Hunter. Just stay here and chill out with the girls. We will take care of it," he replies. He turns and heads back into the house.

"What did he say that made you have to hit him?" she asks.

"It's not worth repeating, Julie. Suffice it to say he is no longer in the band." He stares inside the picture window, waiting to see if the guitar player wants to try a second round.

Julie begins to rub his back, attempting to calm him down. They watch as Franklin and Chris finally help Scratch to his feet.

"I bet the asshole is going to have you arrested," Julie mutters.

"I would count on it," Jenny replies.

The boys help Scratch collect his gear and send him on his way. They join Hunter and the girls on the beach for an impromptu emergency band meeting.

"I hope you have some money for bail because he's going to have you arrested," Franklin says.

"We don't have to worry about that," Julie replies.

"So now what?" Franklin asks.

"Well, now we can call Hunter's friend, Bill," Julie replies. She puts on a defiant smile as if knowing her prayers have somehow been answered.

"Who is Bill?" Chad asks. He looks to Hunter for clarification.

"He's an old friend of mine who just got back into town. He just graduated from Berklee College of Music."

"Berklee? Well, do we want to try and get him here tonight, or should we just say screw it and drink some beers and fire up that there barbeque?" Franklin asks.

"Beers," Chad quickly replies.

"Definitely beers," Chris says. "We haven't had a good beer session in a while."

It isn't long before they all notice a sheriff's car coming down the driveway. Two deputies exit the vehicle and approach the kitchen door as Julie rises from her seat to let them into the cottage. She escorts them through the living room and out onto the patio.

Hunter laughs in knowing both of the deputies by name. "Officer Hoffman. Officer Odell. How are you both doing tonight?" Hunter asks.

"Hunter, what the hell did you do?" Officer Hoffman asks.

"Well, you know when a country boy tells you don't get in his face, it means don't get in his face," Hunter replies.

"You know you broke his nose, Hunter? And he likely has a severe concussion. You haven't been in a fight your whole life. What the hell has gotten into you?" Officer Hoffman asks.

"He was saying very disrespectful things about Julie. When he got in my face, I had enough."

"You can't go beating people up because you don't like what they're saying, Hunter. Come on. You are smarter than that. Why didn't you just ask him to leave?" Officer Odell asks.

"I told him to take the night off," he replies.

"Well, we need you to take a ride with us to the station, Hunter. He's pressing charges. We have no choice," Officer Hoffman informs.

"I understand," Hunter replies.

Officer Odell takes a set of handcuffs from his belt. "I have to put these on, Hunter, but I will allow you to have them in front of you if you like."

"Thanks, Officer Odell," he replies. He offers his wrists for the officer to complete the arrest.

"Is this an inconvenient time to ask you for your autograph, Hunter?" Officer Hoffman asks. Hunter laughs at the wisecrack, but Julie finds little amusement in the witticism.

Officer Odell notices her uneasiness with the situation, and he pulls her aside. "It's just a formality, ma'am. And we have known Hunter for a long time. We're going to process him then take him to Judge Gary up in Newfield for release as both the Ithaca and Trumansburg town judges are away on vacation this week. Do you know where the town hall is in Newfield? You can meet us there in about an hour. It will all be fine, ma'am. Cheer up, all right?"

Julie nods her head as a tear begins to swell in her eyes. The two officers take Hunter to the car and drive off to the sheriff's station.

Julie, Chris, and Jenny proceed directly to Newfield Town Court and wait in the court's parking lot until the deputies arrive. They follow the deputies and Hunter into the courtroom, taking a seat in the back row. The Judge emerges from his chamber and sits down at his desk. "Hunter Watkins, what are you doing in my courtroom, son?" Judge Gary asks.

Well, sir, I guess my attempt at appealing to a man's intellect failed miserably, and then he fell down, sir." The country Judge smiles and shakes his head.

"Hunter, you are charged with Assault in the 2$^{nd}$ Degree. This is a pretty serious offense. You are going to need an attorney."

"Yes, sir, I understand."

"Officer Hoffman, has he been civil with you and Officer Odell this evening?"

"Yes, sir. Hunter has been a perfect gentleman, Your Honor," Officer Hoffman informs the court.

"I would expect nothing less," Judge Gary replies. He begins to sign some of the paperwork.

"Well, I see no need to hold him for bail, do you officers?" he asks. He looks down from the bench awaiting a reply.

"No, Your Honor, I don't think he'll be a problem whatsoever," Officer Hoffman replies.

"Mr. Watkins, you are ordered by the court to keep your distance from the alleged victim. If you see him, then walk away. Do not approach or confront him. Do not contact him in any way as I am putting a temporary order of protection in place against you. Do you understand me, son?"

"Yes, sir, Your Honor. I understand," Hunter replies.

"I am scheduling your court date for August 6th at 6:00 p.m. Officers, please release him from the cuffs." Officer Hoffman takes his key and does as the Judge orders.

"Thank you, Your Honor. Have a nice evening," Hunter says.

"You too, Mr. Watkins." He rises from the bench and returns to his Judge's chambers.

# Chapter 37

## Outclassed by the Outcast

THE NEXT DAY JULIE AND HUNTER arrive at the lake house to work on some material, several hours before the other musicians. "We need a guitar player. Call your friend," Julie says. "Call him right now, Hunter. See if you can get him here tonight. I want him in the band."

"Yes, ma'am," Hunter says. He opens his eyes wide at her order, cocking his head back in surprise as if intimidated.

"And don't forget who came to bail you out. You owe me ... boy," she says.

"I seem to recollect that no bail was required."

"Yeah, well, none-the-less, you are my boy." She laughs as she grabs Hunter by his shirt and pulls him in close for a kiss.

"Since you put it that way." Hunter reciprocates in returning her affection, running his hands down her side. He attempts to wedge his fingers beneath her dark purple yoga pants as he caresses her flesh.

"Mmmm," she murmurs through their kiss. She pulls his hand away and steps back from him. "Maybe later, now call him." She turns away, and he watches her closely, staring at the lower half of her body as she walks toward the kitchen.

"Definitely later," he replies, too quietly for her to hear. He reaches over to the end table and picks up his phone. He dials the number, turning to look out at the lake as the phone begins to ring.

"Billy, it's Hunter. What's going on? Hey, we had a band meeting, and our guitar player unexpectedly dropped out. We were curious if you still wanted to jam and maybe join us this evening out at the lake? Great. We're getting together around six o'clock. We are just before Taughannock State Park. I forget the address. I will text it to you in a minute. Awesome. See you in a bit." Hunter hangs up the phone as Julie comes back into the living room.

"So he's coming?" she asks.

"Yes. He'll be here in a couple of hours."

"Good boy," Julie says. Her playfulness elicits an immediate response from Hunter.

"Boy? Boy? I'll show you, boy." He begins to chase her around the couch, quickly catching her. He lifts her in his arms as Julie lets out a lover's scream.

"No. Put me down." She laughs as she struggles, and Hunter throws her onto the couch, holding her wrists against the plush leather cushion.

"Who's the boy now?" he asks. Julie wiggles and moves her head from side to side as Hunter begins to suck on her neck. After a short struggle, Julie surrenders to the moment as he begins to help her out of her tank top. Just as Hunter takes off her shirt, he looks out the window to see Alex getting out of his car.

"Shit," he says.

"What?" she asks.

"Alex is here," he replies. Julie quickly pulls her top back on as Alex opens the kitchen door.

Alex looks at them through the serving station opening. "Am I interrupting anything?" he asks.

"Nothing I can't do later," Hunter replies. Julie slaps him across his backside as he rises from the couch.

"That's good because we have some things that we need to talk about," Alex says. The seriousness of his tone causes Hunter to look at him with concern.

Hunter joins him in the kitchen. "What is it?" he asks.

"Did you smack your guitar player around last night?" Alex asks. He lays some paperwork down on the countertop.

"He got what he deserved," Hunter replies. Perplexed, he looks at the packet.

"Well, I don't normally get involved with band disputes."

"He's not in the band anymore," Hunter replies.

"Well, that's not the issue now," Alex says. He looks back down at the paperwork.

Julie joins them at the counter. "What is at issue?" she asks.

"I just got done speaking with his attorney this morning. He hand-delivered this cease-and-desist order pertaining to the recordings you have been working on in the studio. You are not to have access to them. Further, he seeks to take possession of the recordings, claiming that his client owns all of the material. You can further expect a cease-and-desist order on playing any of that material out live at any event that you have scheduled until the court rules on the matter."

"What? Court? Hunter owns those songs. He wrote all of them," Julie snaps.

"I am just telling you what his attorney informed me. Looking at the date, he must have planned this for some time as it was dated two weeks ago. I am ordered not to touch the recordings until a judge hears the case."

"That son of a bitch. I'll fucking kill him," Hunter says angrily.

"Calm down. You'll do no such thing. We know you wrote them all. Take it easy. You have plenty of material you can play in the interim. At the moment, I suggest that you find a new guitar player and start writing some brand-new material. Maybe throw in more cover material for the moment. You always wanted to do some Beatles. Pull some old Lennon and McCartney stuff out and make it your own. It will give your band a new flair."

"That's great. That's just great. That son of a bitch." Hunter pounds his fists on the countertop.

"You will need a good attorney. I am sending you over to the Scherer Law Firm. Here is his number." He hands Hunter a card from the firm. "He'll be expecting you. I will obviously be a witness to your defense. I wouldn't worry. We all know who wrote the material. Just tell the attorney the whole story from when you met Scratch and took him into the band. The truth has a way of coming out in these proceedings, so don't get angry. Get even. Do you know what I mean?" Alex asks.

"Yeah. No problem, Alex. Thank you." Hunter looks at the card with rage in his eyes.

"How can he do this? He knows Hunter wrote all the lyrics," Julie asks.

"I don't know. All I know is that it's for real, and you and the band will have to either defend what you have written or let him steal it. Stay away from him, do you understand? Go talk to the attorney and see what he says. It is the only recourse you have at the moment. It seems that Scratch is a very crafty individual, and if he wins, all your material will be his. I had the attorney search for proceedings that he might be involved in. Counselor Scherer advised that at least six other suits exist that he is listed as the plaintiff, just here in the northeast.

"I knew it," Julie shouts. "I knew there was something about him I did not trust."

"I think he has some disputes down south as well, and he likely left there due to some southern boys chasing him out of town on a rail. Now call the attorney's office and make an appointment so we can get moving on finishing the album. Okay, Hunter?"

"Yes. Thanks, Alex. We will call him in a minute."

"Let me know what he says. I have to go."

Hunter walks back to the living room and sits down. Julie curls up next to him and places her head on his lap.

"Do you want me to call my mom?" she asks.

"No, she has enough on her mind." He looks at the card Alex gave him then reluctantly calls the phone number. "Hi," he says. "My name is Hunter Watkins. Yes, I am looking to retain counsel. No, I have not been there before.

Yes, I have the address. I need to speak with an attorney regarding a copyright dispute. Yes, I can be there tomorrow. Yes, ma'am, three o'clock will work fine. Thank you." Hunter disconnects the call and sets his phone on the end table. The two of them sit, staring out at the lake.

"Do you want me to come with you ... boy?" Julie asks. She rolls over on her back and looks up at him to watch the frown disappear from his face.

"You sure know how to cheer me up, don't you," he asks.

"I don't know. Do we still have a few hours before your friend gets here?" she asks. She bats her eyes as she bites her lip, answering his question with a question.

# Chapter 38

## Variation of the Vibe

HUNTER'S FRIEND BILLY ARRIVES AT the lake house right on schedule. Hunter steps out onto the patio to greet him and helps him with his equipment. Franklin instantly notices the guitar player's vintage Steinberger as he pulls it from its case.

"Your fretboard is scalloped, how cool is that! Did you do that or did the factory?" Franklin asks.

"Yes, I did that. It gives me a whole new dimension to playing leads," Billy replies.

"I bet it does. I have never met a guitar player bold enough to do that to his ax."

Bill turns on his amplifier and briefly begins to play. "Hey, Hunter, you and I wrote a few songs that I thought were awesome. I think you called one of the songs 'A Place Called Time' or something like that. I always really dug that song. Do you remember that one?" he asks. He begins to play the arrangement, which appears to refresh Hunter's memory.

"Oh, wow, I almost forgot that one. I can't believe that you still remember it, though. That would be a great song for Julie to sing," Hunter replies. "Let me write the words out real quick for her." He turns to the computer and begins to tap out the lyric sheet.

Bill plays the piece as Hunter writes. The other band members follow the new guitar player, quickly grasping the song's musical structure. Hunter finishes writing the lyrics and prints them off for Julie. He hands it to her, and she begins to read it as Hunter picks up his guitar.

"I love it. You sing it first," she urges.

Bill encourages the creative process to fully come into its own, quickly interjecting, "You should make it your own. It's much better creatively if you try and sing it without his influence."

"He's right. Sing how you feel it, Julie. It will be great," Hunter says in support.

"All right. If you insist," she replies. Julie smiles as she begins to sing the piece.


*A Place Called Time*


*"I've seen fireflies dancing on green oceans,*
*and little girls acting so precocious.*
*Sometimes I need a lot of focus.*
*Once in a while, I feel like life is hopeless.*

*I spent some time down in the gutter.*
*So many things in life that are really getting cluttered.*
*So I just wish well to all others.*
*Though sometimes I feel just like I'm being smothered.*

*Sing it out loud if you want to. Sing it out loud because you ought to.*
*You don't know when your eyes might see no more.*

*So much in life, I wished that I knew.*
*So many things I start and never get to.*

*It gives me cause to sing out these blues.*
*And here I am, writing a silly jazz muse.*

*Sing it out loud if you want to. Sing it out loud because you ought to.*
*You don't know when your eyes might see no more.*
*Sing it out loud, and get close too.*
*Sing it out loud. You're supposed to.*
*You don't know when your eyes might see no more,*
*of here and now in this place called time.*

*So much distraction in interactions, I find it hard to disengage.*
*In all your actions, be the attraction.*
*I keep my opinions locked up in a cage.*

*Sing it out loud if you want to. Sing it out loud because you ought to.*
*You don't know when your eyes might see no more.*
*Sing it out loud. It might make you feel new.*
*Sing it out loud because you're supposed to.*
*You don't know when your eyes might see no more.*

*Sing it out loud. It's a present. Sing it out loud like you're in Heaven.*
*You don't know when your eyes might see no more,*
*of here and now in this place called time.*
*Here and now in this place called time.*
*Here and now in this place called..."*

Bill compliments the girl as they finish the song. "Julie, you have an amazing voice."

The compliment instantly causes a Duchenne smile to emerge on Julie's face. "Thank you," she replies. The group performs the song several more times, then take a quick break on the patio. A sense of genuine camaraderie seems to permeate the encampment.

"I really enjoy your playing style, man. I understand that you went to Berklee. Is that correct?" Franklin asks the band's potential new member.

"I did. It was pricey, but a formalized study in music is an effective way to quickly advance your talents," Bill replies.

"It sure sounds like you got your money's worth. Nice playing with you for sure. Cheers," Franklin compliments as he raises his beer.

"Thanks."

"So you know, Bill, we have an album in the works," Hunter says. He hands Bill a portable storage device. "If you can learn all of these before next week, that would be ideal. The only thing about the material is you have to keep it completely confidential."

"That's not a problem. I can sit down and learn them all. But I have an eidetic memory, so I am good at picking things up from the first time hearing it played. If you play a recording of anything you have, I can cover any of them tonight," he replies.

"Eidetic? What is eidetic?" Chad asks.

"A photographic memory," Julie answers.

"So, you are like a walking computer?" Chris says. He begins to laugh.

"I don't know about that, but I am pretty good at recalling information, I guess," Bill replies.

The band sits and chats with Bill for a few more minutes. It is unanimous in letting him into the group, and they offer the position. He accepts the invitation, instantly placing the morale of the group on an unprecedented high. His talents more than rival that of Scratch. His personality, however, far exceeds that of the band's former member.

"Julie, can you cue up the songs for us, please?" Hunter asks.

"Yes," she happily replies.

They spend the evening working through much of the band's repertoire. Bill quickly captures the very essence of every song, adding much more depth, brilliance, and resonance to the music than the former player had created. By the end of the night, the band has a new sense of direction.

# Chapter 39

## Discomfort from the Decree

HUNTER AND JULIE MEET THEIR ATTORNEY at the United States District Court in Syracuse. The bailiff notices the Judge entering the courtroom, and he turns to announce his entry. "All rise, this court is now in session. The Honorable Judge Christopher David Humble is now presiding."

The Judge steps behind the bench and meticulously arranges the oak gavel and its base to his liking. The opposing parties sit anxiously waiting for him to speak. He takes a few moments to look over the preliminary evidence. "Will both counsels approach the bench, please?"

Hunter and Julie attempt to listen to the conversation. Scratch grins as if he's sure that the news will be favorable to his case.

"Thank you, counselors, you may return to your seats," the Judge says. He begins to address the opposing parties. "I have read this case with interest, and I'm going to proceed with a great deal of caution. I have paid particular attention to both parties' motions, and I am hereby granting a temporary cease-and-desist order against the defendants. I am scheduling a hearing for February 24th, at 12:00 p.m."

"Mr. Watkins and Ms. Christianson, this means that until this matter is settled, that you are both ordered not to play in public any of the material that stands in dispute. I am further ordering that the recordings in the studio are not to be accessed nor altered. You are further ordered to cease and desist from selling any merchandise that conveys any connection to the material in question. You are further ordered not to talk about this matter with any members of the media. Do you understand?"

Hunter nods his head in acknowledgment and lets out a sigh of disgust. "February?" he asks his attorney. The Judge immediately slams his gavel, releasing a loud crack that reverberates throughout the courtroom.

"Counselor, advise your client to control his emotions in my courtroom, or I will assure you that he'll not be playing any of these songs for the next year. Contempt of my court may result in him finding how hospitable I can be when I confine him to the county's public housing facilities. Do I make myself sufficiently clear?" the Judge asks.

The attorney immediately replies in acknowledgment, "Yes, sir. My client fully understands, sir. Thank you." He looks at Hunter, and he begins to whisper. "Whatever you do, remain calm and watch your emotional outbursts. I will handle this."

"I understand," Hunter whispers back.

"Now, are there any other issues before the court?" the Judge asks.

"There is one other item, Your Honor," the opposing counsel says. He stands with some paperwork in his hand. He offers it to the bailiff.

"What is it?" the Judge asks.

"It is a Motion for Summary Judgement."

"Counselor, the defendant is being given an ample opportunity to contend your client's ownership claims. I will give a time where you can file that in February."

"But Your Honor, under section ..."

The Judge slams his gavel on the oak plate, looking very unhappy with the attorney. "Silence!" he says. "I give every opportunity to settle things fairly and amicably in my courtroom as well as provide outside opportunity for two parties to settle things without the court having to impose a decision.

I hold more credentials in law, sir, than you'll ever be lucky enough to achieve, both in practice and here on the bench. I taught procedural law at Harvard, Cornell, and here in Syracuse, sir. So, if I tell you I am allowing the defendant the opportunity to dispute your client's claim, don't challenge it. It means that defendant has the opportunity to dispute your client's claim, period. Do I make myself sufficiently clear with you, Counselor?"

"Yes, Your Honor, sorry, sir. I thank you for your sage advice." The opposing attorney sits back down into his chair.

"Splendid. Now, if there are no further motions, I have a golf date with a dear old friend. Are there any other matters here today, counselors?" he asks.

"No further issues, sir," Counselor Scherer responds.

"No sir, thank you," the opposing attorney quietly replies.

Julie and Hunter follow their attorney out of the courtroom. As they enter the hallway, he advises the two on their case.

"As the Judge's orders are clear, I advise you immediately cut from your repertoire all music that has any connection to this case. Also, I advise that you do not use the band's name either until the matter is settled. Now, I need all original copies of handwritten lyrics, digital copies, or anything else that you might have of relevance. Without establishing ownership before the copyright filing, I'm afraid he will likely end up owning all of your music. I will be in touch if I receive any more paperwork from opposing counsel. In the interim, stay away from this guy. Do you understand?"

"Yes, I do. Thanks, Counselor. We will go through what we have," Hunter replies. Hunter and Julie leave together. Chad and Chris join them outside the courthouse.

"So this means we can't play any of the music? That's bullshit," Chad says.

"We need to start fresh. New material, new look, and a new name, it appears," Julie says.

"You mean we can't even play any of the material we wrote before that schmuck came along?" Chad asks.

"We're ordered to cease and desist from playing all the material in question. So yes, we can't play it," Julie replies.

In spite of the somber mood, Chris attempts to uplift the group's spirit. "So we just get busy writing some new material, that's all. That's all really good stuff, but we can do better. What do you say?" Chris asks.

"That's all we can do. I'm in. Let's start tomorrow, what do you say guys? The lake house, twelve o'clock, are you in?" Julie asks.

"For sure, I'm in," Chad says.

"All in." Chris replies.

"Hunter, what do you say?" Julie asks.

He looks at the three of them for a moment. Anger builds in his eyes as he nods his head. He appears phased by the emotional turmoil, but not defeated by it. "Yeah, I'm in. You bet your ass, I'm in," he replies.


THE TWO LOVERS DRIVE back to Ithaca. Hunter pulls into Stewart Park, parking on the edge of the lake. He drops the tailgate, and the two of them sit on the back of the truck, collecting their thoughts. Julie rests her head on his shoulders, and he puts his arm around her. He looks out at the lake in a glassy stare, and she takes his hand in hers. She breaks the silence as she begins to push Hunter to start thinking about some new material.

"Hunter, we have a set-back, not a knockout," she assures.

"I know. It's just that this crap takes a lot of steam out of me. It seems like it's always two steps forward in life, then bullshit happens, and it's ten goddamn steps backward."

"That's life sometimes, though. You are not the only one in life who has to deal with setbacks. When I first heard about you, I thought, wow, the guy got dealt an atrocious hand. But you know what?"

"What?" he reluctantly responds.

"You started picking yourself back up. That's what winners do. Winners never quit, Hunter. And that's one of the things I love most about you. Some men would have given up, but that's not in your spirit. Is it? You are destined for something big. I believe that God chooses people, special people, to convey words of hope through creativity."

"The creative mind is a blessing as well as a curse. I sometimes wish that I never picked up a stupid guitar."

"I am glad you did. Otherwise, we would never have met."

He looks at her and smiles at her words of truth. "Great point," he replies.

"And your mind is a blessing, not a curse. I believe God chooses people like you for a reason. Sometimes you have to go through a lot of pain to show other people that it is inherently part of life. It is what lets you know that you are alive. I know you have been through a lot. But the difference between you and other people, Hunter, is that you're not a quitter. You are a winner, a leader. And that is one of the many reasons I want to be with you."

Hunter looks at her with the hint of a smile. "That sounds like the same reasons I want to be with you."

"I love you," she whispers into his ear. She kisses him on the cheek, and he pulls her head back onto his shoulder. Desperate to change his depressed demeanor, she lifts her head off his shoulder and displays a look of excitement. "Your guitar is in the truck. Play me a song," she urges.

"I don't know, Julie. I just want to sit here a while and think. I'm not really in the mood right at the moment," he replies.

"Play me a song... boy!"

Her plan works brilliantly, for he smiles, quickly changing his mood.

"What would you like me to play?" he asks. He wedges in between her legs on the back of the tailgate. She folds her arms and rests them on his shoulders. She looks out over the lake as he strums an E minor chord. The 12 strings ring out in an airy restlessness.

"Play for me something uplifting, something new. I don't know. Come up with something. Maybe something that I can write a song to."

"All right, kid. Here is something new," he replies. He begins to fingerpick a captivating melodic progression. Instantly it makes her smile in hearing the soothing and harmonic phrasing. She looks down over his shoulder with a look of amazement as he plays.

"Hunter, do you know that metering is a Waltz?" she asks.

"Nope. I just play what comes in on my mental radio," he replies.

She closes her eyes as he continues to play. "I love it," she whispers.

# Chapter 40

## A Revelation in the Recording

JULIE AWAKENS THE NEXT MORNING wrapped in Hunter's arms. She looks at the writing tablet on top of his nightstand and reaches over to retrieve it and the pen. She rolls onto her stomach, tucking the pillow beneath her arms, and slowly begins to write. Each new sentence she writes appears to flow more quickly than the one before. As she finishes, she looks over at him, kissing him on the cheek as she rises from the bed.

She takes a shower then begins to dress as Hunter awakens from his sleep. She looks at him as he opens his eyes. "Good morning, sleepyhead. Are you going to get around?"

"Yes, I suppose I should. Unless you want to come back to bed, and I can help you out of those clothes."

"No, I don't think so. Maybe later, but we have to be at the lake house, so you need to get moving. Do you want some breakfast?" she asks.

"Yes, I do."

"Well, get up, get showered, and I will take you out to breakfast. So hurry up." She begins to hum the melody Hunter played for her the night before as she turns toward the kitchen. She spends a moment foraging through the cabinets for coffee, humming the melody over and over. Hearing Hunter in the shower, she begins to sing her new song.

She pours the coffee as Hunter comes into the kitchen. He grabs her from behind, kissing her on the neck. She turns around to face him, throwing her arms over his shoulder as he kisses her.

"Good morning," she says.

"Good morning," he replies. He looks at the clock as he takes the cup she poured for him. "It's only 8:30. Why are we getting up so early on a Saturday if we don't have to be there until noon?" he asks.

"Uh, I am taking you to breakfast. Then we have to go to my house so I can get some fresh clothes. Then we will have to go shopping."

"Shopping. What do we have to go shopping for?"

"Uh, we're going to be at the lake house all day. You'll probably want something to eat on breaks, not to mention everybody else. And you will probably want something to drink, not to mention everybody else."

"Oh," he replies. He takes a sip from his coffee. "I guess we better get going then."

"Good thinking, Hunter," she replies sarcastically.

Julie and Hunter spend the morning as planned, finally making their way to the lake house for the songwriting session. The rest of the musicians arrive on time, just as planned. Hunter tunes his guitar and waits for the others. Julie comes up beside him, looking over the lyrics she wrote earlier in the day.

"Can we start with that song you wrote last night?" Julie asks.

"We can, but I have not written any lyrics to it yet," Hunter replies.

I did, and I want to try it."

"Really? All right, sure, why not?" Hunter takes a moment to demonstrate the progression as Julie continues to look over the lyrics. Bill quickly keys in on the chord structure and augments the song, complementing its rich sound. Chris listens and looks at Hunter as he cocks his head.

"It's in triple meter, Chris," Julie informs.

"A waltz?" he asks.

"Yes, isn't it beautiful?" she replies.

"Yes, it is. It's very beautiful," Chris replies. He senses the tempo that Hunter is leading with and begins to play along.

Within a few short minutes, Julie steps up to the microphone and sings her new song from the bottom of her heart.

### The While Time Allows Waltz

*"If I could spend a lifetime in a moment, it's the moments with you.*
*I see you, I know you, and I love you. Light shines all around you.*
*If I could live forever and forever, I couldn't live without you.*
*You're something. You're someone.*
*You're my one, and you're all that is true.*

*I've seen beyond the days gone past. They don't last. They don't last.*
*You and I grow so very fast, so fast, too fast.*

*Help me right now. I am innocence.*
*Hold me right now.*
*Lend me your experience. I am innocence.*
*Love me while time allows.*

*If you could have a wish so enchanted, be granted, that lasted.*
*Would it be here with me?*
*If you could have it all by your side when worlds collide,*
*would you confide all of it in me?*

*I live for the time,*
*I live for your kisses that I've envisioned for life.*
*And I live for your wishes,*
*just to honor and to cherish, and send hope out on the tide.*

*Hold me right now. I am innocence.*
*Help me right now.*
*If you wish and you are curious, I'll be your stimulus.*
*Love me while time allows.*

*If time were meant for kisses and for wishes,*
*I would wish them only with you.*
*I hold you, I touch you, and I love you. I feel so brand new.*
*If hearts were never broken, just awoken, and well-spoken,*
*then I am speaking to you.*
*I need you, I want you, and I love you. Your light guides me to you.*

*Touch me right now. I am innocence.*
*Hold me right now.*
*Lend to me your experience. I am innocence.*
*Love me while time allows.*
*You're the one thing I found so incredibly right."*

"Nice. I really dig the words. When did you write that?" Bill asks as they finish.

"This morning," she replies.

"That was beautiful. I just played that for you last night. You put words in all the right sections," Hunter compliments her. He looks at her as if amazed by what she created.

"Yes, I know. I figured I would take a page out of your book. I even wrote another piece that I want to open every show with from now on. We can do that next if you want to," she replies.

"Can we take a break really quick? Chris asks. "I want to change out this snare skin. It's seen its last song." He begins to look for his drum key. As he reaches into his gear bag, he pulls from it the recording pen, which he had tucked away months before. "Oh, nice, I thought I lost that damn thing," he says.

Julie looks at him to see what he is referring to. "What is it?" she asks.

"It's the recording device I used when we first got together to write songs. I thought I lost it," he replies.

"How many sessions did you record?" Franklin asks.

"Pretty much all of them. The first few months as I remember. I haven't used it much since we went into the studio. After that, I fell out of habit using it," he replies.

"We jammed on a lot of good material. Maybe you captured a few forgotten ideas. We should play it and give it a listen sometime," Hunter suggests.

"Here, plug the sound card into the computer while I change out this drum skin." Chris tosses the device over the drums to Julie.

Julie studies the device and removes the flash drive. She plugs it into the computer and opens the file menu. "Oh, you have quite a few files here," she says to him.

"Yes, that there is. I think the files start around June or July. That's about when I bought it, and we started getting together," Chris replies. He continues to reach into the bag, finally finding the key.

Julie looks at the file dates on the menu. "Hmmm, that's right. We got together at my apartment around the Fourth of July if I remember correctly. The day before, actually, if I am not mistaken. That must be this one," she replies. She double clicks the file, and it opens. A captured conversation seems to refresh her memory as she listens to Chad speaking as it begins to play.

*"Hey, tomorrow night is July fourth. It's the fireworks, and your backyard is the perfect spot to watch them. Maybe we can get that one guitar player from the Scale House up here and rip off a jam. Then afterward we can watch the fireworks. Your place is perfect to see them, Julie. What do you think?"*

"Oh, this is when we did the first take on 'That's Why I Love You.' I remember that afternoon. We had a cookout the next day, remember?" Julie questions. She laughs as she smiles with the delight of the memory. "Here it is. I so love this song," Julie says. She looks at Hunter with a dreamy look in her eyes.

"That's the night I started falling in love with you," Hunter whispers in her ear.

"Funny. It's the same night that I started falling in love with you, too," she whispers back.

She listens for a moment, then looks suspiciously at the computer. "Wait a minute," she says. She stops the file and replays the recording from the beginning.

"What are you doing?" Hunter asks.

"Listen to what Chad says here." She shushes him, putting her finger to her mouth as she plays it back.

*"Hey, tomorrow night is July fourth. It's the fireworks, and your backyard is the perfect spot to watch them.*

Again, she stops the device and looks at Chad. "Do you realize what this means?" she asks.

Chad looks at her as he shakes his head. "No. What is so important about that?" he asks.

"It means Chris established on that recording an actual date where we wrote that song together before we ever brought Scratch here."

It takes Hunter only a moment to realize the relevance. "Chris, I could kiss you. I won't, but I could kiss you," he says. He puts down his instrument and gives Julie a big hug.

"I don't get it. What does that mean?" Chad asks.

Hunter looks over his shoulder at Chad while he continues to hug Julie. "It means that Scratch perjured himself in court by claiming that he wrote that song. They're WAV Files, so the date is on every song and backs up our defense in the lawsuit. It means that son of a bitch is in deep, deep shit for claiming that he wrote them all.

"I recorded almost every song for the album on that device," Chris says. He laughs as he begins to place tension on the drum snare. He rolls his sticks on the fresh drum skin, snapping it hard and abruptly on the last beat.

"I can't wait to see his rat-eyed little face when that turns up in court,"

Franklin says. He reaches over the drums, bumping knuckles with Chris.

"We have to get this to the attorney. Chris, you don't mind if I confiscate this from you, do you?" Hunter asks.

"Hell no. My pleasure. Especially if that little worm squirms in court," he replies.

"Julie, can you make a transcript of this tonight for the attorney's office?" Hunter asks.

"If you buy me dinner," she replies.

"It's a date," Hunter replies. He gives her and the rest of the band a high-five.

The next morning Hunter delivers the transcript and all of the recordings to the attorney. "Will this help our case?" he asks the attorney.

"It not only will help, but it will also likely bear witness to a very embarrassed opposing counsel."

"Good. That would make me incredibly happy," Hunter replies.

"I will ask today for the Judge to move up the date for an emergency session to show cause and remove his cease-and-desist order. Then we can file a motion to dismiss and a motion to transfer the ownership of the material to you, the rightful owner. It likely will cause the speedy end to your nightmare, Hunter. I will be in touch. I am willing to bet the Judge will schedule a hearing in the next several weeks."

"Thanks, Counselor," Hunter replies. He shakes his attorney's hand and leaves the law office sporting a genuine smile.

# Chapter 41

## A Very Sad Adversary

"ALL RISE, THIS COURT IS NOW IN SESSION. The Honorable Judge Christopher David Humble is now presiding," the Bailiff informs the courtroom as the Judge takes his seat.

"You may all be seated," the Judge instructs. "The defense has submitted a motion to show cause for this hearing based on the discovery of new evidence. Before I receive the defense's new evidence, are there any new motions from either party that I should be aware of at this time?" the Judge asks.

"Yes, Your Honor," Counselor Scherer replies. He pulls some documents from his briefcase and hands them to the Bailiff.

"What are you sending me, Counselor?" the Judge asks. He stretches his arm to receive the documents.

"It is a motion to dismiss, sir, as the evidence will show cause."

"A motion to dismiss? On what grounds?" the Judge asks as he looks at the motions.

"Your Honor, we recently discovered this new evidence, which supports my client's assertion that they are, in fact, the rightful owner of the copyrighted material in question. This is based on digital recordings and testimony from the defendants to their authenticity that predates the plaintiffs' copyright."

Scratch's attorney whispers to him. He becomes visibly agitated as he nods to his attorney.

"Attached, Your Honor, is a transcript of conversations that occurred beginning on July 3rd of last year, well before the plaintiff's copyright application. Here is a copy for the court and a copy for the plaintiff." The attorney hands the paperwork to the bailiff.

"I also would like to submit as evidence this digital recording device that my clients used to capture the music and conversations provided in the transcript." He holds out the device for the bailiff. The Judge takes the device and briefly examines it.

"Objection, Your Honor," the opposing counsel counters.

"On what grounds?"

"It's not relevant, Your Honor."

"Overruled."

Counselor Scherer remains stoned faced, quickly glancing at Hunter. "We humbly request, Your Honor, that the court enjoin the plaintiff to assign the copyright in question to our clients." he continues as he hands the bailiff yet another motion.

"Objection, Your Honor," opposing counsel says.

"Overruled."

The Judge begins to read over the transcript. After several minutes he puts it down, taking off his glasses. "I think I have seen enough," he says. The Judge looks at the plaintiff with suspicion. "Will both counselors approach the bench, please?" Judge Humble asks.

The Judge looks at the plaintiff's attorney as he comes close to the bench. "Counselor, this affidavit clearly demonstrates that your client is in jeopardy of committing perjury in my court. This paperwork, Counselor, are witnesses' testimony that they wrote all of the songs in your client's suit and copyright. I do not take kindly to perjury in my courtroom. Do I make myself sufficiently clear?" he asks. He stares down from the bench at the plaintiff like an executioner about to thoroughly enjoy his craft.

"Yes, sir, you certainly do," he replies.

"It presents a prima facie case that demonstrates an intent to mislead this court by your client. Do you want to take a moment and discuss the seriousness of this matter with him, Counselor?"

"Yes, sir. I think that's a great idea, Your Honor," Scratch's attorney replies.

"All right, then, we will take a ten-minute recess, no more, or I will dismiss this lawsuit in your absence with prejudice. Do I make myself sufficiently clear?"

"Yes, Sir," the plaintiff's attorney says.

"All right, please return to your seats." He picks up his gavel as he looks out at the courtroom. "This court will now take a ten-minute recess," the Judge says. He taps the gavel and rises from his seat, immediately turning toward the Judge's chambers.

The attorney motions Scratch to follow him outside the courtroom. Scratch follows him, looking angry and perplexed.


THE ATTORNEY LOOKS around as they enter the hallway. "You have a bit of a problem, Mr. Pocker," his attorney says.

"My name is Scratch."

"Your name will be 'Cell Bitch' if he slams your ass in Onondaga County Jail for perjury. Are these defendants the rightful owners of this material?"

"What do you mean? I wrote it all by my lonesome self."

"Then why is there evidence coming into the court that predates your claim? Now listen, this Judge is going to eviscerate your limey little ass if he finds that they're the rightful owners of all of the content that you claim to own. It seems rather apparent that he already has. Making false statements in a court of law is punishable by up to a year or more in jail, and some incredibly hefty fines as well. If he finds in their favor, and they push the issue, you could even be sued on the grounds of emotional stress and loss of revenue. Now, what is it, do you own the material or not?" the attorney interrogates.

Scratch looks at the attorney with anger in his eyes. "Right, well, what do you want me to do?" he asks.

"I want you to tell me the truth. Did you write these songs, or are they the rightful owners? Which is it?" the attorney asks with little patience.

"Yeah, they wrote them. Didn't think they were really smart enough to—"

"So you are a liar." His attorney abruptly cuts him off in hearing what he needed. "Okay, well then, I advise that you drop this suit right now and the entire copyright process you had me file. Unless, of course, you want to be held in contempt of court for perjury. In which case, you will likely spend at least six months to possibly a year in jail, which may be where you belong, Mr. Scratch."

"Hey, I pay you to be sympathetic. I don't pay you to give me grief or static."

The attorney looks at him with a derisive smile. "Wrong. You paid me to file suit in good faith that you owned this material and wanted it protected. So what do you want to do? Would you like me to proceed with your suit? If so, your retainer is now exhausted, and I will need another $5,000 from you if you wish to proceed."

"Right, well, to hell with it then. Drop the goddamn suit and let them have their stupid songs. They're all cheap, clichéd pieces of shite anyway. Do I need to go back in there with you?" he asks.

"Yes, you need to go back in there with me. After that, however, do not contact my office for anything whatsoever. We will not be representing you in any future proceedings. Do you understand me?"

"Right, not a problem," he replies. No hint of shame or regret in his response exists, and he follows the attorney back into the courtroom.

As the Judge returns from his chambers, the bailiff announces his presence. "All rise, this court is now back in session. The Honorable Judge Christopher David Humble is now presiding." The Judge takes his seat and looks at the plaintiff's attorney.

"Counselor, did you speak with your client, and does he wish to proceed?" the Judge asks. He looks directly at the plaintiff.

"I did, Your Honor, and my client wishes to drop the suit officially as well as transfer all material filed in the copyright application process."

"Oh, my God," Julie says quietly. She hugs Hunter in celebration.

The Judge slams the gavel. "Young lady, you will hold your celebratory responses until these proceedings come to a close. Do you understand me?"

"Yes, Your Honor. I'm sorry, Sir," she replies. She reaches down, tightly clutching Hunter's hand.

"All right. I hereby remove the cease-and-desist order which was in place. Counsel for the defense, I am assuming that you will be representing all future intellectual property rights. Therefore, I will see that the proper transfer is forwarded to your office. Now, as the plaintiff is withdrawing his suit and transferring the copyright ownership to Mr. Watkins it appears there is no further business before this court. I hereby declare this case is dismissed with prejudice. Have a nice day." The Judge taps his gavel and retires to his chambers.

Counselor Scherer pats Hunter on the back as Scratch exits the courtroom quickly. Hunter and Julie hold their heads high. As they walk out of the courtroom, Julie falls into Hunter's waiting arms.

"We won, we won, we won." Julie gives Hunter several quick kisses, exuberantly voicing her pleasure.

"I am very happy for you two," Counselor Scherer says. He shakes their hands in congratulations. "Hunter, I will let you know when the copyright is properly listed in your name. Congratulations, guys," he says.

Jenny, Chris, and the rest of the band exit the courtroom and join Julie and Hunter in celebration.

"Group hug," Chris cries out. Without hesitation, he and the rest of the band surround Hunter and Julie, celebrating the close of their mutual nightmare.

Counselor Scherer escorts the band out of the courthouse. He wedges in between Hunter and Julie as they walk down the steps. "I am incredibly happy for you guys. Had Chris not recorded all those sessions as evidence, then this whole case could have gone completely the other way."

"Can he ever take us back to court, Counselor?" Hunter asks.

"No. Any other court will take into account Judge Humble's ruling. If there is material not covered by the copyright, then he could have grounds for a whole other suit, so be proactive and send me any material as it develops. As for clearing the path to release your album, I am pleased to inform you that your material will now officially and properly be registered. So, I hope for all of you that your disc goes platinum."

"I am not sure that we can ever thank you enough, Counselor," Hunter says.

"Hunter, I would like to ask you and the band a personal favor."

"Sure, what is it?"

"Every year, I put on a benefit for veterans. If you would donate your services, and headline this year's benefit for me, then I will forgo all representation charges up to this point for you."

"I am a Marine. I lost a lot of friends these last few years. You bet we will play it. We will be honored to play for your benefit, sir," Franklin says.

"Great, then I will announce your band next week on the radio show I host."

"When is it?" Julie asks.

"It's on Labor Day weekend at Stewart Park. I know it's getting late in the year, but it is usually a beautiful weekend."

"Looking forward to it. We will all be there," Hunter says.

# Chapter 42

## Order Among the Stars

LABOR DAY ARRIVES WITH WARM temperatures and clear skies. Jenny escorts Chris as his official date, and the band leisurely make their way through the fairgrounds. With a little time to kill, they find a picnic table and take a seat to enjoy some refreshments. Chris, unable to resist his favorite dairy treat, buys two ice cream cones and hands one to Jenny. "I thought this poor little cone needed a pretty girl for an escort," Chris says. He hands her the chocolate treat.

"Thank you," she replies. She blushes as she looks at the cone.

Chris's action registers on Heaven's event monitoring databank. Oliver takes notice to a new alarm that is triggered on the screen.

"Drake, I'm not rightly sure why the system just rebooted and generated this announcement. It is displaying a system command that I have never seen. I think you should have a look at it," he says.

"What?" he asks as he looks over Oliver's shoulder at the monitor. "What have you done? I didn't program that!"

"I didn't do a thing. It just popped up," Oliver replies.

"It says 'click here to proceed.' Did you click there?" Drake asks.

"No, it just popped up, but I can if you want me to," he responds.

"Click proceed then," he says.

"It says, 'Nice job on the new updates, Drake. It was over 99% complete. However, I see that you forgot to install the *Continuance of Angel Mortality and Wings Deferment clause*. I have taken the liberty to install it in your program. That will enable angels on an assignment the option to continue in their current mortal body after successfully completing their mission. Knowing that more than a few thousand angels are on assignment at any given moment, exercising this option provides us the opportunity for our good work to be dispersed amongst humanity for years to come, thus spreading our message of hope and faith. The update I installed will prompt you on an emergency only case-by-case basis and relieve me of constantly having to oversee all of your good work. Again, my congratulations on your accomplishment. Enjoy the new features. Sincerely, God.'" Oliver turns with a look of wonder and amazement upon reading the passage.

"I love it. That, Oliver, is why he is the All-Knowing. If we do our best, He is always there, willing to help us." Drake smiles as he turns his attention back to his hand-held probabilities calculator.

"Hey, it's already working, look," Oliver says with joy. He points to the very first deferment option that displays onto the screen.

"I see that," Drake says.

"Hey, it's about Krystal, I mean Jenny. The first option appearing is for her," Oliver says.

"What does it say, Oliver?" Drake asks. He turns to look back into his hand-held device.

"It says, Drake, that 'the assigned angel is about to be presented with ice cream. Consumption will delete the process of awarding her the *Angel with Wings* status. Press here to send a text message advising her of the '*Continuance of Angel Mortality and Wings Deferment* clause, which will enable her to exercise free will to either conclude her assignment or continue as a mortal.'"

"Huh, how clever. I wish I would have thought of that. Yes, send the text, Oliver."

"Think that's why he is God," Oliver says. He laughs as he looks at Drake.

Drakes points over his assistant's shoulder. "You see that Hallway of Eternity to your left there, Oliver?" he asks with a warm smile on his face.

"Yes. You can't miss it?"

"How would you like to be dispatched to sweep it today?"

Oliver looks down the hallway with a look of apprehension at the suggestion. "That would take forever, Drake."

"Yes, I know. And if you don't start pushing those icon buttons when they pop up, then I will have you pushing a broom. So, if you will, a little less talking, shall we? Send the text now, Oliver," he says, tapping him on the shoulders.

"I'm good at pushing buttons, Drake. I'll just stay here and push them as they pop up if you don't mind."

"Thank you," he replies.

Oliver touches the screen that enables the program's process to complete. Drake walks away as Oliver looks back down the hallway. "Phew," he quietly says in relief as he wipes his forehead. He turns his attention back to the display screen, watching as Jenny sits dumbfounded with the presentation of Chris's frozen gift. Her phone rings with a system-generated auto text. She reads the text in one hand while holding the ice cream cone in the other.

*'Congratulations. You have passed your test on acquiring the status of 'First Class Angel.' However, consuming the ice cream before you will suspend your wings request and instantly transform you into a full-fledged mortal with the identity you have assumed for this assignment. Further, doing so will leave you with absolutely no memory of your past life, your successful assignment, or any memory of Heaven. The suspension of your request will force a reexamination of your application at a later date, which will be based on your new identity. Good luck with your choice, for you have served brilliantly.'*

The text disappears from her screen just as she finishes reading it.

Jenny realizes that she has one nut left in her angelic pouch. She places her phone into her pants pocket and retrieves the hickory nut from her purse. "Oh my God, look at all those fans at the stage," she says. The whole group turns to look toward the bandstand. As they do, she drops the nut onto Chris's back. A rainbow of light scatters throughout the area. Chris shakes his head and turns back to Jenny.

"Are you all right?" she asks.

"I don't think I have ever felt so right. Mainly because you're my date tonight," he replies.

Without hesitation, she looks at Chris with great admiration. She lunges with her tongue for the top of the frozen twisted swirl. She takes a lick then immediately places her lips to Chris's, rewarding him with a chocolate-flavored kiss. Chris blushes as the band carouses at the sight.

"Awww, you two make the most beautiful couple," Julie says. She pushes Chris on the shoulder, smiling at the both of them.

"Can we do more of that later?" Chris asks in a whisper.

"Uh-huh," she replies like an innocent child. She smiles and begins to lick around the outside of the ice cream.

Hunter looks at Julie, pointing across the fairgrounds to her roommates walking toward them.

"Oh my God, is that Nick with them?" she asks.

"It appears that way," Hunter replies.

"He is holding LaShonda's hand." Julie turns back to look at Hunter and drops her jaw as if amazed by the sight.

"I see that," Hunter replies. He grins at the sight.

"She is so going to eat him up," Julie replies.

"Hopefully," Hunter says. The two look at each other and begin to laugh.

The band makes their way to the back of the soundstage. Counselor Scherer thanks each one of them for their service to the event. Acting as Master of Ceremonies, the attorney steps out onto the stage and announces the evening's headline act.

"Ladies and gentlemen, we want to take this opportunity to thank you for all of your support. As we celebrate Labor Day, we hope you give thanks to all the men and women who have so proudly labored in service to our country. Remember, all that you enjoy, and all that you have has been secured by over two hundred years of American Patriots that we call Veterans." The crowd cheers in respect.

"We appreciate all your support for our heroes who have asked so little of their country. They have given so very much, and we thank them for their service, for they help us to believe in that long-held notion, God Bless America!" Again, the crowd responds with applause.

"Our final band tonight are flag-waving patriots, who also love this great country. So without further ado, Ladies and Gentlemen, will you please join me in giving a great big Labor Day welcome to the New York Satellites." The crowd cheers as the band take to the stage. Hunter and Julie smile at each other with excitement in seeing over ten thousand fans gracing the park grounds.

"If this is as far as we ever get, I'll take it," Julie says to Hunter. She grins with a sense of pride as she steps toward the microphone.

"Me too," Hunter replies. "I think, however, that this is just the beginning of the ride, kid." He turns to admire the cheering crowd.

"Hello, Ithaca, New York. How you all doing out there tonight?" Julie engages the fans. The crowd cheers as expected. "Is this the most awesome Labor Day weekend ever or what?" she continues to question with more excitement in her voice. "Are you ready for some Rock and Roll?" she shouts. The crowd begins to cheer with restless anticipation. "All right, New York, then here we go. Let's get ready to Rock and Roll!"

Hunter turns to make eye contact with the band. Franklin, Chad, and Billy nod that they all are ready to play. Seeing this, Chris quickly dictates a four-count, and they begin their instrumentation with passion, precision, and perfection.

The group, united by struggle, bound by a common goal, and determined to give every day their absolute best, begin to play their latest song to their growing legion of fans.

### The Spinning of the Earth

*"I don't think I've ever seen so clearly,*
*walking through life's mist that clouds my eyes.*
*And through my mistakes, I've had to pay so dearly.*
*Kidding myself was my disguise.*

*One too many nights, I sat and wondered*
*just what is this life here all about?*
*I have never known just where to turn to.*
*I have never known which way to go*
*...and then I find you.*

*I can feel the spinning of the Earth,*
*and all of the stars that wrap around you.*
*Now I know exactly what it's worth.*
*I can share a lifetime if you want to.*

*I've been thinking that I must have been blessed.*
*I don't know why I'm just lucky, I guess.*
*Oh yes, I see love spelled out in the stars with you.*
*I see love in the stars.*

*I can feel the spinning of the Earth*
*and all of the stars that wrap so far around you.*
*Now I know exactly what it's worth.*
*I can share a lifetime if you want to.*

*I can feel the spinning of the Earth,*
*and with you it always is the right time!*
*Take this for exactly what it's worth.*
*Love like yours will surely last a lifetime,*
*and beyond the spinning of the Earth."*

# Chapter Titles and Chapter Lyrics

| Chapter | | Lyrics |
|---|---|---|
| 1. | The Consequential Encounter | This Side of the Moon |
| 2. | Music as Magic | Western Town |
| 3. | Cold Winds and Dark Clouds | Long Way Home |
| 4. | All the Queen's Men | |
| 5. | Letting Go | I Stand Down |
| 6. | Golf, God, and Satan | |
| 7. | A Turn in the River | |
| 8. | A Flame on the Rise | Flames on the Rise |
| 9. | A Meeting of Masters | Only Me |
| 10. | An Angel's Arsenal | Find A Way |
| 11. | Must Be Love | That's Why I Love You |
| 12. | Scratch Fever | Satellites |
| 13. | The Melting of an Ice-age | Never Let Go |
| 14. | Halloween with Marilyn | Marilyn |
| 15. | Burning Young Hearts | She Won't Wait for You |
| 16. | The Rat in Strategy | Twisting |
| 17. | Bewildered and Bewitched | |
| 18. | The Show Must Go On | Home to Mama & Cry Myself to |
| 19. | Not Jane Too | Sleep |
| 20. | Pushing Buttons | Calling |
| 21. | While the Cat's Away | Diamonds and Fire |
| 22. | The Hope within a Rainbow | Cyber Girl |
| 23. | The Pounce of the Fox | You're Like a Rainbow |
| 24. | Admission and Suspicion | |
| 25. | Yet Another Attack | Jack Tonight |
| 26. | The Triumph of the Trout | |
| 27. | Hell Gives Up a Hag Stone | |
| 28. | The Sting of the Pain | What Are You Going Through |
| 29. | The Critique of the Critic | Want You to Know |
| 30. | A Walk in the Park | Don't You Run Away |
| 31. | The Mending at Mercato's | |
| 32. | It's All Too Much | Baby Blue |
| 33. | Closure on Connecticut Hill | Hey Dad |
| 34. | Southside with the Angels | A Southside Serenade |
| 35. | If Your Heart is Pure | Girl Like You |
| 36. | A Dear Old Friend | |
| 37. | Outclassed by the Outcast | |
| 38. | Variation of the Vibe | A Place Called Time |
| 39. | Discomfort from the Decree | |
| 40. | A Revelation in the Recording | The While Time Allows Waltz |
| 41. | A Very Sad Adversary | |
| 42. | Order Among the Stars | The Spinning of the Earth |

CPSIA information can be obtained
at www.ICGtesting.com
Printed in the USA
BVHW031302241221
624832BV00005B/20